INDIVISIBLE

A NOVEL BY

JESSICA McQUINN

OMNIFIC PUBLISHING

DALLAS

Omnific Publishing
P.O. Box 793871, Dallas, TX 75379
www.omnificpublishing.com

First Omnific eBook edition, January 2011
First Omnific trade paperback edition, January 2011

Library of Congress Cataloguing-in-Publication Data

McQuinn, Jessica.
     Indivisible / Jessica McQuinn – 1st ed.
     ISBN 978-1-936305-56-8
     1. Contemporary Romance —Fiction. 2. Military Life —Fiction.
     3. California —Fiction. 4. Family Dynamics—Fiction. I. Title

10 9 8 7 6 5 4 3 2 1

Cover Design and Interior Book Design by Coreen Montagna

Printed in the United States of America

For my mom, who is truly my hero.

CHAPTER 1

*S*hit, shit, shit... Gideon Cooper's thoughts danced with images of his gorgeous wife and what she'd be doing for their anniversary.

"Damn it! This is the worst possible day for me to have to tell her this news," Gideon mumbled. He gripped the steering wheel tightly as he ran through all the ways this night could go—none of them ended well.

Gideon knew Charlie would go all out with the romance stuff: candles, the plates they got as wedding gifts, real napkins, and shit like that. But what he was really looking forward to was what she'd do in the bedroom—always his favorite place to be with his wife. Not that they didn't have fun in every other room in the place too...and the car, the laundry room, the pool...

"Shit! There's no way she's going to let me near the bedroom after I tell her the news."

Charlie Cooper stood with her hands on her hips as she surveyed the tiny apartment, making sure everything was ready. This night needed to be perfect. She'd done her best to achieve that goal, and while she wished there was more she could do, she also knew there was no way she could justify spending any more money. Gideon worked so hard, and even though he made more than enough to support them, she felt guilty because she was still in school, unable to contribute to their household. She could always dip into her savings, but Charlie would never do that; Gideon insisted the money she'd put away was for her to finish school—he could take care of them. He was a proud man, and she loved that about him.

As she studied the small table in what they affectionately referred to as the "dining area," Charlie was pleased with the new tablecloth she'd bought that morning. It was a beautiful, rich wine brocade. Her fingers gently slid over the material. She really shouldn't have spent the money for such a silly thing, but it had been on sale, and she'd fallen in love with it as soon as she'd seen it. She'd pushed the limits of the budget a little, but this was a special occasion.

Set atop the new tablecloth were the two place settings of china and three stray pieces of silverware they'd gotten for their wedding. Gideon thought it was silly to keep two spoons and a fork that didn't match anything else, but Charlie couldn't bring herself to return them; she hoped someday they'd be able to complete the set. While their wedding wasn't traditional, Gideon's mother had insisted they register and let all the relatives feel included. Thus the bits and pieces Charlie now had set out on her table.

A bottle of champagne was chilling in the fridge, and Charlie had made her vegetable lasagna for dinner. The smells filling the apartment were heavenly. She had no doubt Gideon would appreciate all the effort she'd put into their celebration. He was always so appreciative of everything she did for him, and for their life together.

Gideon's job was stressful, so on days she didn't have afternoon classes, Charlie made sure she had a good meal cooked and ready when he got home. She worked hard at the one thing she could do for him, which was to make their apartment a home—one he was happy to come back to at the end of every day.

With everything ready, Charlie sent Gideon a quick text to get his imagination working, then decided to relax in a nice, hot bath before she had to get herself together for her husband. The water was as hot as she could stand it, and Charlie added a little bubble bath—vanilla bean, Gideon's favorite scent. Once the bubbles were almost overflowing the tub, she stripped down and lowered herself in. Although she was fairly small, her body displaced some of the water, causing it to run over the sides of the tub. Sinking back into the warmth, Charlie allowed her mind to wander.

Today she and Gideon had been married for one whole year, a fact she was sure surprised most of their friends and family. A giggle bubbled up as she wondered what the betting pool was up to for how long they'd last. It was understandable that no one thought the couple would make it past the first few months; they'd only known each other for three days when they eloped—not technically a great beginning for a long marriage…

…Charlie had been out with friends that Thursday night, celebrating making it through a particularly brutal week of classes. It was the beginning of her junior year at San Diego State University, where she was studying to be a teacher, and this year's workload seemed to be double that of the previous two.

Charlie was only five feet five inches tall, but her confident personality made her seem so much bigger. Her long, strawberry blond hair, sparkling green eyes, and full lips made her the envy of many women and an object of attraction for most men. Usually Charlie spent nights at clubs trying to keep all the pervs and their hands off of her, but when she saw the gorgeous muscled man across the bar, he didn't look like he was mentally undressing her; he looked like he was…caressing her, with just his eyes. Charlie flashed a small smile before turning away. She hoped it would encourage him to come over because she'd never approach a man out at the clubs; she wasn't going to meet her future husband partying in a bar.

The next time Charlie looked up to continue flirting with the blond-haired, dimple-cheeked god on the other side of the club, he'd disappeared. She glanced around, trying to locate him, and cursed herself for being so stubborn and cautious. Her heart broke just a little, and she didn't even know the guy's name. He was gone, and there was very little chance she'd ever find him again. It was San Diego for Christ's sake — not only was there the entire SDSU student body, but University of California, San Diego, and University of San Diego, not to mention all the community colleges, and then throw in the military bases. Charlie was sure she'd never find him again.

"Hey." A deep voice that sounded like sex came from over her shoulder. It was him.

Slowly turning around, Charlie tried not to let her nervousness show. "Hey."

When he smiled at her, Charlie could've sworn her heart actually stopped beating for a fraction of a second. The dimples in his cheeks were mouthwatering, and she wanted to kiss them right then…so she did.

"Well, um, that was…nice." He was still smiling. "I'm Gideon, by the way."

Suddenly, he was kissing her. His kiss was deep and long, his tongue exploring every inch of Charlie's mouth. She knew she should be fighting off this total stranger, but she just couldn't bring herself to do it. Instead, she gave up and went with it, battling his tongue for dominance and tasting his wonderful flavors. He must have been drinking Jack and Coke, because Charlie could taste the sting of the whiskey and the sweetness of the soda.

"I'm Charlie, just so you know," she managed to squeak out once they broke for air.

"Hi, Charlie. Nice to meet you." Those dimples made an appearance again. This time Charlie was more bold and let her tongue slide out from between her lips to run over those small, perfect indentations. Behind her, Charlie's friends gasped at her completely uncharacteristic aggressiveness, but she didn't care. At that moment, she was more sure of Gideon than she'd ever been of anything in her life...

The memory of that night, and the two following it, had gotten to Charlie, and she found her hands had drifted under the bubbles of their own accord.

In hopes of easing the blow—and not the good kind—Gideon had ducked out of work a little early. He was so not good at the lovey-dovey crap, but he knew enough to realize if he came home empty-handed, especially tonight, he wouldn't be touching his wife's amazing body for months.

The flower shop hadn't taken as long as Gideon thought it would. The woman behind the counter was very helpful and easily put together a bouquet of wildflowers—beautiful and unpredictable, just like Charlie. The wrapped bouquet sat on the seat next to him as he tried to talk himself into going inside. All the flowers in the world were not going to help him out of this situation.

Suddenly, the enormity of what he was about to tell Charlie settled over him. Closing his eyes, Gideon rested his forehead against the steering wheel as thoughts of the first time he'd ever seen her whirled in his head...

...When he'd seen her across that bar, the voice in his head and the one in his pants spoke at the same time, both screaming that he needed to make her his. He still wasn't sure which one he'd been listening to more, but there'd been no way he was going to let her get away.

When he made his way over to her and heard her voice, felt her lips, and tasted her, Gideon knew he was going to listen to his heart. After mere minutes, which seemed more like days, weeks, to him, Gideon walked out of the bar with the only woman he ever wanted to spend time with. He pulled her close, making sure every possible inch of her body was in some way in contact with his own. She was his, and he wanted everyone to know it.

"Where are you taking me, Gideon?" she purred as she climbed into his truck.

Good question, he thought. He couldn't take her back to his place.

"Vegas, baby." It just popped out. He didn't even have time to think about it, but once he'd said it, Gideon knew it was perfect. He didn't have to be back to work until Monday morning, so he could have this gorgeous woman all to himself for three whole days.

Hell yeah… Vegas! He knew that was the voice in his pants talking, but the one in his head was totally on board with the plan too.

"V-Vegas?" Charlie stuttered.

Gideon would have settled for a Denny's where they could talk all night if the look in her eyes hadn't agreed with him. Charlie pulled her phone out of her purse and flipped it open. From her side of the conversation, Gideon gathered she was calling her friends and telling them he wasn't some crazy sex fiend who'd kidnapped her. *Well, she was half right—he wasn't kidnapping her.*

Six hours in a car gave Charlie and Gideon time to get to know each other. Charlie told him about her dream of being a teacher for developmentally disabled kids, which impressed him. In addition to her hopes and plans for the future, Gideon learned that since her parents had been killed in a car accident during her freshman year, Charlie's only family was her twin brother, Chance, and his fiancée.

Gideon told her about his job and how much he loved it. Then he told her about his younger brother, Tyson, who was a student at USD, majoring in premed. The two brothers couldn't have been more different.

As they finally saw the glittering lights of the Strip, Gideon thought to himself that he'd never spent a better six hours with anyone in his entire life. Until they checked into the hotel…

The images of Charlie in those first days were fresh in Gideon's mind when he remembered where he was and what he had to tell his perfect wife, today of all days.

"Goddamn it!" Gideon slammed his fist on the dashboard, causing the truck to rock.

Taking a deep breath, he got out and walked slowly to the apartment. He made a decision just as he slid the key in the lock—he wouldn't tell her tonight. He wouldn't ruin this night for her.

"Charlie baby! I'm home!"

The aroma of garlic and tomato sauce was heavy in the air, and Gideon knew immediately that Charlie had cooked his favorite meal. The table was set, but he didn't see her anywhere. The apartment wasn't big, so he didn't have to look too hard to find her.

Opening the bathroom door, Gideon found the loveliest sight he'd ever seen: Charlie with her hair pulled up in a messy ponytail, her eyes closed, her lips parted, and her hand deep beneath the bubbles. The moving water lapped at her perfect breasts, and on the outgoing motion, he caught a glimpse of the beautiful peaks that hardened instantly when the cool air hit them.

"Hey, baby. Need some help there?" Gideon adjusted himself.

A sigh escaped her lips as she opened her eyes to look at him.

"Happy anniversary," she breathed out with a small moan.

Yes it is, Gideon thought. His entire body tightened in anticipation of the night to come.

CHAPTER 2

The sight of Gideon in his work clothes, his black T-shirt pulled taut over his muscled chest, was just the thing Charlie needed to push her over the edge.

"Damn, Charlie! That's just about the best anniversary gift you could've given me. The only thing better would be to know you were thinking of me. Were you, baby?"

Smiling up at him, Charlie moved her glance from his glorious chest down to the obvious bulge in his pants, straining to be released.

"Of course," she confirmed as she stood to get out of the tub. "But if you don't want all the other things I have planned tonight…"

In two long strides, Gideon closed the distance between them, scooping Charlie up in his arms. Her body instantly formed to his, as if they'd been doing this all their lives and she was built to fit with him.

"Gideon!" Charlie swatted at his shoulder. "I'm soaking wet. At least let me get a towel."

"Baby, don't worry about me. Wet is just how I want you."

His mouth was on hers without warning, and Charlie couldn't remember why she was arguing with this gorgeous man who was taking her to his bed. Snaking her arms up around his neck and playing with the short bristled hair at the nape, Charlie wrapped her legs around his waist. She readily granted him access to her mouth, parting her lips and sucking his tongue.

Just as they turned the corner to go into the bedroom, there was a pounding on the front door.

"Just ignore it," Gideon whispered as his tongue traced Charlie's earlobe. "They'll go away."

A low mewling sound escaped from Charlie as she melted into her husband, ready to obey his every directive.

Again there was a pounding on the door. This time, however, it was followed by a voice they both knew.

"Gideon! Come on, bro! Open up! I know you're in there—I can see your truck!"

"Tyson," the couple groaned at the same time.

Gideon looked down at Charlie. She could see every emotion he was feeling play across his face. The want and lust quickly changed into anger, and she knew the twinkle in his eye meant he was thinking of all the ways he could murder his brother.

"Go away, Tyson!" Gideon called over his shoulder, his hands still running up and down Charlie's wet body.

"Gid, come on! Open up!" Tyson begged.

Charlie knew Tyson was not going to go away any time soon, and when Gideon set her on her feet, swearing under his breath, she knew he did too.

"Go. I have to get dinner out of the oven anyway," Charlie said. "We *will* continue this later. Promise." She stretched up and kissed him softly, pushing him toward the living room and closing the bedroom door behind him.

"Dude, why are you all wet?" Charlie heard Tyson ask in the other room.

"What in the ever-living hell do you want, Tyson? It's my anniversary, and I was just about to give Charlie her *huge* present."

"Gideon! Stop it!" Charlie yelled from the bedroom. She tried to block out the rest of their conversation, knowing *that* was probably the mildest thing Gideon would say to his brother.

Grabbing the new pink-lace bra and panty set she'd bought specifically for tonight, Charlie wandered into the closet to find something to wear over it. But she knew Gideon was going to have whatever she put on peeled off of her two minutes after his brother left…

…As soon as the door to their hotel room closed, Gideon's hands had been all over Charlie—sliding up her thighs and under her skirt, slowly undoing each button of the blouse she was wearing. He stood back and admired her after removing each article of clothing. The look in his eyes was more than desire or want; he was in awe of Charlie.

"God, Charlie. I've never seen anything so perfect," he'd cooed, his thumb stroking the sensitive skin under her ear. Charlie melted into him.

The pair never left the room that day, and Charlie hadn't cared in the least. As night fell and the lights of Las Vegas began to shine, Gideon rolled over onto his side. Charlie blushed, feeling his gaze settling on her.

"Charlie," his voice was quiet, reverent.

"Mmm?" She closed her eyes, reveling in the way her name fell from his lips.

"I need to ask you a question."

"What, Gideon? You can ask anything." As if it had its own objective, Charlie's hand moved to run over his huge bicep, coming to rest on the intricate black tattoo of a trident etched there. Charlie loved it and had found herself tracing its lines over the last few hours as they'd talked.

"You know I love my job, right? I told you that serving my country is the greatest thing I could ever think of doing with my life."

Charlie nodded. On the drive, Gideon had told her that after he'd graduated from college with a degree in mechanical engineering, he'd joined the Navy. He felt his skill could serve the country, and he wanted to have a real purpose in his life.

"Yeah, Gideon. It's one of the things I adore about you."

"There's something I didn't tell you about my job." He paused, looking at her.

Charlie smiled to encourage him to continue.

"I'm not just in the Navy; I'm with a special operations unit. I'm a SEAL."

"Oh. Okay. Well, at least the tattoo of a seal on your tush makes sense now." The meaning behind his confession and his need to tell her at that moment completely escaped Charlie.

"I'm a Navy SEAL, Charlie. Do you know what that means?"

Charlie realized apparently she didn't because she obviously was supposed to react differently than she had.

As she shook her head, tears began to well at the corners of her eyes, and she wasn't sure why. Was he trying to scare her off? She'd been stupid enough to think they had some connection. Suddenly she felt very foolish and very naked.

Charlie pulled the sheet up to cover her exposed body, and Gideon pulled his brow together in question. She wasn't going to make this easy for him, and she wasn't going to cry. At least, that was the plan.

With what she hoped was an aloof look, Charlie stared at Gideon, waiting. She could tell he was debating what, and how much, to tell her. To her surprise, he slid his arm around her waist, pulling her to him. It occurred to Charlie that Gideon didn't want to look in her eyes as he told her whatever it was he was going to say.

"Charlie, my job is dangerous. I can be called out at any time to leave for extended periods. I go into war zones, and no one knows where I am. I go to places where people get shot at. It's dangerous…all the time."

"Ah." So he *was* trying to scare her off. "Hey, listen, you don't owe me anything." Charlie tried to pull away from him, but he held on tight.

"Damn it, Charlie! I'm not telling you this to get rid of you." He loosened his grip so he could pull back and look at her.

The tears had started to fall, against her stern demand that they not betray her, and Charlie wanted nothing more than to get out of that room.

Gideon moved a hand up to her chin and tilted her head back, looking into her eyes. He held Charlie there, not with his strength, but with something else she couldn't put a name to.

"I'm telling you this because even though it's insane and we just met, I know I want you in my life…"

"Hey, Charlie!" Tyson's voice echoing from the living room brought Charlie back to the present. "Sorry!" he added — for Gideon's sake, Charlie was sure.

"Hi, Tyson. It's all right. Gideon's just pissed that what's promising to be a *joy*-filled evening will have to wait." She laughed, trying to make light of the situation before Gideon actually hurt his brother.

When she was dressed in Gideon's favorite black dress — short, plunging neckline, virtually backless — Charlie sauntered into the living room with the boys. Gideon's face lit up when he saw her.

"Charlie, dinner smells incredible," Tyson commented as she went to the kitchen to check on the lasagna.

"Don't even try it, Tyson. I know for a fact that you have a kitchen of your own. You don't need to be here for every meal, you know."

"Come on, Charlie. You know I love your lasagna. Please?"

"No freakin' way, Tyson," Gideon quickly replied. "Didn't I just tell you it's our anniversary? And didn't you say you had a date with this mystery girl? So be on your way, little brother." Gideon stood up ready to escort Tyson out.

"You have another date with her, Tyson? When are you going to let us meet her? It's been what, like, almost a month?" Charlie asked. "I think that might be a record for you."

"This one's different. She's smart and sassy and beautiful and doesn't put up with my crap. It took me asking her out for, like, two months before she finally agreed. I don't want to jinx it or have the beast over there scare her off." Tyson's face was plastered with a huge smile as he nodded in his older brother's direction.

Tyson's dating record in the year Charlie had known him had been a jumble of different women, a new one every other day, practically. So to see him excited about a girl after dating her for almost a month was refreshing.

Tyson was good-looking, and Charlie guessed the girls really liked him. He had perfect surfer-blond hair, which he wore longer than his brother's, and endless blue eyes framed by dark lashes — definitely a lady-killer. While Gideon was big and had muscles in every place possible, Tyson was leaner and more classically built. One thing was for sure: Evelyn and Peter Cooper knew how to make beautiful children.

"Tyson." Gideon stood at the door, holding it open. "Get the hell out. Now."

"Can I borrow your truck for my date? It's the only way you're getting rid of me." Tyson flashed a perfect-but-devious smile at his brother.

"Why the hell do you need my truck? You have your shiny little Audi to impress her with," Gideon all but growled at the younger Cooper.

"I want to take her down to the beach and watch the sunset. It's much easier to do in the bed of the truck than through the windshield of my car."

"Fine." Gideon tossed the keys to Tyson. "Now go. And if you bring my truck back with even a hint of a scratch or footprints on the windshield, I will hurt you."

"Thanks, bro." Tyson pocketed the keys and stepped past the door, which Gideon still held open.

Closing and locking the door behind him, Gideon leaned against it with a sexy smile playing on his lips.

"Now, where were we before my asshole brother so rudely interrupted us?" He lunged for Charlie, but she deftly sidestepped his grasp.

Gideon wanted to kill his little brother.

"Charlie, baby, where are you going?" He knew he sounded pitiful, but he just couldn't get the picture of his wife as she stepped from the tub out of his head.

"I made your favorite dinner, Joe. I worked hard all afternoon, and we're going to sit down and enjoy our anniversary meal."

Gideon watched her ass sway back and forth as she marched into the kitchen. At that exact moment, he heard Tyson squeal out of the parking lot in his truck.

Yeah, he was definitely going to kill him.

Realizing Charlie wasn't going to get naked for him again anytime soon, Gideon decided to change out of his uniform and get more comfortable before dinner.

"Fine. Hey, babe, do I have time to jump in the shower real quick?"

"Yeah. Go ahead. Dinner will be ready in about fifteen minutes," Charlie answered from the kitchen. Gideon wondered if she was bending over, checking on the lasagna or maybe getting something out of the fridge, her dress lifting a little so he could get a peek at that exquisite ass. His imagination got the better of him, and he felt his pants get tighter for the second time in under an hour. It was time to head to the shower.

Ten minutes later, after a very cold shower, Gideon stepped out of the bathroom dressed in just a pair of jeans. The table was set with their meal and a bottle of champagne, and Charlie was in the kitchen on her tiptoes trying to get two of their three champagne flutes off the top shelf. Her dress was perilously close to exposing that fine rear end Gideon had been dreaming about earlier.

"Baby, I don't deserve you. You know that, right?" He walked up behind her, wrapping his arms around her waist and nuzzling her neck.

Charlie sighed heavily at his closeness. That small noise drove Gideon crazy, but he didn't want all her hard work to go to waste, so he tried to control himself.

"Let me get those for you." He reached up and easily took the glasses down.

"Thanks." Charlie kissed him softly and went back to the table. "Well, are you ready for your first anniversary dinner?"

Gideon pulled out her chair for her to sit down.

"What a gentleman."

Her smile melted his heart, and he was so happy he'd made that plunge in Vegas. Gideon knew there was no way he could live his life without Charlie. As he gazed at her beautiful smile, he couldn't help but remember that glorious weekend a year ago…

…They'd been wrapped around each other, simply talking for several hours. Gideon couldn't fight the thoughts that played in his head. There was something about the woman in his arms that just fit. She made him feel like he was now the man destiny had scripted him to be.

It was during that quiet time that Gideon's heart decided to speak without his permission. "I think we should get married," he blurted.

"What? You want to marry me? Now?" Charlie's voice was high-pitched, and Gideon could hear the disbelief lacing it.

"You're right; it was a stupid idea." Defeated and on the edge of humiliation, Gideon turned to get out of bed, but he felt something stop him and pull him back down. He couldn't bring himself to look at her, sure he'd made an ass out of himself.

Charlie's lips were on his ear, her tongue darting out to run circles around it. She definitely had Gideon's attention again.

"Yes."

It was more of a breath than a word, and Gideon wasn't sure he'd heard her.

"What?"

"I said 'yes.' I will marry you."

Gideon immediately crashed his lips to hers, wanting to hold on to that moment forever. The most beautiful, perfect woman — for God only knew what reason — had just agreed to marry him.

"I know it's so fast, but when you were telling me about your job, and I thought you didn't want me, I felt lost. I feel like I belong with you."

"Okay then." He stopped, not knowing what to do next. "What should we do now?"

"Well, we could just go to one of those places and have Elvis marry us."

Charlie was smiling, but Gideon knew no woman dreamed of a wedding performed by a dead icon while wearing two-day-old clothes.

"No. We're going to have a real wedding. A very quickly put together wedding, but a real one. I love you, Charlie…um, this is awkward, but I don't know your last name."

Charlie giggled. "Yeah, I guess we kind of forgot about that. Let me start—Charlotte Esther O'Connor. Very nice to meet you." Her smile was infectious, and Gideon could tell that although this was moving fast, she was as sure of everything as he was.

"Charlotte Esther? Seriously?"

"My grandmothers' names. Could have been worse—my brother is Chancellor Mortimer. So all in all, I got off easy."

"Makes sense, and you do have it better than your brother, I have to say. I guess it's my turn, huh?"

She nodded, her eyes never leaving his.

"Okay. Nice to meet you, Charlotte Esther O'Connor, or should I say, the future Mrs. Gideon Isaac Cooper?"

"Gideon Isaac? So, wait…your initials are G.I. and you're a Navy SEAL?" Charlie began to laugh.

"What? I must be missing something here." Gideon tried to figure what was so funny. He knew his name was a little unusual, but nothing like Mortimer.

"Oh, I can't believe you've never seen this…G.I." She paused and gave Gideon a hard stare, willing him to understand the reason behind her fit of giggles. "G.I. Joe? You know—gung-ho Army guy? Barbie's much cooler and more masculine boy toy? Well, at least in my world he was. I used to steal Chance's G.I. Joe and make him go on dates with Barbie. You are totally my G.I. Joe… Yeah, my Joe."

"I think I like being your anything." Gideon leaned in and gave her a passion-filled kiss, staking his claim to the beautiful woman in bed next to him. The fact that she was totally naked didn't go unnoticed as he began to think about branding her even more thoroughly as his.

"Charlotte Cooper? Charlie Cooper? Mrs. Cooper? I could get used to that," she suddenly said as she pulled away from his kiss to look him in the eye. Her gorgeous green eyes were glazed over slightly with pure love, and he couldn't imagine anything more beautiful.

"So could I." Gideon didn't think he could possibly be happier…

"How was work today? You seem a little distracted. You ate your entire meal without a word. Did you even hear anything I said to you?" Charlie's warm voice pulled Gideon from his reverie and reminded him he hadn't had a great day at work and there was something he'd have to tell his wife, eventually.

"Just thinking about how beautiful you were when we got married and how the happiest moment in my life was when you said 'I do' and became my wife." Gideon couldn't have felt more sappy if he tried.

"Oh, Joe," Charlie exclaimed and threw herself into his lap. Fortunately, they'd finished the meal while Gideon was lost in memories, because he couldn't wait any longer to have his wife naked and underneath him.

With Charlie still held tight to his body, Gideon stood and headed for the bedroom.

"Wait, I have to clean up." Charlie tried to wiggle her way out of his grasp, but Gideon was not letting that happen.

"Tomorrow." He leaned in and kissed her deeply, allowing his tongue to slip into her mouth and trace every inch of it. In return, Charlie ran her fingers lightly over his bare chest.

When he kicked the door to the bedroom open, Gideon heard a small gasp from Charlie. Walking over to the bed, he gently laid her down, and she stretched out on the king-size mattress. It was one luxury Gideon had insisted on. He was a pretty big guy, and when he had Charlie on the bed, he needed a lot of room.

Slowly, Gideon crawled up his wife's lean body, gently planting small kisses along the way. He let his hands trail behind his mouth, up along her thighs, pushing her dress further and further up. When she moaned, Gideon fell on her beautiful lips and kissed her while his fingers played along the edge of the lace that covered her perfect, warm place where he needed to be.

Reaching up, he slid her pink panties down over her hips as she lifted off the bed for him. As the smooth expanse of her skin came into view, Gideon went weak and let out a low hiss.

Moments later, they were both completely stripped down — the dress tossed in the corner, her bra thrown on top of it — and Gideon was making love to Charlie, his wife and, in his opinion, the most perfect being God had ever created. He could never be more content in this world. As they each found release, Gideon cried Charlie's name, but never closed his eyes because he only ever wanted to see her under him…as long as they both shall live.

Gideon rolled to the side and pulled Charlie to him, tucking her into his body. Gently, he kissed the top of her head. His heart was heavy with the news he had to tell her, but there was no more putting it off. The longer he waited, the more upset she'd be. Charlie would hate that she'd lost a day already.

"Baby," Gideon whispered tentatively.

"Mmm?"

"I need to tell you something."

"You know you can tell me anything, Joe. I love you." She stifled a yawn and snuggled in closer to Gideon. "This is my most favorite place to be in the whole world. I can't imagine not being able to do this every night."

That certainly didn't help. "Do you remember when I explained to you how, with my job, I could be called away at a moment's notice?" Gideon began.

In the darkness of the bedroom, he felt her body tense next to him, and her head brushed against his chest when she nodded.

"Well, I just found out today that I have to leave in three days on a six-month deployment."

CHAPTER 3

"What did you just say?" Charlie tried to pull herself away from Gideon, but he wrapped his other arm around her and pulled her tighter into his massive form.

"I said I have to leave for a six-month tour in a little less than three days—if I were counting down."

Charlie felt tears beginning to sting the corners of her eyes.

Gideon rested his chin on the top of her head, his hands rubbing her arms in a futile gesture of comfort. Charlie couldn't breathe; she couldn't think. She just lay frozen in Gideon's hold. Quickly, disbelief turned to anger, and she wondered how long he'd known about this.

"Three days? Three days, Gideon?" The pitch in Charlie's voice was approaching hysteria, and she knew it, but she was unable to fight the emotion that bubbled to the surface. "How long have you been keeping this from me? Huh?"

Gideon's grip slackened, and Charlie sat up. She stared into his eyes, anger and hurt burning in her own.

"Baby, I told you, I just found out today. I didn't want to ruin our anniversary, so I waited to tell you."

"Well, brav-fucking-o, Gideon. Thanks for not ruining our anniversary. Great job." After giving him two thumbs up, Charlie moved to get out of bed. She needed to be away from him.

Before Charlie could extricate herself from the tangle of sheets, which seemed to have conspired with her husband to keep her in place, she felt his strong hand slip around her wrist.

"Let go of me." The words were harsh as Charlie bit them out through clenched teeth.

"Charlotte, what is the matter with you? You knew what I did when we got married. I explained my job and how important it was to me. I gave you an out. I gave you a chance to walk away from me. You accepted me, and you accepted this life."

The fact that he used her full name pissed Charlie off even more. He was trying to make her feel like a child, and he knew, more than anything, that would only make things worse. It was like he was *trying* to make her mad.

"Don't you do this, Gideon. Don't throw those things back at me. You know as well as I do that when you told me all of that, I really had no idea what it meant. I didn't know I'd have to let the person I love more than anything else in this world go off to God knows where and let people try to kill him." The tears flowed freely, and Charlie made no move to brush them from her cheeks.

The worst part of it for Charlie was that he was right. Everything Gideon had said was true. He'd explained to her how dangerous his work was, but it didn't seem real at the time. Even with troops still occupying countries in the Middle East, Charlie never truly thought he'd have to leave her.

"Come on, Charlie. You can't possibly be so upset about this. I mean, it isn't like I've never left before."

"Yeah, a week here or two weeks there for training, not a mission you may not come back from." As the words left her mouth, Charlie watched his expression change to one she couldn't understand.

"Charlie, come on. I'm a SEAL. You didn't really think I was training, did you?" His tone was full of accusation, like she'd been playing this game with him all along.

Charlie's eyes narrowed, and she rolled her hands into fists. "Are you telling me you've been lying for the entire year we've been married? Is that what you're saying, Gideon. What else do you lie about?"

"You know I can't tell you where I go or what I do. I thought you understood when I went on 'training exercises' that I was really working. I didn't know I was lying, truly. I would never lie to you, Charlie. On that first night, I swore to myself I wouldn't ever do that to you." He hung his head and looked almost ashamed.

For a tiny fraction of a second, Charlie felt bad for him. A tiny second.

"Gideon." She took a deep breath, trying to get her emotions under control before continuing. "I guess I'm the schmuck here. Because I actually thought you were out in the middle of the desert playing war with your buddies, but instead you were really in a war. Stupid me." The mix of emotions was overwhelming, and Charlie wasn't sure if she was supposed to be mad, sad, or embarrassed for being so naïve.

Finally, she succeeded in getting out of the bed. Everything inside her was fighting. Her heart wanted to stay and wrap her arms around Gideon, try to keep him with her and not let him go. Her head, however, was pissed off and wanted to be as far away from him as she could get. With both sides raging, Charlie stood, frozen and naked, waiting to see which was going to win.

"Charlie, I don't know what to say about this anymore. I genuinely believed you knew what I was doing and why I never really told you any specifics about what I did while I was gone. I'm sorry for that. But I can't tell you those things. If you want to call it lying, then so be it. I'm not going to apologize for my job. It's who I am — a part of everything you love." His tone was beginning to change from comforting to harsh and bitter.

Charlie's head won the battle. Grabbing her dress off the floor, she quickly pulled it over her head as she stalked to the door.

"Come on, Charlie. Don't do this. Not on our anniversary."

Gideon was begging from the bed; he hadn't moved an inch to come after her. Charlie suspected his body was fighting the same war hers had, and like her, his head was winning.

"Gideon, I need to be away from this for a while. I'm not going to leave the house. Please, just give me some time to think."

Charlie pulled the door closed behind her and hoped with everything she had that he'd listen to her. Leaning against the door for a moment, she heard only the sound of Gideon's voice as he cursed under his breath and the soft rustle of sheets being straightened out. He was going to stay put.

Charlie could see the dining room table from where she was, stuck against the bedroom door. The idea that she should clean flittered through her mind and was quickly dismissed as she walked to the freezer and took out a carton of Ben & Jerry's Chubby Hubby.

With ice cream and a spoon in hand, she found the couch in the moonlit room. Sitting in the near darkness in her anniversary dress with the carton of ice cream, she let the tears fall. She wondered what had happened. Had she and Gideon just had their first real fight? Charlie couldn't think of another time when she'd been this angry with Gideon.

Glancing over at the table, still set from the meal, Charlie couldn't help but remember their whirlwind romance. Her life was perfect now — at least it had been until just a little while ago. It was amazing how easily she'd known she'd found the person God put on this planet just for her…

…The wedding had been organized to take place on Saturday evening, to give their families time to get there. Gideon had immediately called his brother to be his best man, telling him not to call their parents because he figured it would be better to ask forgiveness than permission.

Charlie called her brother and his fiancée Gabriella. Chance would give her away, and Gabby would be her maid of honor. Charlie knew if she and Gideon were planning a big, traditional wedding—like the one Gabby was driving everyone insane planning right now—she'd be missing her mom and dad, but without Gideon's parents there either, it seemed easier somehow.

"You know, Joe, I'm fine with the quickie Vegas thing," Charlie had protested when he called down to the front desk to find out if the wedding chapel would be available for a half hour the next night.

"No, Charlotte O'Connor."

Charlie cringed at the use of her given name. The only people who ever called her that were her grandparents and her teachers on the first day of school.

"Uh, Joe?"

Gideon looked at her with a smile on his lips. She could tell he liked that she'd given him a nickname, even if it was kind of goofy and had no meaning to anyone but the two of them.

"Yes, baby?"

"Can you please not ever call me Charlotte? I hate the name, and the grandmother I'm named after was a nasty old lady who hated children."

Gideon chuckled and pressed his gloriously soft lips to hers before pulling back to look her in the eye again. "Okay, Charlie O'Connor, but when you become Mrs. Cooper, I want it to be something you're proud of, not something you have to try to explain to our kids one day. I know it won't be perfect, but I want it to be special."

Several hours later, Charlie was sleeping in Gideon's arms when a loud pounding on the door nearly caused her to leap out of bed.

"Gideon, you jackass, open up."

"My baby brother," Gideon confirmed with a roll of his eyes before getting up and pulling on his pants. "Hey, baby, why don't you go in the bathroom and put on one of those robes? I don't want my brother seeing all your goodies and trying to steal you away from me."

"Like that could happen," Charlie scoffed as she rolled herself out of bed and headed into the bathroom. As she pulled on a robe, she heard what sounded like a brawl in the other room. Flinging open the door and taking in the scene, Charlie noticed a stunning, raven-haired beauty standing in the doorway, looking as shocked at the two brothers as she was.

"Gideon! What the hell is going on?"

"Let….me…up…asshole," the man struggling underneath Gideon managed to say.

"Fine, pussy. Get your ass up and meet my bride-to-be." Gideon stuck his hand out to help his brother off the floor. "Tyson, this is Charlotte, uh, Charlie, your soon-to-be sister-in-law." He reached out and wrapped an arm around Charlie's waist, pulling her to him.

Tyson took several long looks up and down her body, a small smile breaking out on his face.

"Ahem." There was a loud clearing of a throat behind the small group. The beautiful woman stood there like a statue, never moving.

"Oh, yeah, Gideon, this is Mercedes. I thought I might need a date for this affair." Tyson winked at Gideon.

Mercedes moved into the room, giving off an air of coolness.

As Tyson and Gideon began discussing the room arrangements, there was another knock. Gideon pulled the door open to reveal Charlie's brother and his fiancée.

To see Gabby and Chance together was always a shock for Charlie, even though they'd been together almost three years—since they were freshmen in college. Chance, Charlie's twin, looked a lot like his sister with the same green eyes and spattering of freckles over the bridge of his nose, but his hair was more red than blond. And while Charlie had a small, almost petite frame, Chance was built more like Gideon, with a wide chest and broad shoulders. At almost six feet four inches tall, he only barely topped his fiancée's willowy height. In sharp contrast to Chance's pale Irish look,

Gabriella was a beautiful Hispanic woman with long, dark hair that fell in waves to her hips.

"Charlie! *Hermana!*" Gabby wrapped her arms around the woman who was not only going to be her sister, but was her friend as well.

"Are you really getting married, Lottie?" Chance looked at her with his piercing green eyes.

"Yeah, Chance. I love him."

It was all she had to say. A big smile spread across his face. "All I need to know," was his only reply…

Looking down into the empty ice cream carton, Charlie instantly regretted eating the whole thing. It wasn't going to help the situation; Gideon was still leaving. Setting the container on the floor beside her, she curled onto her side and pulled the afghan draped over the back of the couch down on top of her. The wetness from her cheeks made the leather couch slick, so Charlie grabbed a throw pillow to put under her head. She was sure sleep would evade her, but she closed her eyes in a vain attempt.

Fuck!

Gideon rolled over, pulling the sheets up as the door quietly clicked into place behind his wife. He knew sleep wasn't going to come, and he wanted so badly to chase after her and scoop her up to bring her back to their bed.

Not a good idea, his inner voice whispered. He may have been married for only a year, but after watching his parents for the past twenty-seven years, he'd learned a few things about angry women. When they told you to leave them alone, you did.

Charlie had said in no uncertain terms that she needed to be alone, and even though it was going to kill him to do it, Gideon knew he had to give her that. She needed to find a way to deal with what was happening to their lives, and he could only hope it didn't involve leaving him.

As he lay in the dark, alone, all Gideon could do was think about what had just happened, and the more he went over it, the more pissed off he got. None of this was his fault. He didn't do anything wrong tonight. Why was she so mad? She'd accepted him and everything that came with his job when she agreed to marry him. Gideon had been totally honest about how dangerous his job was, and she still married him.

Instead of sleeping, Gideon's thoughts turned to their wedding day…

…Gideon took Tyson and Chance down to the front desk to get rooms for them.

"So little brother, what's with the tight ass?" Gideon asked once they were in the elevator.

"Dude, don't talk about her like that. You never know, she might be the one." He laughed.

Both he and Gideon knew she wasn't. Tyson had always had horrible taste in women. He was a smart guy, but he chose to date girls who were less than stellar in the brains department. Now that Gideon had found perfection in Charlie, he couldn't help but want the same for his little brother. He wanted him to find a girl who was his equal.

"So the first words out of your mouth about the woman I'm going to marry in just a few hours' time were 'Where's the skank that has you doing something as stupid as getting married?' and what I said was offensive?"

Gideon saw Chance stiffen. His hands clenched and unclenched as his breathing fell into a pattern of slow, in-and-out, steadying breaths.

"Yeah, sorry about that," Tyson apologized. "I do have to say I'm impressed she has you obeying already."

"Nothing I wouldn't do for her, man."

Gideon saw Chance's smile return and found himself hoping Charlie's brother would approve of him.

"Good to know," Chance said quietly.

At Chance's response, Gideon wondered if he'd passed some sort of test in that brief exchange…

The alarm started blaring, and Gideon was back in the aftermath of his and Charlie's first fight. Pulling himself out of bed and cautiously opening the bedroom door, he heard the shower running and knew Charlie hadn't slept either. She never got up this early.

Gideon wasn't quite sure what to do next. They'd never fought like this, and he didn't know how to approach her. Slowly he opened the bathroom door, deciding to go with some lovey dovey, hoping she'd come to her senses. Gideon pulled back the shower curtain just as Charlie bent to turn off the water.

"Oh, baby, I was just coming to join you." He flashed the biggest, sexiest smile he could.

Charlie just stared at him.

"Can I have a little privacy, please?" Her voice was cold and pissed off.

Still wanting things to be normal, Gideon stepped in closer and tried to give her a hug. She was having none of it and moved out of his reach. In that moment, he knew it was going to be a very bad day. He didn't believe her words at first, but the fact that she wouldn't let him touch her screamed loud and clear, so Gideon turned and left Charlie to her routine.

The rest of the morning didn't get any better, with only a few words spoken, and when Gideon tried to kiss his wife good-bye, she turned her face away and only offered her cheek. He didn't know what to do to fix this, considering he hadn't done anything wrong. Gideon's mind raced as he pulled the door closed harder than he'd intended to and heard Charlie whimper inside.

As he walked down the stairs, he looked forward to the haven of his favorite thing in the world — next to Charlie, who was not available to him. He'd almost forgotten he'd lent Tyson his truck until he saw it.

"I am going to murder him. I am going to string him up by his balls and let him suffer for days." The words left him in a quiet hiss.

Sitting where his pristine truck had been the previous night was a filthy pickup, covered cab to bumper in mud and muck. Tyson had definitely picked the wrong day to piss Gideon off. Pulling out his phone, Gideon called his brother. He knew it was early, and he was probably waking him up, but oh well, too bad for him.

"What?" Tyson's sleep-heavy voice barked when he finally picked up.

"Tyson, you ass. You're going to fix my truck, and then I'm going to hurt you." Gideon hung up. He didn't care about the explanation or want to hear any excuses. He'd let Tyson worry about what he might do to him for a while. Tyson knew Gideon's size combined with his training meant it was more than a mere threat — it was a promise.

Once at work, Gideon figured he needed to tell his parents he was leaving in two days. They'd want to see him before he left, and his mom needed time to pull a gathering together, or she'd kick his ass.

It was a relief for Gideon to have physical training first thing in the morning. With all the damn drama going on at home, losing himself in a three-mile run and an hour of free weights was definitely welcomed. After PT, Gideon had some time before the briefing on the situation his team was heading into, so he decided to call his mother.

"Hey, Mom." Gideon tried to be light and not show how much strain had entered his life in the last twenty-four hours. He hoped his mom hadn't already talked with Charlie. He knew he'd be in big trouble if she knew how pissed Charlie was. Even though Gideon was Evelyn Cooper's son, she loved Charlie like she was one of her own too. Having two sons, she'd always missed out on all the girlie stuff, so when he brought Charlie home as his wife, Evelyn immediately embraced her as a daughter.

"Hi, Gideon. What are you doing, sweetheart?" When his mom called him sweetheart, Gideon knew she hadn't talked with his wife, and he felt his chest ease with relief.

"Well, I have some news. Now, don't get mad." After springing it on Charlie, Gideon decided to take a different approach with his mom.

"Is it that you're going to kill your brother? Because really, Gideon, I don't think a big pile of metal is worth Tyson's life. Do you?"

Gideon immediately thought what a fucking pussy his brother was to call and tell on him. That was going to earn him some extra punishment.

"No, it isn't about Tyson's upcoming beat-down. But, in answer, he was warned about what would happen if he brought my truck back in anything less than the condition it was taken in. Putting that aside, I have to leave on Friday."

"Where are you going, dear? Are you and Charlie finally taking that long-postponed honeymoon? Are you going to work on giving me some grandbabies?"

"No, Mom. I have to go away for work. I'm going to be gone for six months." He hated to blurt it out, but when she got started on the grandkid thing, there was no stopping her.

"Oh." There was a long silence before his mom started again. "Okay, so you and Charlie need to come for dinner tonight then. I'll have your dad put something on the grill. We can invite your brother, and Chance and Gabriella, of course." The list kept going on and on, and Gideon understood that this was her way of dealing with him going away. She'd done it every time he left on a long tour over the past four years.

"Okay, Mom. I'll call Charlie and tell her. We'll be there around six. I'll have her call Chance. You're going to have to call Tyson, though. I don't think he'd pick up for me."

Evelyn laughed, trying to act like everything was normal. Gideon knew the routine. While he hadn't been gone much in the last year, he'd left for months at a time before Charlie, and every time, his mom took on the same chipper persona. He let her fuss over him — it was what she needed to do to be okay, and Gideon got that. But Charlie's reaction was something new, and he still had no idea how to deal with it.

"Bye, sweetheart. See you tonight. Give Charlie my love."

"Bye, Mom."

Gideon sat with the phone in his hand for a few minutes before working up the nerve to call his wife. It took reading the text she'd sent the day before a couple of times to convince himself that she really loved him and was just scared right now. Finally he hit the speed dial and waited, hoping she'd actually answer.

"Hello." The chill from her voice reached right through the phone and squeezed his heart. Normally, when she knew it was him, she'd answer with "Hey, sexy." Not today. Gideon decided to match her tone, reminding himself he hadn't done anything wrong.

"Charlie, I just got off the phone with my mom. She wants everyone to come for dinner tonight."

"Okay." The one word conversation irritated him more than a little.

"Can you call Chance and Gabby to invite them too? Six o'clock at my parents'." He wanted to apologize and tell her how much it was killing him to be fighting like this — but he didn't say it; he hadn't done anything wrong.

"Sure."

"All right then. That's all, I guess. I love you, Charlie." Gideon couldn't keep up the mad thing with her any longer. He was sure he sounded pitiful, but he knew she was hurting more than anything else. Unfortunately, they didn't have time to let her work through this; Gideon was leaving in two days.

"Yeah. Me too. Bye." The phone clicked off.

Dropping the phone, Gideon laid his head down on the desk. He had to figure out how to change this before he left; having it hanging over him while doing his job could actually kill him.

"Cooper, come on. Briefing's starting." Gideon looked up to see one of his team standing there.

"Boyd, I thought you weren't going with us on this one? Docs didn't clear you."

"Doesn't mean I'm not still part of the team, though. I'll be the contact here."

"I'll be there in a minute." Gideon needed to gather himself together. There was no need for the other members of the team to think he was going to be a problem on the mission. After a few minutes, Gideon took a deep breath and headed into the war room to get the information he'd need to stay alive and come back home to Charlie…if she was still his home.

CHAPTER 4

Gideon couldn't remember a shittier day—and he got shot at for a living. Sitting in his still-filthy truck—Gideon was saving that little job for his baby brother—a sense of déjà vu washed over him. He'd been doing the exact same thing the previous day: sitting in the car, dreading going into the house.

Unable to decide if this feeling of dread was better or worse than the one from the day before, Gideon let out a long breath. Yesterday he'd been going into things blind, not knowing how Charlie was going to react. This time he could prepare himself. One thing his SEAL training taught him: know as much about what you're going into as you can.

The only thing Gideon knew for sure was that Charlie was still pissed. He'd been texting her all day, but got absolutely nothing in return. The texts had become more and more explicit, just trying to get a rise out of her, but still nada.

Dragging his weary ass out of the truck, Gideon climbed the stairs to the apartment. He held a tiny nugget of hope that Charlie had come to terms with what was happening, even just a little bit. Deep down Gideon knew she wasn't really mad at him. She was just scared, but he didn't know how to comfort her. If she'd break down and cry, he could hold her and tell her how much he loved her. The anger, though, made it impossible to get near her. She was fighting him with silence, and there was no combating that.

He wished dealing with women could be like fighting a war. With an enemy, he could usually predict from history or basic knowledge of human nature what they were going to do and adapt—learn how to fight them. He was a SEAL: He entered buildings and camps where people wanted him dead, and he fixed the problem — whatever the problem was. But women never reacted the way he expected.

Unlocking the door, he instantly knew Charlie was not any better than when he'd talked to her that morning. The apartment was deadly quiet, and she sat on the couch in cut-off sweats and a thin tank top, her hair pulled up in a loose ponytail. There were open textbooks strewn around her, and she typed furiously on her laptop. She didn't even look up as Gideon came in.

"Hey, babe." Gideon tried to smile, but the one-sided effort he'd been working all day was wearing on him. He felt the smile falter.

"Hi." Charlie was back to the one-word answers.

It was almost five, and with traffic they had about a forty-minute drive north to Gideon's parents' place in La Jolla. He didn't think she was exactly ready to go, and although apparently he wasn't always real smart when it came to dealing with his wife, Gideon knew not to point out that Charlie wasn't dressed for a family dinner. In her current mood, that might just get him killed. And wouldn't that just be the most ironic way to go — not at the hands of an enemy, but those of the woman he loved.

"I'm gonna change for dinner," he tried to hint as he headed to the bedroom.

"K."

One-word answers had just moved to one letter; that didn't seem like progress.

Dejected, Gideon wandered into the bathroom and turned on the shower. He needed to relax and think of what he could do to turn this shitty situation around. The problem was he was totally out of ideas, and as the hot water ran over his body, he gave up. All that mattered now was getting through tonight and tomorrow, then he'd be gone. The idea that Charlie was going to let him leave without making up made his lungs feel heavy and tight in his chest. Slumping against the shower wall, he gave himself over to the pain.

When Gideon stepped out of the shower into the steamy room, he resolved to put on a happy face for his family tonight. They didn't need the added stress of knowing what was going on between him and Charlie. Of course, he'd have to talk to Charlie about that. Back in the bedroom, Gideon dressed, working out in his head what he'd say to her. When he walked into the living room, he was surprised to find her dressed and ready to go. He didn't realize he'd been in the shower that long.

"We have to go, Gideon. We're going to be late." Her voice was clipped and harsh. This was not *his* Charlie.

"Yeah. Okay." Gideon followed his wife out the front door and down the stairs. She looked at the truck and the state it was in, and immediately turned toward her little Honda. Instinctively, he reached out to catch her hand and stop her. Charlie froze and pulled her hand out of his. That one hurt.

"We're taking the truck." He was back to pissed off now. His own wife didn't want him to touch her? Well, fuck her.

"It's a mess, Gideon. I'm not showing up at your parents' house in that thing."

"Yes, you are. Don't worry, it'll be clean by the end of the night." Gideon stalked over to his truck and got in, not bothering to open Charlie's door. He was done. No more.

He waited a heartbeat and turned the key in the ignition to let Charlie know he was serious. She needed to get her ass in the car. The door creaked open, and she slipped into her seat, buckling her seat belt. The look on her face was one of embarrassment and disgust.

As they pulled out of the parking lot, the silence in the car was tense. Being completely stubborn, Gideon didn't want to be the one to start the conversation. Even though he knew they needed to talk about how they were going to act around the family, he wanted her to suffer for a little while. He knew it was wrong. Didn't care.

After about ten minutes of fiddling with the radio and finding nothing she wanted to listen to, Charlie finally turned and looked at Gideon. It was the first time she'd actually looked at him all goddamn day.

"Why the hell did we have to take your disgusting truck? I feel gross, Gideon." There was a whine in her voice he'd never heard before. It made his skin crawl. This definitely wasn't *his* Charlie.

"Because Tyson did this shit to my car, and he's going to clean it. I mean, I'm leaving the day after tomorrow, and I need to know he did his penance for leaving it in this condition."

Charlie turned away quickly.

"Charlotte, we need to talk about tonight," Gideon started, enjoying it a little bit when she stiffened at the use of her real name.

"What about it?" Charlie bit out.

"I don't want my mom to know we're fighting. With me leaving, it would kill her if she thought there was something wrong between us." He hazarded a glance over at her.

She was staring out the window, her arms crossed over her chest.

"So, back to the lying thing, Gideon?"

"Yeah, if you want to look at it that way. I guess I want you to lie. For my mom, please." He knew there was nothing Charlie wouldn't do for Evelyn. She loved her like a second mother, and the thought of hurting her would keep Charlie in line.

"Fine. For Evelyn." And that was the end of the conversation. All of five minutes had passed, and just by Charlie's posture, Gideon knew there wasn't going to be anything else said for the rest of the drive.

Watching the traffic stop and go, stop and go, Gideon's mind wandered back to that day a year ago when he'd first seen her standing at the end of the aisle in the chapel at The Venetian. No woman could have looked more beautiful than the one who appeared when the music started…

…"Damn, bro. You're one lucky son of a bitch," Tyson whispered as he clapped a hand to Gideon's shoulder. Not trusting his voice, Gideon just smiled and nodded. He was unable to pull his eyes away from his bride as she seemed to float down the aisle, holding tightly to her brother's arm. His breathing halted for a long moment.

When after what seemed like an eternity Chance placed Charlie's hand in his, Gideon wanted to cry. He didn't, of course, because he wasn't that kind of pussy, but he wanted to. The smile on her face as she looked at him was blinding. Gideon was so caught up in her that he paid no attention to what the officiate was saying. It took Tyson giving him a smack to bring Gideon back.

"Oh, sorry, what?" He felt like an asshole, but Charlie's smile never faltered.

"Do you have rings to exchange?" asked the small man in front of the couple.

"Um, yeah."

Tyson handed over the rings.

Gideon took the rings and followed the little man's instructions, repeating all the words about the ring being a sign of his love for her as he slipped it on her hand. Once the band was on her finger, Gideon held up one finger to stop the preacher guy.

"Um, I want to also put this ring on Charlie's finger. Since we never got engagement rings, I want you to have this one too." It hadn't come out right, but from the look on Charlie's face, it didn't matter. Her eyes grew wide as she took in the perfect princess-cut, two-carat diamond, surrounded by emeralds the color of her eyes.

"Oh, Gideon." It was just a whisper, but he heard it, and his heart soared. Every time he heard his name fall from her lips, he melted just a little. Maybe he *was* that kind of pussy.

After that, everything seemed to go by in a blur. Gideon remembered saying "I do," and he'd never forget the look in Charlie's eyes when she looked at him and said the same thing...

As Gideon finally pulled into his parents' driveway, he looked over at his wife and wondered if she'd ever again look at him the way she had on their wedding day.

When Charlie and Gideon arrived, Charlie looped her arm through Gideon's as they walked up to the house. His look of surprise only served to infuriate her more, and she thought for a few seconds about pulling her arm out again. But Charlie was going through the motions for Evelyn, and there was no way she'd make her feel bad tonight. Charlie's stomach knotted at the thought that this could be the last time Evelyn saw her son.

Charlie knew being mad at Gideon was wrong. She wasn't really that mad—a fact she could only admit to herself. No, it wasn't anger. Charlie was scared to death. She wondered how fate could hate her so much, how just when she was the happiest she'd ever been in her life, it might all get taken away.

Charlie was afraid, but she'd never let anyone see her like that. Being angry was much easier and safer than letting people know she was weak and frightened.

As the couple approached the huge wooden door, Charlie remembered the first time she'd met her new family...

...After the wedding, Charlie and Gideon had spent the rest of the night and the next morning in bed together. They had no idea what everyone else did, and honestly, Charlie couldn't have cared less. It wasn't until Gideon mentioned that they should probably head home that the reality of what they'd done hit her.

"Charlie, baby, what's wrong?" Gideon asked as he ran his hands over her back.

"Joe, I—I'm worried about your parents."

"Oh, Charlie, trust me, Evelyn and Peter are going to love you. All my parents want is for Tyson and me to be happy, and you make me happier than anything ever has."

He kissed the top of her hair and held her against him for a few minutes. The panic began to fade. With Gideon's arms around her, nothing could scare her.

"Come on, let's get going so we can make it home in time for Sunday dinner."

The drive back was just as nice as the trip to Vegas. Even though they were married, there was still a lot the couple didn't know about each other. The conversation kept Charlie's fear at bay until Gideon pulled into the driveway at his parents' house. It was huge!

Charlie mentally kicked herself for not realizing when they got off the freeway in La Jolla that she'd gotten herself into something bigger than she could've ever imagined. The enormous house that loomed in front of her had the butterflies flying again.

"This is where you grew up?" The mixture of surprise and fear in her voice was evident, and Gideon was at her side in an instant to wrap his arm around her. Taking Charlie's left hand, he brought it to his lips and brushed a gentle kiss over the new rings there.

"I love you, Mrs. Cooper. There's nothing to be scared of. Really. My parents are going to love you as much as I do."

Charlie rolled her eyes.

"Okay, maybe not as much as I do, but they're going to love you. Trust me." Gideon dragged her up the long walkway to the front door.

Opening the door, Gideon's big voice filled the entire house as he yelled that he was there to eat. Charlie slapped at his chest.

"Gideon, shouldn't you be a little more formal here?" Charlie whispered. The huge open interior was intimidating.

Before Gideon could answer, his parents came into the front hall.

Gideon pulled Charlie closer, sensing her fear. An attractive woman with her blond hair pulled up in an elegant sweep came to a halt right in front of the couple, appearing to evaluate whether

Charlie was worthy to be in her son's presence. In a moment of panic, Charlie hid her left hand behind her back, not wanting to spring that on them before she'd even said hello.

"Well, Gideon, who is this lovely young lady?" His mother's face lit up with a genuine smile. Charlie was surprised by the friendly greeting after the onceover. She hoped her new mother-in-law still thought she was "lovely" after she found out how Charlie had seduced her son.

"Mom, Dad," Gideon paused for a second. "This is Charlie. My wife."

Charlie wanted to curl up and hide, or turn and yank that giant wooden door open. It seemed to her that this was something a person should ease in to — not toss out there like, "I bought a new car!"

"Charlie, this is Evelyn and Peter, my parents."

"Your wife?" Peter was the first to speak.

The question wasn't harsh or unfriendly, just a question like, "How's the weather?" Charlie braced herself for the storm.

Then Evelyn stepped right up to her. Charlie moved further into Gideon, not sure what his mother was about to do.

"Gideon, let go of her already. I want to give my new daughter a hug."

Evelyn smiled. Never in her wildest dreams had Charlie expected to be welcomed so genuinely and warmly.

A loud chuckle echoed in the hallway as Gideon released his wife, and Charlie felt his mother's small arms wrap around her.

"Welcome to our family, Charlie…"

Gideon opened the big wooden doors and announced their arrival, much as he'd done that day a year ago. Despite her current tangle of emotions, Charlie was still so thankful that there'd never been any lectures about how crazy it was to get married after only knowing one another for just a few days, no questioning as to why Charlie would want to marry their son, no hinting that she was after their money. Charlie had been welcomed into the family. Evelyn and Peter always made her feel like she'd been missing and they'd just found her.

About ten minutes later, Chance and Gabby arrived, and not long after that Gideon, who'd been pacing by the door and peeking out through the leaded glass every few minutes, bolted outside. He didn't tell Charlie where he was going and hadn't even glanced back at her before the door closed behind him. That only served to move Charlie from hurt toward actually being angry.

His recent revelations about where he'd been while she thought he was training, combined with his leaving her standing alone in front of the entire family, made Charlie wonder for the first time since marrying Gideon if maybe they'd rushed into things.

A short time later, still sulking, Charlie sat in a lounger by the pool, watching her family move around her. Evelyn had embraced Chance and Gabby like they belonged to her as well. Since their parents' death almost three years ago, Chance and Charlie had only had each other. It was nice to be part of a family again. Having Evelyn and Peter in her life was important to Charlie in a way Gideon would never understand.

Everyone was acting normal—and even seemed happy. Charlie couldn't understand how the hell they could just laugh and smile and act like Gideon wasn't getting ready to leave. To go fight for someone he didn't even know. And maybe not come back to them…to her.

A low sigh escaped as Charlie leaned her head back against the chair and tried to think of the happiest day of her life. She needed to find a way to keep up her pretense.

"What you thinkin' about, Lottie?" Charlie didn't have to look over to the other lounge chair to know it was Chance. He was the only one in the world who would dare call her Lottie.

"I was thinking about how lucky we are that when I married Gideon we got Evelyn and Peter in the deal. I mean, they just welcomed all of us and made us feel like part of their family."

"So are you doing okay with all this, Lottie?" Chance's voice dropped to a whisper. Charlie could never hide anything from him.

"No, no, I'm not, Chance. I'm so mad right now—and scared. But I can't let him know how scared I am. I can't send him away thinking about me like that."

"So sending him off thinking you're mad is better?"

Charlie hated that Chance was the logical one. She'd only wanted to vent, and he had to go and be all wise and crap.

Suddenly, Charlie felt a light hand on her shoulder. She hadn't noticed Evelyn standing behind her. It didn't matter anymore whether she was scared or mad. Now that Evelyn had heard, Gideon was going to be pissed.

"Chance, I'm wondering, would you mind if I stole my daughter-in-law from you for a minute?" Evelyn asked.

"No problem, Evelyn. I think I need to rescue Peter anyway. Looks like he's getting some 'lessons' from Gabby." Chance got up, gave Charlie a small kiss on the top of her head, and winked at Evelyn before walking over to where Gabby was standing with Peter. "Baby, let the man cook in his own house," he said. "He's a surgeon, for God's sake. I think he can figure out how to marinate a steak."

"Come inside with me for a minute, hon." Evelyn held her hand out to help Charlie off the lounge chair.

Charlie followed her mother-in-law through the house into her small study off the main living room. When she sat on the couch, Evelyn sat down beside her and took Charlie's hand in her own.

"Charlie, honey, I want you to know that you're my daughter now. I don't ever want you to be afraid to talk to me."

Charlie tried to fight the tears she felt welling behind her eyes.

"Let me tell you something about my boys. Don't get me wrong—I love both Tyson and Gideon more than anything in this world. But I learned long ago that I have to love them without expectations."

"I'm not sure what you mean, Evelyn." Tears started to run down her cheeks, and Evelyn softly brushed them away.

"Are you and Gideon fighting?"

"Sort of." Charlie was unsure what she should say after what Gideon had said in the car. "I just don't know, Evelyn. I'm so worried about him. He's going to leave me, and what if he doesn't come home?" The tears were flowing freely now, and she couldn't have stopped them if she'd wanted to.

Evelyn pulled Charlie to her, letting her daughter-in-law lean against her shoulder and cry.

"Let me explain Gideon to you, Charlie. Ever since he was a little boy, he's always done what he wanted. Not in a bad way, mind you. While he didn't always listen to his father and me, he was a good boy for the most part. But when he set his mind to something, he got it done. When he wanted to start on the varsity football team as a sophomore, he did it. When he wanted to get into USC, he did it."

She stopped and smiled. Charlie smiled a wet smile too, thinking of Gideon and his determination.

"So, I've had to learn to live with Gideon's decisions and understand that while he may seem crazy and go off half-cocked, everything comes together in the end," she continued. "Didn't you ever wonder why when he brought you home as his wife I hugged you and you were my new daughter? No questions asked?"

"Well, as a matter of fact, I was just thinking about that earlier."

"It was because I trust Gideon and know that everything is going to turn out right. You have to know that too, Charlie. It's the only way to live with Gideon."

Evelyn's smile grew wider, but this time Charlie couldn't return it. All she could think was that he might never come home.

"How can this turn out right? He's going away to be shot at."

"Charlie, do you trust Gideon?"

"Yes, of course."

"Do you know how much he loves you and that he'd do anything to come home to you?"

"Yes, but —"

"There are no buts, honey. This is Gideon. I suspect that his devotion and total commitment are what you fell in love with. Am I right?" Evelyn gave her a hard stare.

As much as Charlie wanted to argue, she was right; one of the reasons Charlie fell in love with Gideon was his commitment and pride in what he did for the country. Evelyn's words made her see how stupid she'd been.

After giving her mother-in-law a quick hug, Charlie wiped her eyes and got up off the sofa, determined to find Gideon and make things right.

"Thank you so much, Evelyn. I'm so lucky to have you."

"And you do have us, honey. Both Peter and I are here for you whenever you need us." She pulled Charlie into a tight embrace and kissed her on the cheek.

"I think I need to go find my husband," Charlie whispered.

"Good idea."

CHAPTER 5

"Shit." The word was let go on an exhale as Tyson forgot about the gorgeous woman sitting next to him.

"What's wrong?"

Tyson looked over to see Paige's huge brown eyes staring back at him, and he lost his train of thought. It wasn't the first time that had happened.

"Uh, nothing really. Just that my brother brought the truck." He pointed to the dirt-covered metal beast sitting in his parents' driveway. "And he didn't clean it. That doesn't bode well for me."

When Tyson glanced over again there was a smile creeping across her face. Paige Halloran was the first woman he'd ever dated who he thought he could have real feelings for. Usually after about two dates, Tyson had to get rid of a girl. They just got so boring. Sometimes he'd keep one around a little while longer if he wanted to get her in bed, but for the most part, he never went out with a girl more than twice.

Paige was different. He wanted to know everything about her. Of course, he wanted to get her into his bed too—with the legs she had… He daydreamed about having them wrapped around him as she panted his name. But there was so much more than that. Unlike the other women—who were all about appearances and status—Paige was actually interesting.

Gideon had tried to explain how he felt about Charlie right before the wedding, but Tyson just didn't get it. Gideon was a stud, that was a well-documented fact, and Tyson worshiped the guy. His hero was getting married to some chick he met in a bar not even two days before. At the time it just didn't make sense. But when he looked at Paige, Tyson thought he was beginning to understand it a little better. No way was he ready to marry her, but the idea didn't send him running the other direction either. That was progress.

Although the couple had been dating nearly a month, he hadn't been brave enough to bring her home to meet his parents. Ever since Gideon showed up married one Sunday night—and effectively took all the "when are you going to find a nice girl" attention off himself—Tyson had been the sole focus of his mother's invasive questions. Until now he hadn't been sure Paige could handle that kind of pressure. And he didn't even want to think of what his brother might tell the first girl to hold his attention for more than a day or two.

"Why is your brother's truck such a problem?" Paige asked.

"Here's the thing. Other than Charlie and his job, Gideon's greatest love is his Ford SuperCab F-150. It was the first substantial thing he ever bought with his own money."

"And?" she prompted.

"When I borrowed it last night, he made some threats about what would happen if I brought it back in anything less than the condition I took it in. I got a nice little wakeup call from him this morning, threatening me."

Tyson expected her to gasp and worry for his safety. Instead she laughed. And while it was one of the most beautiful sounds he'd ever heard, he was taken aback by it.

"Why are you laughing?" A hint of the irritation he felt crept into his voice. She was supposed to be horrified that he was being threatened, indignant even.

"You're afraid of your brother? I think that's funny."

Tyson looked up to see Gideon marching toward his car.

"Really, you think it's funny? *That* is my brother." He pointed to the gigantic pile of muscle and pissed off stalking down the walkway.

"Oh my," Paige squeaked out.

"Tyson!" Gideon's voice boomed as his face lit up with a smile. "So glad you could make it. I got a job for you."

Shit! Tyson wasn't sure if he said it out loud, but he didn't look at Paige to find out. Opening the car door, Tyson stepped out. He walked around and opened Paige's door like the gentleman his mother had raised him to be (of course, this was the first time he'd actually put the training into practice), then took Paige's hand and helped her out.

"Gideon, this is Paige Halloran. Paige, this would be my obnoxious, pain-in-the-ass older brother, Gideon."

"Is this the girlie who helped you fuck up my truck last night?"

Gideon was never one to mince words.

"Nice, Gid. You just met Paige, and you start talking like a sailor, and yet you wonder why I haven't introduced her before. Mom would kill you if she heard you talking like that in front of our guest. Hell, Mom would kill you if she heard you talking like that period."

"What? Are you going to tell Mom on me again, Ty?"

"Yeah." Paige's voice broke into the siblings' spat. "I was with Tyson when your car got dirty."

Tyson looked at her in amazement. Most people were so intimidated by Gideon's size that they barely spoke when they first met him. Paige was almost challenging in her response.

Tyson saw the puzzled look on Gideon's face turn into a smile, and then he laughed.

"Good to know, good to know. So you can help him while he cleans the entire thing — inside and out."

"Gideon, you can't be serious." The younger brother slid his hand into Paige's and headed toward the house, but Gideon's meaty hand pressed against Tyson's chest, stopping all forward movement.

"Oh, serious as a heart attack, little brother. I want my baby shining when I leave here tonight. And, by the way, I'm leaving specific instructions with Charlie that while I'm gone no one — and that means you — drives the truck."

Gideon's mention of the fact that he was leaving was a jolt to Tyson. He hated when his brother left. He understood why Gideon did what he did — he was proud of his big brother. But God, he hated when the guy left.

"Fine. But you have to explain to Mom why I'm out here instead of being the life of the party inside, and why you're making our guest wash your car."

Gideon laughed out loud, and Paige jumped a little.

"Holy Christ, man. You scared me." She gave him a playful slap on the arm. "Warn a girl before you make a noise like that. I thought there might be a moose in heat somewhere close."

Another booming laugh filled the air as Gideon pulled Paige into a quick hug.

"I like this one, Tyson. Maybe I should take her in to meet the family while you get to work. Then I won't have to explain to Mom why your little friend here is washing my truck."

Tyson could only watch as his brother and girlfriend walked into the house with Gideon's big arm resting across her shoulder.

"Have fun, little brother. Oh, and it better be spotless, or else."

Unfortunately, Tyson knew what "or else" meant, and he didn't feel like being Gideon's punching bag tonight. That could get humiliating in front of Paige.

Looking down at the supplies Gideon had left next to his truck, Tyson sighed. But then he decided that in exchange for the night he spent with Paige in the bed of the truck, this was more than worth it.

Just as Gideon walked into the house with his arm around Paige, the door to his mother's office opened to reveal Charlie and Evelyn. Paige was laughing at the bit of information Gideon had just given her: Evelyn had dressed Tyson in girl clothes as a baby because she'd wanted a girl so badly. The blonde's head was thrown back, and Gideon's face had relaxed into a smile, which he welcomed after the day he'd had.

"Ah, he's trying to kill me," Gideon heard Evelyn whisper under her breath.

Immediately Gideon's smile faded, and he dropped his arm from Paige's shoulder. Before he could process what was happening, Charlie had run to him, throwing her arms around his thick waist and pulling herself into him as close as she could get. Hesitantly, Gideon let his arms slide around her and placed small kisses on the top of her head.

"I'm sorry, Joe. I'm so, so sorry. I love you." Charlie sobbed into his chest, and Gideon's heart soared at the use of his nickname. No one else in his life called him that, and to hear it again let him know they'd be all right.

"I know, baby. I love you too."

Gideon was so caught up in having his wife's body against his again that he'd completely forgotten about the stranger standing in the middle of all the drama—until she cleared her throat.

"Oh, sorry. Mom, Charlie, this is Tyson's new friend, Paige."

"Hi," Paige said.

Evelyn stepped forward and put an arm around Paige's shoulder, pulling her into a hug.

"Hi, dear. So nice to meet you." She looked over at Gideon. "Where's your brother? I think your father is just about ready to serve dinner."

"Oh, Gideon here has him playing car wash," Paige informed her.

"Gideon Isaac Cooper. You go right out there and tell your brother to come in. Your truck can wait." Evelyn gave him a stern, motherly look. Gideon cursed silently, hoping Tyson had gotten at least some cleaning done, because there was no way he was going to defy his mother.

"Fine," Gideon mumbled. "But I'm leaving here with a clean car tonight," he called over his shoulder as he walked out.

Moments later, as Gideon stood on the porch watching Tyson work just a little more, he heard the door open again. "Give him a few more minutes," Charlie whispered as she came up behind him, sliding her arms around his waist and resting her cheek in the space between his massive shoulder blades.

"Sounds good to me." Gideon turned and leaned down to brush his lips against Charlie's.

His world was right again. Gideon's mind exploded at the sheer pleasure of having his wife back in his arms. "Let's go home, babe," he whispered in Charlie's ear as he leaned in to kiss her neck.

Charlie's head tilted back to allow better access as a small giggle rang out into the night.

Gideon wanted to be at home in bed with his wife straddling him. He *needed* to see her with her head thrown back, screaming his name.

"Joe, we can't. You know that. There's a house full of people wanting to say…"

She paused, and Gideon saw her eyes glisten slightly. He knew she couldn't say the words.

"It's okay, Charlie." Gideon pulled her closer. This was something he couldn't control for her. There was no way for him to stop the hurt, no matter how badly he wanted to. Every fiber in his body was on fire, itching to protect her.

The pair stood entwined for a long moment, neither wanting to let go.

"Oh, for Christ's sake!" Tyson's voice broke into their perfect moment as he sauntered up to the porch, wiping his hands. "You'd think after a year, you two would be able to keep your hands off each other. Get a room!"

Gideon's mouth opened, ready to fire back one of the thousand rude remarks floating through his head, when he felt Charlie's finger against his lips.

"Allow me, Joe." She gave him a brilliant smile. "Fuck off, Tyson!"

Simple, to the point. Gideon liked it, and he wanted to take Charlie right then and there, brother or no brother standing in front of them. With that thought in mind, his hands began to wander up Charlie's body.

Tyson clutched his hand to his chest. "Charlie, I'm hurt, dear sister-in-law. Has my asshole brother finally lured you over to the dark side?"

Charlie just smirked at him, then snuggled back into Gideon's chest.

"Is my truck back in pristine condition, Ty?"

"Yes. Knowing Paige was being mauled by you was great inspiration." Tyson began to tuck his T-shirt back into his jeans. "What did you do with her anyway?"

"Mom was taking her for introductions. Can't wait for her to meet Gabby. You know how she loves to share family stories." Gideon couldn't help but laugh at the thought of Gabby telling Paige all the stupid things Tyson had done over the last year.

"Shit. I better get in there before she starts telling her about New Year's." Tyson flung the front door open, and before it had even swung closed he was sprinting through the house, headed for the gathering out back.

"You know, as much of a pain in the ass as my brother is, he did have a great idea." Gideon trailed kisses along Charlie's jaw line as Tyson's words rang in his head.

Charlie looked up at him, her brow furrowed in confusion. It was rare that Gideon gave Tyson credit for anything.

"What fabulous words of wisdom did Tyson accidentally utter that have you so, um, worked up?" She dragged her fingertips over the strained material of his pants.

He groaned at the sheer ecstasy of having his wife finally touch him again. Gideon knew underneath she wasn't okay yet, but as long as she was talking to him and, most especially, touching him, everything else could wait.

"Well, he suggested we get a room." Gideon raised his eyebrows suggestively. "And what do you know? My bedroom is right upstairs."

There was no giggle this time, but a big burst of laughter. Instantly, Gideon's body reacted, claiming her mouth with a kiss so passionate, he was sure she wouldn't say no to the suggestion. When he was finally able to release her lips, her gaze locked on his. She moved a hand to rest on his cheek.

Hells yes! I'm going to have my wife naked and moaning in total euphoria in just a few minutes, he thought as the warmth of her hand seeped deep into every pore of his body.

"Yeah, don't think so, Joe. Remember last time we tried that?" Charlie kissed the tip of his nose. Sliding her hand back down his neck and arm, she grabbed Gideon's hand and began to pull him into the house.

Of course Gideon couldn't forget the one and only time they'd tried to get busy in his old bedroom. It was that first night he'd brought Charlie home as his wife, and during dinner he realized they had nowhere to stay as a married couple. The fact that he lived in the barracks on base and she lived in the dorms had completely slipped their minds in the haze of love.

His parents had graciously offered them his old room, Heidi Klum poster and all — a detail Charlie had never let him forget. The problem came when his mother walked into the room with clean linens to find Gideon with his hand obviously up Charlie's shirt. Gideon thought it was funny until Charlie told him in no uncertain terms that he wouldn't be getting any until they had their own place. Gideon had greased a lot of wheels so the couple could move into an apartment the very next day.

Gideon was laughing as he and Charlie entered the backyard where their family was gathered. He grabbed Charlie around the waist and pulled her back to him, and he may have accidentally let his hand settle on her perfect ass. She wouldn't be getting very far from him for the rest of the night. Gideon knew he only had a short time left to hold her.

"Good God, Gideon," Tyson complained when he noticed his brother practically mauling his wife.

Gideon shot Tyson a look to let him know he was completely serious about wanting to hurt him. He figured having Paige there made the threat all the more frightening.

"That's right, little brother," he said. "Keep it zipped."

Gideon noticed his mom watching and tried to play it off like he was just having a brotherly moment with Tyson. He knew she hated that they fought, but he thought she'd be used to it by now. She always said it had started the day she brought Tyson home from the hospital. Whether it was Gideon trying to get Tyson to "ride" in the dryer or Tyson stealing Gideon's toys — they'd fought.

In the end, however, Gideon loved his brother, and there was nothing he wouldn't do for him. And Gideon knew the same went for Tyson. They could have their little wars, but when it came down to it, they loved each other, and Gideon hoped his mom knew that.

Gideon was grateful his mom had been able to give him the one thing he needed most before he left — his Charlie back. He didn't know what they'd talked about, but whatever had been said in that office was exactly right. Charlie leaned back against Gideon as he smiled at his mom, silently promising not to let her down when it came to Charlie and their future.

The night was slowly coming to an end, and no matter how much Charlie tried to keep it at bay, time kept creeping forward. After her talk with Evelyn, Charlie had spent the entire evening at Gideon's side. She'd already wasted an entire day being mad, and she wasn't going to lose even one more minute of her time with him.

Throughout the night, Charlie had watched Tyson and his new girl-friend. Paige was pretty, with long blond hair and big brown eyes. And she was smart—so not Tyson's usual type. Charlie remembered, with a shudder, the skank he'd brought to the wedding. There was still some deep-seated hostility toward him for that little treat. But this girl was sweet and stood up to Gideon, which Charlie really liked.

When everyone began to gravitate toward the door, Gideon wrapped Charlie in his arms as they waited in the entry hall for the rest of the family. Tyson came in holding Paige's hand. Behind him, Chance and Gabby were talking with Peter, while Evelyn stood staring at her sons.

"Dude, I'll miss you." Tyson clapped Gideon on the shoulder, and Charlie let go of him, even though her heart ached when she did.

"Yeah, sure. You'll just miss my truck." Gideon smiled. "Seriously, I want you to watch out for Charlie, okay? Chance, I know I don't need to say that to you, right?"

Charlie rolled her eyes. Like she needed to have those two boys look-ing out for her. She was a married woman who could take care of herself.

"You know I will." Chance flashed a smile at his sister.

"You can count on me too. You know that, Gid."

Tyson and Gideon stood awkwardly with Tyson's hand resting on Gideon's shoulder.

"Oh, cut the macho bullshit, boys, and just give each other a hug." Paige spoke the words everyone else in the room was thinking.

Charlie decided she really did like this girl for Tyson. Seemed like she could keep his skinny ass in line.

"Amen," Charlie added with a special smile for Gideon, which let him know if he didn't hug his brother, there'd be hell to pay. She was pretty sure they really did want to hug anyway.

Charlie saw Evelyn wipe a tear away as she watched her sons embrace. Charlie knew what she was thinking—the same thing Charlie was: This might be the last time they hugged. The smile on Evelyn's face, however, never faltered. She was playing her part perfectly, and Charlie vowed that she would too.

Turning back to the scene in front of her, Charlie offered Paige her hand.

"It was really great to meet you, Paige. Sorry you had to meet the family at such a crazy time."

"I had a great time. I know I don't know you very well yet—" she looked over at Tyson for just a split second "—but if I can help while Gideon is gone… Well, just let me know."

Just as Charlie had been, Paige seemed instantly absorbed into their family. Tyson was back at Paige's side, his arm around her waist as she shook Gideon's hand and said good-bye.

Gideon and Charlie were the last to say good-bye to Evelyn and Peter. And even though she kept her brave face on as the front door closed behind them, Charlie knew Evelyn's night was going to end in a lot of tears, just as she was sure every one of hers would for the next six months.

But Evelyn had Peter to help her through it, Charlie would be on her own.

CHAPTER 6

The ride home was just as quiet as the one to dinner, but for different reasons. The couple's hands were clutched together with Gideon's thumb constantly tracing circles on the back of Charlie's. She wondered what Gideon was thinking that kept him so quiet. Since she'd met the man, he'd never gone this long without talking. That had Charlie worried.

"We're home, babe." Gideon released her hand so he could get out of the car. He came around and opened her door, lifting Charlie out of the truck and carrying her all the way up the stairs to their apartment.

"Joe, can we talk? I need to talk." Charlie suddenly felt the urgency to share what she was feeling.

"Of course, baby. Whatever you want to do."

Sitting on the couch and kicking off her shoes, Charlie snuggled into Gideon's warm, hard body and let him wrap his strong arms around her. She needed to feel him like this.

"What do you want to talk about? I'm pretty sure I know, but I want to hear what you're thinking."

Charlie sighed, not sure if she was going to be able to tell him how scared she was, how absolutely terrified she was to let go of him.

"First, I want you to know how sorry I am for the past day or so," she started, already holding back tears.

Gideon pulled her closer. He stayed quiet, letting Charlie get out what she needed to. Charlie was thankful for that. If he'd tried to comfort her or explain right then, she wouldn't be able to go on.

"I love you so much. I feel like we just found each other and now… now…" The tears began to fall, and she let them. "Now you're going away. Leaving me."

"Oh, Charlie. I'm not leaving you. I wou—"

"I know you aren't leaving me in that way. But you won't be here every night when I fall asleep. The last thing I think about every night is how safe I am in your arms. How we fit perfectly together, like God made us for one another. And you won't be here when I open my eyes in the morning. Those things will be gone."

Gideon's hand caressed her arm, and Charlie felt his breath as he sighed.

"You, Gideon Cooper, are my whole life. I can't lose you. I'm so torn because what you do is who you are, and I could never ask you to not be you, not do your job. But damn it, I want to kick and scream and beg you not to go. My heart and my head are in two different worlds, and I don't know how to bring them back into alignment."

Charlie's body slumped and huge, wracking sobs caused every muscle to jerk and twitch while Gideon held her. His strong arms kept her against him as he whispered how much he loved her and that there was no way their story was over. These things only made Charlie cry harder, a feat she'd been sure was impossible. She cried until there was nothing left.

When Charlie opened her eyes after what seemed like only minutes, the sun was coming up. The last day they had together was starting, and Charlie had wasted the whole night crying.

"Morning, babe." Gideon's breath was hot on her ear.

"I'm so sorry, Joe. I ruined another night." Charlie wanted to cry again, but she knew she was done. Gideon wouldn't see her cry again before he left. That much she could give him.

"Charlie, you don't ever have to apologize for telling me how you feel. I want you to know that. I love you, and what hurts you, hurts me."

Turning her body so she was facing him and lying on his chest, Charlie stretched up and slowly kissed his neck and chin, where rough stubble had grown during the night. She finally reached his mouth, and he welcomed her warmly, parting his lips and allowing her to slip in her tongue. Charlie moaned.

"Fuck, Charlie. We can't start this."

Charlie pulled back. "Wh-Why?" She'd thought yesterday was behind them.

"Oh, baby. No, no, no. I have a team meeting in like forty-five minutes. It's our last one before we ship out. I have to get a shower and get my ass to the base. I love you."

He kissed Charlie lightly and extracted himself from her grip, stretching what she was sure were very sore muscles from the way they'd spent the night.

Charlie suddenly felt empty, but she remembered the vow she'd made only moments ago. Sadness and fear would not creep into their last day together. Today she'd make sure Gideon had something to think about while he was gone, something he wanted to live for.

To change the path her mind kept wandering, Charlie started planning her going-away gift for Gideon. She needed to do something he'd remember, something he'd never expect her to do.

The few men Charlie had been with before Gideon hadn't been anything memorable. Most had been concerned only with their own outcome, in the literal sense, and Charlie had been left less-than-impressed by the whole process. So when she met Gideon, her world was rocked off its axis. He was the first guy to give her an orgasm. He was the first guy to pleasure her, and he was the first guy who truly made love to her.

Charlie's lack of experience, however, had made her a little timid in the bedroom. She was good at flirting with her husband — Charlie knew just what to do to turn him on — but once they were naked, it was all Gideon. He was in charge. But tonight, Charlie wanted to give him something he'd never expect.

Gideon couldn't stop his knee from bouncing. Every once in a while it knocked against the underside of the table, causing the coffee in the cups above to slosh all over.

"Shit, Coop."

"What the hell, man?"

Gideon shrugged. There was no way in hell he'd tell them the reason for his nervous knee bounce. He'd let them think he was getting worked up over the mission, but in truth, it was all Charlie's fault.

Gideon felt his phone vibrate against his hip again. In the few hours he'd been in the briefing, Charlie had texted him six — make that seven — times.

Oh sure, she'd started out innocently enough. Her first message simply said: *I luv u.* That one made Gideon smile, knowing he was lucky enough to have the smartest, most beautiful woman in the world loving him. The second message was about the same: *I miss u.* Then about ten minutes later, a third one came: *Miss u. Want u.* Not too bad, but enough to cause some blood to rush from one head to the other.

It was the next text that started Gideon's knee bouncing: *I want u. ALL of u. Cum home soon.* The fact that he hadn't touched his wife in two days was not helping the situation. Considering he was in a room full of guys, Gideon didn't think sporting major wood was going to go over too well. Thus, the knee bouncing. He'd hoped concentrating on something besides Charlie's incredible naked body writhing in total ecstasy—*okay, that image* so *did not help*—would keep his body under control.

Fifteen text-free minutes later, Gideon had everything back under control. Of course, that's when he received yet another message from her. Actually in the span of five minutes, Gideon's phone vibrated three times.

The first text was fairly innocent, or so he thought: *Which do u like better?* While he was confused, he was more relieved at not having to talk himself out of another embarrassing display of his body's total lack of control. He settled into his seat, focusing on Lieutenant Dallas Walker, the team leader, once again.

The comfort was short lived, however. Moments later his cell vibrated again. This time it was a picture of Charlie in the most amazing piece of lingerie Gideon had ever had the pleasure of seeing. She wore a black leather, lace-up corset type thing with a black thong and garter belt. The little hook things on the garter belt hung loose, but he could picture those thigh-high nylons attached. Gideon let out a groan, and his knee went into overdrive, knocking against the table so hard that three of the coffee cups actually fell over.

"Problem, Lieutenant?" Walker asked. His eyes were hard, and Gideon knew he was pissed.

Gideon was second in command for this mission, so it was important that he show himself as a leader these men could trust and obey without hesitation. Hesitation could get someone killed. Gideon was pretty sure pitching a tent during the briefing and being so distracted he didn't even know what they were talking about was not the way to build that trust.

"Sorry, sir. Leg cramp," Gideon lied, reaching down to rub his calf to make it more believable.

Another vibration in his pocket caught Gideon by surprise, even though he should have expected the "other choice." He was afraid to look this time, sure he'd actually have to get up and run out of the briefing or else pass out from the blood rushing from his brain to below his belt.

Gideon's hand wrapped around the tiny cell phone as he debated his options. He wanted to look. He had to look.

He shouldn't have looked.

It was Charlie in yet another incredible outfit. This one was pink lace. It was a one-piece job that pushed her boobs together so they were almost spilling out. His girl had a nice rack, but to see them on display like that…

He got so excited, he must have squeezed too hard, because the small metal object shot out of his grip and skidded across the polished wooden table. It landed right in front of Cody Boyd, face up. Everything seemed to move in slow motion as Gideon dove across the table to grab his phone before the other man got his hands on it. He wanted to keep his wife's incredible body out of his buddy's head. No such luck.

"Damn, Coop. I knew your wife was hot, but holy shit — she is smokin' in that little number." Boyd sneered at Gideon as he held the phone just out of reach.

"Gimme my fucking phone, Boyd." Gideon's voice sounded menacing even to his own ears. Having another man look at Charlie in that outfit was sickening. No one was ever supposed to see her like that but him.

"Break it up you two. Boyd, give Cooper his phone back," Walker ordered.

Boyd flipped the phone to Gideon, who caught it with one hand, clearing the screen as he slipped it back in his pocket. Lieutenant Walker glared at Gideon the entire time. Gideon knew he was going to get bitched out, but he hoped the lieutenant would wait until they were on the transport tomorrow. Then Walker could have his undivided attention for several hours.

"Okay, SEALS, that's it for now. I want all your asses on the tarmac at oh-eight hundred tomorrow morning. I ain't waiting for none of y'all. Now, get the hell out of here. That's an order."

Gideon was the first one out of his seat and through the door.

"Yo, Coop. Gotta fire in your pants?" Boyd called from behind him. "I know I do after seeing that picture of your wife. Better be careful — I might just steal her away while you're gone."

Gideon stopped dead in his tracks and turned on his heel.

"First of all, you stay the hell away from my wife. Second, I catch you even *smiling* in a way that makes me think you're picturing her in your head, I'll put a hurt on you so bad, your mama will double over in pain. You reading me on this one?" Gideon's breath came in short bursts as he punctuated each word with a finger in the guy's chest.

"Hey, back the fuck off, Cooper. I was just kidding." Cody put his hands in the air in surrender. By this time, the entire team was standing around the two men. Gideon knew he was out of line, but no one disrespected his Charlie.

"Go home to your wife, Cooper. *Now*." Gideon held Walker's stare for a second before turning around and roughly pushing his way out the glass doors into the parking lot.

On the way to his truck, Gideon felt the vibration in his pocket again and groaned in anticipation of what his vixen of a wife was going to show him this time. Glancing at the screen, he couldn't help but smile: ***It's time for a little JOY.***

In the first few weeks of their marriage, when the couple was still learning about each other, Gideon found out Charlie had a hard time talking about sex and telling him what she wanted and how she wanted him to do it. Instead, Charlie always came up with little euphemisms for different acts. One night while watching TV, they saw a silly skit about older women who chased younger men, and one of the women said she gave a "blow joy." Charlie had flown into a fit of laughter at the idea that the act *was* more of a joy than a job, and she'd used the phrase ever since.

Whenever Charlie was being particularly naughty, she'd sidle up to Gideon and say things like, "You bring so much *joy* to my life, Joe." Or "What a *joy* it is to be married to you." That was her way of telling him she wanted to fool around. It made singing Christmas carols with the family a little awkward, though. Gideon nearly peed himself the first time his mom gathered everyone around the piano and told Tyson to play "Joy to the World," and when the next song she wanted to hear was "Ode to Joy," Gideon had to leave the room. Even Charlie couldn't keep a straight face.

Since they'd seen that show, Gideon had never heard his wife say "blow job." Even if they were sitting around with Gabby and Chance or Tyson and whatever chick he was dating at the time, she'd only say "blow joy."

Glancing down at his phone again, Gideon replied to her latest text: ***On my way. U naked when I get there.*** Fortunately at midmorning the traffic was light, and the drive from Coronado Island to their apartment near the university was fairly quick, leaving Gideon with little time to think about Boyd's remarks.

Once he parked, Gideon realized that for the first time in two days he wasn't worried about going inside. Today he was in a hurry to get to his beautiful wife. Hoping she'd taken his text message to heart, Gideon took the stairs two at a time. He unlocked the door, and as he let it fall open, he heard low music playing. There seemed to be no other sounds in the apartment.

Charlie appeared in the bedroom doorway, and Gideon's heart nearly stopped at the sight of her. On her head was his dress uniform hat with her hair pulled up under it so her elegant neck was exposed. She wore one of Gideon's camouflage uniform shirts with only one button fastened over her breasts. The pink lace of the second outfit peeked out from where the shirt fell open. Gideon's body hardened for her like never before—and that was saying something.

"Hey, sailor. You got a minute to help a girl out?" Charlie cooed as she came toward him.

"Are you trying to kill me, baby? Because between this outfit and the texts during our final planning meeting—"

"Oh my God, Joe! I didn't think you'd still being in your meeting! I'm sorry. Did you get in trouble? What if you missed something important?"

"Hey." Gideon reached out to capture her hand in his, easily pulling her to him. "Don't. Be here with me right now. I'm fine. See? Perfectly fine and alive, standing right here with you."

"Well, I definitely need you alive for what I have planned."

Gideon breathed in as she regained her previous seductress persona and slipped a single finger into his waistband, slowly moving it from side to side. She stretched up on her toes and ran her tongue around Gideon's ear. Her breath was hot and felt like heaven against his cheek. He imagined what other things she would do with her tongue and other places her warm breath might glide across.

Charlie gently tugged Gideon's hand, pulling him to the bedroom. He went willingly. Once in the room, Charlie lifted his T-shirt up his body, kissing his bare chest as she exposed each inch. The feel of her tongue as it brushed over his skin was mind numbing.

When the shirt was completely off, her hands came back to trace his muscles. Gideon couldn't help but shudder at the sensation of her hands on his body. Reaching for her, he intended to rid her of her own uniform, but she lithely danced out of his grasp. Gideon looked at her with puppy dog eyes.

"Eh, eh, eh—you don't get to touch until I say you can touch." Charlie wagged her finger at Gideon. "Are you going to follow the rules, Lieutenant?" she asked, a hint of a threat in her tone.

Not trusting himself to actually speak, Gideon simply nodded. He was going to be a good boy and do whatever he needed to do to make sure he got to be naked with her for the next several hours.

"Good. Now lose the pants, sailor."

Gideon happily obliged, immediately starting to undo his belt. Finally, he was able to get the zipper down and let the pants fall to the floor.

Charlie inhaled deeply at the sight of his ready state straining against his boxer briefs. Stepping into him, her hands moved to Gideon's waist and grabbed the waistband of his drawers, yanking them down in one smooth motion. Gideon couldn't hide how much he wanted his wife at that moment.

Charlie raised her right hand to her forehead and gave a salute.

"What's that about, baby?" Gideon smiled at how adorable and hot she looked trying to play soldier.

"You're saluting me, so I thought I needed to salute too." She nodded toward Gideon's saluting soldier. Her hands slid up his body and came to rest in the middle of his chest. With one push, Gideon fell back onto the bed. Charlie crawled up his body, kissing every inch of his skin and driving him crazy.

Gideon wanted her *now*. But Charlie was having none of it. As he dragged his hands up her sides and tried to guide her to his waiting arousal, she sat up.

"I told you, Gideon, I am in command here. You will follow my orders. Since you can't play by the rules…" She reached under the pillow and pulled out a silk scarf.

Catching Gideon off guard, Charlie was able to pull both of his big hands together, wrap the scarf around them, and quickly knot it through the brass bars on the headboard. Gideon had to admit she did a decent job on the knot, but being a SEAL, he didn't see how this would be a problem for him. He'd just let her think she'd gotten the best of him for now.

"You, Lieutenant Cooper, are now my prisoner of war."

"Hells yeah!"

It was sometime later that Charlie's body, completely spent, fell forward onto Gideon's chest, where she stayed for several minutes. She was safe and happy in that moment with her husband's arms wrapped tightly around her, still connected to him in more than just a physical way. Gideon was her world. Nothing was as important to Charlie. She'd make sure he wanted to come home to her more than anything.

After several minutes in the security of Gideon's embrace, she was still bothered by how easily he'd escaped her capture in the middle of a very *joyful* time. Charlie finally found the strength to roll off his hard, muscled chest, but stayed pressed against him, his arm curled protectively around her.

"I have just one question for you, Lieutenant," Charlie whispered.

"What's that, babe?"

"How much do you want to come home to me?"

Gideon didn't answer. Instead, he pulled her in closer, nestling her under his chin. That was all the answer Charlie needed.

CHAPTER 7

Gideon's lips grazed Charlie's neck, moving slowly down to her collar bone and onto her shoulder. Charlie's mind quickly turned to mush under Gideon's expert lips. Then she remembered what was happening that day—how her entire life would change in a matter of hours—and she didn't want to wake up. Maybe if she didn't open her eyes, the day couldn't start and Gideon wouldn't leave.

When she could no longer fight reality, Charlie made the decision to do as Evelyn had told her. She wouldn't let Gideon see her fear or sadness, only the happiness she felt to be in his arms. She wouldn't dwell on the bad, but focus on the good. Later, when he was gone and she was alone, she'd give herself over to her darker emotions. For now, however, she'd play the part.

"Mmm, Joe." Charlie stretched out, feeling her husband's body behind her. His impressive hardness pressed into Charlie's backside.

Rolling over so his elbows were propped on either side of her head, Gideon leaned in to kiss her lightly, and Charlie felt the safety and security he always provided wash over her. Although this was going to be the worst day of her life, she still felt comforted in his arms. Allowing herself the pleasure of roaming his amazing body with her hands and eyes, Charlie finally came back to stare into his steel gray eyes.

They held each other's gaze for a long moment. Charlie didn't want to look away…ever. If she stopped looking at him, he might disappear, and she'd never find him again.

"I love you," Gideon whispered against Charlie's lips just as she felt him enter her.

Time seemed to stop. Nothing mattered other than being with Gideon.

The couple moved together in a rhythm that mirrored Charlie's heartbeat and breathing. It was as if they'd always been meant for loving each other. This was the moment Charlie would hold on to while Gideon was gone.

I'm going to have years and years with this wonderful man. I'm going to have years and years with this wonderful man. I am going to have... If she didn't tell herself that over and over, Charlie knew she'd never make it through the next hour — let alone the next six months.

With their gazes locked, never wavering, Charlie focused on Gideon and keeping the rhythm he'd created, so he became part of her. Finally, Charlie fell over that perfect peak of pleasure and watched Gideon as he followed soon after. In his eyes she saw them: their past, their present, and their future.

In that look, Charlie knew she had to trust him to do everything in his power to come back home to her. She did trust him; it was the people he'd be fighting she didn't trust. They wouldn't know she'd die if he didn't come home; they wouldn't know everything that would be lost if Gideon were no longer here with her. And, even if they did, she was sure they wouldn't care.

Gideon stared into the endless green of his wife's eyes, trying to preserve the image to carry with him into that long stretch of time he was trying to avoid thinking about. Life without Charlie in his arms was a life he truly wasn't sure he could live. She was like air for him.

I will come home. In his mind, Gideon vowed this — not only to her but himself.

Being away from Charlie, even just for those two- or three-day mini-missions had been harder than Gideon would allow himself to admit. When the team returned to the base, Gideon would skip the showers and head directly back to Charlie. Being away was physically painful. It wasn't until he could hold her in his arms, smell her wonderful scent, and kiss those perfect lips that he was whole again.

Gideon had watched and memorized every expression on Charlie's face as she quietly rode out the waves of ecstasy to the end. She'd never closed her eyes, never broken from him. When he'd followed shortly after, it had been one of the most intense releases he'd ever experienced. Sex with Charlie was beyond words — indescribable under normal circumstances — but this time had been like the joining of their lives, their future.

When the two finally broke, Gideon sighed at the exact moment he heard Charlie gasp. He wasn't ready to let go of her yet. They lay together, simply holding each other, until Gideon knew he couldn't put it off any longer. He rolled over, pulling her with him. In one smooth motion, Gideon's feet hit the floor and he pushed both of them up off the bed. Charlie instantly wrapped her legs around him, not ready to lose the contact either.

"Gideon, what are you doing?" Her light giggle filled the bedroom, and Gideon's mind catalogued the sound. He hoped he'd be able to recall it with perfect clarity while he was away.

"I'm not ready to let go of you, and I have to get my shit going." Gideon smiled down at her as he walked them into the bathroom. "My ass is already in trouble because of your texts yesterday. If I show up late…" He kissed the tip of her nose as he bent down to turn the water on.

"Joe, put me down! We can't take a shower like this."

Wondering if his wife was actually crazy, Gideon tested the waters before stepping in, still holding her to him. He couldn't give her up. He knew he'd eventually have to let her go, but for now, he wanted her one last time.

As he pressed Charlie against the cold shower tile, her back arched, and her beautiful breasts pressed against his chest. While their earlier lovemaking had been intense and perfect, this time the pair gave themselves over to the passion and fear. The sound of Charlie screaming Gideon's name echoed in the small room. Another detail he committed to memory for later use.

Carefully setting her down, Gideon pulled his wife to him and wrapped his arms around her. They stood for a long time, the water sprinkling down on them, the only other sound in the room their synchronized breathing.

God, please let me come home to Charlie. Not for myself, but for her. I don't know if she's strong enough for this. Don't let her suffer while I'm gone, Gideon silently prayed as Charlie clung to him.

Time had seemed to stop while Charlie and Gideon were together that morning. But once they got out of the shower, it seemed to be on fast forward. Suddenly the couple was in the truck, with all Gideon's gear in the back.

Charlie wondered how Gideon would live for six months out of one duffle bag. Maybe he'd be back sooner. Maybe it would only be a month. She could handle a month. A month seemed like nothing in comparison.

"What are you thinking about, baby?"

"Nothing." Charlie tried to lie even though she knew he'd never let her get away with such a simple response to a question she couldn't answer fully and truthfully, even if she wanted to.

"Bullshit. Charlie, you have to tell me. I don't want to leave knowing you're hiding something from me."

"Why? What difference does it make? You're leaving, and my worrying about it or being sad about it doesn't change it. You'll be gone in an hour."

The tears started despite Charlie's promise to herself that she wouldn't do this. She didn't want Gideon to leave thinking about her with tears and a scared look in her eyes. She wanted to be strong for him.

Gideon took the next exit and gently pulled over to the side of the road. He moved his hand to cup Charlie's cheek.

"Charlie, I need you to tell me things. I know my mom told you to have a brave face and not let me see you scared."

Charlie's head snapped up. "I, uh, I don't…"

"Baby, I know my mom is scared out of her mind every time I leave. I know my dad has to comfort her for days after I'm gone. He tells me about it. I've never told her because I want her to have that. She needs to think I think she's strong for me." Gideon brushed a tear from Charlie's cheek.

"Why?" Charlie's voice caught in her throat.

"She's my mom. She's one of the strongest women I know. The crap she's put up with over the years from Tyson and me—she deserves my respect. I know how proud she is of me. But I also know how worried she is. That's the look I see in your eyes right now. Like you don't think I can handle your fear."

"I don't want you to think of me like this when you're gone. When you picture me, I want to be happy and laughing, not the way I've been the past three days."

"Oh, Charlie. This is part of you. When I picture you in my head, you're always beautiful, but not to have everything—the good, the bad, everything—would mean I didn't have all of you."

Gideon brought his other hand up so Charlie's face was captured between the two.

"I'm so confused, Joe. I love you so much, and my heart is hurting. I want to scream and shout and beg you not to leave me. But I know that won't help; it'll only make you feel worse. At the same time I want to throw my arms around your neck and cover you with kisses and tell you how proud I am of you."

Charlie had to stop and take a huge breath as she felt herself start to hyperventilate.

In that small pause, Gideon's lips met hers, and she took the opportunity to put everything she was into that kiss. She wanted him to know everything she was feeling, to absorb how much she loved him and worried for him and wanted him to come home and spend the rest of forever with her. When they finally broke the kiss, Gideon leaned his forehead against his wife's as he held her in place.

"You are my wife, Charlie Cooper. Our life together is the single most important thing in this world to me. I need you to always tell me what you're feeling or thinking. Evelyn is my mother, and I respect the hell out of her, so I let her think I don't know how much this hurts her. It's the least I can do. But you—I will never let you get away with putting on the brave face for me. I can't change who I am, and I can't change what's about to happen—"

"I would never ask you to change who you are," Charlie interrupted. "I love everything about you, and even this thing makes me respect you so much and love you."

Gideon's mouth turned to a small frown. "What the hell is wrong with women? I'm trying to give you a kick-ass going away speech and tell you how strong you are, and you can't help but interrupt me." He leaned in and kissed her softly as he smiled.

"Sorry." She tried to sound thoroughly apologetic, but the crack in her voice and a new wave of tears ruined her plans.

"Charlie, you're strong. We'll get through this. I'll call when I can."

The expression on Charlie's face changed so quickly it took Gideon a second to realize he'd said something that shocked her. He dropped his hands from Charlie's cheeks.

"What's wrong?"

"What do you mean you'll call when you can? I thought I'd at least get to talk to you."

"Charlie, I'm going into a war zone. It's not like I can carry my cell with me. I thought you'd have understood this. I'm sorry."

Gideon did look sorry, and Charlie wasn't willing to jeopardize these last minutes with him by fighting over something they couldn't change.

It was Charlie's turn to comfort her husband. Gideon had looked away, not wanting to see the hurt that kept creeping into her expressions. Charlie placed a hand against his jaw and turned him to face her again.

"I'll take what I can get, Gideon, and not complain about it. The only thing I want is for you to concentrate on being safe. I don't want you to worry about me. I want you to worry about you and your team."

He smiled at her, and Charlie's heart leapt and came crashing back, only to break into a million pieces. She knew he wanted her to tell him things, but she wouldn't do that anymore. She wouldn't let him know her fear and worry because Evelyn had been right; the only thing he needed to worry about while he was gone was himself.

"Let's get this show on the road. I don't want you getting into any more trouble because of me." Charlie flashed a smile and nodded at the clock on the dashboard. When she got home, she'd give herself over to the turmoil inside, but for now she'd be strong.

Gideon got back onto the freeway. Charlie's hand was firmly wrapped in his, and he pulled it to his lips to kiss it.

"Midterms are just around the corner, right? At least you'll have lots of time to study." Gideon gave her a half-smile that was returned with the same amount of enthusiasm.

"Way to look on the bright side. Midterms are in a few weeks. I have two papers and two actual tests, so it shouldn't be too bad."

"So, do you think Gabby and Chance will have their Halloween party again this year?"

"Gabby mentioned the other night that they were. I doubt I'll go, though."

"Oh, you have to go!" Gideon's voice boomed in the small space of the cab, and Charlie jumped.

"Why? I doubt I'll be in any kind of mood to be at a party. I mean, Halloween is only a few weeks away."

"Charlie, you have to go. I know Tyson and Paige will go, and I need you to be my eyes and ears on this one. I'm putting the responsibility of keeping Tyson in line all on you."

"Just what I need," she joked. It felt all wrong.

"Seriously, Charlie, I like that girl, and my brother is a dumbass who will totally screw this up if he doesn't get some guidance. You don't want him to find another Mercedes, do you?"

Charlie cringed at the thought of spending the rest of her life with a Mercedes-ish girl as her sister-in-law. That would totally ruin the holidays—every year.

"Fine. I'll try to go. That's the best I can do."

Gideon looked over and smiled. Charlie was glad she could make him smile that way. It was a smile he put on only for her.

The conversation had distracted Charlie enough that she was surprised to see the signs for the base appear. Her heart stuttered, and it took everything in her not to burst into tears. There was silence for the next several minutes as they drove across the base. Neither trusted themselves to speak. Now that they were at the base, it was real.

Gideon pulled onto the tarmac where the rest of the team was waiting for their instructions. There were only three other wives there. The majority of the team was single. The other couples were huddled together, away from the rowdy group of guys.

The truck stopped, and Gideon opened his door to get out. Charlie stayed where she was. Her mind screamed that if she didn't do this, if she didn't say good-bye, he couldn't leave. She heard Gideon pulling his bag out of the back, and still she stayed where she was.

It wasn't until he opened the passenger door that Charlie knew her plan would never work. He was leaving in a matter of minutes, and she couldn't stop him. Glancing over, Charlie saw the other wives, who she'd met only a handful of times at squadron functions, clinging to their husbands, tears streaming down their cheeks. One couple even had a baby; the soldier cradled a small blanket-wrapped bundle in his arms. A second woman was pregnant, and her husband's hand moved constantly over her huge belly. Charlie realized he was going to miss the birth of his child, and her stomach turned over as she wondered if one day she'd be one of *those* wives.

The last couple Charlie recognized as Zoe and Jaylon Fox. They were a sweet newlywed couple, having gotten married not long after her and Gideon. Jaylon was Gideon's closest friend on the team, and Charlie had spent the majority of the last party talking with Zoe. She really liked her. Tears rolled over Zoe's cheeks at she hung on to Jaylon.

Gideon wrapped Charlie entirely in his arms. She buried her face in his chest and couldn't help the tears that flowed from her eyes. His hand moved in circles over her back, and he whispered in her ear how much he loved her over and over again.

"All right, team!" The voice of the team leader, Lieutenant Walker, broke through the sorrow and chaos as twelve men snapped to attention. All talking ceased, and every husband—though each remained next to his wife—no longer held her, including Gideon. Instantly Charlie's body ached at the distance between them. He was Lieutenant Cooper, Navy SEAL, now not Gideon, Charlie's husband.

"Finish up your good-byes. I want the team on the transport in five minutes."

Walker turned and walked up the ramp to the giant plane that would take this group of boys and men to whatever godforsaken, war-torn country they were off to protect.

"I love you, Charlie. I love you more than anything in this entire world." Gideon leaned in to kiss his wife. "I will come home to you. I make you that promise."

He looked into her eyes, and Charlie knew he truly believed the words he'd just said. But she also knew he was making a promise he had no control over.

"I love you, Joe. I'll be here when you get home."

After one more bone-crushing hug and a deep, passionate kiss, Charlie watched him turn and walk toward the airplane. She stood in the same spot, following his every move, memorizing each small gesture.

"Don't let Tyson drive my truck!" Gideon's lips pulled into a huge smile as he walked backward up the ramp onto the transport. "I love you, baby. I'll call you soon!"

Then he was gone.

Gideon watched as Charlie got back in the truck. He knew she was about to lose it. It was killing him that she felt like she needed to be strong for him. Charlie *was* strong, and she didn't need to hide her fear from him. He loved her all the more, knowing she worried about him so much.

As the others filed into the plane, Gideon needed to do one last thing to take care of his wife. Pulling out his phone, he called the only person he could trust with Charlie's safety.

The phone rang a few times, and Gideon was afraid he wouldn't pick up. His backup plan was Tyson, and that wasn't much of a backup at all.

"Hey, Gideon. What's up?"

"Chance, thank God you answered. I really didn't want to call Tyson for this." Gideon's voice was thick with emotion. "I only have a minute to talk."

"What do you need?"

"I need you to come out to Miramar to get Charlie. Like, now."

"That bad?"

"Yeah, I think so. Damn it! I should have thought of this." Charlie had been so upset the past few days, he should have known she'd break down. "Just come get her. She won't make it home by herself."

"I'm on my way."

"Take care of her, Chance."

Before Gideon could get his brother-in-law's response, the team was on the plane, and he had to disconnect and check in his phone with the communications guy. He had to trust another man with the job he'd promised to do on his wedding day, and that was the hardest thing he'd ever done.

Charlie waited until the plane was out of sight before giving herself over to the emotions she'd been pushing away all morning. Her entire body convulsed as each sob escaped.

When the shrill ring of her phone started, she actually screamed it startled her so badly. Even after seeing it was her brother, she didn't want to answer. She wasn't sure she could talk, but she also knew he'd keep calling until she answered.

"H-H-ello?" Charlie managed.

"Lottie?"

And with just that word from her twin, she began to settle down. The tears wouldn't stop any time soon, but she thought she'd be able to pull herself together enough to make it home.

"Lottie, Gideon just called and asked me to come get you. I'm already in the car. Gabby will drop me off at the front gate. None of us want you to drive home."

Charlie was disappointed in herself. She thought she'd hidden exactly how broken she was from Gideon. But if he'd called in backup to get her home, he knew.

"Uh-huh."

"I'll call when I'm there. Please try to calm down for the next couple of minutes, then come and get me. I'll drive you home, and Gabby will pick me up."

"Okay." Charlie's powers of speech were failing her, and she had to work hard to even understand what Chance was saying.

When Chance was gone, Charlie sat in the silence of the truck cab, her crying the only sound. She began to pray, silently. *God, please bring him back to me. Give me the strength to be what he needs me to be.*

A short time later, Charlie slumped over the wheel, her forehead resting on it as she sat in Gideon's truck, which she'd parked on the side of the road just outside the base gates. She'd barely made it out before giving up and deciding to wait for Chance and Gabby.

Chance tapped lightly on the window. "Lottie, you need to let me in."

Charlie's head slowly turned to look at him, and Chance took a step back. She could imagine what she looked like after her crying jag—makeup streaked down her cheeks and bloodshot eyes. Leaning back, Charlie unlocked the door and slid over to the passenger side.

After Chance lifted himself into the cab of the truck and sat down, he reached for Charlie, pulling her into a hug. She stayed there a long time, her body shaking with each new wave of sorrow that attacked her. Chance just let her cry, and she was thankful for that.

After almost an hour of sobbing into Chance's shoulder and chest, Charlie pulled herself away from him and sat up in her seat, fastening the seatbelt.

"Take me home, please."

A few minutes later, as he pulled the car onto the highway, her breathing evened out, and she fell into an emotionally exhausted sleep.

CHAPTER 8

As soon as they were airborne, Walker unstrapped, and as he was getting up, he looked directly in Gideon's eyes. His head jerked toward the rear of the aircraft where huge crates of equipment were stacked. Gideon knew immediately what he wanted. It was time to pay for yesterday's distraction with a little piece of his ass. But when he conjured up the image of Charlie in that pink number, he decided it was more than worth the verbal ass-kicking he was about to take.

Reluctantly, Gideon unhooked his straps and got up to follow. Glancing over at the other members of the team, he was suddenly in a hurry. At least three of the new guys were turning an alarming shade of green. Walking to the rear of the plane and laughing to himself about the newbies, Gideon remembered his first time, and he cringed at what was to come. Fortunately, the noise inside the plane was loud enough that he wouldn't have to hear the rounds of retching that were sure to be coming soon. And as a bonus, the others wouldn't hear the dressing-down he was about to get.

Gideon stepped around a crate to face his waiting team leader.

"Lieutenant." Gideon addressed him formally with a salute, trying to redeem himself.

"Cut the crap, Coop." The set of Walker's jaw was hard, but there was a twinkle in his eye. "You know I have to get on you for the little stunt yesterday."

"Yeah, I was kinda expecting it." Gideon held his superior's gaze, letting him know he'd accept whatever was due him.

"Look, I get it. First long deployment since you tied the knot. Been there." Gideon nodded and waited for him to continue. "Now I got a kid—a kid, Cooper."

Gideon instantly pictured Charlie, her belly huge with his baby. Just the thought had his blood rushing south, only to do an about face when he then imagined having to say good-bye to Charlie with a baby in her arms.

"This is it for me. I'm getting out when we get home. So you, my friend, need to get your shit together, 'cause you're going to be it, man. These guys need to respect you and be able to trust you with their lives. Playing on your phone during a briefing isn't how to get that done."

"I'm sorry about that. It will never happen again." Gideon was truly ashamed, and knowing this was his last mission with a man he liked and respected made him feel even worse. Lieutenant Walker was completely right, Gideon had to grow up.

A clap on the shoulder let Gideon know that was the end of the lecture — not as bad as he'd thought it was going to be.

"So, how's daddyhood treating you?" Gideon had completely forgotten Walker and his wife had a new baby. Again, he felt his heart clench when he thought of leaving Charlie and his child.

"Good, good. Of course, Ginger does all the work. I get to do the fun shit." His eyes glazed over for a brief second, and Gideon wondered where his thoughts went. "When I get home, she might be walking. That's what made me realize I was done. I don't want to miss any of her other firsts if I can help it."

He turned and walked away, leaving Gideon alone to contemplate his future for a few moments. He wondered if he could survive a civilian job. Would he be happy knowing someone else was doing *this* job? Did he trust someone else to do this job?

When Gideon finally returned to his seat, he tried to sleep, but the sounds of the new guys puking were not exactly conducive to that goal. Only after a few hours of letting his mind wander, thinking about the future and what it held for his family, was Gideon able to block out the sounds and drift off.

His dreams were vivid and disturbing. He saw Charlie crying, holding his dog tags in one hand while the other ran circles over her pregnant belly. She fell to her knees, her body trembling. His parents stood in the background. Evelyn was held up by Peter, who had a tear rolling down his cheek. Behind them were Tyson, Chance, and Gabby, all with tears in their eyes. Waking with a start, Gideon's heart raced, and tears threatened to make him look like a total pussy in front of his team.

Fortunately, as he looked around at the others, he saw that no one was paying attention to him. Half the team was asleep, and those that weren't were holding bags to their faces.

The plane landed in Thailand the next afternoon. Gideon wanted so badly to call Charlie but knew they'd be in a briefing before the team headed out again. There'd be no time for even a quick hello. After filing off the aircraft, the group gathered to find out their next move. Walker was immediately on the phone with the mission contacts. The plan was to meet a Navy ship and have it take the team to a drop-off point. Gideon kept the group together while they waited for transport to the ship.

"Team!" Walker shouted to be heard above the still-running engine of the plane. "We have a SNAFU! Our ship is delayed. We won't be able to meet them until tomorrow, noon."

Everyone looked at one another, waiting for the rest of the instructions. Gideon was sure they'd be stuck in some crappy motel room for the night, so he was surprised when the team leader said, "We're going to check into a motel, then you boys can have tonight out on the town. Make it count, because it will be your last for six months."

After Gideon picked his jaw up off the floor, he sidled over to Walker and whispered, "Going soft in your old age?"

Walker let out a big laugh, causing all the others to turn and look. "That must be it, Cooper. The catch is you need to go with them. I think a few may need to be babysat."

Gideon groaned. He was totally screwed. The only thing that could save him would be convincing Fox to come too. Then at least he'd have one guy to hang with who wasn't trying to get laid.

"All the team needs to be back, tucked in, and kissed goodnight by oh-one hundred hours. You got it, Cooper?"

"Shit. Yeah. Not sure how I'm going to manage that, but I also don't want to tell them they can't go."

The bus that was to take the team to town pulled up, and Gideon formed the plan to get Fox to go with him. It would take some smooth talking and maybe a bribe or two.

As they got on the bus, Gideon made sure he lined up right behind Jaylon. Once they boarded, Gideon took the seat next to him and started a conversation. It took only the short ride into town to get him to agree. As Gideon had thought, there was a small bribe—and a little begging—involved. He promised they'd get to call their wives prior to releasing the young and single into the bars.

Before sending everyone to their rooms, Gideon called the guys to a meeting to lay down the rules for the night. Eight SEALs dragged their asses into the lobby of the motel, all grumbling under their breath about having a babysitter.

"All right, assholes." Gideon called the room to attention in his own special way. "Here are the rules for our night out on Uncle Sam."

A unified groan echoed in the room.

"Okay, okay. I know you all think you're grown up, but there are a few of you—" he gave a quick sweep of the room and found the newbies, holding their gaze for a brief second "—that have never been here and need some help navigating the treacherous waters of the bars and, more importantly, the bargirls."

A few snickers erupted, but Gideon quieted them all down with a wave of a hand.

"So here are the rules that you *will* follow, or I *will* personally kick your ass. I'm not going to get my ass handed to me because one of you dumbfucks messes up. First, you'll be within my line of sight at all times, unless I know about it first."

Again a groan spread across the room. This time, however, a simple look shut them up.

"Second rule: We *will* be back here by oh-one hundred hours. If I have to look for you, I will mess your shit up. Those are the rules. If you can't follow them, keep your ass here."

"Can we take a piss on our own, or will we need to have a chaperone for that too?" one of the guys actually had the balls to ask.

Gideon glared at the SEAL for a long moment before allowing a smile to slide onto his face. If Walker was going civilian, Gideon had to make sure these men would listen to him. Tonight was definitely a test.

"Okay, get the fuck out of here and go get ready. We're leaving for town at oh-eight hundred. You aren't at my room, your ass is staying here."

Gideon barely avoided being trampled by the mad dash for the rooms. Stepping aside, he allowed the young guys to storm out. Then he picked up his duffle and headed down the hall to his room. Fox followed and opened the door across the hall. Before ducking into his room, Gideon looked over at Fox and laughed as he saw his new "partner in parenting" give a small shake of his head.

"I know, dude. This is going to be one long night." Gideon laughed. "But, like I promised, we'll call home first. So these idiots are going to have to wait until we're done. Did I forget to mention that to them?"

Jaylon laughed and Gideon joined in, not really feeling the mirth, but pleased he was going to hear his wife's voice in just a few short minutes.

CHAPTER 9

"*Oh, Tyson,*" Paige had been moaning his name as her naked body writhed under him.

"*Tyson, Tyson…Tyson!* Tyson! Get up and talk to your mother!" His mother's voice broke into his dream as she yelled through the answering machine.

Nothing took care of morning wood like hearing his mother's voice.

He had much better ways to remedy the problem, but even though he spent every possible waking moment with Paige, Tyson was still sleeping alone. He didn't know what he needed to do to get the woman into his bed. It had never been this difficult for him before. Sure, he'd felt the soft, smooth skin of her bare stomach and had even been able to cop a feel, but that was pretty much it. The only time Tyson ever got any further than second base was in his dreams.

And now Tyson's fantasy time with Paige was ruined because he would forever associate naked, hot-for-him Paige with his mother's voice.

I'm going to need therapy after this! Tyson thought. He wasn't sure he'd ever be able to get it up again.

Blindly, Tyson reached for the phone on the nightstand. As much as he loved his mom, he couldn't keep the irritation out of his voice.

"What do you want, Mom?"

"Tyson Lawrence Cooper, why don't we try that again?"

Tyson felt the ball of guilt he'd known since he was a small child form in the pit of his stomach. He took a deep breath, trying to find his happy place. Unfortunately, his happy place had been naked and hovering over Paige, which was now a scary place.

"Sorry, Mom. How about this? Morning, dear Mother. To what do I owe this glorious phone call at—" he sat halfway up to see what time it was "—seven twenty in the morning?"

"That's a little better, I guess."

Tyson knew he'd have to do something for her later to make up for being such a dick.

"Really, Mom, I'm sorry. You know I'm not a morning person."

"I know, Tyson, but I have something I need you to do."

Tyson's day started to brighten as he realized he wouldn't have to work too hard to make up for his behavior. He was never very good at thinking up shit like that.

"Anything for you, Mom."

"Tyson, I want you to go over and check on Charlie. I tried to call her all day yesterday to make sure she was okay, but she never answered her phone. I'm worried."

Evelyn's voice was heavy with concern, and Tyson was suddenly annoyed with his brother for putting their mother through this. It was bad enough she always had to worry about Gideon when he left, but now she had to worry about Charlie too? Sometimes Tyson thought Gideon was selfish in his need to help the world.

"I'm sure she's fine, Mom. She's just crying in a corner."

"Tyson! You need to go check on her. Now. I called Chance, and he said she was so exhausted from breaking down after Gideon left that she'd probably sleep for hours, but I'm worried."

"Okay, okay. I'll go over there." Tyson pulled himself out of bed and stumbled into the bathroom. He wanted to borrow Gideon's truck anyway, so why not kill two birds with one stone?

"Thank you, Tyson. Please tell Charlie to call me. I'd go over there myself, but I don't want to be *that* mother-in-law. I love you, Son."

"Love you too, Mom."

Tyson's shower only took a few minutes, especially since his mom had ruined his fantasies and there was no need to linger today. He was out the door and on his way to Gideon and Charlie's place by eight.

As long as he was doing penance, he might as well go all the way, Tyson thought, so he stopped to pick up some coffee and a Danish for Charlie. He was pretty sure she'd make him hurt if he showed up on her doorstep this early in the morning empty-handed, no matter how upset she was about Gideon leaving.

Once armed with goodies, Tyson slid back into the car and headed toward the apartment. He decided to call Paige. It was still early, but she had morning classes, and he thought—or hoped—she'd be up already. The phone rang several times before it went to voicemail.

"Hey, it's me. If you don't know who 'me' is, then don't leave me a message."

"Morning, Paige. I just wanted to hear your voice. I'm running an errand for my mom." Tyson thought that might help him out with her. What woman can resist a guy who loves his mom? "I'll call you later. Maybe we can meet up tonight?"

As he pulled into the parking lot at the apartment complex, Tyson saw that both cars were parked in their spaces. As he headed up the stairs the fear began to creep in. He didn't deal with emotional women well. Hell, usually as soon as a woman actually exhibited feelings, he ran for the hills.

As he knocked loudly on the door, Tyson heard hushed voices on the other side and wondered who the hell could be in there. Wonder turned to surprise when the door opened and Paige stood in front of him.

"Um, hey?" He was at a loss for words—something that didn't often happen to Tyson Cooper.

"Tyson? What has your ass on this side of town? I mean, isn't it a little early for you to be out and about, considering you don't you have classes until this afternoon?" Paige's smart-ass wit was already in high gear. No surprise there.

"I tried to call you," Tyson blurted, immediately feeling like an idiot.

"I saw, but I was busy with Charlie. So, you came bearing gifts?" Paige nodded at the coffee and the bag in his hands. Opening the door wider, she allowed Tyson to pass, and he headed to the kitchen with the breakfast he'd brought.

"Uh, yeah. I'm sorry—I didn't know you'd be here. Wait, why are you here?"

"Well, first, don't worry, I'll just take yours."

Paige took one of the cups out of the holder and brought it to her lips, where she gently blew on it. Tyson's body reacted immediately, and he was relieved that he wouldn't need therapy after all.

"Second, I called to check on Charlie yesterday because I knew Gideon had left, and she seemed like she needed someone to talk to."

"My mom was worried. Why didn't she answer the phone?" Tyson was well aware that he was deflecting—he felt like a total asshole for not thinking about Charlie at all the previous day. Judging by the look on Paige's face, she was thinking the same thing.

"She didn't want to talk to anyone. I was easy to talk to and cry with. Sometimes talking to a stranger is the best therapy."

Finally, Paige stood on her tiptoes to give Tyson a small kiss on the tip of his nose.

"Where is my lovely sister-in-law?" After Paige's encouraging kiss, Tyson felt slightly better, but still a bit like an ass for not checking on Charlie on his own.

"She's in the shower. I think she's doing better this morning. Last night was not good."

Just the look in Paige's eyes let him know how bad it had been.

Tyson admired his older brother. He did. Gideon's sense of duty and his love of his job was awe-inspiring. He hoped to have half the enthusiasm for his medical career his brother had for the Navy. But things had changed in Gideon's life, and Tyson thought leaving Charlie alone and hurting so badly was inexcusable. Once again, Tyson cursed Gideon for trying to be noble and save the world instead of saving his own wife.

Before Charlie, only their small family missed him and would suffer if he one day didn't come home. But once he married Charlie, he brought so many others into this — Charlie, Chance, Gabriella — and what if they had kids in the future? Would he leave Charlie with a baby and the possibility of him never coming home?

The bathroom door opened, and Charlie came out wrapped in a towel.

"Tyson!" She ran to the bedroom and slammed the door. "What are you doing here so early?" she yelled. Tyson laughed. While Charlie was beautiful, she had nothing to worry about — he was completely entranced by Paige.

Paige's hand was swift and lethal as it came up to smack the back of Tyson's head. He wondered how she knew he'd just been imagining *her* in a towel.

"Ow!" he blurted, rubbing the spot where she'd whacked him. "What was that for? It's not my fault Charlie runs around with nothing on in front of company."

That earned yet another slap to the head.

"Tyson, I wouldn't have come out in just a towel if I'd known you were here. Trust me." Charlie stared down her brother-in-law as she came into the living room, fully clothed. While her voice sounded rough from crying all night, her tone was lighter than Tyson had expected.

"My mom called and was worried about you. She woke my ass up from a fantastic dream."

He smirked at Paige, who returned a small smile.

"She asked me to come check on you. Can you please call her and let her know you're okay?"

"I know. I felt bad for not answering when she called, but I just couldn't put on the brave face for her. I'll call her right now."

As Charlie went to talk with his mother, Tyson turned to focus his attention on Paige. He pulled her into his arms and held her to him before kissing her.

"Why don't you come over to my place tonight? I have something I want to show you," he whispered into her ear as he brushed his lips over her neck. Tyson felt her shiver.

"Yeah, sure. You have something to 'show' me? Please, Tyson. Do you really think I'd fall for that? Besides, Charlie, Gabriella, and I are going out tonight. Girl's night." Paige wiggled out of his arms with a smile playing on her lips.

"I know, Evelyn. I'm sorry. I was wiped out," Charlie said into the phone. "Yeah, I'm going to go to dinner with Gabby and Paige tonight… Yes, Tyson's Paige." She looked over at the couple on the other side of the room and smiled.

Tyson cursed under his breath. He could expect an interrogation call from his mother later.

Paige looked at her watch. "I've gotta get going. I have class in half an hour."

Charlie looked over and mouthed "thank you" while continuing her conversation. "I promise, Evelyn. Really, I'll be there tomorrow night."

Tyson walked Paige to the door and gave her a small kiss before watching her walk down the stairs. When he turned back, Charlie was just hanging up the phone with a look of exasperation.

"She's just worried about you. I mean, good Christ, she woke my ass up to come over here."

"I know, but it's going to be hard to be around her and talk about Gideon being gone. Don't get me wrong—I love Evelyn. She's like a mom, not a mother-in-law, but I need to adjust before trying to be normal around her."

This was a different side of Charlie, one Tyson had never seen. She was so open and vulnerable. While he'd seen her be candid and honest in her opinions, until now Charlie Cooper had never been scared.

"If you want, I'll come to dinner tomorrow and run some interference with my mom for you."

"Tyson? I never knew you had the ability to think of someone else's feelings."

Her tone was joking, but Tyson knew there was a hint of truth there too.

"Ha ha ha. Well, if you want to face Evelyn and Peter on your own…"

"No, no, no. You're going to be there, or I will sick Paige all over your ass."

Tyson smiled at the image she planted in his head.

"Ew. Tyson, pull your mind out of the gutter for just a few minutes."

"Hey, you're the one who mentioned Paige and my ass in the same sentence. Not my fault."

"Okay, Tyson, I can't deal with your sick and perverted mind right now. You've done your good deed for the year. You're free to go."

She was smiling, sort of, so Tyson knew she wasn't really mad at him.

Just as he was about to ask about taking Gideon's truck, the phone rang. Charlie groaned, but when she looked at the caller ID, a huge smile crossed her face and her eyes began to tear up.

After quickly accepting the collect charges, Charlie exclaimed, "Gideon! I love you. I miss you. Where are you?"

Tyson headed for the door, certain this was a conversation he didn't want to overhear.

"Just a minute, Joe. Are you leaving, Tyson?"

"Yeah, I'll call you later. Oh, and I'm taking the truck!" Tyson yelled the last part, knowing Gideon would hear and be through-the-roof irate. Grabbing the keys off the counter, he beat feet to the door.

Pulling the door closed behind him, Tyson heard Charlie trying to calm Gideon down. He laughed at the torture he could inflict on his brother from halfway around the world.

"Charlie, do not let him take my truck!" Gideon screamed into the shitty, circa-1982 phone in his room, wanting Tyson to hear him. Suddenly his door flew open and the entire team stood there with huge grins on their faces, making like they were checking their watches.

He knew it was getting close to time to leave, but after a quick shower it had taken him almost a half an hour to get a line to the United States. He didn't give a shit. They could wait while he talked to Charlie. The bargirls weren't going anywhere. Through the open door he could see that the idiots had busted in on Jaylon too.

"Gideon, he's already gone. Your truck will be fine."

Charlie's sweet voice brought him back to the conversation. He tried to ignore the stirring mob in the hall.

"No, I left specific instructions that he was not to drive my truck while I was gone."

"Gideon Isaac Cooper. Do you want me to go and stop him? Huh? Do you want me to hang up this phone and go chase after your brother over your car?"

"No, of course not, baby. I'm sorry." It was beyond embarrassing to be groveling to his wife with these guys listening to every word.

"That's better," Charlie cooed into the phone, and he almost got hard right then and there. "Now, tell me where you are."

"Can't give specifics, but there was a SNAFU and our ship is late coming in, so I have to babysit the guys in the bars tonight."

Gideon shot a death glare at them, warning them not to speak a word.

"Poor baby. Did I mention that I love you?"

"Yeah, but I love hearing you say it, so that's okay."

The assholes started making kissing sounds and *awww*-ing.

Charlie could hear the guys giving Gideon shit about talking on the phone with her. It didn't matter. All she cared about was hearing his voice, and her heart soared.

"Tell those morons to shut the hell up, Joe."

Gideon laughed, and then Charlie heard the muffled sound of him talking to them. She couldn't hear every word, but picked out a few like "kick," "ass," "kill," and "die." There was an extra flutter in her chest at hearing the man she loved not only stand up for her, but show everyone how he felt about her.

"Okay, Charlie, I don't think we'll be hearing from them anymore. I had to threaten each of their lives, but I think we're good."

"Tell me again why they're even standing around listening to our private phone call." Charlie had been so excited to hear his voice that she hadn't paid any attention to the actual words he'd said.

"I'm in charge of these idiots for the night. I get to make sure they don't come down with the clap while we're out on our mission."

He gave a small laugh, and Charlie imagined him glaring at the young guys she'd seen the day before on the tarmac.

"I'm sure you can find a way of having fun." She tried to sound chipper but knew it wasn't really coming through in her voice.

"Back to my question—what the hell was Tyson doing at the house so early in the morning?"

"Well, since you're gone, I thought I'd try the next best thing."

There was an uncomfortable silence, and Charlie worried she'd pushed too far. "What do you think, Gideon?" she said. "Your mom made him get his ass out of bed and come over here when I didn't answer the phone."

Gideon released a huge breath. "Don't say shit like that, Charlie. I hate the thought that I'm so far away and can't protect you."

"Are you kidding me? Did you for even a minute think I was serious? Come on, Gideon."

"Not really, but you hear lots of stories. I never worried about them before, other than to feel sorry for the poor schmo whose wife or girlfriend finally confessed to him."

"Gideon, I love you. I'm not going to be inviting your brother, or anyone else, into our bed."

"I know. I'm stupid. Forgive me?"

Charlie could hear in his voice how flustered he was and felt sorry for him. While she wanted to be mad and act indignant, she decided to let him off the hook.

"Paige came over last night and stayed with me. I really like her, Gideon."

"Come on, Cooper! There are hot *señoritas* waiting for us in the bars! Let's go!" someone in the background yelled.

There was a muffled sound like Gideon was covering the phone, and Charlie felt a little sorry for those guys.

"Sorry, baby. I do have to go."

A small lump formed in Charlie's throat at the thought of hanging up. It had only been a few minutes, and with the awkward almost-argument about how Gideon didn't trust her, her heart was heavy.

"Off to find the *señoritas*, Gideon?" She was suddenly angry. Her husband wanted to get off the phone with her to go to the bars with these guys!

"Stop it, Charlie. You know I don't want to. I could stay here all night and talk to you. But I have a team of horny guys standing around me, and if I don't get them near some women, I'm worried for my own safety." Gideon tried to joke, but that wasn't going to work.

"Oh, please, Gideon. They're grown men. I mean really, if they're old enough to be sent into a war, I think they can conduct themselves for a few minutes without you guarding them."

"You'd think that. But no. They're like children."

"Whatever. Just go. I have a class to get to anyway."

"Charlotte. Don't be this way, honey. I love you. I'll call again tomorrow before we leave."

"If you can squeeze me in." Charlie felt a little bit of guilt for being so bitchy, but first he chose his job over her and left. Now he was choosing his buddies over her and going barhopping rather than talk to his wife.

"I do love you so much, baby." Gideon ignored Charlie's last statement—or at least wanted to make her think he had.

"I know. Bye."

She waited a fraction of a second for him to say good-bye before hanging up.

Grabbing her books and heading out the door, Charlie hoped to lose herself in school. That went by the wayside, however, as she felt the all-too-familiar tears begin to slide down her cheeks. Charlie Cooper resigned herself to another shitty day.

Gideon was fuming when he hung up the phone. He took a giant step forward, murder written all over his face, only to have Jaylon hold him back.

"Goddamn it! I'm going to strangle each and every one of these dickheads. Or maybe just the one who was stupid enough to yell something about girls while I was on the phone with my wife," Gideon hissed.

"You can't touch them, Cooper, as much as I'd love to see you do it. Zoe was none too happy with the way things were going down either, but you just can't."

"No, you're right. But I can make sure whoever yelled 'hot *señoritas*' doesn't even sniff getting laid tonight."

A smile emerged on Gideon's face, and Jaylon nodded. This would keep their minds occupied with something other than how angry their wives were. Gideon only hoped Charlie would have calmed down some by the time he could call the next day.

With an evil grin firmly in place, Gideon turned to address the team. The looks on their faces were fearful, and he chuckled to himself. He knew they should be scared.

"Okay, assholes. We're going to have a teambuilding exercise here—one designed to test loyalty to the team over yourself." Looking over at Fox, whose grin matched his own, he continued. "I want to know who the jerkoff was who thought it would be funny to talk about chicks while I was on the phone with my wife."

The entire group began looking around as if Gideon was talking to someone else. Their heads swiveled in every direction, trying to avoid looking at him.

"That's fine, boys. Here's what will happen tonight. No one will get within licking distance of any of those bargirls. Fox and yours truly are going to make it our personal mission to ensure that if you're having a good time, it will be stopped."

"Fuck."

"Dude."

"You've got to be kidding me."

"The only way to stop this is for one of you to 'fess up. Then I'll focus solely on you for the night. Otherwise, we play the game with all of you. And I don't want any tattletale whiney asses ratting on anyone. That's the pussy way out."

Gideon knew the best way to go about this was to get the dickhead's team members to force him to confess. But how long would it take and how many women would he and Fox have to shoo away before they got the guy to cop to it?

"So that means no one gets a blow job, hand job, whatever. Just consider yourselves on unemployment for the night—no jobs for any of you!"

In one uniform movement, all heads turned and all eyes landed on one guy, the culprit. Gideon should have known Doran would be the fuckup. He often wondered how the hell Doran had gotten through SEAL training. The only possible explanation was the guy's daddy was an admiral somewhere. Trying to keep his cool, Gideon pretended he hadn't just seen them all rat out their teammate. Knowing Doran was going to have a crap night made Gideon a little happier, but he still wanted to snap they guy's neck for making Charlie unhappy.

With the plan set in motion, Gideon and Jaylon gathered everyone together and headed into town. They easily found a bar that wasn't too crowded. It was the same as any other bar on the street: neon signs, loud music, and scantily clad working girls jostling to get to the patrons.

After walking in as a group, they pushed two tables together so they could have enough space for all of them to sit. Immediately three girls in tube tops and short shorts came over to cozy up. The team all looked over at Gideon, but he wasn't going to stop it just yet. He had a plan.

"You want to buy me a drink?" Gideon heard the girl closest to him purr into one of the new guys' ears. The girl's ass rubbed against the guy's crotch, and Gideon knew it wouldn't be long before Doran was punished by his buddies.

"Um, sure?"

After a few minutes, a few more girls came over, repeating the same scene. He waved off the girls who approached him. He knew what they were looking for in the end wasn't a drink.

That's right boys—spend your money and get nice and worked up. One by one, Gideon watched his men fall into a false belief that he'd forgotten his promise. Standing up abruptly, Gideon clapped his hands to get their attention. All heads snapped toward him, and looking in their eyes, he knew it was exactly the right time.

"All right, men. Let's go. Time to move on."

Gideon turned toward the door. Groans and a lot of creative swearing in both Thai and English rang out behind him.

"Don't give a shit. I'm in charge of this little party, and I say it's time to go…unless one of you has something to tell me?" Gideon had to hold his laughter in, as once again, Doran was stared down by the entire team.

With heads bowed, adjusting their pants as they walked past, Gideon saw a few of the guys actually smack Doran in the back of the head. He wondered if this guy was asinine enough to keep going with his silence. Judging by the looks on the faces of the others, Gideon guessed it wouldn't be too much longer.

There was one thing that Gideon felt bad about: They were ruining the girls' business. It wasn't their fault they weren't going to make money off a table full of soldiers. Throwing a few twenties on the table, Gideon smiled and apologized to the girls. They couldn't have cared less as they grabbed the money and moved onto the next table.

It took two more bars, and two more rounds of Jaylon and Gideon causing eight cases of blue balls for them to finally catch on. By the third bar, most of the guys had stopped buying drinks for the girls and instead waved them away before they even got close. Oddly enough, Doran was one of the only ones who still had a girl on his lap.

The fact that Doran was the kind of guy who'd allow his teammates to suffer for him made Gideon very nervous about taking him into the field. Based on the looks the others were giving him, they were thinking the same thing. Gideon made a note to have a little talk with the moron in the morning—set his ass straight.

It was just before one in the morning when Jaylon and Gideon delivered the entire team back to the motel as they'd promised. Every last one of them was tucked in, minus the good-night kiss, by curfew. While Gideon was disappointed in Doran, he was proud of all the men who didn't rat him out. *Karma is a bitch.* He knew this would come back and bite Doran in the ass.

CHAPTER 10

Opening the front door, Charlie flung her book bag across the room, and it slammed into the wall. She flopped on the couch and laid an arm over her eyes. It was good to finally be home. But without Gideon it just seemed like a place to be, not a place to live.

As predicted, Charlie's day had been shitty. With midterms coming fast, all her professors were cramming in as much as possible. The events of the last few days had already put Charlie behind, so now she was drowning. There were, however, two bright spots in her day. The first was practical work. Three days a week Charlie got to be in a classroom with five second-grade students. She felt guilty for missing the last session, and it had been a few days since she'd seen them. Still, when Charlie walked into the classroom, the children threw their arms around her with abandon, and all her stress melted away. She loved her kids.

The second good thing was that she ran into Zoe Fox on campus. Fortunately, it was right after her practical, and Charlie was still in high spirits. Both women had breaks before their next classes, so they'd been able to get off campus for lunch together. Charlie was relieved to talk to someone who truly understood what she was feeling. Of course Gideon's family missed him, but not the way Charlie did. It had only been a day, but she already missed his touch. She missed the way he'd say her name first thing in the morning. She missed seeing him come through the door in his uniform. She missed his arms around her. She missed his lips on hers.

"Did Jaylon call you this morning?" Charlie asked as the two sat down at a booth in the back of the pizza place they'd picked for lunch.

Zoe rolled her eyes. "Yes. I swear I wanted to kill him."

"I know. Why would they call us with those idiots in the background screaming crap about finding women?"

"Because until recently they were those idiots, and they don't know any better." Zoe laughed and Charlie joined in for a brief moment. Then the image of Gideon with another woman flashed in her head. She shook it away.

"Um, you don't think—"

"Charlie! Pahlease. I've seen the way Gideon looks at you. There's no way he'd ever want or need another woman. Trust me. This may be the first long deployment since Jay and I got married, but we dated for years. I remember the first time."

"So you completely trust Jaylon?" Charlie worried she was being a little too forward, but she needed to know. Having Gideon halfway across the world had her questioning so much about their relationship. "I don't mean to pry, but Gideon and I only knew each other for two days before we got married, and so we don't have that history to rely on."

"You guys only knew each other two days?"

Charlie was suddenly embarrassed. She looked down.

"No, no, no. I didn't mean that in a bad way. I'm just impressed that there's so much love there after such a short time. I could never be so ballsy to jump in that quick. I admire you for that, Charlie."

"Well, when I saw him, every other man disappeared. I'll have to tell you the story sometime—it's quite interesting. But please, Zoe, tell me how you trust him so much. It's not that I don't trust Gideon, I really do, but as far as I know he's never had other…options."

"Charlie, just because there are options doesn't mean he'll sample them. You have to trust his love for you. It's a leap of faith, but the reward is a long, happy marriage."

She reached out and laid her hand on Charlie's. Charlie did feel a little better. She knew Gideon loved her. And truthfully, she had just as much opportunity to cheat as he did, and she wasn't going to, so she needed to trust that he wasn't either.

After the pizza was placed on the table, the two dug in and a comfortable silence settled between them. By the time there were only a few slices left, Charlie felt much better and was thankful for having run into Zoe.

"Hey, my brother's wife and Gideon's brother's girlfriend have insisted on taking me out tonight for a girls' night. Do you want to come?"

"I don't know. I mean, I don't even know…Gideon's cousin's sister's…"

Charlie laughed. "Well, my sister-in-law is Gabriella—she and my brother *finally* got married a few months back. We've been friends forever, and I love her. Lots of energy, so she'll be fun tonight and maybe take our minds off our men."

"Where are you all going? I'm really not into the frat bars in town or anything."

Charlie could tell Zoe was trying to find excuses so she could stay at home and miss Jaylon. If her friends weren't going to let Charlie do that, then she wasn't going to let Zoe do it.

"Honestly, I have no idea where we're going tonight. They won't tell me, but they know better than to take me to some pick-up bar. That's *so* not what I need."

Zoe took a few moments to think about the offer. Charlie watched as her dark eyes glazed over. The expression on her face changed from doubt to acceptance in the span of about a minute.

"Okay, I'm in. But seriously, if they take us to Pacific Beach, I'm going to turn around and go home."

"Great! I'll call and let you know what time. I think they'll at least tell me that."

Once finished with lunch, the two had headed back to campus to finish out the day. A few grueling hours later, Charlie was now finally able to lie back and relax on her couch. Being alone in the apartment was probably not the best idea, however. Guilt over being so bitchy to Gideon that morning had started to creep in. It hadn't been his fault, and Charlie allowed herself a little laugh when she thought about how mad he probably was at those idiots and the price they'd no doubt paid. Gideon was almost diabolical when it came to plotting revenge.

Charlie glanced at her watch and tried to do the math to figure out what time it was wherever he might be. Could she expect a phone call any time soon? The best she could figure, it was either the middle of the night or possibly morning.

She'd just closed her eyes to take a few minutes and try to find a happy place, when she was startled by the sound of the apartment door flinging open. She rolled off the couch, landing flat on her ass, as Gabby burst in without so much as a knock. Paige was close behind with a big smile on her face.

"Come on, Charlie. We're going out. Go get changed, quick," Gabby ordered.

To look at her, no one would ever guess how bossy Gabriella could be. Her soulful brown eyes, framed by night black lashes, gave her an air of shyness and a demure demeanor. It amazed Charlie that her smart and opinionated brother put up with Gabriella's need for total control.

"What? It's, like, not even four in the afternoon, Gabby. Are we hanging with the elderly tonight? Gotta get somewhere for the early bird special?" Charlie asked from her position on the floor.

"We have a little bit of a drive. So get a move on, please." Gabby's foot was tapping. "I'm going to pick out something for you to wear, but you need to go do something with that." She waved her hand at Charlie's messy ponytail.

Charlie looked over at Paige, hoping she could help talk some sense into her. How long could Paige have been under Gabriella's influence? Maybe Charlie had a chance to pull her to her side.

"Don't look at me, Charlie. I'm here for moral support. This is all Miss Bossypants' idea." That was all Paige said — no hint of where Charlie was being whisked off to or anything.

"I have to call Zoe Fox. I invited her this afternoon." Charlie wasn't sure if Gabby even heard her, but she whipped out her phone and dialed Zoe.

"Charlie! Get your ass in here and start getting ready, *chica!*" Gabby's accent was more prominent when she was excited.

Paige took the phone out of Charlie's hand as Zoe screamed Charlie's name. Charlie was totally confused as to who she needed to respond to first. Paige took over and introduced herself on the phone, and Charlie gave her a smile for rescuing her before heading into the bedroom.

"Get in that bathroom and do something with your hair and makeup. You look like you rolled out of bed and left the house."

Gabby's tone was condescending, and Charlie was starting to get annoyed. Her husband had just left for six months, for Christ's sake. She had every right to wallow for a few days, and it had only been a few hours.

"Gabriella, stop." Charlie grabbed her sister-in-law's shoulder mid-clothes fling and held her still.

Paige walked in on this scene and chuckled. "So that's how you stop her. I was wondering if she had an off switch or would eventually just run out of batteries."

All three women broke out laughing. The tension in the room lifted, and Charlie thanked God she'd asked Paige to come with them. She needed the balance of Paige's wit to Gabby's intensity.

"Zoe's on the way, Charlie. I explained the situation, and she said she wouldn't leave you alone with Gabby and not to worry."

Paige's voice was so deadpan that Charlie didn't know if she was joking. Gabby didn't look so sure either.

"Okay." Gabby took a deep breath. "I'm sorry. Now, seriously, go fix your hair. We're just doing dinner, so you don't have to worry about anything too fancy."

For the first time Charlie took in what Gabby and Paige were wearing. She was surprised to see just simple jeans and T-shirts.

Based on the clothing choices of the planning committee for the night, this couldn't be that bad, so Charlie gave in to Gabby's demands and went into the bathroom to get herself together. She almost jumped when she saw her reflection in the mirror. Obviously she'd have to apologize to Gabby for all the mean things she'd wanted to do to her earlier. She'd been absolutely right — Charlie was hideous.

"Charlie, come on. If we don't get going by four, we're going to be in traffic for hours." It had only been five minutes and looking in the mirror for the final time, Charlie was impressed that she could go from hideous to acceptable so quickly.

"Gabriella, where are you taking me that might take hours?" Charlie asked. She walked into the bedroom to find Paige lounging while Gabby made a last-minute switch of Charlie's shirt. Paige shook her head.

"It was just a figure of speech, Charlie," Gabby explained as she handed her sister-in-law her outfit for the evening.

Charlie was happy to see her favorite comfortable jeans and a simple red tank to go with them.

Shooing Paige and Gabby out of the room so she could change, Charlie heard a knock at the door and figured one of them would let Zoe in. Their voices carried through the small apartment, and Charlie could hear them all talking as she slipped on the jeans. Minutes later, Gabby ushered everyone out the door, and Charlie barely had time to make sure she'd locked the deadbolt as she was practically pushed down the stairs to the car. The four women piled into Gabriella's Land Cruiser.

Gabby turned up the radio, and they were off. She got on I-5 going north, and when they passed San Clemente, Charlie again questioned where they were headed. Gabby smiled as she looked at Charlie in the rearview mirror.

"We're going to the happiest place on Earth."

"Disneyland?"

Paige turned in her seat and looked at Charlie, rolling her eyes and giving the other girls a quick smile. "I tried to talk her out of it. I wanted to do dinner and rent movies, but that got shot down pretty quickly."

"Disneyland is where we go when things aren't good. You just can't be sad at Disneyland," Gabby informed them with a touch too much enthusiasm. "I think they actually kick you out if you aren't happy."

If Gabby's belief about the "law of Disneyland" was true, there was a good chance their asses would be escorted off the premises before they even made it through the turnstile, Charlie thought. The empty feeling she'd had since Gideon stepped on the plane seemed to grow as she thought about even trying to act happy. When she looked up, Paige caught her eye and twisted her face into a grimace. Charlie almost wanted to laugh.

"See, Paige doesn't want to go either," Charlie pointed out.

"Sure she does." Gabby turned to glare at Paige.

"Come on, Charlie. This will be fun." Charlie could tell Paige was trying to sound enthusiastic to avoid Gabriella's ire.

"Now that we have that settled, and everyone—" Gabby paused to glare at Paige "—is in the proper mindset for our little adventure, I have a question."

Charlie knew from experience that what followed was not going to be pleasant.

"How is Tyson in bed?"

"Gabriella! That's a totally inappropriate question!" Charlie came to her new friend's defense. "Besides, I happen to know she hasn't slept with Ty yet. Which, given Tyson's history, has to mean something."

Paige didn't answer, but turned to look out the window.

"Okay, seriously, Paige, how have you managed to resist, *the* Tyson Cooper?"

Gabby turned her head away from the road and toward the passenger seat, which was scary, because Charlie could see brake lights in the distance.

"Well, we've only been dating for, like, a month, and I'm not really ready to make that kind of commitment yet. It's not for lack of trying on his part, though." Paige smiled as she continued. "It's actually kind of fun to see how creative he can be. So far, though, not too much thought has gone into his plans."

The women in the car laughed, even Charlie and Zoe.

"You gotta love a Cooper man," Charlie said through her giggles. "Gideon's idea of romance is throwing me over his shoulder and taking me to the bedroom, and Tyson isn't half as smooth as his brother."

"Well, his most recent attempt involved showing up at my apartment with roses and a bottle of champagne to celebrate our one-month anniversary. I was actually a little insulted that he thought that would work on me. Don't get me wrong, when he isn't working so hard at being Tyson Cooper BMOC, he's smart, interesting, and definitely se—"

"Oh, Gabby—" Charlie leaned up between the front seats and pointed across four lanes of traffic "—there's the exit."

Everyone in the car immediately understood the need for those over-door handles. Each woman clutched one in a death grip as Gabby careened across the highway with horns blaring, fingers flying, and people yelling.

"Zoe, are you all right?" Charlie reached over and rubbed her friend's arm. She looked like she was going to be sick after that little maneuver, and Charlie made a mental note not to ride Big Thunder with her.

"I'm fine. Just thought we might die right there. Give me a second—and find me a drink when we get to the restaurant—and I'll be fine."

"Gabriella, you are *so* not driving home tonight," Paige declared. "I'll volunteer to be the designated driver. I'm not in the mood to spend several weeks in traction because you're more concerned with my boyfriend's bedroom prowess than where we're going."

"First of all, we're all alive, are we not? So there's no need to criticize my driving skills. And you didn't finish your sentence. Here, let me help you out. You were saying, 'and definitely…'"

Paige burst out laughing. "Okay, you got me. Tyson is damn sexy," she finally admitted.

"It runs in the family, believe me. I almost attacked Gideon the first time I saw him. Hell, I married the guy after spending two days in bed with him," Charlie confessed.

"Well, that little bit of information makes me think maybe I'm stronger than I'd been giving myself credit for," Paige said.

As if on cue, her phone chirped. She flashed the girls a hard smile that earned yet another round of laughter. The others instantly knew it was Tyson checking up on her.

Leaning back into the worn leather of the couch, Tyson sighed. He couldn't remember the last time he'd been home alone on a Friday night. He was Tyson *fucking* Cooper, for God's sake. Women fell over themselves to be with him. All he had to do was look at a girl and her panties would practically fall to the ground. And, man, did he ever take advantage of that.

Thinking back on all of the girls he'd used and never called back after he got into their pants, all the girls who thought he was worth giving it up for, Tyson realized the irony of the situation. Now the one woman he wanted on this entire planet was barely letting him feel her up. The fact that he couldn't manage to close the deal with Paige was baffling to him.

He glanced at the pile of textbooks in front of him. He knew he should just suck it up and study, but his mind kept wandering back to Paige. And not to visions of her in his bed or shower or the backseat of his car like it normally did. This time he genuinely wanted to talk to her and make sure she was okay.

Which is why he finally picked up the phone and called her, even though he knew she was out with Charlie and Gabby, and he'd been specifically told not to call her tonight. He thought maybe just hearing her voice would help focus him again so he could get back to studying—and he'd score some points when he asked about Charlie.

"Tyson."

Paige sounded angry when she answered, but he could hear the girls laughing in the background, so he knew she was putting on a bit of an act.

"Hey, beautiful," Tyson purred, completely ignoring Paige's tone.

"Tyson." Paige's tone thawed a bit, and he smiled at how well he could read her already. After only a month, he could push the right buttons. "Why are you calling me when I told you I was going out with Charlie?"

"Ouch. That hurts, baby. I was just calling to see how all you ladies are doing."

"Other than Gabriella almost killing us, we're doing wonderful. And no, I'm not telling you where we are or where we're going, so don't even ask."

Paige had shot down his next question before he could even get there. It seemed she was beginning to understand him too.

"Gabby's driving? If I'd known that, I never would have let you go. She's crazy behind the wheel, and I don't want to lose you."

"I heard that! And I'm an excellent driver, Tyson!" Gabby shouted.

Tyson's response was a loud, genuine laugh.

"So, how's Charlie doing?"

"Why? Does *Evelyn* want to know?"

Paige's response pulled him up short. Did she really think he wouldn't ask about his sister-in-law on his own? Tyson cared about Charlie. Of course he could have called and asked her how she was doing on his own, but he hadn't.

Actually, if his mom hadn't gotten his ass out of bed that morning, Tyson would have gone the whole day without thinking about what Charlie was going through. It probably would have been days before it occurred to him to stop and see her. And then it really would have been to borrow Gideon's truck.

Even Charlie knew he was a selfish bastard. He remembered her comment that morning. "*I never knew you had the ability to think of someone else's feelings.*" Charlie would probably never call him if she needed something. That wasn't right. He wanted to be someone she could rely on. He wanted to be there for her when Gideon couldn't be. He wanted to be more like Gideon.

"No. Actually *I* want to know." Tyson tried to keep the hurt out of his voice.

"Well, I think she's doing okay…I think. I've heard her laugh, so that's good."

"I'm fine, Tyson. Where's Gideon's truck?" Charlie called out.

Tyson exploded into laughter, gasping as he said, "Well, my brother definitely has her well trained. And if she has enough of her faculties to ask about the truck, I'm guessing she's going to be okay."

"So what are you doing to keep yourself busy tonight?" Paige asked.

"I'm home alone, missing you."

Paige laughed. He couldn't believe he was sharing his feelings, and she was laughing at him.

"You are so corny, you know that? Really, what are you doing?"

"I'm serious. I'm sitting at home. Okay, well, I'm trying to study for midterms, but thoughts of you keep popping into my head, and then I'm distracted. You know…if you were here with me, maybe I could concentrate better?"

"I'm pretty sure me being there would have the opposite effect, because I know I'd be focused on distracting you."

Paige's voice had suddenly taken on a lower, sultry tone Tyson had never heard before—from her. It gave him hope.

"Paige, don't tease me when I know I have no chance of even seeing you tonight, let alone touching you. I'll just stick to the fantasies of what I'm *going* to do to you once I *do* get to touch you. I have a very vivid imagination."

Tyson waited for her reply. It didn't come, and he began to worry. Had he said the wrong thing? It wasn't as if he hadn't been dropping big hints and talking in innuendo since their second date. It had never left Paige speechless before.

"Paige? Baby? Did Gabby crash the car? Are you okay?"

"I'm here. Sorry. I was a little mesmerized by all the lights."

"Lights? Did Gabby take you guys to Vegas? I'll kill her."

All Tyson could think about was how *he* behaved in Vegas. He'd have been all over Paige the minute he saw her—just like all the other men there. Suddenly, "What happens in Vegas, stays in Vegas" didn't seem like such a brilliant tagline, though he'd certainly loved it when he'd been the one tossing it around.

"I've gotta go, Tyson. Call you in the morning."

The phone disconnected, and he was left with the image of Paige in a short skirt and barely there top, her head thrown back in laughter while some douchebag leaned in to whisper in her ear.

"I am so fucked," Tyson moaned as he fell back into the couch with the phone against his chest.

Half an hour passed as he played out different scenarios in his head involving Paige in Las Vegas. He was going to go crazy if he didn't do something to distract himself. Then he realized he hadn't called his mom to find out how she was.

Actually he never called his mom to find out how she was when Gideon left. He just assumed everything was fine. His dad would take care of her. But what if she needed more than that? What if she needed to know she had another son who could be there for her? Could he be someone she was proud of too? Yeah, he could. He would be that for her.

It hit Tyson like a ton of bricks: He was an arrogant ass, and that needed to change. If Tyson wanted a woman like Paige to be with him, he had to be Tyson, not Tyson *fucking* Cooper.

CHAPTER 11

Disneyland. Who else but Gabriella would think of driving all the way to Disneyland just to cheer her up? Charlie dearly loved her sister-in-law, but she was a little crazy. And she knew her brother *had* to love Gabriella, because only someone who truly loved her could live with her.

"*Vamanos, chicas.* Our reservation is for six thirty, so we're right on time."

Downtown Disney was a jumble of restaurants and stores. They could have eaten at one of the "grown-up" restaurants. But no. Gabby had chosen the one with animatronics and a thunderstorm that rumbled through every fifteen minutes. Thankfully she listened when Charlie begged to sit on the patio where the group could hold a conversation without lions roaring or gorillas thumping their chests.

Dinner passed comfortably with lots of laughter and good conversation. Paige was bombarded with questions about Tyson, which she deftly sidestepped. Charlie had to admire the way Paige was with Tyson. Deep down there was something good and caring in him. How could he and Gideon come from such great parents and he not have something special too? If anyone could bring it out in him, it would be Paige.

After wandering through the retail maze of Downtown Disney, the women finally made it through the turnstile and into "The Happiest Place on Earth." Charlie didn't know how happy she was, but it was nice to spend time with her friends and forget about real life for a little while. There certainly wasn't any better place to do that than Disneyland.

"Where to first, girls?" Gabby asked the group, standing in the middle of Main Street.

"Pirates of the Caribbean," Charlie offered.

"Small World," Zoe said at that same time.

Then they looked at Paige, waiting for her input.

She just stared back at them.

"I got nothing. I've never been here before, so I'm at your mercy."

The other three stood frozen, jaws hanging open.

"Wh-What do you mean? You've never been to Disneyland? Were you an abused child, Paige? Seriously, who hasn't been to Disneyland?" Gabby was incredulous. Never going to Disneyland was the worst life any child could have endured.

"I didn't grow up here. I moved here for college, and I guess I've just been a little too busy to drive all the way up here for a few roller coasters."

Paige's tone was more defiant than apologetic. This was not going to end well. Charlie needed to head things off before Gabby lost her mind, as she was prone to do when someone insulted her beloved Disneyland.

"A few roller coasters?" Gabby stared down Paige.

"Well, Paige, you have no idea what you've been missing." Charlie stepped between Paige and Gabby.

"Really! Come on, we only have a few hours before they close, so we need to get Paige on all the icons of Disney." Zoe seemed to sense the tension too and tried to help.

Charlie laid a calming hand on Gabriella's shoulder, and Zoe began extolling the greatness of each ride. Soon the mood lightened and the group moved on. Surprisingly, they were able to hit every major ride over the next few hours, and Paige seemed to enjoy herself on everything from The Matterhorn to Space Mountain to the Haunted Mansion.

As it got close to time for the final parade and fireworks, the women made their way to Main Street to find a spot. Of all the rides and activities at the park, the parade was Gabriella's absolute favorite. She always had to have the best seat, which meant everyone with her had to sit on the curb for half an hour.

When the parade finally started—and their butts hurt from staking their claim—Gabby jumped to her feet, clapping her hands wildly. Paige shook her head and laughed. Behind Paige, Charlie noticed a group of younger guys weaving their way through the crowd. It was obvious where they were headed.

Sure enough, as soon as the guys got to the group of women, they divided up and each approached one. The music from the parade was so loud they had to shout their lame pick-up lines.

"Hey, beautiful! I noticed you standing here all alone and wanted to keep you company!" the guy who apparently had picked Charlie shouted at her.

Charlie didn't want to even bother with him, but she knew if she didn't respond, he wouldn't go away. Raising her left hand, she politely showed him her wedding ring. Out of the corner of her eye, Charlie saw Zoe and Gabby doing the same thing. Poor Paige actually had to talk to her guy. Charlie couldn't hear her, but from the way she was standing and the look on her face, the guy was going to feel like he'd just been castrated.

Unfortunately the one hitting on Charlie didn't take the hint and kept trying to talk to her. She felt her phone vibrate in her pocket and wondered who would be calling tonight. Charlie's heart leaped when she saw the international number on the screen.

Moving away from the crowd, she flipped the phone open, a smile filling her face. The idiot frat boy, however, decided he was going to follow her. Apparently the genius couldn't take a hint.

"Gideon! Oh, I'm so sorry!" Charlie screamed hoping Gideon could hear her over the music blaring in the background. She kept moving to find a quieter place, only stopping when she found a spot where she could finally hear her husband. Looking behind her, Charlie groaned as she saw the loser still following.

"Hey, baby. No, I'm sorry. That was stupid. I love you. I miss you," Gideon told her.

Charlie wanted to cry, but knew she couldn't let Gideon know how miserable she really was—even at the happiest place on Earth.

At that moment, the guy trying to hit on Charlie decided to be a bit more bold. "Come on, gorgeous. Let's go somewhere more private."

"Who the hell is that, Charlie? Where are you? I can hear music. Are you out at a club?" Charlie could hear the hurt in his voice and it killed her.

Gideon seethed. If he could, he'd have reached through the phone and wrapped his hands around that asshole's neck. Sadly, he couldn't do anything about it.

Forcing himself to take a few deep breaths, Gideon reminded himself that he trusted Charlie. She'd never cheat on him. He knew that. But not being there to prove how much he adored her had his mind running in directions it normally wouldn't have.

"Hold on a sec, Gideon."

He could still hear her as she spoke to whoever that guy was.

"Look, asshole, I tried to be polite, but you just can't take a hint, apparently. If you didn't get it before, I'm married. See? Ring. So I'm not interested. And my husband—did I mention he's a Navy SEAL? Yeah, he doesn't take very kindly to morons who bother me when I've told them to piss off."

Gideon was instantly hard. There wasn't anything hotter than a beautiful woman telling a guy off because she only wants to be with you.

"Okay, I'm back. Had to get rid of a pest." Her voice was light, and Gideon felt better about the two of them. He needed this conversation to go better than their last. He didn't know when he'd talk to her next. The team's ship was already in port. When Charlie hadn't picked up on the home line, he'd stolen a few minutes on one of the phones in the offices around the pier so he could call Charlie without it having to be collect. He didn't know whose phone it was, but they were going to be a little surprised when they got the bill. Unfortunately, Gideon only had a few minutes before they were called to assemble.

"Baby, I love you. I needed to tell you that."

"I know. I really am sorry I got so pissy this morning."

Gideon didn't want her to spend these precious seconds feeling bad about anything. He just wanted to hear her voice and know she was going to be okay. He wanted to know that she loved him and for her to know he loved her.

"I only have a minute, baby. I just wanted you to know I miss you."

"I know, Joe."

There was his name, the one only Charlie called him. It made him happy to hear her use it.

"And I love you more than anything in the world. I'm counting the days 'til you come back to me."

"You never answered my question—where are you? I can hear music, but it doesn't sound like a club."

"Well, that's a long story, but Gabby decided to bring me to Disneyland."

"Disneyland? Only Gabriella."

"I know, but we've had fun. Can you believe Paige had never been? When you come home we'll all have to come here. Make a weekend of it."

Glancing out the window, Gideon saw his team starting to gather to board the ship. He cursed under his breath.

"Baby, I'm gonna have to go. I love you so much. I'll call you when I can. Take care of yourself."

"Love you, Joe."

"Bye, Charlie."

Gideon stayed on the line a second longer, hoping to hear her voice one last time. Instead he heard her sigh as she hung up.

Knowing Charlie had people to take care of her while he was gone was the only reason this whole thing was even bearable. Throwing his duffle over his shoulder, Gideon turned and went to join the team. Unconsciously, he began whistling. He'd talked with his baby. She loved him, and she was, if not exactly happy, at least getting by with the help of friends. The only thing better would have been holding her himself, but Gideon was happy with what he had…Charlie.

CHAPTER 12

It had been almost two weeks since Gideon left, and in that time it had become somewhat expected that Tyson and Charlie would be at the Coopers' for dinner every Wednesday and Sunday.

During their second Sunday dinner together, Evelyn Cooper looked around the dinner table, and a feeling of contentment washed over her. Not happiness. Her gaze settled on the empty seat next to Charlie. She couldn't truly be happy until Gideon was back home—so she'd have to settle for contentment.

"So, I'm thinking of going into oncology," Tyson announced as he reached over and took Paige's hand in his.

Evelyn liked Paige. Any girl who could cause Tyson to change so drastically was tops in her book. Over the past few weeks, Evelyn had seen him check on Charlie, making sure there was nothing she needed. And she herself had seen her youngest son more in the past two weeks than she had during the entire previous six months. She was so proud.

It wasn't difficult to understand why Tyson acted the way that he did. It had been hard to grow up in Gideon's shadow. The first question teachers, coaches, and even other kids often asked him was, "Are you Gideon Cooper's brother?" That happened for a few years before Tyson realized what they meant when they said it: "Oh, boy. Here's someone who'll be perfect and smart and do everything I ask. A leader." Poor Tyson. He was doomed before he started.

Evelyn knew this was what had made him the Tyson he'd been for years now: the self-absorbed, inconsiderate boy. He wanted to be the opposite of his brother. Of course, there was only so far Evelyn would allow that to go.

She knew how smart he was, so good study habits and good grades were always required. And she never allowed him to be disrespectful of women in front of her, which, based on comments from Gideon, explained why he'd never brought a girl home before. But she'd always hoped someday he'd find the real Tyson again.

"Tyson, oncology is a tough field. You sure you don't want to think about general surgery?" his father asked.

Tyson's face fell for just a second before he quickly recovered.

"Peter." Evelyn gave him a look that said, "wrong, wrong, wrong." "I think it's wonderful that Tyson has been thinking about a field of study. I'm proud of you, Tyson."

Paige seemed to realize quickly that a change of subject would be a good idea. Unfortunately, she chose the one subject everyone else had been avoiding all night.

"So, Charlie, how is Gideon doing?"

The rest of the table stopped breathing for a split second.

"Oh, I'm sorry." Paige quickly apologized, realizing her mistake.

"No, it's okay, Paige," Charlie responded.

An obvious friendship had formed between the two, and Tyson had mentioned that Charlie talked about Gideon with Paige. Evelyn was glad Charlie had someone to talk to.

"Actually, I just got a stack of letters from him today. And I mean a *stack*. The boy must have nothing better to do than write to me."

She laughed, and it was a nice sound. In all the times Evelyn had seen her over the past weeks, this was the first time she'd laughed.

"Wouldn't it be better if you got them, like, one a day? Why the hell a stack at a time?" Tyson asked.

"Well, it's not like he can just waltz over to the post office and drop the letter in the mailbox, Tyson. He has to wait until someone comes to get it or they're on a base of sorts." Charlie added an "idiot" under her breath, causing Tyson's smile to widen.

"I just sent him a little care package the other day," Evelyn added.

For some reason, she felt the need to stake a claim on her own son. It was the strangest feeling. She loved Charlie. She loved that Gideon had Charlie. But he'd been hers first, and she was a little jealous that she'd only gotten one phone call and three letters that arrived the day before — hardly a stack. Evelyn knew her envy was wrong, but she couldn't help it.

"Me too," Charlie replied. "I sent him a Halloween package, a bunch of little bags for all his team with stupid Halloween stuff and candy in them. And of course magazines and a hefty supply of Reese's Peanut Cups for Gideon. He loves those things."

Evelyn felt more guilt as she listened to her daughter-in-law. She tried to ignore the tiny piece of her that was jealous, because the bigger part was overjoyed that her son had found this woman to love him.

The next day Tyson stopped after his last class to check on Charlie. He was planning to make it quick because Paige was meeting him at his place when she was done for the day. He was more than eager to get home to her.

Dinner with his parents the night before had been rough in places. He'd felt bad when Paige brought up Gideon. It was always the elephant in the room when they were together as a family. But leave it to his woman to bring it up and have Charlie actually laughing. It was just one more reason Tyson adored her.

Of course, the fact that Paige's hand had been moving perilously close to his straining zipper under the table didn't make things any easier. For the past few weeks Paige couldn't seem to keep her hands off of him, which was kind of funny considering that on the night Paige and Gabby took Charlie to Disneyland, Tyson had decided to stop scheming to get her into his bed. He didn't want to be *that* Tyson anymore. He wanted to be something more for her. He wanted her to want to be with him.

That resolve had lasted all of about a day. But apparently Paige had had some sort of realization too, because the next time Tyson saw her, she'd turned into a little vixen.

The morning after Paige's little excursion with Charlie and Gabby, a persistent knocking had woken Tyson from yet another wonderful dream about Paige naked. Needless to say, he was none too happy about having his Paige time interrupted again. Yanking open the door, he was about to give whoever it was hell, when recognition finally made its way to his brain. Standing in front of Tyson in a bathrobe and slippers and her hair pulled up in a ponytail was Paige. She had a box of doughnuts and two cups of coffee in her hands.

"Thought you might like something sweet this morning." She held out the coffee. Tyson took it with a smile, stepping to the side so she could come in.

Paige stepped into Tyson's hard body, and he had to count to ten to calm himself down. He'd never been this close to Paige in this state. When she stretched her body up, causing glorious friction over his about-to-explode erection, and her lips softly brushed his ear, Tyson groaned.

"Tyson, I want you. I want all of you. I know who you are, and I'm not worried about us and our future. I trust you. Please, Tyson, take me to bed."

All resolve was gone as Tyson leaned in and attacked those perfect, full lips of hers. Paige eagerly met his kisses with her own and allowed his tongue entrance when he dragged it across her bottom lip. Her taste was like cotton candy: sweet and sticky and melt-in-your-mouth. Tyson knew right then he never wanted to taste another woman.

Scooping her up in his arms, Tyson carried Paige into the bedroom, the sound of her laughter filling his apartment and his heart.

The memory of that day and all those since had Tyson walking with a bounce in his step as he made his way from the car down the sidewalk, heading for Charlie and Gideon's place. This was another aspect of his life that had changed in incredible ways. Since Gideon had been gone, Tyson had realized he needed to be there for Charlie. So he and Chance traded off checking on her. The two men teased her about needing them to open jars or kill spiders. Of course, she'd just roll her eyes, but Tyson suspected she liked that they were checking up on her.

He'd just rounded the corner, and Charlie and Gideon's apartment came into view. He froze. A guy in a uniform was coming out the door. Something was wrong. Something had happened. His stomach began to churn. Then the guy lifted his head, and Tyson saw a smile on his face. Relief washed over him. If Gideon had been hurt, or worse, the guy wouldn't be smiling. Would he?

Then his motions caught Tyson's attention. He was tucking in his shirt and zipping up his pants. Both men reached the bottom of the stairs at the same time. When the stranger saw Tyson, he looked up, and the smile got bigger.

"Great day, huh?" he said and walked toward the parking lot.

Charlie was cheating on his brother? Gideon was off risking his life to serve his country, and his wife was here screwing the guys who didn't go? Tyson thought he was going to be sick. He felt like his feet were glued to the spot where he was standing. It was a good three minutes before he could even think about moving. His eyes darted from Charlie's door to the space where the guy's car had been just moments before.

He tried to convince himself Charlie would never cheat on his brother. He wanted to believe that, but as the scene played through his head again—the guy in uniform, whistling as he tucked and zipped, coming out of *that* door—Tyson couldn't come up with another possible explanation.

Finally he was able to make his feet move, and he turned to head back to the car. There was no way he could even look at Charlie right now. Tyson worried about what he might say or do if he were to go up to the apartment. He needed to think.

Sliding into the silence of the car, Tyson sat with the keys in the ignition for several minutes. It was too hard to make himself believe Charlie would do this to Gideon. This would kill him. As he sat there, Tyson reached for the door handle several times, ready to march up to the apartment and confront Charlie. Each time, however, he stopped.

When he was finally able to turn the key and actually focus enough to drive, he pulled out of the parking lot, squealing of the tires. On the drive back to his place, Tyson noticed he was gripping the steering wheel so tightly his knuckles had turned white. There was a real possibility he was going to break the damn thing in half.

Feeling the anger building up, Tyson knew he couldn't go home. There was a chance Paige would be there, and he didn't want her to see him like this—or run the risk of taking his bad mood out on her. He bypassed the exit to his apartment and kept driving until he got to the beach.

Tyson pulled into the parking lot, which was mostly empty—just as he knew it would be. Although the weather in San Diego was exceptional all year long, late October would be pushing it to take a dip in the ice-cold waters of the Pacific. The only people crazy enough to even attempt swimming at this time of the year were surfers and tourists. The surfers wore wetsuits, and the tourists…they just made him laugh.

Allowing these trivial things to occupy his mind, Tyson got out of the car and headed to the nearly deserted beach. This was where he came to think and be alone. Right now, he most certainly needed to do both of those things.

He kicked off his shoes as he stepped into the sand, and the feel of the cool grains sliding between his toes brought a small sense of comfort. Tyson picked up his shoes and trudged across the beach to the small outcropping of rocks he liked to think of as his own personal spot. He'd been coming to this place since he was sixteen. Once he had his license and could escape the watchful gaze of "big brother Gideon," Tyson had jumped at the chance to get away.

In this spot, he'd sit for hours—just thinking about things: girls, school, his future. Loads of shit that in this moment seemed trivial and unimportant.

Finding his favorite rock, Tyson climbed up and perched himself with his legs pulled up to his chest. The wind blew slightly, and he tasted salt. He watched as the sun began to sink into the water, causing the sky to fill with pinks and yellows and oranges. The sight was breathtaking, and he thought for a minute about Paige and how he wanted to share this spot with her. He'd never wanted anyone to even know about his rock, but Tyson knew he would share it with her. He'd been thinking he wanted to share a lot with her, that he wanted what Gid—*Shit!*

Like a punch in the gut, Tyson was suddenly reminded why he'd come here. What did he need to do about the situation he'd just walked up on—or did he even want to do anything? He wasn't ready to deal with this. For Christ's sake, he'd just started acting like a grown up about two weeks ago. How the hell was he supposed to deal with his brother, who was off fighting for his country while his wife was screwing his buddy? This was so unfair…for everyone.

Tyson weighed the options. He figured there were three ways to go. First, he could tell Gideon. It would destroy him. There'd be nothing he could do while stuck overseas, so it would eat him up and possibly get him killed in the process. So door number one was a definite no.

The second choice would be to confront Charlie. Of course she'd deny it. She'd never tell Tyson she was screwing around on Gideon. And then where would he be? Charlie would still be a part of the family, and she'd be glaring at him over dinner at his parents'. Then his mom would want to know what was going on. Keeping something from her was next to impossible, so eventually he'd have to tell her. And that would get back to Gideon finding out, because there was no way she wouldn't tell him. So again, a big no.

Tyson's last option was to try to act like he knew nothing. It would be difficult, but he thought he could pull it off. He'd just wait it out and tell Gideon when he got back. That way the situation could be taken care of without endangering his brother's life.

This seemed the most logical of all the options. He'd just have to watch Charlie a little more closely over the next six months, and when Gideon came home, he'd tell him what he saw. It would still kill him, but at least not physically. The biggest problem with this plan was being around Charlie and acting civil toward her. He didn't know if he could do that, but he had to try, for everyone's sake.

The final decision Tyson had to make was how much he should share with Paige. He knew keeping something from her wasn't going to be good for their relationship, but he also knew if he told her, she'd confront Charlie, and then they ended up back with Gideon finding out while he was in the field.

Tyson couldn't tell Paige. He hoped she'd forgive him in the end, but he had to do this for his brother.

Having made a decision, Tyson felt lighter and ready to go home. The sun had completely set, and the beach was almost pitch black as he walked back to the parking lot. Fortunately, every year his mother put one of those little key chain flashlights in her sons' stockings at Christmas. Using it, Tyson could just barely make out the ground about a foot in front of him.

When he got back to the car, he checked his phone. He'd left it in the cup holder on the console because taking it with him would have defeated the whole concept of time by himself. There were three missed calls and two texts, all from Paige. A pang of guilt washed over him. He was new at this "good boyfriend" shit, and it occurred to him now that he should've called her and let her know he wasn't going to be home right away. He quickly dialed her number.

"Wow, Tyson. So nice of you to call."

At Paige's icy greeting, Tyson wondered exactly how long he'd been out on the rocks. Glancing at the clock on the dash, he realized his internal argument had lasted almost three hours.

"I'm so sorry, Paige. Really." He couldn't tell her what he'd been doing or why, and he felt like a total dick for that.

"Where are you? I sat in your apartment for hours, Tyson. You said you were going to check on Charlie, like, forever ago."

Tyson could hear the worry in her voice, which only made him feel worse.

"I went for a drive. I needed to think about things. I'm really missing Gideon."

"You know, Tyson, I understand that. You can talk to me. I shouldn't have to beg you to tell me what's wrong. I thought maybe you were chang-ing, but whatever. I'm home now, and I think that we need a night apart."

Tyson was silent for a second too long, debating whether or not to just tell her what he'd witnessed earlier. Apparently she took that as a sign he agreed with her.

"Yeah, okay. I'll talk to you tomorrow, Tyson." And she was gone.

He let his head fall against the steering wheel and banged it there a few times.

"I'm such an asshole. I should just tell her."

Once he'd started the car and was driving toward home, he decided to call Paige again. Tyson had worked up the courage to tell her the truth, but when she answered the phone with a curt "What, Tyson?" all he wanted was to make her not be mad at him anymore. He didn't think accusing Charlie of screwing around on Gideon would produce the results he was looking for.

"I'm sorry," was all he could come up with. It wasn't much, but it was heartfelt, and he hoped she could hear that in his voice. Tyson didn't know where their relationship was going yet, but the thought of Paige angry with him made him nervous. "Paige, I'm so sorry. I have some things I'm working through. This 'good boyfriend' thing is still kind of new to me. I'm gonna screw up sometimes."

"I know. I'm sorry too. It's just sometimes those things I've heard girls say about you come rushing back, and I get scared."

Paige sounded as nervous as Tyson felt, and he wanted to believe it was because she wanted this to work out as much as he did.

"I swear to you, I wasn't with anyone. I just needed to think. It kills me to think I may have screwed this up with my own stupidity. I can't promise it won't happen again, but I promise I'll try my hardest not to make you worry about me or my feelings for you." Tyson held his breath.

"How long will it be before you get here, Tyson?" Paige asked, her voice lowering to that sexy timbre that made all the things he thought about doing to her on a daily basis seem within the realm of possibility.

Lifting his hand, Tyson knocked on her door. "Not long at all."

CHAPTER 13

"Ahhh."

The breath escaped in a whoosh as Charlie flopped onto the couch, preparing to study for her psych midterm. She couldn't bring herself to open her book bag though. Instead she grabbed a letter off the stack that had arrived a few days ago and settled in to read Gideon's words:

Charlie,

Baby, I miss you more than I could ever put on a stupid piece of paper. I miss everything about you. It's only been a few days, and I'm having withdrawals. How am I going to make it six whole months?

It's pretty much the same thing here every day. I get up... yadda yadda...I wish I could tell you what we do, but I can't.

Oh, I didn't tell you what happened to Doran after I had to punish everyone for their stupidity. I wish I wasn't second in charge, cause I would have loved to be part of that little night maneuver. So, anyway, the next morning, we all report to the ship to leave, and Doran won't take his hat off. I knew immediately the guys had done something as payback. Everyone was pushing him to take off his hat and laughing. finally someone called him a pussy, and he felt the need to prove he wasn't. He is, but that's beside the point. The letter "A" was shaved in the back of his head, and then it looked like they took red permanent marker and colored it in. I can only guess that the "A" stood for asshole. That was fucking brilliant.

There was a loud rapping at the door. Charlie had been enjoying getting lost in Gideon's mind and wasn't at all happy with the interruption.

She already knew who'd be at the door. It was either Tyson or Chance. Since Gideon had left, one of them stopped by to check on her every day, asking if she needed a jar opened or a spider killed. Like that was the only reason Charlie wanted Gideon around. There were about a dozen or so more reasons she could think of that neither her brother nor Gideon's could help with.

A smile crept across her lips as the image of the couple's last night together swam through her mind. Another loud knock pulled her back to the present, and she formed a few new ideas about what she wanted to tell her dear brother or brother-in-law to do.

But when Charlie pulled the door open, a total stranger stood there—a stranger in a military uniform. Charlie's heart stopped.

Oh. God. Oh. God. Gideon.

With a sinking feeling, Charlie realized the last time Gideon had called was three days earlier.

No. No. No. No.

The stranger in front of her, sensing her panic, quickly stepped to Charlie, laying his hand on her arm, which she realized she'd wrapped around her body. Closing the door, the man smiled down at her, and she thought it was odd that someone about to tell her that her husband had been hurt or—*oh God, oh God, oh God*—killed would be smiling.

"No. Oh, I'm so sorry." His hand moved back and forth over Charlie's arm as he steered her to the couch. "I always forget about the uniform. I'm so sorry. I'm not here to tell you anything about Gideon, I swear. He's fine."

Charlie finally let out the breath she'd been holding since opening the door. The man now sat next to her with an arm around her shoulders.

"Wh-Who are you then?" she choked out.

"Oh. I'm sorry. Man, I keep saying that, don't I?" He seemed as flustered by the situation as Charlie. "My name is Cody, Cody Boyd. I work with Gideon."

"Um, okay. Why are you here?" It sounded rude, but now that Charlie had her senses about her again, she was irritated that he'd scared her so badly.

Cody looked at Charlie with a smile, and she felt a chill run up her spine. There was something about the way his lips curled up over his teeth that made her uncomfortable.

"Well, aren't you direct?"

"Oh, now it's my turn to be sorry. I didn't mean to be rude." Charlie's mind was working on the quickest way to get him out of her home. Her inner self was starting to tingle, and she didn't like it.

"Gideon called the office today and asked me to come check on you. Didn't he tell you?" The smile was still in place, but his eyes didn't seem right.

"You talked to Gideon?" Charlie's heart began beating faster at just the thought of her husband. "So he's okay?"

"Yeah, he's fine. I can't tell you where they are or what they're doing, of course, but he wanted me to check on you and see if there was anything I could do for you." His hand was still moving up and down her arm, and she suddenly felt panicked.

"So, why are you here? I mean here in San Diego. Shouldn't you have gone too?"

Something wasn't quite right about this whole thing. Gideon would never have asked someone she hadn't met to come to their home. He knew Tyson and Chance were making daily visits.

"I've been having some health issues, and the doctors wouldn't clear me to go on this mission, so I'm riding the desk back here."

"Well, that makes sense." Charlie wanted to finish the conversation and send him on his way. "Thanks for coming. I'll tell Gideon you did your duty, but really, I'm fine." She made a move to stand and get away from Cody.

"Are you sure?" His hand caught Charlie's wrist and pulled her back to sit in his lap. "I know how lonely it can get when the hubby is gone for so long."

His hands slid around her waist, one moving up to her breast.

"I know a fine woman like you has needs. Needs I can help take care of."

His breath was hot on Charlie's neck, and she felt her stomach turn.

"Please, just leave. Please." Charlie tried to make her voice louder, but the feel of his hands as he held her in place was making her sick, and she was afraid to speak any louder than a whisper.

"I know you want this." His hand stopped on Charlie's breast, and he grabbed the nipple roughly.

Charlie gasped at the pain.

"See? You liked that."

Tears began to form, and as she squeezed her eyes closed, they started to run down her cheeks.

"Oh, don't cry. And if I was you, I wouldn't scream either. I don't want to hurt you. I just want to take care of your needs…like your husband asked me to."

His grasp on her momentarily loosened, and Charlie made the decision to run for the door. Surely someone would see or hear her if she could get to the door. But before she could make it even two feet, his hands were in her hair, and Charlie felt herself pulled back through the air.

Landing with a huge exhale of air against his chest, Charlie crumpled to the floor. He leaned down and got within inches of her face. His breath was hot and putrid as he spoke in an almost-whisper.

"Naughty, naughty, Charlotte. I thought you were smarter than that. I thought you were going to follow my instructions."

Tears streamed down her face as she realized what was going to happen next. Charlie had read about things like this and seen on the news about women who were attacked. Whenever she saw those stories, she always thought, *Why didn't they fight back? How can you let someone do that to you?* Now she understood.

When Charlie looked into the eyes of the man pinning her to the ground, his hands groping at her body as he worked to get her clothes off, she knew he would hurt her, badly, if she did anything other than give herself over to what was happening. At that moment, Charlie's only goal was to live—live and see Gideon again.

Charlie went numb as he crawled over her. Her mind drifted to another place as he touched her, causing her skin to crawl. His hands were rough and his nails too long. She occupied her mind thinking about other things instead of what was happening to her body. His breath smelled of cigarettes and coffee, and Charlie knew she would never again smell either of those things without her stomach rolling.

"Ooh, you're perfect. I knew as soon as I saw that picture you would be," he rasped as he pushed himself into her.

Tears slid down Charlie's face. She looked up at the ceiling and listened to his noises. She focused on a small crack, following it from just over the window in to the small kitchen on the other side of the room.

"Yeah, baby. You know you like that."

Charlie noticed that the table in the dining area was lopsided as she tried to look anywhere but at what was on top of her. *I'll have to figure out how to fix that.*

"Uh. Yes. Oh. God." With a final thrust, the act was done, and the weight that had kept her on the floor was suddenly gone.

Not wanting to see his face again, Charlie kept her eyes closed. Still unable to face the ache of her body, she was acutely aware of the sounds around her. From the rustle of cloth and the clanging of a metal belt, she knew he was pulling up his pants, his breathing still coming in bursts, but beginning to even out. Outside she heard a car door slam and then a dog bark. Life was still going on like normal outside her apartment.

"I thought you'd be more of a fighter. I'm a little disappointed. You do have one of the finest bodies I've ever seen, though." He then leaned down and put his mouth right to Charlie's ear. "Now, here's how this will work: You keep your mouth shut, and I don't come back. I hear that you breathed one word of what happened between us — well, just remember, I know where your precious Gideon is. We wouldn't want *anything* to happen to him, now would we? Besides, no one would believe you weren't begging for it."

Charlie laid on the floor, exposed, eyes closed. She didn't say anything.

Suddenly, the toe of his combat boot made sharp contact with her hip. She winced in pain.

"You got it?"

She nodded, never opening her eyes.

Seconds later, Charlie heard him whistling as he opened the door to leave. *He* stopped, and she panicked, thinking he was coming back for more.

Please just leave. Please just leave, Charlie chanted over and over in her head.

"Oh, let me lock this."

Charlie heard him turn the door lock.

"Don't want any unwanted visitors to get in."

Even with her eyes closed, she knew he was smirking.

She heard him start whistling again as he pulled the door closed and left her crumpled on the floor. Charlie rolled over onto her side and pulled her knees up to her chest, then finally allowed her eyes to open a tiny bit. Lying on the floor, just a few inches from Charlie was Gideon's letter. Her heart broke open at the thought of him knowing what had just happened.

She'd never tell him. It would destroy him to think that because he was gone, this had happened to her. From where she lay, she could read the last lines of the letter.

> Love you always, baby. Until I come home and see you again, never forget how much I love you.
>
> Joe

Charlie could do nothing but lay there sobbing until she had nothing left to cry.

CHAPTER 14

The entire apartment was dark when Charlie was finally able to pick herself up off the floor. She didn't know how long she'd been there, but she knew she needed to get in the shower and wash *him* off of her. His stench clung to her, and her stomach churned at the memory of what *he* had done. The tears started again. She was surprised she had any left.

Charlie double-checked the locks, checked in the closets, under the bed, and in all the other shadowy spots before heading to the bathroom. Her mind told her *he* had gone and locked the door behind *him*, but she wasn't sure she could trust her own memory. Would she be able to stay in the apartment? All she could see was his face looming over her. Instead of warm and happy memories with Gideon, all she had now was fear and shame.

As Charlie headed into the bathroom, she tried to avoid the mirror. Her entire body ached, and she was afraid to see what *he* had done to her. Unfortunately, habit got the better of her, and when she glanced toward the mirror, what she saw horrified her.

She was almost prepared for disheveled hair and black circles ringing her eyes where mascara had run. But stepping back, Charlie could see a bruise forming on her hip where *he* had kicked her. Angry red marks encircled her wrists. Turning her head, she saw a huge red mark on her collarbone. She was disgusted that the sicko had actually marked her like that. That, coupled with the bite marks she could see on her breasts, brought on a wave of nausea, and she stumbled to the toilet.

After several minutes of dry heaving, Charlie felt it was important to finish her assessment of the damage. Steadying herself with both hands on the counter, she leaned into the mirror. She couldn't see any more physical damage, but every single muscle and bone in her body ached, and, of course, the space between her legs where *he* had assaulted her was the worst. The idea of *him* touching her that way brought on another round of dry heaves.

She sat on the bathroom floor with her head against the porcelain of the toilet and waited for the nausea to pass. She thought about the look she saw in her own eyes as she'd stared in the mirror. They didn't seem like her eyes. A stranger stared back at her from inside her own body. The eyes in the mirror were hard and sad—that wasn't her.

She finally pulled herself up off the floor and turned on the shower. She knew she should call the police and not take a shower. Her mind, the logical part, told her to go to the emergency room, but she couldn't. The other side of her, her heart, won over. Charlie couldn't bring herself to admit to anyone that she'd been so stupid and weak. She couldn't cause Gideon such pain and guilt. How could she have let this happen?

After making the water as hot as she thought she could stand it, Charlie stepped into the spray and allowed it to wash over her. She thought about how everything in her life had changed in such a short time.

Why hadn't she fought harder? She should have done something to stop *him*. The whole thing played over and over in her head as she washed away all traces of *him*. Charlie tried to identify the moment she'd let *him* do this to her. The instant she'd given up and let *him* take her future from her. She *let him* do this. If only she hadn't opened the door for *him*, if only she hadn't invited *him* in, if only she hadn't let *him* put his hands on her…if only.

Charlie slid down the wall to sit on the floor of the tub. She pulled her knees into her chest and wrapped her arms around them. Once again, tears she didn't think she had left rolled over her cheeks. It was time to figure out what to do next.

She couldn't even think of telling Gideon while he was gone. The guilt and anger he'd feel would be so distracting. He'd be in danger. No, that was definitely out of the question. His beautiful face floated through Charlie's mind: the man she loved more than her own life, the man she knew would protect her at any cost, the man she could *never* tell—even after he returned. Charlie knew that for sure.

Was there anyone she could tell?

The idea of telling Evelyn or Peter was too horrifying even to contemplate. The way they'd look at her and treat her if they knew…no. Charlie shook her head, dispelling that thought.

Gabby? Chance? Tyson? Paige? No. She tried to imagine the looks in each of their eyes when she told them what *he* had done to her…what she'd *let him* do to her. Charlie didn't think she could spend the rest of her life seeing that every time they looked at her. These people were her family, her friends—people she'd have to see every day. There'd be no avoiding them.

The only thing she could do was to lock this away and deal with it only when she was alone. *Well, you're very much that for a while,* Charlie told herself as another round of tears mixed with the water washing over her.

Charlie stayed in the shower, scrubbing her entire body over and over again, but never seeming to get completely clean. When the water finally started to run cold, and her fingers and toes looked more like an old woman's than her own, she knew she had to get out and face life again.

Throwing back the shower curtain, Charlie kept her eyes closed for a minute, worried *he* might have come back. Slowly, she opened one eye and then the other before letting out a slow breath.

How the hell was she going to stay in the apartment if she couldn't even go from room to room without worrying *he* might be there waiting for her?

Charlie thought about taking Peter and Evelyn up on their offer to stay with them, but the idea of opening the door and going outside was far more frightening than staying there behind locked doors.

Her fuzzy pink robe—which she loved and Gideon hated because he said it covered up too much of her body and made her look like an old lady—hung on the back of the bathroom door. Slipping it on without even drying off, Charlie left her hair hanging loose and damp around her shoulders. She hurried past the mirror on her way out of the bathroom, unable to look at herself again. After another search of the house, she headed to grab the phone, planning on settling into the couch for the rest of the night. There was no way she'd sleep. In fact, she wasn't sure she'd ever sleep again.

As Charlie took the phone out of its stand, she noticed the blinking light. There were three messages. Pressing the play button, she waited. The first was a hang up. Next she heard Paige's voice, and it made her feel a little better.

"Hey, Charlie. Um, Tyson said he was headed over to see you a couple hours ago, and I haven't heard from him since. If you see him, give me a call and let me know. And if you're there right now, Tyson, call me so I can bitch you out for being gone so long. I'll talk to you later."

The mechanical voice of the answering machine told Charlie Paige had called at 6:22. Tyson was supposed to be coming to see her? She wondered if he'd come when she was lost to the world and hiding from everyone after *he* left. Or had he not come at all?

Charlie's mind was still occupied with wondering about Tyson when the next message began playing.

"Charlotte, just checking in with you."

It was *him*. Charlie's whole body began to shake, and she felt the now familiar stirrings of dry heaves forming in her stomach.

"Wanted to remind you to keep our time together this afternoon our secret. We wouldn't want Gideon to get hurt."

Immediately, Charlie's hand reacted and hit the delete button just as her head screamed for her to wait. It was too late. By the time she realized she could use his words as evidence against *him*, the number staring back at her from the phone was a zero. She'd erased the message. Her survival instinct was too raw, and hearing his voice had triggered the need to make it go away. Charlie wanted to kick herself. She wanted to scream. She wanted to throw up. She wanted her life back.

Charlie clutched the phone more tightly. Her stomach was churning, and while she didn't think she was going to be sick again, she needed to sit before her knees failed and she ended up on the floor.

Making her way to the couch, and keeping an eye on the locks of the door the whole time, Charlie dropped to the cushions. She sat with the phone in her hand and the TV on just loud enough that she could also hear every other noise in the apartment.

It was going to be a very long night.

Gideon's unit had liberty, and they were actually back in the civilized world. Usually when Walker let them have down time, it was twelve hours in the fucking desert. Not a whole lot to do with your liberty in the middle of a bunch of sand dunes. But today they were in a real city. Gideon couldn't have been happier.

The first thing he did was walk into the nicest hotel in town and plunk a wad of American currency on the counter to get the biggest and the best room they had. Gideon wanted to take a real shower and send his clothes out to the laundry. He planned to order several beers and a steak from room service and sit on the king-size bed with a remote in his hand. It didn't matter that he couldn't understand a goddamn word the people were saying; he wanted something to remind him of home.

But after he took a shower, the first thing on his list was to call Charlie.

It had only been two weeks, but they were the longest two weeks of Gideon's life. He wasn't sure how he was going to make it another five and a half months. He'd been talking to Jaylon, who'd given him some advice, but Gideon still wondered at how he and Zoe had survived doing this over and over for the past three years.

Taking his key from the clerk, Gideon headed to the elevator with a spring in his step. Glancing back, he saw Jaylon walk into the lobby and had to laugh that he'd had the same idea for his liberty.

"Too late, Fox," Gideon called. "I already got the best room in the joint."

He stepped onto the elevator and caught Jaylon giving him the one-finger salute. Gideon chuckled. The younger guys had headed straight for the bars, and Gideon was so glad he was done with all that crap. The elevator ride was slow going, and he groaned. The thought of a hot, steamy shower all by himself was making him antsy. When the doors finally opened at the top floor, Gideon found the room easily. Unlocking it, he strolled in, threw his bag on the bed and went straight to the bathroom.

Cranking the water, he stripped down while it warmed up. Gideon sighed loudly when he finally stepped under the showerhead and felt the heat penetrating his skin. He took his time under the warmth, letting it run over all his sore muscles. His mind wandered to his beautiful Charlie, and he missed her so much his body ached, as usual.

Eventually, Gideon forced himself to leave the shower. He had twelve hours and figured he could manage another one later. Making a beeline for the phone, he jumped through all the hoops to place the call. After the second ring, he began to worry maybe she wasn't home. Finally, she picked up, and Gideon's heart filled with the sound of her voice as she tried to rush the operator in order to get to him.

"Charlie!" Just hearing her voice washed him in a warmth the shower could never achieve.

"Oh, Gideon." Charlie burst into tears.

"Baby, what's wrong? Don't cry, Charlie. Please."

A ball of guilt twisted in his gut as he heard how unhappy she was. He hated being gone.

"Gideon…I-I-I…"

"I know. I hate being away from you too. I miss you every minute of every day, baby."

There was a long pause, and Gideon heard Charlie take a deep breath. He made a note to write Tyson and make sure he was looking in on Charlie like he'd asked him to. A letter would take forever, but he wasn't going to waste any of his phone time on his brother. That was reserved for Charlie, with a call to his mom every other time too.

"I'm fine, Joe." She took another deep breath.

Gideon could tell she wasn't fine, but he also knew Charlie was too stubborn to admit that. She was putting on the brave face for him, the one she'd learned from his mom.

"Where are you?"

"We got liberty, and I'm in a hotel room. I just had a shower and in a little while I'm going to have a steak and a beer."

"Really?" There was still a high pitch in her voice that Gideon knew meant she was holding back tears.

"Baby, tell me what's wrong. I know how hard this is."

"Gideon, I'm fine. I just miss you. I haven't been sleeping very well without you. So I'm tired. That's all."

"Are you sure? I mean, I'll kick Tyson's ass when I get home if he was being a dick to you or anything."

"No. Tyson actually has been really great since you left. I think Paige has something to do with it."

Gideon could almost hear the smile in her voice now — almost.

"Hey, Gabby and Chance's Halloween party is in a few days, right? I can't wait to get a picture of you in your costume."

Gideon had gotten a glimpse of the angel costume Charlie was planning on wearing before he left. She'd bought it thinking he could go as the devil.

"Yeah, I don't think I'm going to go." Charlie sounded sad again.

"Come on, baby. I don't want your life to stop because I'm here instead of there. I want you to go."

"It won't be fun. I'd rather just hang out with your parents and pass out candy."

"Charlotte." He knew using her real name would irritate her, but he also knew it would get her attention.

"*Don't* call me that." Charlie's voice was quiet, but Gideon could hear the venom in it. She'd never gotten so angry when he'd used her real name before. He wasn't sure why she was so adamant this time, but decided to press on.

"Okay, um, anyway, as I was saying, I want you to promise me you're going to that party."

It was painful for Gideon to think her life was on hold because he wasn't there. Charlie loved Halloween, and he knew she wanted to go to her brother's party.

"Fine. I'll go."

Gideon wasn't sure he believed her. There was no emotion behind her words, but what could he do from the other side of the world?

The couple talked for a long time after that. Gideon tried to make Charlie laugh, telling her about how the guys were still torturing Doran and all the crazy shit they'd done. Gideon almost felt sorry for the idiot. If he wasn't such a douchebag and deserving of everything they did, Gideon might have put a stop to it. Finally, when his stomach started to rumble and he did the math to figure out it was after midnight for Charlie, Gideon tried to say good-bye.

It was the hardest good-bye so far, other than the day he left. For some reason, Charlie seemed even more reluctant to get off the phone than usual. As much as Gideon would have preferred to talk to her the entire time he was free, he knew she needed to get some sleep. She was studying so hard for her midterms, and he didn't want to be the cause of her not doing her best on them.

When they finally hung up, Gideon called room service to order a meal. Sitting back against the headboard, he flipped on the TV. The channels were all in a foreign language, but it didn't matter. He was comfortable, his food and a beer were on their way, he'd had a shower, he'd talked with Charlie, and he knew she was safe.

Gideon felt fan-fucking-tastic.

CHAPTER 15

Four days, three hours, and fourteen minutes. That's how long it had been since what Charlie had categorized in her mind as *the incident*. After spending the entire night awake on the couch clutching the phone, she'd realized she couldn't stay in the apartment. Fortunately, Peter and Evelyn were thrilled when Charlie asked if she could stay in Gideon's old room for a few nights. She told them she was having a hard time sleeping without him in the apartment. Considering she hadn't had a good night's sleep since he left, it wasn't a lie.

She found it much easier to pretend she was fine around others, and it was important to her to be the same Charlie she'd always been. She only allowed herself to think about *the incident* when alone. Showering had become an especially horrible time. She was alone, and the sound of the water allowed her the freedom to let everything go. The loss of control was terrifying, so now she showered quickly, trying to stave off the breakdown that was always on the edge of bursting through.

The harder thing was hiding how nauseated she was all the time. She hadn't been able to hold down a single thing in the past two days. Just the thought of food made her stomach turn, and she tried to come back to the house well after Evelyn would have served dinner, using the excuse of a study group or a meeting with an advisor. It had only been a few days, and Charlie already knew she needed to get out of the house before her mother-in-law realized what was happening. Peter was a doctor, for God's sake. Charlie could only get away with not eating for so long.

Standing in front of the closet, she knew she had to hurry up to get to Chance and Gabby's for the Halloween party. She didn't want to go. Just thinking about being in a room with people who were going to touch her made her break out in a cold sweat. But she'd promised Gideon she'd go, and given all the lying she was already doing, she wanted to be honest with him about this at least.

However, she couldn't wear the skimpy dress she'd bought for her costume. So Charlie stood in front of Gideon's old closet trying to figure out what to wear instead. Not only had she promised her husband, but when Gabby called earlier, Charlie had reassured her that she'd be there. If she disappointed Gabriella, her sister-in-law had ways of making life miserable. *More miserable*, she thought as that day again flashed in her mind and she had to run for the bathroom.

Back in front of the closet, Charlie found an old white dress shirt of Gideon's and decided to pair that with the rest of her costume, rather than coming up with something new. She put on the shirt, which fit like a dress, and added white leggings, a silver halo, and wings. Dressing as an angel felt like a joke. Charlie was anything but an angel; she was dirty now.

On the drive over to the party, Charlie formulated a plan to say hi to everyone and then get the hell out, hoping no one would notice she'd left.

She parked and steadied herself in the car for a moment. Even so, when she walked into Chance and Gabby's townhouse, her heart beat faster, and her stomach tied in knots. Chance was in the middle of the room with Gabby by his side. They looked perfect as Robin Hood and Maid Marion. Charlie thought about how much crap Gideon would have given her brother for wearing tights, and a smile found its way to her face. As she approached the couple, she heard Tyson giving Chance all the ribbing Gideon should have been doing. She stood back for a few minutes and listened to the very normal conversation her family was having. *I'll never be normal again*, she thought.

"Nice tights and dress, Chance." Tyson smiled at the irritated look that passed over Chance's face.

Charlie was sure her brother had put up a fight with Gabby over this costume—at least she hoped, for the sake of his manhood, he had.

Tyson wore scrubs and a white coat and had a stethoscope draped around his neck. Paige was suitably dressed as a naughty nurse in a barely there skirt with thigh-high stockings, a blouse unbuttoned obscenely low, and white, strappy high heels.

"It's not a dress, Tyson. It's a tunic." Chance tried to pull himself up taller and look very manly, but no matter how he sliced it, he was wearing tights and a dress.

"Whatever gets you through the night, man." Tyson laughed as his hand clasped Chance's shoulder in an effort to hold himself up.

"I think it's great that you'd wear something like that for Gabriella. She makes a lovely Maid Marion," Paige commented, throwing a hard glare at Tyson.

"I do, don't I?" Gabby chirped as she slid in next to Charlie's twin, picking his arm up and draping it over her shoulder. "And Chance is a fabulous Robin Hood."

"Hey, Chance, Gabby," Charlie said. She turned to greet Tyson and Paige, but they were gone.

Gabby made a move to escape Chance's embrace, and Charlie tensed in fear. *Please don't let Gabby try to hug me, please don't let Gabby try to hug me,* she silently begged.

In the past days, the only people who'd touched her were Peter and Evelyn, and it took all Charlie's strength to get through that without bursting into tears. The bruises on her wrists were faded enough that only she knew they were there, but the one on her side was still huge and painful. It was much harder to get over the fear and shame than the physical pain.

"Charlie, um, what happened to the dress we bought for your costume? That was gorgeous, and you looked incredible in it." Gabby bounced over and kissed Charlie on the cheek while checking out the substitute outfit. Charlie made an effort to not wince when Gabby touched her, thankful she hadn't tried to pull her into an embrace.

"Oh, I forgot it at the apartment, and I've been staying at Evelyn and Peter's. This is just as good. Did I just see Tyson and Paige?" she quickly changed the subject.

"Yeah, the little perv made Paige dress like a naughty nurse. Can you believe she did it?" Chance offered.

"Jealous are we, Chance?" Charlie poked him with her elbow. Falling into routine was getting easier, and she stood talking with Chance for a few minutes. She felt almost normal again, like she belonged there. Then someone bumped Charlie from behind and she froze. By the looks on Chance and Gabby's faces, it was an uncalled-for reaction.

"Charlie? What's wrong?" Chance's voice was low and heavy with concern.

"N-Nothing. I guess I was just so caught up in our conversation, I was startled. That's all."

They both looked at Charlie, and it was obvious they didn't believe her.

"I think I'm going to look for Paige and Tyson. I've been here a while already and haven't seen them."

Charlie quickly turned to head through the crowd, being careful not to touch or make eye contact with anyone. She offered only a wave or a hurried hello when caught by someone. In reality, she had absolutely no intention of finding anyone. Her stomach had started churning and tears collected behind her eyes. She was in no condition to talk to Paige or Tyson. Instead, Charlie headed up the stairs to Gabby and Chance's bedroom and locked herself in their bathroom.

After a few rounds of dry heaves, Charlie fell back against the glass shower door and pulled her legs up to her chest. The tears came hot and fast.

Charlie couldn't understand why this had happened to her. Just a few weeks ago her life had been perfect: she had the man she loved more than anything beside her, she was going to school for something she truly loved and believed in, and she and Gideon had talked about starting a family one day. And now…now everything was wrong.

A knock on the door startled her.

"Charlie? Are you in there?" Paige's voice was muffled through the door.

"Um, just a minute." Charlie looked at herself in the mirror. She couldn't let Paige see her like this.

"Charlie, please open the door." She jiggled the door handle. "Charlie, if there's something wrong, you have to tell me."

"I-I can't." She hadn't meant to say anything, and she hoped Paige hadn't heard the whisper that escaped.

"Yes, you can. Please open the door."

Charlie didn't know why, but for some reason she reached over and unlocked the door. Paige slowly pushed it open and gasped. Suddenly Charlie regretted letting her in. On Paige's face was a hint of that look Charlie never wanted to see.

"Oh, Charlie. Please tell me what's wrong. This is more than not sleeping. This is more than Gideon being gone. Please, let me help." Paige cautiously approached the other woman like she was a wounded animal who might bolt at any moment. And to be fair, Charlie's mind was already working, trying to find a way out.

"I…can't." Charlie's back hit the wall and she slid down, tears streaming.

Paige lowered herself to the floor next to Charlie and wrapped her arms around her friend. Charlie flinched slightly, but Paige didn't let go.

Although Charlie remained stiff in the embrace, Paige held her close as her tears fell and sobs wracked her body.

Paige mumbled "Oh, Charlie" over and over. Time seemed to stand still, and the two women sat on the bathroom floor, not talking.

When Charlie finally started to settle down, Paige released her and went to the sink to get a wet washcloth. Coming back, she lifted Charlie's chin and wiped the streaks of mascara from her cheeks. Paige's big brown eyes never left Charlie's. For the first time in two days, Charlie felt safe. She wanted to tell Paige.

"Paige, I have to—"

"Come on, let's get out of here. We'll go to my place. I know something's wrong, and obviously you don't want anyone else to know. So I'm going to take you to my apartment, and then if you want to tell me, you can. If not, that's fine too. But let's get out of here."

Charlie wasn't sure if she'd be able to work up the nerve again to tell her later, but the thought of leaving the party spurred her into action.

As they walked through the bedroom toward the door, Tyson turned the corner and they almost ran right into him.

"Pa—" He stopped when he saw Charlie. The look on his face was almost one of disgust.

Charlie had no idea what he could be so angry about.

"Tyson, I'm taking Charlie home. She's not feeling well." Paige stepped forward and kissed him lightly on the lips. "I'll call you tomorrow."

"Yeah." Tyson's eyes never left Charlie.

"You know what, Paige? I feel better. I'll just go to the Coopers'. You stay and have fun."

Charlie tried to make it out the door, but Paige's hand reached out and grabbed her.

"No. Come on, Charlie. Tyson is a big boy. He'll manage one night without me."

The women walked out the door and down the stairs, but Charlie was pretty sure Tyson never stopped glaring at her. She tried to convince herself it was because she was taking Paige away for the night, but the pit of her stomach said there was something else. Charlie just didn't know what that something else was.

Once back at her place, Paige showed Charlie around before giving her a pair of pajamas. Then she allowed Charlie some time in the bathroom to freshen up and wash her face. Charlie still didn't know if she'd be able to tell her, but for the first time she felt almost truly normal.

Eventually the pair ended up in Paige's bed with the blankets pulled over them, the TV on, and the lights turned off. *Sixteen Candles* played, and both pretended to watch it, but neither was laughing in the appropriate places.

"So, things with you and Tyson seem to be going well?" Charlie asked, trying to break the tension filling the room.

"Yeah, believe me when I say I'm more surprised than anyone." Paige laughed. "You know, the first time I saw him in my Spanish class, I got all hot and bothered real quick. Then I found out who he was and how he treated girls, and I swore on everything holy that I'd stay far away from him. You can see how well that turned out."

"It's hard to resist the Cooper men." Charlie offered a weak smile.

"Tell me about it. I promised myself I wouldn't do it, and here I am worried he's mad that I left him alone on Halloween. You don't think he'd take any of the other skanks at the party home, do you?"

"Paige, I've seen the way he looks at you. Tyson has *never* looked at a girl like that in the year that I've known him. You have nothing to worry about. Besides, I think he's a little afraid of you."

They both laughed a little at that.

"It's nice to hear you laugh, Charlie." Paige's tone got more serious, and her voice was quieter. "I want you to know you can talk to me. Something happened. I can tell. You were doing so well the other night at dinner, but now…"

"I-I don't know what to say, Paige."

"That's fine. I just want you to know I'm here for you."

Silence settled over the room again as a few tears slid over Charlie's cheeks. She sniffled, and Paige turned to her.

"Paige, I…" She couldn't do it.

Paige, to her credit, sat quietly, allowing Charlie the time she needed.

"I…I mean…a few…" She started again, only to lose her nerve and her voice at the same moment.

This time Paige leaned in and wrapped her arms around Charlie. Unlike the last time, Charlie didn't flinch or stiffen at the contact. It was nice. She liked knowing someone cared enough about her to want her to be safe. Paige remained quiet, waiting for Charlie to find the words she was so desperately needed.

"A man came to the apartment a few days ago." Charlie stopped to take a deep breath. "He was in uniform, and said he worked with Gideon, so I let him in. And then…he…" She couldn't say the word. If she said the word, it would make it true.

"Oh my God. Why didn't you tell someone?" There was fear and anger in Paige's voice. She understood what Charlie was trying to say, even without the words.

"He knows where Gideon is. He knows what they're doing; he can get Gideon hurt or killed."

Charlie broke down for the second time that night, and once again, Paige let her go, simply stroking her hair as she gave herself over to the hurt and shame.

At some point, Charlie fell asleep, her body simply exhausted. Paige never asked Charlie for details, and she was thankful. Instead, Paige simply asked questions about what Charlie was planning to do. There were no lectures about going to the police — although she did make the suggestion. But when the idea was rejected, she let it go.

With sun shining through the bedroom window, Charlie woke, feeling somewhat refreshed for the first time in weeks. Talking with Paige had eased some of the pain, and she'd slept all night without waking up in a cold sweat for the first time in two days. Feeling safe, Charlie didn't want to get out of bed.

Paige rolled over with a stretch and groan.

"Morning," she said.

"Morning."

After lingering for a while under the warmth of the comforter, the women finally crawled out of bed and took turns in the shower. When Charlie was dressed and ready to head back to the Coopers', she found Paige at the kitchen bar, a cup of coffee in her hand. There was a second cup on the counter, but even the thought of taking a sip made Charlie's stomach heave in protest. The smell of coffee was something she'd never be able to tolerate again.

"Charlie, sit down. I want to ask you a few things."

Paige slid the cup over, and Charlie quickly pushed it away before she had to run to the bathroom.

"No coffee then?"

"Yeah, haven't been able to keep much down lately." Even though Paige knew about *the incident,* Charlie found herself playing the part of "normal Charlie."

"I know you don't want to tell anyone about this," Paige began.

Charlie took a deep breath. This was a mistake. She never should have told her. Now everyone would know. "Please don't tell anyone," she said quickly. "Especially Tyson. I have to trust you, and I do. But I don't think I could take it if Tyson knew. I told you why I can't tell Gideon." Charlie spewed everything she could think of, trying to convince her not to talk.

"I promise I won't say anything to anyone. But I need you to do something for me. I want you to go to see a professional."

Charlie made an effort to protest, but Paige held up her hand.

"Please hear me out. I thought about this for a long time last night after you fell asleep. I know you're blaming yourself right now, and you need to have someone to talk to who can help you. This wasn't your fault, Charlie."

"My father-in-law is a respected member of the medical community here, and my brother is studying to be a psychiatrist. Don't you think they know people and this would get back to them? I know there's the whole doctor/patient privilege thing, but they'd know I was seeing someone. I can't take that chance."

"You can go to L.A. I'll drive you. But you have to talk to someone. Otherwise I think that this, combined with Gideon being away, may kill you. You can't eat and you can't sleep. You need help—more help than I can provide."

Charlie knew Paige was right, but she couldn't imagine sitting in an office telling someone what had happened to her. Then she looked in Paige's eyes and saw nothing but concern—no judgment, no pity, only worry.

"Okay. I'll go to someone in L.A. I'll try it once, but if it's too much, I'm not going back."

"I think that's fair. One other thing." There was a catch in Paige's voice, as if she was scared to say the next thing. "I think you should see a doctor too. You need to be checked for any permanent damage or, um, STDs."

"No way. That would definitely get back to Peter. The fact that his daughter-in-law is being checked for diseases while his son is deployed? Not happening." That item was non-negotiable.

"What if you saw someone in L.A. for that too, just this one time? We could get the appointments on the same day. I'll be there with you, Charlie, but you need to do this. He may have really hurt you."

Tears started to fall from Paige's eyes, and Charlie knew they weren't just for her, but for everyone who cared about her. They didn't have to know, but they were still going to be affected.

Charlie decided she couldn't be that selfish. And if *he* had passed something on to her, she could never let this hurt Gideon. Paige was right. The only way to be sure was to see a doctor. Charlie just wasn't so sure she'd be able to get through an exam without screaming, crying, or throwing up.

"Fine," Charlie whispered

Just the thought of having to tell a total stranger what *he* did to her, and then letting a doctor touch her, probe her, had Charlie in a cold sweat.

"Charlie, I just want you to know this wasn't your fault." Paige looked deep in Charlie's eyes and nodded, encouraging the other woman to do the same. But she couldn't. "I'm here for you. Know that at least. If you need me, just call."

After giving Paige a hug, Charlie went back to Peter and Evelyn's feeling a little bit better, but knowing it wasn't over. It would never be over.

CHAPTER 16

5:27
5:29

5:33

Every time Charlie looked at the clock on the dresser, it got closer and closer to the time she'd actually have to get out of bed. She wondered for the millionth time why she'd let Paige talk her into this trip to L.A. Three days ago she'd thought Paige was right about her needing to see someone, but as time crept forward, not so much.

Charlie's stomach clenched, and she knew what was coming next. Catapulting herself out of bed, she ran for the bathroom. This was pretty much the routine. As soon as she became aware of herself every morning, she'd remember what had happened and immediately begin vomiting.

When she finally felt like she was done, she splashed water on her face and opened the bathroom door to find Paige leaning against the wall, waiting.

"Charlie? Are you all right?" There was true concern in her voice, and it made Charlie feel the tiniest bit better about the day.

"No, but that's nothing new." She tried to smile but felt the tears pushing behind her eyes. It seemed too early for crying; that wasn't part of the routine. Crying was reserved for the shower, for alone time.

Paige had stayed the night at the apartment. It was the first night Charlie had spent there since the long night on the couch clutching the phone, and the only way she'd done it was with Paige.

"Charlie, honey, I know this is going to be a rough day. Well, okay, I don't know, but I can imagine. You need to know I'm going to be with you every step of the way. I'll be wherever you need me to be."

Paige wrapped Charlie in a hug as the tears escaped.

"I-I-I know. Th-Th-ank you." Charlie couldn't manage anything more.

"Okay, we better get this show on the road. With traffic, who knows how long it will take to get to L.A. We can leave early and grab coffee and a bagel on the way. So you jump in the shower first."

Charlie knew better than to get in the shower at that moment. The tears would flow and, given the circumstances of the day, she didn't know if she'd be able to stop them.

"No, you go first. It won't take me long." Charlie turned and headed back to the bedroom.

Sitting down on the bed, she took a deep breath. It suddenly occurred to her that she hadn't heard from Gideon in a few days—not since *that* day. Her heart plummeted into her stomach. There were letters from him every couple of days, but Charlie hadn't heard his voice in more than a week.

Running to the phone to check the caller ID, she wasn't sure if she wanted him to have called and worried when she wasn't home, or not to have called and then she'd worry something had happened to him.

Not called, she decided. She hated the idea of him trying to do his job and getting killed while he was worried about her. Charlie would rather worry about him.

Flipping through the numbers, she cursed when she saw he'd called the day after the party. She hoped he just thought she'd stayed over at Gabby and Chance's place and wouldn't worry about her. By the time Paige emerged from the bathroom, Charlie had thoroughly convinced herself Gideon would have figured she was with her brother, safe and sound. He wouldn't be distracted by her welfare. Everything would be fine.

"Okay. Your turn," Paige called.

"Uh, okay." Charlie was still working out the details of Gideon's safety.

"What's wrong?"

"I missed a call from Gideon. I was just wishing I could hear his voice." She knew he wouldn't have left a message because he called collect, but she wished she could have at least heard him say something through the operator.

"Charlie? Can I say something?"

Charlie looked at Paige and knew immediately what she wanted to say. She couldn't let her say it. She wasn't up to hearing about how she should tell Gideon, how he needed to know.

"Not right now. Please, Paige. I can't right now." Charlie hoped she hadn't hurt Paige's feelings, but she just couldn't hear the words.

"All right. Not right now. But I'm gonna keep asking." Paige smiled to let Charlie know her feelings weren't hurt.

The drive north took longer than usual as Paige had to pull over three times on the way for Charlie to be sick on the side of the road. Still, they made it in plenty of time, and at 9:45, Paige left Charlie at the door of the therapist's office. She'd offered to come in, but this was something Charlie needed to do on her own. It warmed her to think Paige would have sat in the room with her, holding her hand, had she asked. Charlie would never ask.

When Paige headed back to the car, Charlie remained in the hall with her hand grasping the door handle. It took a few minutes before she pushed it down and swung the door open. When the door silently shut behind her, Charlie's stomach turned over. She had to force her feet to move toward the receptionist.

"Hi, um, Charlie O'Connor. I have a ten o'clock appointment?" It was a question, not a statement. Deep down, she hoped she was wrong and the girl behind the desk would tell her she didn't have her scheduled.

"Okay, she's finishing up right now. Why don't you have a seat, and I'll call you back in a few minutes."

No such luck!

Sitting down, Charlie mindlessly flipped through a magazine, plotting how much or how little she'd tell this lady. Surely she wouldn't tell her the whole thing. This woman was a stranger. There was no way she could tell her what had happened.

"Charlie O'Connor?" A woman in a nicely tailored skirt and jacket with a fabulous pair of Manolo Blahniks scanned the room from an open door. She couldn't possibly be the therapist.

Standing up, Charlie headed toward the woman, her stomach in knots and feeling like she needed to find the bathroom again.

"Hi, Charlie. I'm Dr. Lassiter." She extended her hand to Charlie before turning down the hall to a comfortable room with a big soft sofa and a coffee table. Charlie followed. It was more like a living room than an office.

"So, Charlie, tell me what I can help you with." Her face was very open and, for some reason, Charlie felt at ease.

An hour later, Charlie opened the car door and slid into the seat. Paige looked at her. There were questions in her eyes she wouldn't ask. Charlie's eyes were rimmed with red, and her nose was still running a little bit.

"So, are you okay?" Paige finally asked.

"Um, not yet, but I think maybe one day I might be." Charlie gave Paige a watery smile. By that Charlie hoped Paige knew she'd not only told Dr. Lassiter everything, but she was planning on coming back. Things weren't going to get better right away, but now there was a small glimmer of hope that they could.

The one thing the therapist wanted that Charlie had flat out refused was to tell her family—most especially Gideon. She would never let Gideon know what happened. She couldn't survive if Gideon looked at her differently or blamed himself for what happened. Fortunately, Dr. Lassiter had let that go, but Charlie suspected it would come up again.

"Well, I'll take that." Paige smiled. "How about lunch?"

"Sounds good," Charlie said, although her stomach clenched at even the thought of putting any food in it. "Let's go to Jerry's on Beverly. Then we can go over to Beverly Center for some of that retail therapy you were talking about." She tried to be Normal Charlie.

Having Paige know everything made Charlie less guarded around her, and she decided that wasn't a good idea. She worried that one day Tyson or Gabby would be around and she'd forget about being normal because Paige was there. Then something would slip out. That couldn't happen.

"Sounds perfect." Paige started the car, and the women headed toward the heart of the city and Charlie's favorite restaurant.

After lunch, where Paige watched as Charlie picked at a salad, only eating a few forkfuls before pushing it away, the pair headed over to the Beverly Center to window shop.

At two o'clock they were on the way to Charlie's ob-gyn appointment. The butterflies worked furiously as Paige maneuvered through the afternoon traffic.

What if he did give me some sort of disease? What could I do? Would I have to tell Gideon then? Will this be the thing that forces my hand? Charlie couldn't stop the string of questions that ran through her head.

By the time the car stopped in front of the office building, Charlie was in full-blown panic mode. This morning she'd thought this was the better of the two ideas, now she wasn't so sure. Paige had said that she'd wait in the car, and Charlie was grateful not to have to ask her to. She wanted to do this on her own.

This office was much busier than the last one, and Charlie thanked God for that. She could get lost in the chaos. Babies cried, pregnant women looked miserable—easy to be anonymous.

After signing in with the receptionist, Charlie sat down with the paperwork. Since she was a first-time patient, they needed the full history.

`Why are you being seen?`_______________

Charlie was stumped on just this simple question. How could she tell the doctor she wanted a full battery of tests for every imaginable disease without sounding like a total tramp or telling her what happened?

Charlie made the decision to go with tramp. That would be easier than the truth.

`First day of your last period?`_______

Charlie dug her calendar out of her purse and flipped to October. She stared at the tiny book for a minute, searching for the telltale dot. There wasn't one. She flipped to September and the dots were there. Counting the days forward…twenty-six, twenty-seven, twenty-eight…she should have started her period the week Gideon left. With everything going on at that time, she hadn't even noticed when she didn't.

The whole appointment passed in a haze of wonder and fright. Charlie wasn't sure if she'd be happy or scared to find out she was…pregnant? She was pretty sure she asked the doctor all the right questions because she found herself with a few pints less blood by the end of the whole thing. They were running lots of tests. Charlie's stupor was actually a blessing—she was so worried about being pregnant she almost forgot to be scared of the internal exam. While her tears had flowed silently through the entire thing, Charlie survived.

Using a lame excuse that she was leaving on a cruise the next day, Charlie was able to get them to rush the test results. She sat on the table wringing her hands while she waited for the doctor to come back in. Since she'd gone with the whole tramp thing, she could read the look on the doctor's face when she opened the door and slipped in, and she knew a lecture was on its way.

"Charlie, I have all your test results, but I really think we should talk before I give them to you." The woman stared directly into Charlie's eyes, and she wanted to tell her the truth so she wouldn't think badly of her, but the truth would open a whole new set of issues.

"I know what you want to tell me, and I assure you, this was a one-time thing. That's why I came in. I'm really normally very responsible."

The doctor looked at Charlie skeptically before starting. "Okay, well then I guess I'll save my speech for now." Taking a deep breath, she continued, "First, all the tests for any kind of STD came back negative. I think you got pretty lucky there. You know that, right? I do recommend, however, that you continue to be tested over the next several months, just to be sure."

Charlie nodded, letting out a huge breath of relief. She wouldn't have to tell Gideon.

"But given some of the problems you've been having—vomiting, exhaustion, not to mention the missed period, we also ran a pregnancy test. And that came back positive."

Running her fingers over the bruise on her hip, Charlie cursed *him* and thought about how just a few inches over and *he* could have taken one more thing from her. Quickly recovering before her thoughts got too carried away, Charlie smiled at the doctor as she tried to listen to the woman's instructions.

She walked out of the office in a total daze, promising the doctor she'd make a follow-up appointment. The poor doctor was totally confused by Charlie's reaction, given that she thought her patient was a party girl who had one-night stands.

When she got back in the car, Charlie didn't tell Paige about the pregnancy. This was something for her and Gideon, and she wanted him to know first. Silently she prayed that Gideon would call later. Her stomach did a flip when she realized she was going to have to stay in the apartment, in hopes that he'd call.

On the ride home Charlie told Paige about the rest of the results, and her friend seemed almost as relieved as Charlie was. Charlie stared out the window for a lot of the drive, watching the world whizz by and thinking about the small human growing inside her. Gideon's baby. For the first time in weeks, Charlie was happy.

The phone rang for the third time, and Gideon was beginning to get anxious. It had been a week since he'd talked to Charlie, and he needed to hear her voice. Letters just weren't enough. The last time he'd called, she hadn't been home, and he couldn't even leave a message. Finally, someone on the other end picked up.

"Yes, yes, yes," Charlie yelled at the operator, trying to speed things up.

"Charlie." Gideon sighed heavily into the phone.

"Oh, Gideon. I miss you so much. You have no idea. I have so much to tell you."

"Slow down, baby. I just want to make sure I tell you how much I love you. I only have a few minutes."

"What? What do you mean you only have a few minutes?" Her voice went up a few octaves, and Gideon could tell she was moving in the direction of pissed off. He really didn't want a fight. The team was getting ready to leave on another high-risk mission, and Gideon didn't think he'd be able to talk to her for a few weeks.

"Please, Charlie, my time on the phone is almost up. There's a line of other guys who need a turn. We're going out tomorrow, and I'll be out of touch for about two weeks. I just wanted to let you know so you didn't worry."

"Cooper! Come on, man. I want to call my girl too." Gideon flipped the guy off before returning to the conversation with his wife.

"I'm sorry, Gideon. I have to tell you something before you go, though."

Out of the corner of his eye, Gideon saw Doran walking toward him. He knew it was the other man's turn, but Gideon *so* wasn't ready to let go of Charlie. Holding up a finger in the international sign of "just a minute," Gideon hoped Doran would cut him a break.

"Charlie, I love you, but I really have to go. I'll be dreaming about you."

"Gideon, we're having a baby!"

Doran's finger reached out and pushed down the lever, disconnecting Gideon from his wife. When he saw the smirk on the prick's face, he almost punched the asshole in the head.

"What the fuck? Do you know what you just did?" Gideon began frantically dialing the operator again.

The operator informed him that because of a storm she could no longer get a connection to the States. That was the bitch about having to rely on the communication systems of third-world countries.

"Dude! Cooper, what the hell, man? It's my fucking turn to make a call."

Gideon threw the phone at Doran, knowing he wasn't going to be making any calls, and walked away. If he'd stayed anywhere near the moron, he'd have to kill him, and he wasn't in the mood to make it look like an accident.

As Gideon walked in circles around the camp, Charlie's words ran through his head. *Gideon, we're having a baby! Gideon, we're having a baby! Gideon, we're having a baby!*

His lips slowly drew up into a smile until he could feel the crinkle of it beneath his eyes. He was going to be a dad. Gideon's heart swelled, and he suddenly had a new reason to get his ass back home in one piece.

CHAPTER 17

Gideon was waiting, yet again, for his turn on the phone.

It had been two weeks since that tool, Doran, hung up on Charlie. Unfortunately, because Gideon was Doran's superior, he couldn't come right out and beat his ass like he wanted to, but he did have other ways of torturing him. After Gideon told Walker what the sneaky little prick had done, the team leader offered to look the other way while Gideon took out all his frustrations on the idiot. The idea was truly appealing, and Gideon considered it for a minute, but knew he couldn't do it. He respected his job and country too much to do something like that. He had created a plan for payback, though.

While the unit had been out in the field, Gideon had taken every opportunity to bring Doran with him on patrol, which usually consisted of very long hikes through the desert with very little water…for Doran. Gideon made sure the moron led the way, but he directed from behind. This was Doran's first time in the desert, and he didn't know all the signs for some of the more scary creatures that called the hot sand home. Several times the guy ran screaming in the other direction as a giant scorpion emerged from its lair. Gideon would just stand, laughing his ass off.

On the last night in the field, the pair was out on patrol when Doran missed a step and went tumbling down a huge sand dune—cursing the entire time and drawing the attention of the people they'd been looking for. When the shooting started, the rest of the unit was alerted, and backup came quickly. The team hunkered into the top of the dune and returned the enemy fire.

In the end, Doran was shot in the shoulder and had a broken leg. They decimated the enemy when the team split up and half the unit moved to take them from behind. Several were mortally wounded, but Gideon's men took their leader into custody. Mission complete—on so many levels.

"Cooper! The phone's yours."

"You thinking about your girl or the fact that Doran got choppered out an hour ago?" Fox asked as Gideon passed him on the way to the phone.

"A little of both," Gideon replied. He smiled as he picked up the phone and waited for the international operator to connect him to Charlie.

Gideon knew she'd stayed with his parents right after he left and wondered if maybe she was there again as he listened to the phone ring. He didn't want to have to talk to his mom before he heard Charlie's voice. He loved his mother, but right then, he wanted nothing more than to hear Charlie's sexy voice and make sure she and the baby were okay.

Just as Gideon was about to give up and resign himself to calling his parents, he heard Charlie's voice, breathless and worried, on the other end.

After waiting through all the operator crap, Gideon said, "Charlie! Are you okay? You sound out of breath."

"I was walking downstairs, heading to your parents', when I heard the phone. I had to run back up. I didn't want to miss your call."

"You shouldn't be running, should you? I don't want anything to happen to the, um, well, baby."

Charlie's honest laughter made Gideon's heart sing. It'd been forever since he heard her laugh.

"Gideon, you can say it. We're having a baby." Charlie's voice carried her excitement.

"So, tell me what's happening. I want to know everything."

"Yeah, what happened last time? I barely got out our news, and you were gone."

"Dickhead Doran disconnected us. I couldn't get another connection because of a storm. I'm so sorry. But if it makes you feel better, Doran got shot."

"No! Gideon, that does not make me feel better. You didn't shoot him, did you?"

"No. I'm pretty sure it wasn't me." Gideon let out a loud laugh.

"Was anyone else hurt? Are you okay? Oh, Gideon. I can't stand to think of you getting shot at."

"Don't worry about that, baby. I'm not a total moron like Doran. I ain't gonna get shot. I'm gonna come home and be a daddy." Although Gideon was still wrapping his mind around that fact, he liked the way it sounded. "Now tell me all about it. How are you feeling? Do you want to eat weird things like potato chips and chocolate sauce?"

"Ew. No. In fact, if you keep talking like that I might have to hang up and run for the bathroom. I was really sick for a while, but the doctor gave me some medicine, and I've been better. Still having meat issues though."

"What does that mean?" Gideon was perplexed. He didn't know what to make of "meat issues" and was frustrated he couldn't be there to help her when she was feeling so bad.

"I can't stand any kind of meat. Just the thought turns my stomach."

"Maybe the little critter is a vegetarian? What does the doctor say? When's the baby going to be here?"

"Well, I've only been to the doctor twice. The first time was when I found out, and then the next time I got all the prenatal stuff. They gave me these vitamins that could choke a horse, and I have to take them every day. Then they pulled out their little wheel and figured out when the baby was due."

"And?" Gideon was sure his beautiful-but-devious wife was actually trying to torture him.

"The 'critter,' as you so eloquently put it, should be here around June fifteenth."

"Good deal! I'll be home way before that. Don't want the critter to get here without me."

That would ruin him. He thought of Klausen, whose wife just had their baby the previous week. He hadn't even known right away because they were on the high-risk mission and out of communication. Gideon never wanted that to be him.

"So, I wanted to ask you something." Charlie's voice got quieter.

"Okay. You can ask me anything, you know that."

"I was thinking maybe I'd look for a bigger apartment? With the baby and everything, I thought we may as well get things ready as soon as we can."

She stopped talking and seemed very apprehensive. Gideon wondered what had her so nervous. She had to know he couldn't deny her anything.

"That's a great idea, baby. You can get Chance and Tyson to help you move." Gideon actually loved this idea; coming home to a new place Charlie had created for their growing family made going home sound even better than it had just minutes before. Sure, Gideon would rather have a house—and one day they would—but for now a nice, big apartment with a nursery would be perfect.

"Really? So it's okay?"

Gideon had never heard Charlie like this. She'd never worry about asking him something like that. In fact, before he left she wouldn't even have *asked*, she'd have told. He could only blame himself for that change.

"Yes, Charlie. I think it's a wonderful plan. Are you sure you're up to doing it though? Why don't you get my mom or Gabby to go with you?"

Gideon's time on the phone was about up, and Charlie sounded tired. She needed her rest, especially now, and he didn't want to keep her up. But he had one more question for her.

"Charlie, I'm gonna hafta go here in a minute, but I wanted to know if you've told anyone about the baby. I just don't want to get you in trouble by saying something to my mom."

"Well, I was going to ask you about that. I kind of want to wait a few more weeks. I was thinking that if you can call your parent's house at Thanksgiving, the whole family will be there, and we could tell them together."

"You, my beautiful, perfect wife, are a genius. They usually give us extra time on holidays. Maybe I can even get to a computer and do a video uplink. I'll check in to that."

"Oh, Joe, that would be the best! To tell you the truth, I think your dad knows; he's a doctor after all. But as far as I can tell, Evelyn is clueless."

"I love you, Charlie. I have to go now, baby. I want you to get some sleep. You're in charge of that baby—until I get home anyway."

"Yeah, right. I'm pretty sure I'm in charge of this baby for the next seven and a half months, and another eighteen years after that. I love you, Gideon. When will I talk to you again?"

"We're pretty stable until after the holidays, so I can call a little more often."

"Oh, Gideon. That's great. Hopefully I'll have some news on an apartment soon."

The excitement in Charlie's voice brought on yet another round of guilt for being away from his family at the holidays, while his wife was pregnant. He was so torn between serving his country and caring for his wife and child. Why was it so hard to do both?

"I love you. I have to go."

"Bye. Love you." And she was gone.

Gideon's heart was heavier than when he'd first picked up the phone to call home. It was a weird feeling. He thought talking to Charlie would ease his anxiety about the baby and her health, but learning about how sick she'd been only made things worse.

Gideon just had to wait for Thanksgiving and maybe the chance to see his family. A video uplink never truly eased the pain of being away, but Gideon looked forward to seeing his mom's face when he and Charlie told her she was going to be a grandma. She'd be over the moon.

CHAPTER 18

The smell of warm pumpkin pie wafted through the house as Charlie made her way down the stairs, and she was thankful it didn't send her stomach rolling as it would have just a few days before. She'd once again spent the night with her in-laws, this time under the guise of helping Evelyn with Thanksgiving dinner.

Over the past week and a half, Charlie had found various excuses to stay either with Gideon's parents or with Gabby and Chance. On the nights she knew Gideon would be calling, Charlie tried to convince Paige to stay at the apartment with her. She usually did. But there were a few nights she couldn't, and Charlie spent those nights exactly as she had that first night — sitting with the phone clutched in one hand and the remote in the other, staring at the door and the window alternately, and not sleeping.

Stopping in the foyer, Charlie checked the mirror that hung near the door. There was a good chance she'd actually see Gideon today, and she wanted to look perfect. It had been almost two months since he left, which meant four more before she could touch him or smell him or hold him.

Smoothing a hand over her hair, Charlie leaned in to get a better look at herself. Her eyes were only slightly red, and she'd done a pretty good job covering up the dark circles that were now ever present in the hollows under her eyes.

Finding out about the baby had helped some in dealing with everything else. She was able to focus on the pregnancy *instead* of everything else. Days were better than nights. Night time was still hard. Every time she closed her eyes, Charlie could see his face and the sneer on his lips as *he* touched her. Sometimes she could even smell his breath. The only reason Charlie slept at night was because she was so exhausted by the baby growing inside her.

She was barely hanging on in school. Her midterms didn't go very well—she'd been a little distracted. The only class she was managing to keep her grade up in was her practical. When she could lose herself in the joy Hayley felt reading her first book or in helping Luke put a puzzle together, nothing else seemed nearly as important.

Fortunately all the professors knew Charlie, and after her midterm grades put her average in the toilet, they were allowing her to do some extra credit to bring her grades back up. She hadn't told Gideon yet, but she'd already decided to take the next semester off. He wouldn't be happy about it, but she could use the baby as an excuse.

Another thing that seemed to be helping was seeing the therapist. Unfortunately Dr. Lassiter still insisted Charlie tell Gideon about *the incident*. Not going to happen. But talking with her was helping Charlie find herself, so she was pretty sure she'd keep going back anyway.

"Charlie, honey, is that you?" Evelyn called from the kitchen.

"Yeah, Evelyn," she answered as she rounded the corner. The fact that she was going to be cooking had Charlie dreading the day. For the most part, she was okay with food now, but meat was still not one of her favorite things. She hoped to avoid that part of the preparations.

"Oh, good. Charlie, can you put the potatoes on?"

Potatoes she could do. Unfortunately Charlie glanced over at Evelyn, who was elbow deep in raw turkey, and her stomach didn't appreciate the view. She was forced to make a quick exit to get a breath of fresh air.

"Sorry, Evelyn. I forgot something upstairs," Charlie apologized quietly when she came back to the kitchen.

"What? I'm so crazy this morning, dear. I feel like I'm going a hundred different directions. But the turkey is in the oven, so as long as it cooperates and cooks, this day will be fine."

Evelyn's smile was radiant. It was obvious she loved having a house full of people, and while it was hard not having Gideon with them, Charlie and the rest of the family would help fill the void.

Charlie hadn't told anyone Gideon was planning the video conference. It was going to be a great surprise. He was more excited than Charlie was. Absentmindedly, Charlie rested her hand on her belly. Fortunately, she caught herself a second before Evelyn turned around.

"Did you get the potatoes on, Charlie?"

"Oh, yeah. I was just about to."

Peter strolled in and wrapped his arms around his wife's waist, pulling her to him and peppering her neck with kisses. It was sweet and kind of creepy at the same time. Charlie felt so close to them it was like watching her parents make out.

"Peter! Stop! You'll embarrass poor Charlie." Evelyn tried to pull away, but she wasn't trying very hard. Charlie envied her the feeling of her husband's arms around her.

Pressure behind her eyes warned Charlie that tears were starting to form again. She quickly distracted herself by getting water in the giant pot and hauling it to the stove. Peter saw her struggling with what could only be called a vat and released his hold on Evelyn to help.

"Charlie, you shouldn't be carrying something so heavy." He gave a small wink, and Charlie knew her suspicions were true — Peter knew about the baby. "You'll throw your back out; it weighs a ton."

At least Evelyn still had no idea. She couldn't have kept her cool if she'd known.

"Thanks, Peter."

"Okay, you." Evelyn pointed at Peter. "Out of my kitchen. Go find some sort of sporting event on the television to watch. And call your son. Tell him to get over here."

"Yes, my love." Peter leaned in and kissed her before leaving the women to finish the dinner preparations.

What seemed like hours later, the house was full of family, and everyone gathered around the table awaiting the turkey. Charlie glanced around the room, thinking it should make her happy to see so many people she loved, but it only served to emphasize the fact that the person she loved most in the world was missing.

Evelyn came into the dining room holding the turkey on a giant silver tray. She set the platter in front of Peter, who immediately started to carve it. But being a surgeon apparently didn't necessarily translate into great carving skills.

After saying Grace over the meal — thanking God for family and friends, and most especially for keeping Gideon safe — the food was passed. Charlie said her own little prayer for the health of the baby and the ability to deal with the turmoil that was her life at the moment. When she opened her eyes and looked up, Tyson, who was sitting across from her, glared at her with what looked like unadulterated hatred.

For the past month or so, Tyson had been keeping his distance. And when he did come in contact with her, he was actually rude. She'd been attributing his attitude to the fact that he missed Gideon almost as much as she did, and being around her was probably painful. Of course, she'd also been monopolizing Paige lately, and Charlie was sure that wasn't earning her any brownie points with her brother-in-law.

"So Paige went home?" Charlie finally asked Tyson after gathering herself and moving past the death stare.

"Oh, yes, Tyson. You did tell Paige we would have loved for her to be here with us? She's part of our family now." Evelyn beamed.

"Paige went to Minnesota. She was feeling like she'd been ignoring her parents lately." Tyson's voice was harsh.

"So, Charlie, have you found a new place?" Evelyn asked, changing the subject after Tyson's unfriendly response.

"Yes. I can move in this weekend. Chance and Tyson are going to help." She was excited about the new place for reasons no one at the table would ever know.

Tyson's head snapped up. The look on his face was one of confusion.

"No one asked me if I could help you move. Nice of you to just assume I'm available."

"Tyson! Of course you'll help your brother and Charlie move," Evelyn scolded him.

At least he had the decency to look ashamed.

"I thought Paige asked you. I'm sorry. She said she was going to tell you about it. Don't worry. Chance, Gabby, and I can handle it."

Charlie felt tears pricking at the back of her eyes. She didn't want to ruin the meal for everyone, so she willed them away. It was getting easier to do.

"No. Tyson, you have a few hours to spare this weekend, I'm sure." Peter stared hard at Tyson, who had no other choice but to agree.

Tyson nodded slightly, but the look on his face never changed.

"Tell them about the new place, Charlie." Gabby's voice chimed from the other side of Chance.

"Well, I mentioned to one of my professors that I was looking for a new place to live, that we wanted more room, and how I was disappointed we couldn't really afford a house right now." With Gideon's salary, that wasn't totally true, but he wanted to have a huge down payment when they bought a house, so for now they were renting.

"Keep going, Charlie." Gabby had been with Charlie when she looked at the place, and she was a little jealous of the deal she was getting.

"So, my professor tells me about a small house he has in Pacific Beach that he wants to rent out. He's getting married, and they're going to live in his new wife's place. In fact he's pretty much already living there. He says he isn't ready to totally give up his house, just in case. I guess when you wait until you're almost fifty to get married, some habits are hard to break."

"Can you believe it?" Gabby's tone was playful—with a touch of envy.

"Gabriella," Charlie admonished. "Okay, so the house is, like, a block from the beach, has two bedrooms, and a nice little backyard. And the best part is, he's only asking that we pay the mortgage."

"Why would he do that?" Tyson practically spit the words between clenched teeth.

"Um, he just knows me, and he knows Gideon is responsible. He wants someone who'll take care of the property for him and not throw wild parties." Charlie's voice had gotten much quieter, and she was pretty sure everyone at the table was feeling as uncomfortable as she was. That was her inspiration to change the subject and tell them about the first surprise of the day.

Charlie took a deep breath and refocused her gaze on Evelyn, who looked mortified that Tyson was behaving so badly at Thanksgiving.

"I do have some more good news," she said.

All eyes focused back on Charlie, except Tyson's, which stared at his empty plate.

"At five o'clock, Gideon will be doing a video conference with us on the computer."

"Oh!" Evelyn's hand flew to her mouth.

"And that's in about fifteen minutes, so I'm going to go into Peter's study and get everything set up. You have a web cam, right, Peter?" Charlie asked.

"Of course." He nodded.

Excusing herself from the table, Charlie made her way to Peter's study and fired up the computer. The butterflies in her stomach were doing double time; just the thought of seeing Gideon's face after such a long time made her nervous.

After finding the right website and turning on the web cam, she sat by herself, gathering her thoughts and feelings. Then Charlie heard his voice. Lifting her eyes to the computer, she couldn't help the smile that spread across her lips. There on the screen was her husband, the person who meant the most in her life.

"Baby!" His smile was just as big as Charlie's.

"Gideon. Oh…" Tears streamed down her cheeks, and there was nothing she could do to stop them.

"Don't cry, Charlie. I can't stand it when you cry."

"I'm crying because I'm so happy to see you." Charlie wiped the tears with her hand. It wouldn't do to have the whole family see her like this.

"I'm glad I got you by yourself. You look beautiful. Lift up your shirt a little."

"Gideon! I am not flashing you!"

"No. I want to see your belly. I want to see my baby."

Charlie's smile widened, and she thought she might pull a face muscle. She complied with his request, lifting her shirt to reveal a still-flat stomach. No one would guess she was pregnant.

"Hi, baby." Gideon wiggled his fingers at her belly.

The damn tears started again.

"Joe, I have to get everyone in here. Say good-bye to the critter."

"Fine, go get them. Bye, bye little Gideon."

Charlie raised an eyebrow. "Little Gideon?"

"It has to be a boy. I don't think I can handle being dad to a girl. I'd have to hurt any boy who even looked at her. So I decided we're having only boys."

"Well, good luck with that. I love you."

"Love you too. Go get the masses." He blew a kiss.

A minute later, Charlie was back in the study with the entire family behind her. Evelyn gasped when she saw Gideon on the screen. Turning to see her face, Charlie saw Tyson smiling too. It was the first time in weeks she'd seen him smile.

"Son." There was a glint in Peter's eye as he greeted Gideon.

"Hey, everyone," Gideon called from the other side of the world. "Happy Thanksgiving."

Everyone shouted their greetings, and Gideon smiled big — not as big as when he'd first seen Charlie though, and that made her happy.

"Okay, I'll talk to everyone, but Charlie and I have something we want to tell all of you together." His eyes drifted to his wife, and he gave a slight nod. The two had decided to tell them at the exact same time, but in that moment, Charlie wanted him to do it. She wanted him to be the proud daddy he was. This was his moment. Charlie would have the family for the next four months; he only had them for the next few minutes.

"You tell them, Gideon," she said.

"You sure, babe?"

"Absolutely."

"Will one of you please tell us something before all the time is up?" Evelyn almost shouted, causing everyone to turn and stare. Evelyn never yelled.

"Okay. Well…Charlie and I…I mean…not me, really…mostly Charlie…"

"Oh, for the love of God." Evelyn once again let her impatience seep out.

"We're having a baby," Gideon finally spit out.

The room erupted in squeals, and everyone moved to hug Charlie — everyone except Tyson, who turned and walked out of the room.

CHAPTER 19

The weekend after Thanksgiving, while Tyson wished to be wrapped around his woman, he was instead helping his cheating sister-in-law move into a new house.

After the surprise announcement, Tyson had bolted. He couldn't stand there and play happy for the family. Not when he knew there was a possibility the baby wasn't Gideon's. Once he was outside, however, he didn't know what to do. Spotting his car, he'd decided to just go. He'd ended up driving for hours, going nowhere in particular. At some point, he'd realized he was almost to Santa Barbara, and as much as he wished he could keep driving all the way to Minnesota to find Paige, he'd turned around.

Tyson regretted that decision on the day of the move. It was getting harder and harder for him to act normal around Charlie. Having Chance there made it a little easier, but Tyson still barely talked to her. Fortunately Gideon and Charlie didn't have too much stuff, and the move was done pretty quickly. As soon as he could, Tyson rushed out of the house, not worrying about saying good-bye or sticking around for the pizza and beer Charlie had ordered.

Paige came home the day after Tyson helped Charlie move, and he couldn't wait for her plane to land. After Thanksgiving, he wanted to know something was still right with the world. Eventually he saw Paige's silky ponytail bobbing in the crowd, and his breath caught for a moment. She was as stunning as ever.

When Paige saw Tyson, she flung herself into his arms, and their lips instantly melded together. Tyson took a moment to hold her and revel in the feel of everything shifting back into place in his world.

After loading her bag into the car, they headed to his place. He wasn't about to let go of Paige right then. On the ride home, Tyson told Paige about Charlie and Gideon's big news, although given how much time she and Charlie had been spending together, he was sure she already knew. Judging by Paige's reaction, however, Tyson had been completely wrong. Her eyes got wide, and a worried look crossed her face. Recovering quickly, she began asking questions about Charlie and the pregnancy. Tyson didn't know too much though. He was trying not to know too much.

A few days later, Tyson still couldn't stop thinking about Gideon's excitement when he'd told them all about Charlie being pregnant. It kept him up at night, and it was starting to affect his life and school. He made the decision to talk to Gideon, even if it was just to feel him out on how much he might know or suspect. Maybe Tyson was making himself sick over nothing and Gideon already had an idea about Charlie's affair. He tried to convince himself of this as he walked into his parents' house.

Tyson heard his parents talking in the family room and headed in.

"Are you okay? You seem a little far away lately," Peter asked his wife as Tyson entered the room.

Quickly glancing at his mother with concern, all he could see was light in her eyes and a smile that lit up the room. There was absolutely nothing wrong with Evelyn Cooper — yet.

"Oh, yes. I'm absolutely wonderful. I'm just so happy for Gideon and Charlie. I can't wait to start getting things ready."

Tyson cursed Charlie again as he realized what he was about to do was going to destroy his mother.

"Tyson, how are you, Son?" Peter greeted his younger son with a shake of his head at his wife's grandbaby fever.

"Okay."

"How is Paige, Tyson?"

Evelyn hadn't seen Paige since before Thanksgiving, and Tyson felt bad about that, but with all the time she'd been spending with Charlie, he'd hardly seen her himself.

"She's great. I just dropped her off at the campus. She has a study group tonight." Then he quietly added, "at least that's what she says."

"There's fresh apple pie in the kitchen. Would you like a piece?" Evelyn asked. Tyson knew she was trying to keep him there and feed him like when he was a kid and came home from school. Instead of plying him with warm cookies and milk, however, she was using her apple pie.

"No thanks, Mom. I just wanted to stop by and ask you a question." Tyson stood in front of his parents, his hands in his pockets, his eyes focused on nothing in particular.

"What can we do for you, Tyson?" Peter asked, all business just like his son.

"I was just wondering if you ever know when Gideon is going to call. I mean, does he have days that he calls you or is it just random?"

"Oh. Well, it's really just random. I never know when he'll call," Evelyn answered.

"Okay. The next time he calls, can you ask him to call me?"

Peter and Evelyn glanced at each other for a moment.

"Of course. Is there anything we can do?"

"No. I just need to talk to Gideon. All right, I gotta go study. I love you." He leaned down and lightly kissed his mom's cheek before he was out the door.

"I love you, Mom," Gideon said as he hung up the phone. Even though he could tell it was hard for her to do, Evelyn had cut her call short so he'd have time to call Tyson. Apparently there was some major crisis he needed to talk to Gideon about.

Gideon couldn't imagine what kind of problems Tyson could be having, but his mother had almost begged him to call, and he couldn't say no to her when she started with all the "he's not like you, Gideon. It took a lot for him to ask me to have you call. You are his big brother, after all."

Checking the time, Gideon decided he could give his baby brother a few minutes, but that was it.

Tyson sounded surprised Gideon had actually called as he answered the operator's questions and then said, "Hey, Gideon."

"Hey, little brother. Mom said you were in dire need of some awesome advice from your much wiser and better-looking big brother."

"Um, yeah." Tyson sounded confused, and Gideon wondered if he'd wasted his time calling.

"What's up, Ty? I don't have a lot of time allotted for the phone, and I still have to call Charlie. I thought I'd get your little problems out of the way first because I tend to get carried away when I can get time with my wife and baby. I mean, really, how bad could your issue be?" Gideon laughed.

"Well, I do need to talk to you about something, but I'm not sure where or how to start."

"Just spit it out, man. I thought we had the whole girl parts and boy parts and where they go talk a long time ago. I mean, I know Dad had the official talk, but come on, mine was *way* more helpful. So it can't be how to get into Paige's pants that's the problem. Oh shit! Is Paige pregnant?"

"What? No. No, she isn't pregnant. As I recall your little instruction included an hour-long section about wearing a raincoat, or some shit like that."

Gideon laughed with Tyson as he remembered being sixteen and telling his twelve-year-old brother how to put on a condom. Tyson hadn't paid that much attention, more concerned with video games than girls, but Gideon thought he'd given some great gems Tyson would need one day.

"Then let's get this show on the road," Gideon urged, anxious to get to Charlie and the critter.

The line was silent for a few seconds, and Gideon thought maybe the call had been disconnected until Tyson finally said, "Never mind, bro. It's not important."

"So you wasted my time for nothing? I know that isn't true, little brother. I can hear in your voice that there's something wrong. You always sucked at lying. Remember the time I got caught sneaking in at, like, two in the morning and actually convinced Mom and Dad that we were both out and had just been playing football in the fields? I was so close to getting us off the hook, and then you tried to help me out. Damn. I got grounded for like a month because you can't lie for shit."

Gideon heard a deep intake of air and knew Tyson was finally going to get to the point. "I saw a guy coming out of your apartment a few months ago, and I think Charlie's been cheating on you."

"What? What the fuck are you talking about, Tyson? Charlie would *not* cheat on me." He could feel the heat burn in his face. Charlie would never cheat on him, and Tyson knew that too.

"One day, not long after you left, I headed over to your place to see if Charlie needed anything. As I got to the stairs, I heard the door open, and out walked a guy, zipping up."

"Fuck."

"He saw me, but obviously didn't recognize me. He was whistling as he zipped up his pants. He smiled at me before heading into the parking lot. He was in uniform, Gideon."

"Are you sure he came out of my apartment? I mean, the guy next door is a Marine. It could've been him." Even to himself he sounded pitiful, like he was trying to find the loophole in the story.

"No. I saw him pull the door closed behind him. It was definitely your place."

Gideon was silent. His mind worked overtime trying to process what Tyson had just said. There was no making sense of it. His Charlie wouldn't do that.

"Gideon? You okay?"

"What's this really about, Tyson? What, did Charlie piss you off because she's spending too much time with your precious Paige? Is that it? You felt the need to tell me this load of shit about my wife now? I can't fucking believe you."

Gideon hung up. *Fucking Tyson!*

He needed time to think. He needed to talk to Charlie. Tyson had been mistaken about what he'd seen, he was sure. He just needed to talk to Charlie.

Picking up the receiver, Gideon was about to call her, but he just couldn't do it. Tyson's words rattled around in his head. *I think Charlie's been cheating on you. I think Charlie's been cheating on you. I think Charlie's been cheating on you.* The words produced images of his Charlie naked under some other man. He wanted to hurt someone. He wanted to hurt Tyson.

There was just no way Charlie would fuck someone else.

Slamming the phone back into the cradle, Gideon turned and walked out of the communications tent. He had to think. His mind scrambled for a reason Tyson would say something like that.

Charlie and Paige had been spending a lot of time together, but would Tyson actually make this shit up because he was jealous? Gideon knew the answer to that; his brother was selfish and focused when it came to something he wanted, and apparently Charlie was interfering with that something.

He refused to believe Charlie was screwing around.

But the more Gideon thought about it, the more small things from over the last months started to run through his head. Charlie had seemed different when he talked with her on the phone. He could never figure out what it was, but now he wondered if it was guilt.

Then Gideon was assaulted with visions of what Charlie had looked like before he left — the total devastation in her eyes when he told her he had to leave, her anger over the whole situation, and finally the heartbreaking scene at the airstrip. All he could picture was Charlie in the truck, hunched over the steering wheel, her entire body shaking. He'd had to call her brother to come get her, for Christ's sake.

How could Charlie cheat on him?

Gideon walked to the far edge of camp, his head spinning. Nothing made sense anymore. If he could have, he would have wandered into the desert. He needed to be completely alone…to think.

He replayed the conversation with Tyson over and over. His brother had asked to have Gideon call him, then said there was nothing wrong. Gideon had forced the issue. Tyson had been hesitant to tell him. If he were lying, wouldn't he have just come out and said it?

After pacing the fence for God only knows how long — it could have been minutes or maybe hours — Gideon plowed right into Jaylon Fox. He hadn't even seen his buddy, and he nearly knocked him on his ass.

"Hey, Coop. Walker sent me over to check on you. I think he's worried you might start taking guys out. We've been watching you pace for like two hours. Looks like you got something you might need to get off your chest, man."

"Tell Walker I'm not planning on taking anyone out. I don't even have my weapon." Gideon raised his hands and turned around so everyone could see he was unarmed.

"Dude, I've been in combat with you, a weapon wouldn't be necessary." Jaylon laughed. "But seriously, you got something you need to talk about?"

"What, like I'm a total pussy who can't handle shit?" The tone of Gideon's voice was harsher than he'd planned, but he hated being treated like a pansy, especially with all his team members around.

"Yeah, 'cause so many people would mistake you for a pussy. Come on. What the hell happened? One minute you were on the phone with Charlie, and the next you're walking the fence for two hours. Is the baby all right?" The question was halted, like Fox was afraid to even ask it.

Gideon took a deep breath. He didn't want to say the words because then they might actually be true. As long as he kept it to himself, Gideon could choose to believe what Tyson said wasn't true. If he told Fox, he might confirm it. Maybe Zoe had seen something, and he'd been keeping it from Gideon?

"First of all, I wasn't on the phone with Charlie. I was talking to my brother." Gideon started to talk, still not sure if he was going to actually say the words.

"Oh. Well, are the parents okay? Something happened. I've never seen you wander off for hours at a time. You missed your watch time—you know that, right?"

"What?" Gideon looked at his watch. He'd never missed a watch. Ever. "Fuck!"

"Don't worry, we got it covered. It's not like any of the guys had anything better to do. I mean, we're kinda stuck here, right? So, what did your brother tell you that has you so in your head?"

Fox wasn't trying to pry, but it still felt strange for Gideon to talk to a team member like this. Usually when he had a problem, he talked to Charlie. That wasn't going to work on this one. Or he could always talk to his mom, but Gideon couldn't imagine telling her this. She loved Charlie, and he couldn't hurt her until he knew for sure what was going on.

"Okay, well, he…fuck. I can't even say it." The urge to punch something was overwhelming.

Looking over at Fox, who stood patiently waiting for him to continue, Gideon wondered why his friend was a SEAL. He didn't seem the type. Gideon always thought he'd be better suited for an office job somewhere. He was smart and fast though, and there'd been plenty of times Gideon was glad Fox was covering his ass.

"He told me he thinks Charlie is cheating on me." Gideon finally blurted. His heart felt like someone was driving a wooden stake through it when he said the words. Now that they were out there, he couldn't take them back, and he hated them.

"Bullshit!"

Gideon was startled by Fox's reaction, and it took a few minutes of staring at the other man to pull his shit together and continue the story.

"He said he saw a guy in uniform coming out of my apartment."

"So fucking what? That could have been anything, man. That could have been someone from the base who needed some info about you. You don't know."

"He was zipping up." Gideon watched the expression on his buddy's face falter for a split second before he composed himself again.

"Still, I don't believe it. I've seen the two of you together, man. She wouldn't cheat."

He sounded so sure of himself, but Gideon had seen this too many times, and he knew Jaylon had too.

"Remember Matthews?" Gideon asked.

Fox froze at the mention of their former team member. There was a long silence as they thought about what had happened almost two years ago.

They'd been in a jungle somewhere in Asia for four months. It was a tough assignment. The entire team was constantly wet, and the bugs were everywhere. Everyone was miserable except Matthews. He seemed to be constantly smiling, and they all knew why. Right before leaving he'd married his high school sweetheart. If the guy wasn't on patrol, he was on the phone or writing letters.

About a month and a half into the stint, Matthews started getting pictures of his wife that made the men he showed them to a little uncomfortable. She said she was getting ready to go out with her girlfriends, but the outfits she wore were more appropriate for earning money on the side by selling a little bit of what was clearly on display. Of course no one wanted to tell the guy there was no way she was just going out with girlfriends.

Then Matthews started getting letters from old friends back home who told him they'd seen her out at local bars, practically screwing another guy. He was in complete denial. He refused to believe the eyewitness accounts, instead saying they were all just jealous and wanted to break them up.

When the tour was up and they all went home, he found an empty bank account, and his parents informed him his wife had disappeared with his best friend. Then Matthews put a gun in his mouth.

Gideon didn't want to be Matthews.

Fox looked at his teammate and friend, and didn't know what to say. The entire team had been devastated when Matthews killed himself. No one ever talked about him or even brought up his name.

"That's what I thought," Gideon said.

"No. I still won't believe it, and you shouldn't either." He clapped Gideon on the shoulder and turned and walked away. Gideon saw him stop and say something briefly to Walker. He assumed, since the lieutenant nodded and headed into one of the admin tents, Fox had convinced him he wasn't about to massacre the entire camp.

Gideon thought about what Fox had said, but he wasn't about to show up at his own house and find all of his stuff, including Charlie and the baby, gone.

The baby…fuck! He didn't even want to think about that possibility. How long had Charlie been cheating on him?

Just hours ago, Gideon's life had been close to perfect. With one phone call, that was gone.

CHAPTER 20

Christmas was only a few weeks away, and Charlie still had a few more things to pick up. The only people left on her list were Tyson and Peter. Gabby too, but she didn't count because Charlie had no idea what she to get her and would have to wait until she could get some ideas from Chance.

As Charlie lay in bed, she decided to visit Horton Plaza and call Gabby to meet for lunch. From the way the sun was lighting the room, Charlie could tell it was going to be a nice day—perfect for the outdoor atmosphere of her favorite shopping center.

She'd made a decent amount of progress in therapy and could now be alone in the new house—only thinking about *the incident* maybe ten or so times a day. But showering was still dangerous territory, so she sped through that as usual. She wasn't ready for maternity clothes just yet and instead threw on a pair of designer sweats and a baggy T-shirt. As she stepped out the door and headed to the car, she thought about how lucky she was to live in San Diego where she could go Christmas shopping in a T-shirt.

The mall was crowded as Charlie had expected, but she was able to find a space in the parking garage. The mall included everything from Coach to Macy's, so Charlie had a huge selection and began to wander. She decided to get a new book bag for Tyson. She'd seen his, and it was a wonder he could carry anything in it. The straps were threadbare and hardly attached to the satchel. She thought leather would be ideal for him—maybe even something he could use when he was done with med school.

As Charlie searched the leather store for the bag she envisioned for Tyson, she suddenly felt someone standing very close behind her. She froze. It was the smell that hit her first, then when *he* spoke, all the blood in her body turned to ice.

"Well, well, well." His hot breath hit her neck, and her stomach had an instant reaction. She had to work hard not to throw up right in the store. "Aren't you even going to say hi to me? That's kind of rude, don't you think?"

Just leave, Charlie. Just turn around and leave. He *isn't going to do anything to you in public.* The words were there in her head, but Charlie's body was stuck in place. The familiar feeling of helplessness washed over her, and her knees threatened to buckle. She had to get away from *him*, but her body betrayed her, staying frozen in fear.

"I said it was rude to ignore an old friend." His tone was harsh, his lips at Charlie's ear.

"Hi," she whispered, bile rising in her throat.

"That's better. I miss you. Why did you move away?" Charlie's mind raced, and her body finally started to catch up. Stepping away from *him*, she set the leather bag down and headed for the door. She didn't want to see *him*. His voice and scent had been too overwhelming. If she had to look in his eyes, she knew for sure she'd break down.

Charlie's heart raced and her stomach rolled as she pushed the glass doors open and stepped out of the store. Finding a bathroom, she hurried inside, barely making it in time to vomit in the sink. When Charlie finally glanced in the mirror, she didn't recognize the person who stared back at her. Her face was pale, and sweat beaded along her hairline. Her eyes were wide, and the only thing she could think was *Thank God* he *didn't touch me.*

After staying in the bathroom for several minutes, Charlie splashed water on her face before going back out to the mall. Looking around, she didn't see any sign of *him*, so she headed to her car. Every footstep in the parking garage made her heart beat a little faster. Charlie knew *he* wouldn't touch her in the store, but this was different. This was more private. Quickly finding the car, she jumped in and locked all the doors before even putting the key in the ignition.

As she sped out of the garage, Charlie called Gabby to cancel their lunch plans. She couldn't see her now. If Gabriella saw her this shaken up, surely she'd question her. Charlie was so tired of lying.

She checked the rearview mirror the entire drive home and even passed her exit, getting off and back on the freeway to make sure *he* wasn't following her. Once she was parked in the driveway, Charlie practically sprinted to the house and fumbled with the keys as she tried to unlock the door. A car drove by, and she glanced up, praying it wasn't *him*. It was a minivan with three kids jumping around in the back.

"Shit!" She couldn't do this again. She needed to feel safe in her home.

The door finally opened, and Charlie slammed it behind her, making sure to double lock it. She grabbed the phone and took up her usual position on the couch. It was difficult to watch everything in the house, but she did the best she could, trying to focus so she wouldn't go into hysterics. She thought about calling Paige, but didn't want to hear the whole go-to-the-police argument. If Paige knew she'd seen *him*, she'd definitely start in with that one.

Charlie sat for well over an hour, not moving an inch. When the phone rang in her hand, it scared the life out of her. She screamed and tossed the thing across the room. Realizing how ridiculous she was, she quickly retrieved the phone and cautiously glanced at the caller ID. It said "International Operator."

The voice of the operator eased her fears, turning them into excitement. She knew she needed to turn on the "happy Charlie" for Gideon. He didn't need her fear to be part of what he had to worry about.

She waited for Gideon to talk, not trusting herself yet. Until Charlie heard his voice and let it wash over her and seep into her heart, she was worried she might blurt out everything that had happened since he'd left. It took longer than she thought it should for him to speak, and Charlie suddenly thought maybe it wasn't Gideon…maybe this was *the* phone call?

"Charlie?"

"Joe?"

"Uh, sorry. I wasn't expecting you to answer."

"What does that mean? Why would you call if you didn't expect me to answer?" Charlie's fear was quickly turning to anger.

"I mean, this was the first chance I've had to call, and I was worried you wouldn't be home at this time of day." Gideon seemed detached somehow.

"Oh." She decided to let him tell her what he needed to, praying silently he hadn't been hurt.

"Um, yeah, I know I was supposed to call last night….but, something happened and I…I just couldn't."

"Gideon? Are you hurt? Please tell me. I can't take this slow-reveal crap. Just come out and tell me." Charlie realized someone was yelling, and it was her. The events of the day were building up, and she could feel the explosion about to happen.

"No. I'm not hurt. I just couldn't call last night. That's all."

"Okay. I was just worried about you."

"Were you?"

"Of course I was! I worry about you every second of every day. All I think about is losing you." Tears streamed down Charlie's cheeks, and she made no effort to wipe them away.

"I'm sorry, Charlie. There's just some stuff happening here. I have to go."

"Wait! I have to tell you something." She couldn't let him hang up without telling him about her doctor's visit.

"What?" he asked, his voice flat.

"I went to the doctor yesterday and found something out about the baby—or I guess I should say 'babies.'" Charlie waited to see if he'd pick up on the correction she'd just made.

"So tell me." He was barely listening. On a normal day, Gideon would have been yelling with joy into the phone.

"Okay, then. I was hoping this would be good news, but now I'm not so sure." Her tears still flowed, and Charlie could tell her voice was starting to carry the heaviness of the breakdown lurking somewhere in the future. "Well, I tried to give you a hint, but whatever. We aren't having one baby—we're having two. Twins."

The silence at the other end was so complete Charlie thought they'd been disconnected. It took a few moments before Gideon spoke again, but when he did, he was *her* Gideon again.

"Seriously, baby? We're having twins? Holy shit!"

Hearing Gideon excited about the babies was what Charlie needed. It was what she'd been living for lately.

"Yes, Joe. The doctor heard two heartbeats, and I'm having an ultrasound next week to make sure, but she said it was very distinct."

"Baby, I have to go. I'm sorry. My watch starts in, like, five minutes. I'll call when I can."

"I love you," she said, just as the phone went dead. She didn't know if he heard her, and she realized he hadn't said he loved her.

When Tyson's alarm went off, he groaned as he rolled over, automatically reaching for Paige. She wasn't there. He'd completely forgotten she hadn't come over last night, claiming she needed to study.

Ever since Thanksgiving, things had been different with Paige. Tyson was keeping so much from her, and it was tearing them apart. The news of Charlie's pregnancy had pushed him over the edge, and he was taking it out on Paige. Whenever she mentioned Charlie's name, Tyson's entire personality changed. He knew it, but there was nothing he could do to stop himself.

Now that Paige had only one more final before the end of the semester, and he was just about through as well, he was determined to make things better between them. Paige would be his full-time job. He tried to push thoughts about the previous night and the phone conversation with Gideon out of his head. What's done was done. There was nothing he could do to change it.

Finally rolling out of bed, Tyson jumped in the shower. He had Christmas shopping to do. Normally, his mom did the majority of his shopping and put his name on the stuff she bought, but he was going to get Paige something special on his own.

He'd never had a girlfriend at Christmas because he lived by the rule of "No Holiday Hos." Before Paige had waltzed her beautiful ass into his life, he always had the year planned out: no chicks at Valentine's Day (they want you to buy them flowers and shit) and single for the entire summer, which meant he could do who and what he wanted. But Tyson always had a girl for Halloween, because you only got invited to the best parties if you were part of a couple. Then he'd break up with her before Christmas, thus avoiding having to buy a gift.

But now he wanted to buy something special and beautiful for Paige. Hell, he wanted to shower her with gifts. Although when Tyson recently decided to surprise her with a trip to San Francisco for a weekend, she practically bit his head off, accusing him of trying to buy her or some shit. Tyson just didn't get women. They needed to come with their own "How To" booklet. Of course, a booklet would only tell a guy enough to get himself in trouble; women needed their own wing in the library.

A few hours later, Tyson found himself at the mall, in a jewelry store of all places. He looked into the glass cases and pondered each piece. When he got to the engagement ring section, he took a deep breath and skipped right over to the watches. He was in no way ready for that…yet.

Just as he was about to walk out of the store, he saw the perfect thing: a thin platinum chain with links so delicate they looked like they'd fall apart if breathed on too heavily—but in reality it was very strong, just like Paige. In the center of the chain hung a small, intricate piece that looked like the infinity symbol, but was looped over itself again and again. More than infinity. The small charm was encrusted with tiny diamonds. They were all different shapes, yet they fit together in the most impossibly beautiful and unassuming way. It was Paige—simple, unique, and beautiful.

Feeling pretty proud of himself for finding a gift to convey everything he felt about her, Tyson strolled through the open air of the mall with the bag swinging in his hand. Then he noticed Charlie heading into the leather store.

Curious, Tyson stopped in front of the store and peered in the window. He watched as Charlie picked up a nice leather satchel and turned it over to examine it. That was when he saw *him*—the same guy who'd come out of her apartment a couple months ago. The guy moved behind her and whispered in her ear.

Tyson couldn't watch anymore, so he turned and went to find his car.

No matter what his brother thought, Tyson knew Charlie was cheating on him, and he hated her for it.

CHAPTER 21

Over the past weeks, Tyson had stopped checking on Charlie, and Paige was starting to notice. Every time she mentioned she was spending time with Charlie, his face turned into what he was sure was a grimace. Paige hadn't called him on it yet, but he knew it was coming. The only good thing was that since Charlie moved, Paige hadn't been spending every night with her. But she hadn't been spending them with him either.

The couple was curled up on Tyson's couch, watching one of his favorite movies — one with lots of shooting and sex. Paige was snuggled into Tyson's chest, her legs curled under her, and his arms held her close.

"Hey, can we go to the mall tomorrow?" she asked quietly.

"Seriously? It's like two days before Christmas. Do you know what that place is going to be like?" Tyson actually never wanted to move from where they were right now. For a few hours, it had been only the two of them — no Charlie to think about, no Gideon to worry about, no one else.

"So? I'll have my big, strong bodyguard with me to push all those nasty people out of the way." Paige tilted her head back and looked up at him, flashing her best smile.

"You know I can't say no to you. You don't play fair." He leaned in and gave her a nice slow kiss before sitting back and focusing on the movie once again. "I thought you were done shopping."

"I still have to get something for Charlie. I'm having a hard time with her."

Tyson's arms tensed. "Oh," was all he said.

"What's wrong with you, Tyson?" Paige asked, her tone heavy with irritation.

"What? Nothing."

Paige pulled away and scooted to the other end of the couch, facing him. "Bullshit, Tyson. Every time I mention Charlie's name, you get a scowl on your face and stop talking."

"No, I don't."

"Yes, you do. I'm sick of it. She's your brother's wife and my friend. Tell me why you're so pissed off at her," she demanded.

"I'm not mad at Charlie. It's just that you've been spending a lot of time with her." Even he didn't believe the words coming out of his mouth.

"And?"

"I just don't think Charlie is the kind of person you should be hanging around with so much."

"What the fuck are you talking about?"

"I just don't want you to go out with Charlie anymore. That's it. I don't want you to be friends with her. I don't want you to go shopping with her. I don't want you to see her." He was shouting.

Paige's face instantly changed from questioning to irate, and Tyson realized he might have gone too far.

"Oh, really? You don't want me to be friends with Charlie? Well, let me tell you something, Tyson Cooper." She was so angry she had to stop to take a breath. "You're not in charge of me. It's not your job to tell me who I can and can't be friends with."

"I just…" He couldn't finish. The words were right on the tip of his tongue, but he couldn't bring himself to say them. This was something between Gideon and Charlie now.

"What, Tyson? You think I'm not smart enough to pick my own friends? You're jealous that I'm spending time with someone other than you? How ridiculous is that? You have no right to tell me who I can hang out with."

Before Tyson could reach over and grab her, Paige was up off the couch and walking toward the door.

"Fuck. Paige, don't go." Tyson had gotten up too. His hands were stuck deep in the pockets of his jeans, and he was glaring at Paige. "I'm just trying to protect you."

"Protect me? Protect me from what? I don't need you to fucking protect me from anything—and most especially not Charlie." Paige turned to open the door.

Tyson wanted to ask her not to go, to beg her to stay with him, to tell her how much he cared about her and wanted her in his life. But he didn't do any of those things. He just stared at her.

Paige stared back at him for a few seconds, tears streaming down her cheeks. With her hand on the doorknob, she turned back to Tyson.

"Just so you know. I'll be at your parents' house on Christmas. I'll act like this—" she waved a finger between the two of them "—is still something. I'm not going to let you ruin everyone's Christmas by being the total asshole you're being at the moment."

With one last glance, Paige pulled the door open. Usually he'd sit back with relief and watch a girl go, but this time he didn't want that to happen. He wanted Paige to stay.

"Paige, please—"

The door clicked shut, and she was gone. At that exact moment Tyson knew without a doubt that he loved her. And if he wanted to keep her in his life, he was going to have to tell her everything.

Jumping up off the couch, Tyson yanked the door open and burst into the hall, only to see the elevator doors close in front of the woman he loved. The only woman he'd ever loved.

It was all Charlie's fault.

CHAPTER 22

As Charlie pulled into the already overflowing parking lot, she tried to talk herself into being happy tonight. It was Christmas. However, it wasn't going well.

It had been two weeks since she'd told Gideon about the twins, and she'd only talked to her husband three times since. She knew he was all right because the caller ID registered his calls every couple of days. For some reason, he always called when she wasn't home, and on the days she was home, he sounded more surprised than happy. Those few phone conversations had been short, and he hadn't asked about the babies or talked about what they were going to do when he got home. Charlie thought maybe the idea of having two babies was too much. He'd been so excited when it was just one baby, and now he barely talked about them, even when Charlie brought it up.

The church was already hot and uncomfortable, with stragglers trying to find spots in the overly populated pews, when Charlie finally pulled herself together and went in. She dreaded the smoke and foul-smelling incense that would soon be part of the pageantry. Despite the throngs of people, she knew exactly where to find Gideon's family. Her family. Unlike their children, Evelyn and Peter were at All Saints Episcopal Church every Sunday. Evelyn's family had been founding members of the church, and she and Peter had practically paid for the entire Social Center themselves. This earned them the second-row pew at all the services. Everyone knew not to sit in the second row — that was the Coopers' pew. The only thing better, in Evelyn's eyes, would have been that front pew, but that was occupied by the very, *very* old Mrs. Sandridge. The Sandridge family, along with Evelyn's family, had spent a lot of money and pulled a lot of strings to get the church built years and years ago.

Charlie smiled as she thought of Evelyn just waiting for Mrs. Sandridge to die so she could move to that front pew. Evelyn had once confided that all the Sandridge children had married and moved away, and since Mr. Sandridge went to that "big poker game in the sky" about ten years earlier, there was no one left to lay claim to that front pew. It was funny to Charlie that Evelyn was so concerned about all this stuff. In her everyday life, she was so different. Sure, she enjoyed being the wife of Dr. Peter Cooper, but she was so smart and kind, and she never threw her status around to get things done…except in church.

When Charlie finally made her way to the second row, she looked down the bench and was surprised to see Tyson, but not Paige. The last time she'd talked to Paige, she said she'd been invited to church and to spend the night at the Coopers'.

"Where's Paige?" Charlie asked as she scooted past Peter and Evelyn to sit next to Tyson. It didn't escape her notice that Tyson moved a little farther down than he needed to.

"I'm not sure, but she said she wouldn't be able to make church tonight." Evelyn frowned slightly before continuing. "She said she'd come for dinner tomorrow, though."

Something wasn't right. Paige had been way too happy about being included in the Cooper family Christmas.

"What's going on?" Charlie whispered, leaning over to Tyson.

"Nothing." His voice was rough.

"Bullshit!" Charlie countered, her voice louder than she had intended.

People from several rows looked over. Evelyn was mortified. Charlie gave a weak smile in apology before turning back to Tyson.

"Where's Paige? Why isn't she here?"

Tyson kept his gaze focused on the altar, never answering the question and seeming to indicate that Paige's failure to show up at church was somehow Charlie's fault.

Well, that just wouldn't do. Charlie wasn't going to let the rest of her family be miserable too. There was nothing she could do about Gideon not being there, but there sure as hell was something she could do about Paige. She quickly stood and slid back past Evelyn and Peter. When Evelyn looked up at her with a questioning raise of her eyebrows, Charlie leaned down and told her, "I think I have to get out of here. I'm sorry. The smoke and the smell of the incense are making me sick." For extra emphasis she patted the small bump of her stomach.

Evelyn smiled before squeezing Charlie's hand in understanding. She felt a twinge of guilt for lying to her mother-in-law in church, but there was a kernel of truth in what she'd said, and she needed to talk to Paige.

Twenty minutes later, with a force she didn't know she was capable of, Charlie pounded on Paige's apartment door. It was after midnight, and she worried her friend would be asleep. Paige pulled the door open and a look of shock registered on her face.

"Jesus Christ, Paige! You don't open a fucking door at midnight without knowing exactly who it is," Charlie immediately yelled.

"I thought it would be Tyson," Paige tried to explain, but quickly realized the reason for Charlie's anger. "Oh, shit! I'm sorry. You're right, Charlie."

Once they were in the apartment with the deadbolt securely in place, Charlie pulled Paige into an embrace. "I'm sorry…it's just…well, you know…"

"I know."

"Okay, well, this is awkward now." Charlie laughed a little. The smile on her face was forced, and her eyes were still bright with fear and anger.

"Um, yeah. Why are you at my apartment at midnight on Christmas Eve?"

"Because your ass is supposed to be sitting in the Cooper pew with the rest of us, not worshipping at the altar of Ben & Jerry's." Charlie took the ice cream container out of Paige's hand and turned it to read the label. "Cherry Garcia. I'm a Chubby Hubby girl myself."

"I couldn't make it?" It was more of a question than a statement.

"Yeah, that's a load of crap. So tell me what stupid thing my dickhead brother-in-law did. I mean, he hasn't been himself for a while. Honestly, I'm a little relieved you're having problems with him too. I thought it was just me."

"Glad I could be of service," Paige replied, not even trying to hide the sarcasm in her voice.

"Oh, please. You know what I mean. I'm not at all happy there's a problem between you two. First of all, I fully plan on you and me being sisters, and since Chance seems totally in love with Gabby, that leaves Tyson."

Paige smiled.

"And second, it will hurt Evelyn to find out there's something wrong between you and Tyson. I don't think she'd be able to handle it, what with Gideon gone and all." Charlie's voice caught.

"How's the baby?" Paige asked. Charlie knew she was trying to deflect the conversation.

"They…um, fine. I went to the doctor a few weeks ago. They did another ultrasound, but I had to look away so I wouldn't find out the sex. Gideon wants to be there for that." Her hand rubbed her belly as she thought once again about how her life had changed so drastically in such a short amount of time. "Now, why the hell are you here wallowing instead of suffering with the rest of us at church?"

"I'm going to be there for dinner tomorrow. I would never hurt Evelyn, but Tyson and I had a fight, and I think we broke up."

"Oh, baby. I know Tyson is miserable right now. I just saw him in church, and he's so unhappy he wouldn't even talk to me." Charlie wrapped her arms around her friend, pulling her into a hug.

"I don't think so. I mean, the fight was really big, and I said some things…he would never want to be with me again." Tears had started to escape, and Paige pulled back from Charlie.

Charlie pulled Paige's arm and guided her to the couch. She sat down and yanked Paige onto the cushion with her.

"So, tell me." Charlie turned to look at Paige, folding her legs underneath her.

"It was a fight…what more can I say?"

Charlie wasn't buying that for a minute. There was more.

"What did you fight about?"

"God! He was just being an ass and got all caveman telling me who I could—" Paige stopped suddenly and looked at Charlie.

Charlie knew where she was going, but didn't want to push the issue. She knew Tyson didn't like that she'd commandeered Paige over the past few months.

"I don't think it was about anything. I think I was looking for a way out," Paige blurted as more tears began to fall.

"Okay, I get that. But why? You two are great together."

There was a moment of hesitation, as if Paige wasn't sure if she wanted to trust Charlie. Watching the other woman, Charlie simply waited.

"I cheated on Tyson."

"When? How? Why?" Charlie couldn't believe Paige was capable of such a thing.

"I was home for Thanksgiving, and I went to a party with my ex."

"Was it a date?" Charlie tried to keep her expression neutral, knowing how hard it was for Paige to tell her this.

"No! His family and mine are close, and we had Thanksgiving dinner together. It was awkward, but what could I do? When he told me about the party, I was excited to see the few friends I actually have back home."

Once the words started flowing, Paige couldn't stop them. "I still don't know how it happened, but by the end of the night, I was tucked between Alex's legs, leaning against the couch in KerryAnn Adams' basement. He had his arms around me, and his lips kept brushing across my neck. I knew it was wrong, Charlie. I swear I wanted to stop, but all the feelings from the past were there, and I guess I just kind of fell into the moment."

"Did you sleep with him, Paige?" Charlie needed all the facts before she could even begin to form a plan to help her friend. If she'd gone to this guy's bed, Charlie didn't think there would be any hope for her and Tyson. The Cooper men didn't share. Gideon had once told her about a girlfriend he had in college who cheated on him. He cut all ties and never talked to her again.

"No! Oh, God! No. It was only the kissing. After that night, I asked Alex to drive me to the airport—it was time to talk. I told him that while I'd always love him for what we'd been, it would never be the way he wanted because, well, I'm in love with Tyson, Charlie.

Charlie wrapped Paige in a warm hug and held her while she cried herself out.

After a long while, Charlie broke the silence. "You're going to have to talk to Tyson about this."

Paige groaned.

"I know it'll be hard, and he's going to blow up."

"Wow, that's encouraging. Maybe I could just avoid him for the rest of my college career instead?"

"*But*, he'll forgive you. I'd totally lead with that whole 'I love you' thing though." Charlie smiled, and Paige gave a small chuckle as she wiped the last of the tears from under her eyes.

"You're right. I'll tell him."

"Good. And one last thing—when he starts yelling, just ignore whatever he's saying and get to the end. Cooper men tend to get pretty dramatic, so Tyson will go over the top."

The two women sat quietly for a few minutes before Charlie suddenly popped off the couch and said, "Let's go."

"Where exactly are we going at two in the morning on Christmas, Charlie?"

"Back to Peter and Evelyn's, of course."

"Um, why?"

"Because you need to be part of the Cooper Christmas. If you aren't there, Tyson will be pissy, Evelyn will be sad, and hell, I need some happy in my life. So go get some real pajamas on." Charlie looked down at Paige's old, holey sweats and ice cream-spotted T-shirt. "I know you bought some just for tonight."

"How did you know?"

"Please, Paige. Even after a year, I buy a new set for Christmas at the Cooper house. I mean, I love Evelyn, but she's still my mother-in-law, and there's no way I'm going to let her see me in my regular nightwear."

Ten minutes later, Paige was ready to go and climbed into Charlie's car. Paige had wanted to drive her own car, but Charlie wasn't going to give her an easy out. She did promise to bring Paige home if things didn't go as she'd predicted, but Charlie wasn't worried. The fact that Tyson had been so upset at Paige's absence let her know he was head over heels for her too.

As they drove through the dark, deserted streets, the silence in the car was oppressive. Charlie finally broke the quiet when she cleared her throat and said, "Paige?"

"Hmm?"

"I think you should wait to tell Tyson your story."

"What? No, I have to tell him. I can't hide from him anymore," she protested.

"Listen to me. Tyson is going to overreact. We've already established that. He's going to scream and yell, but in the end, that's all he's going to do. I think he loves you, and all you did was kiss this guy, so he'll get over it pretty fast."

Paige was shaking her head.

"He's so miserable right now. There's no way he'll let you walk away from him for even a second. And he will forgive you."

"You can't know that. He may decide he never wants to see me again."

"I've watched a parade of bimbos come and go over the past year, and trust me when I say there's no way he can give you up. He'll forgive you."

"Whatever."

"So just hold off on telling him." Charlie immediately held her hand up to stop what she knew was going to be a protest. "Please. Just for one day. Trust in the fact that he loves you and won't let you go. Be happy with the family for the day, and then tomorrow you can tell him."

"Okay, fine," Paige agreed.

"Thank you," Charlie said just as the car came to a stop in the Coopers' driveway.

It was almost three in the morning, and Charlie was exhausted. Paige followed her into the house and up the stairs, where Charlie pointed to a door across the hall from the one she'd just opened.

"Heidi Klum? Really?" Paige whispered across the hall before ducking through the other doorway.

Charlie rolled her eyes and slipped into the room, closing the door quietly behind her after whispering goodnight. Even if she couldn't sleep next to the man she loved tonight, at least Paige could be with Tyson.

After changing into her own newly purchased nightgown, Charlie slipped into bed with a sigh. "Good night, little critters. Merry Christmas," she whispered to her bump.

CHAPTER 23

As the light filtered into Tyson's room, he groaned and cursed. It had been a miserable night, and he really wasn't in the mood to celebrate anything with the family, especially not with Charlie. He wanted to stay in bed and go back to dreaming about Paige.

The dream had seemed so real. He could have sworn he smelled her and held her and kissed her. He sat up to look at the clock on the dresser. It was eight a.m., and he flopped back onto the pillows. Paige's scent billowed around him just as the bathroom door opened, and in stepped a vision. Tyson was pretty sure he wasn't still asleep and dreaming. This Paige was real, and she couldn't have been sexier if she'd tried. She stood in the doorway, leaning against the jamb, her hands planted on her hips and her hair in a wild tangle. If Tyson didn't know better, he'd say they'd had wild sex during the night. But the ache in his groin told him they'd done no such thing.

"Are you going to sleep all morning? Don't you want to see what Santa brought you?" Paige's smile was as bright as the sun that filled the room, and Tyson was momentarily speechless as he realized how much he needed, not just wanted, this woman in his life.

"I already got what I wanted. Now get your ass over here so I can unwrap my present." Tyson knew things weren't completely right between them, but he was willing to forget that for a few hours. They'd be fine. He could feel that in his soul, and he wanted her to be in his arms again.

Paige rolled her eyes, and Tyson laughed.

"You're so cheesy, Tyson."

"I can't help it. I'm turning all girly because of you. This is all your fault."

He sat up and held his arms open for her to come back to bed. But Paige didn't move, and Tyson's heart sank.

"Tyson." Her tone had changed dramatically. "We still have to talk. I'm sorry I walked out. It was wrong, but until we can talk about what happened, I'm not going to sleep with you. I want to know where we stand before I fall into bed with you again."

"So…talk."

"Not here, not now. We're going to go down and have a lovely Christmas with your family, and then later we'll talk. I don't want your mother any more upset today than she already will be with Gideon gone."

"So this is all about my mom?" Here he'd thought Paige had crawled into his bed not so many hours ago because she wanted to be with *him*—not his mother.

"No. This is about us." She stepped away from the bathroom and sat down next to him, snaking her arms around his neck to thread her long fingers into his hair. Tyson sighed. He'd missed her touch.

"Goddamn it, Paige. I don't get it. Why are women so fucking complicated?" He didn't realize he'd said it out loud until Paige let out a sexy laugh that rang through the room.

"I love you. As much as I try not to, I do." Paige's lips met his in a gentle caress, and Tyson had to use every fiber of inner strength to stop himself from trying to get her naked and moving under him.

"I love you too. I don't ever want to be away from you like that again."

Tyson ran his hands over her back. It wasn't the way he'd planned on telling her he loved her, but she'd said it first, and he wasn't going to make her feel awkward. And he did, in fact, know that he loved Paige Halloran.

In an easy movement, Paige's hand found Tyson's, and she pulled him off the bed. A small smile played on her lips as she raked his body with a hungry gaze. She pushed Tyson toward the bathroom with instructions to get himself together so they could go downstairs. The smile on Paige's face told Tyson she was excited for the day, so he headed into the bathroom.

A few minutes later, with Paige's hand firmly in his own, Tyson thought about how perfect the day was going to be. Christmas carols already filled the house, and Tyson could smell his mom's famous cinnamon rolls baking in the oven. He couldn't remember a Christmas when these two things hadn't greeted him as he came down the stairs.

Even when he and Gideon were kids and got up at the crack of dawn, running as fast as they could to see what had been left under the tree, their mom was always up ahead of them, and the smell of her baking wafted through the house. Of course, when they were young, they couldn't have cared less about the music and the food; their sole purpose was to get to the presents.

Tyson smiled as he remembered how every year, instead of ripping into the piles of gifts, he and Gideon would stack them and count them over and over to see who had the most. Gideon's pile always seemed bigger than Tyson's, and it took several years for the younger Cooper to figure out his brother just asked for bigger shit so his pile would seem like more. He wished so badly his brother was here.

Just as that thought entered Tyson's head, he heard a soft sound on the stairs behind him and turned to see Charlie coming down. There was a smile on her face, but her eyes were red, with dark circles under them. And instantly Tyson's happy memory was gone, replaced by the vision of that guy coming out of his brother's apartment.

"Morning you two. Sleep well?" Charlie winked at Paige, who blushed for no reason, considering her little speech about not letting Tyson in her panties until they'd talked.

Tyson's stomach turned in knots. He was so conflicted. As much as he wanted to snap and tell Charlie to leave Paige alone, he also wanted to thank her. He was pretty sure she'd been the one to bring Paige to him last night.

Hearing the kids coming down the stairs, Evelyn came out of the kitchen, wiping her hands on her apron. When she saw Paige, her face lit up.

"Oh, Paige! I'm so glad you're here." Evelyn pulled Paige to her.

While the Cooper family had once headed directly into the living room to dig through the presents, now that everyone was older, they tried to make the magic of the holiday last as long as possible. Tyson walked behind his two favorite women as they went to the kitchen to dig into those wonderful cinnamon rolls.

"Peter, will you look who snuck in to make our Christmas almost perfect?" Evelyn announced.

Peter sat at the table in the alcove of the kitchen, a cup of coffee and the newspaper in hand. He smiled to see Paige being guided by his wife. Tyson felt pride swell in his chest at the thought that his father approved of Paige.

Tyson watched as Paige and Charlie chatted easily. Charlie reached for her third roll, but pulled her hand back when she saw Tyson watching her. Catching his reflection in the window, he realized why she decided against taking it. He was actually sneering at her. Not wanting to ruin his mother's day, he decided to work harder to not show his feelings about his cheating sister-in-law today.

"It's so nice to finally be able to enjoy food again," she said, blushing. "I stopped throwing up all the time a while ago, but it's only been in the past couple of weeks that I've actually wanted to eat."

Tyson actually felt a little bad for her. "Then eat up, Charlie. Mom's cinnamon rolls are the best around. Too bad she only makes them for us at Christmas."

Once the plate was empty and everyone leaned back, rubbing their full stomachs, Peter announced, "All right, time to open those presents under the tree."

The whole table got up in one motion and moved into the living room. Evelyn needed every inch of the cathedral ceiling to house her Christmas tree. It was an extravagance she gave in to every year. She supervised the decorating, of course, but left the ladder-climbing to professionals.

With everyone gathered around the tree, Evelyn started to dig through the huge pile of gifts. Tyson wondered who the hell all the presents were for. He was sure there were some for Gideon, and they'd stay wrapped until he came home, but there still seemed to be hundreds of gifts under the tree.

As the gifts were being handed out, Tyson noticed the pile in front of Charlie growing exponentially. Although he was supposed to be all grown up, the sight brought back those childhood feelings about Gideon's giant pile of presents, and jealousy burned in the pit of his stomach. He tried to calm himself by running a hand over the small wrapped box in the pocket of his robe. He'd put Paige's gift there instead of under the tree because he wanted to be the one to give it to her.

Tyson's attention shifted when Charlie started to open some of the gifts stacked at her feet. She laughed as she read the gift tag on the first one. "To Grandbaby Cooper."

Tyson was sure his mom had lost her freakin' mind. It occurred to him, suddenly, that Charlie and Gideon's issues were going to ripple through the entire family. Hell, they'd already started to weigh on his relationship with Paige. Evelyn would be crushed beyond repair to find out the baby wasn't Gideon's.

Tyson had never wished more that he could change just one day in his life. He wished he'd never gone to check on Charlie that day. He wished he didn't know what he knew.

"Evelyn! You're crazy!" Charlie laughed as she opened the box and pulled out a small piece of clothing. Paige oohed and aahed, but to Tyson it just looked like a towel of some sort. "I love this, Evelyn. It's so soft." She brought the towel thing to her cheek and rubbed it.

Charlie's eyes closed, and a tear trickled down her cheek. Tyson thought he was going to be sick to his stomach. But remembering the promise he'd made to himself earlier, he made an effort not to show his true feelings. Then Charlie spoke, and his tenuous grasp on his emotions grew even more perilous.

"I hope they had another one at the store, though."

Evelyn looked at her with confusion and hurt.

The heat rose in Tyson's face, and he felt Paige's hand squeeze his. She must have noticed his reaction, and she knew he was about to blow.

"Because I'd hate for one of the babies to have something so beautiful and the other to miss out." Charlie beamed as she waited for the room to process what she'd just said. It took Paige only a heartbeat, and she gasped. As soon as Evelyn understood, she flew across the room to wrap Charlie in a hug.

"Are you saying I'm not only going to have one new grandbaby in a few short months, but two?"

"Yes." Charlie smiled at everyone in the room, but stopped when she got to Tyson. He tried to hide what he was thinking, but by the way Charlie's face dropped, he knew he was a second too late.

"That's wonderful, Charlie," Paige offered, and Tyson nodded, not trusting himself to open his mouth and speak.

"I was going to wait for Gideon to tell everyone, but with all this stuff—Evelyn you know you shouldn't have!—I thought I needed to mention something now."

When Tyson was able to pull his shit together, he realized he needed to change the flow of the conversation. Digging into his pocket and pulling out Paige's gift, Tyson casually wound an arm around her shoulder and opened his hand so the box was right in front of her.

"Oh, Tyson. I left your present at my apartment. I'm sorry."

"Don't worry about that. You being here with me is more than enough," he whispered in her ear.

Tyson knew everyone was watching them. With his heart beating a rhythm he could dance to, he watched Paige slowly, so goddamn slowly, unwrap the gift.

When she opened the black box, she gasped.

"Oh, it's beautiful."

"Let's see, Paige. I want to see how well my son did on his own," Evelyn prompted.

Paige gently took the necklace from its case to show around the room.

"Tyson, that is exquisite." Charlie seemed genuine in her admiration.

Tears spilled over the edges of Paige's eyes and tracked down her cheeks. Tyson reached out to wipe them away. Her hands came up to his face and held him still, looking straight in his eyes. She leaned in and kissed him softly, whispering words of love against his lips.

"Paige, I love you. Forever."

Tyson fingered the infinity charm hanging on the length of platinum chain so she'd understand. This only made her cry harder, and he hoped that was a good thing.

Once all the gifts were opened and Evelyn had inventoried each piece of baby paraphernalia so she could go back to get doubles, everyone went back upstairs to get ready for the rest of the day.

Charlie showered quickly. Not only did she want to be ready in time to help Evelyn in the kitchen, but she was worried the nightmare that had woken her that morning would return and break her. She didn't want anything to ruin the day. Until last night, it had been two weeks since the last nightmare. The last one had been after the encounter with *him* at the mall, and honestly, she hadn't thought about *him* too much since then. She didn't know why the nightmare had come this time. She just wanted *him* to go away forever.

As she closed her eyes and took a deep breath, trying to rid her mind of the things that haunted her whenever that moment came back—his voice, his smell, his touch—the most amazing thing happened. The babies moved. It was just a flutter, but she knew instantly what it was.

Setting her hand on the small bump, she willed them to do it again, wanting to make sure it had actually happened. After a few minutes, when she was about to give up, another flutter moved through her. It was the most incredible feeling she'd ever experienced. It made the whole pregnancy real. It made her forget about *him*.

Chance and Gabby arrived around three for the huge meal Evelyn had made. Now that Charlie had felt the babies move, it seemed like that's all they did. But she mentioned it to no one. She wanted to tell Gideon first.

Several times during dinner Evelyn tried to get Charlie to go against Gideon's orders and have an ultrasound so she could find out the sexes of the babies. Charlie adamantly refused. Evelyn might have been able to skirt

Gideon's request that they wait for him before doing anything for the babies under the guise of Christmas, but Charlie wouldn't find out the sex of the babies without her husband next to her.

Just as everyone was finishing dessert, the phone rang. All conversation stopped, and Evelyn jumped out of her seat to run for the phone. Charlie knew it would be Gideon. She smiled at just the thought of being so close to talking to him.

"Oh, Gideon." Evelyn's voice carried into the dining room.

Charlie couldn't wait to hear his voice and tell him about the new development with the babies. She was sure this was the thing that would get him excited again—to know they were moving around and pushing each other out of the way.

Evelyn was gushing to Gideon, and when she mentioned the twins, Charlie cringed, hoping he wouldn't be too upset that she'd told them.

Eventually, Evelyn came into the dining room and handed the phone to Peter. Charlie's bladder was starting to protest, and now that the babies were moving, she was even more uncomfortable. But she wanted to wait until after she talked to Gideon.

When Peter finally said good-bye, Charlie held her hand out for her turn. Peter looked at her with a sad smile on his face.

"Oh, sorry Charlie, he asked to talk to Tyson." He handed Tyson the phone. Charlie realized Gideon was saving her to talk to last…and the longest.

Charlie couldn't hold it anymore and had to practically waddle with both knees pulled together to the bathroom to avoid an embarrassing situation. She was in the bathroom for only a few minutes, but when she walked back into the dining room, Evelyn had the phone again.

"Okay, dear. I love you too. Merry Christmas." And she hung up.

When Evelyn looked up at Charlie and saw the pain and confusion on her face, her smile turned to a frown.

"I didn't get to talk to him. I was in the bathroom," Charlie stammered.

"I'm sorry, Charlie. I thought you talked to him after Peter. He said he had to go on duty. I'm sorry."

Turning, Charlie walked out of the room.

Just as she made it to the first step, there was a commotion behind her, and she stopped to try to understand what was happening.

Gabby's accented voice drifted out to her, and Charlie could picture her sister-in-law's fierce expression as she said, "Evelyn, I'm sorry. I like you a lot, but your sons are being asses. I've kept my mouth shut for the past three months, but I can't any longer. Gideon, who claims he loves Charlie, leaves her here alone for six months. He just springs this shit on her like it's no big deal, and then she's supposed to jump up and down because the man she's chosen to spend her life with will be off getting shot at?"

Charlie was about to continue up to Gideon's room when she heard Tyson snort.

Gabby had a few words for him as well, and Charlie stood, numb, on the third step as she listened to her sister-in-law say the things she'd only dared to think.

"Tyson, I don't know what your problem is, but you've been treating Charlie like crap for months now. She's married to your brother and all alone. I'd think you could do a little more to help her out."

This quickly digressed into an onslaught of Spanish, which Charlie could only guess was not very kind words about Tyson. At that point Charlie climbed the stairs and crawled into Gideon's bed, her knees pulled up under her belly, and her hands cradling her head. It was in this position that Gabby found Charlie about ten minutes later.

"Charlie, *querida?*" She sat on the edge of the bed and rubbed Charlie's back. Gabby cursed in Spanish under her breath.

"Why, Gabby? Why didn't he want to talk to me? I don't understand."

"Come on. Let's go home. You don't have to stay here." Gabby ran to the bathroom and got a wet washcloth to wipe Charlie's tear-streaked face. Charlie was grateful for Gabby's help. She didn't want to walk out of the house looking like the hurt and beaten-down woman she seemed to have turned into.

When the two women appeared at the top of the stairs, Chance was pacing the tiled floor of the foyer, his face twisted into a mask of anger and hurt. Then Evelyn came into the foyer, wringing her hands. Charlie was embarrassed and deflated. She didn't know why Gideon wouldn't want to talk to her, but she couldn't face his mother at this moment.

"Evelyn, thank you. Charlie is coming home with us. And again, I'm sorry, but until you can figure out what the hell your sons are doing, I'm going to do my damnedest to keep Charlie away from all of you. She's hurt and fragile right now, and if something like this were to happen again, she wouldn't survive it. So, next time you talk to Gideon, you tell him exactly what he's done to his pregnant wife tonight."

Gabby turned and left the Cooper house, her arm wrapped tightly around Charlie.

CHAPTER 24

Paige stared at him, her eyes wide. Evelyn came back into the room and collapsed in her chair. Tyson realized he might have made a mistake. The silence was eerie. Tyson watched as Paige began to fidget with her napkin, and he sensed her need to be anywhere but there. He wanted to talk about their relationship and head off any thoughts that might be bubbling up in that too-smart head of hers, so he stood and pulled Paige up with him.

"Well, now that Paige has been thoroughly inducted into the Cooper world, I'm going to take her home." Tyson tried to break some of the tension, but no one even cracked a smile.

"Evelyn, Peter, thank you so much for inviting me. I, well, it was nice," Paige said before following Tyson out of the dining room and up the stairs.

Once the bedroom door closed behind him, Tyson wrapped Paige in his arms and kissed the top of her head. He whispered an apology. Paige pulled away and gathered her stuff, throwing it haphazardly into her bag. Tyson sat on the edge of the bed with his eyes trained on her as she scurried around the room.

"Can you believe Gabby?" Tyson finally asked.

"Don't," Paige said through clenched teeth. "We'll talk about this when we get to my place. We have lots to talk about."

Tyson's face fell. It was going to be a long night.

Following Paige down the stairs, Tyson called to his parents that they were leaving. No one answered. Paige allowed Tyson to hold her hand as they walked to the car, but when he leaned in to kiss her, she hesitated.

He was hurt, and at this point he was too tired to hide it. He was certain whatever they had to talk about was going to change everything.

Tyson kept a death grip on the steering wheel as he drove to Paige's apartment. He was deep in thought, working out exactly what he was going to say and trying to predict what arguments Paige would offer and how to counter them. That's how Tyson worked. When he was young, his mom used to tell him he should be a lawyer, the way he puzzled everything out. The thing working against him right then, however, was that he had no idea what Paige was going to say. He couldn't create a good defense if he didn't know what the offense was going to look like.

Eventually they made it to Paige's place and, trying to be a gentleman, Tyson took her bag from her as he wrapped his free arm around her waist. She let him. He was surprised she let him touch her after the way she'd acted when he tried to kiss her, but he tried not to show it.

Paige unlocked the door and flipped on the lights once they both stepped in. Tyson didn't know if it was a good sign or a bad sign that she wanted to talk at her apartment. On the one hand it would be easy to kick him out after she broke up with him, but on the other hand, she could have just done it on the ride over and never let him in. He was confused.

"Paige, please. Let's just talk now. I want to get this done so we can get back to us. I've missed you." His voice was low and unsteady.

When he dared to glance over at her, he saw she was fingering the necklace he'd placed around her neck earlier that day. Tears clung to her dark lashes.

"I know I've been an ass around Charlie, but there's—"

"Tyson, please let me say what I need to." Tyson braced himself for the words he knew would pierce his heart.

Paige sat on the couch and scooted so her back was against the arm rest. Pulling her legs up underneath her, she took a deep breath and looked him right in the eye. "First, I love you."

"I love you too. You know that."

"Please let me get through this before you say anything. If I stop, I won't be able to start again."

"Christ, Paige! Just tell me already! I can't take any more."

"Okay. At Thanksgiving, when I went home, my dad invited the Baylors over for dinner. You remember I told you about Alex?"

Tyson nodded, and his teeth clenched. He already didn't like where the conversation was going.

"Well, he invited me to a party while I was home, and since I hadn't seen so many of my friends, I said yes. I don't know what happened. I swear. One minute I was talking and telling stories with my old friends, and the next I was being held by Alex."

At this point, Tyson launched himself up off the couch and began pacing the living room. Tears flowed down Paige's cheeks.

"And then he kissed me. And I kissed him back for a minute before I realized what I was doing."

"Did you fuck him, Paige?" Tyson's voice came in a whisper. Paige stood from the couch and tried to wrap her arms around him, but in the same way that she'd pulled away from him earlier, he stepped back.

"No! All I did was kiss him…once….I'm sorry. I don't know…I was tired…and he was familiar. But then I realized he wasn't you, and I didn't want anyone else but you. I'm sorry."

"I knew it!" he exploded, and Paige jumped back in surprise. "I knew she'd do this. I knew you two hanging out was bad! That whore Charlie! This is all her fault. I should have stopped this earlier, and then you'd never have kissed him."

"What the hell are you talking about? My kissing Alex has nothing to do with Charlie. Why would it?"

"Because she's cheating on Gideon! She's fucking some other guy while my brother is serving our country. I hate her." Tyson's face was red, and his eyes were wild.

"Charlie would *never* cheat on Gideon. She loves him."

"Bullshit! I saw it. I saw the guy coming out of their apartment. He was zipping up his pants! She fucked another guy just days after Gideon left. And now she's pregnant? How does she even know that it—or I guess *they*—are Gideon's and not this other guy's?"

Paige stood frozen in front of Tyson.

He was glad he'd finally told her. Now she'd understand why she needed to stay far away from Charlie. "She's a whore, Paige. Don't worry. As soon as Gideon gets home, she won't be around us anymore."

A long silence that hung in the room. Suddenly Paige was right in Tyson's face, and she didn't look ready to make up or apologize.

"She was raped, you ass!" Paige screamed.

CHAPTER 25

Charlie noticed Chance checking on her, glancing in the rearview mirror every few seconds. She was in shock after the events of the evening. Since getting in the car, she hadn't said a word, hadn't moved. She didn't know what to do or say. The impossible had happened, and her life actually had gotten worse. Gideon didn't want to talk to her. What more could happen?

Gabby sat beside Chance, her body shaking slightly from the adrenaline that must still have been coursing through her. Charlie watched her brother turn to look at his wife and knew both of them were just as confused as she was.

"Where are we going?" Charlie asked.

"We're taking you to our house tonight, *hermana*," Gabriella answered in a low, even voice.

"No."

Both Gabby and Chance's heads snapped around. Thank God the roads were empty, or Chance probably would have driven right into the back of someone.

"Lottie?"

"No! I want to go to my house." Charlie's voice was quiet, but solid. She wanted to be in her own house, near the phone. The idea that Gideon might call her there had been playing in her head for most of the ride.

"Honey, you don't want to go back there right now. Just come home with us and stay in the guest room." The look on Gabriella's face was one Charlie had never seen in all the years she'd known her. Gabby was strong and brave in all things. There was nothing that couldn't be looked at positively. She didn't worry about a problem, only found a solution. But now she seemed scared.

"No! Why doesn't anyone listen to me? I want to go to my own home. I want to sleep in my own bed, the bed where…" Charlie didn't finish her sentence, but slumped back into the seat as exhaustion washed over her.

"Okay, we'll take you home, Lottie," Chance soothed.

Chance's words allowed Charlie to relax for a minute. From the backseat she watched as Gabby and Chance stole glances at one another. Charlie wanted to tell them there was nothing they could do. This was her life, her problem, her burden. Nothing anyone else did would change what she was experiencing.

Once they arrived at the small house by the beach, Charlie practically sprinted to the front door, trying to get in before her brother and his wife could follow. Unfortunately, she was still shaking and had a hard time getting her key in the lock, allowing Chance to get beside her as she fumbled. Tears streamed down her cheeks, and she mumbled curses under her breath. Chance finally took the key away from her and opened the damn door himself, stepping back to let the two women in first. After closing the door and locking it, Chance followed Gabby into the living room and sat on the couch.

"You two don't have to babysit. I'm an adult, you know."

"We know that. We just love you and want to help," Gabby offered.

"Oh, really? Well, let's see. Can you change the fact that my husband is gone? Can you bring him back to me or even promise me he's going to be coming back? No? Okay, how about changing the fact that my brother-in-law has been treating me like I have a big scarlet 'A' on my chest? Can you fix that, Gabriella? No again? All right, moving on then. Can you change what he—"

And right there, in the middle of her rant, Charlie stopped. Like a deflated balloon, her desire to fight or argue just collapsed. The events of the day finally defeated her. "I'm going to take a shower. You two do what you want." Charlie waved her hand at the pair in dismissal before turning and heading down the hall.

Instead of the quick and utilitarian showers Charlie had become accustomed to, this time she welcomed the opportunity to be alone and allowed herself to feel. She didn't want to face her brother and Gabby, and hoped they'd get tired of waiting for her and leave.

The water had run cold, and Charlie sat in the tub with her knees pulled up against her, her body shaking with sobs when there was a knock on the door and Gabby burst in without an invitation. Stifling her tears, Charlie groaned.

"You've been in here for like half an hour."

"Goddammit, Gabby! Can't you just leave me alone? I just want to be alone!"

Tyson's mouth was moving—he could feel it—but nothing was coming out. Had Paige just said Charlie was raped? He wasn't buying it.

"Is that what she told you?"

"Yes, as a matter of fact. And damn it, I swore I'd keep her secret, but you were being so mean and you were so wrong. She's hurting. He really hurt her." Paige sank into the chair and pulled her knees up to her chest, wrapping her arms around them.

"Paige." Tyson walked over to kneel in front of her. "Obviously she knows I saw the guy. He must have told her he saw me, and that's why she's saying this. I saw him, Paige. He didn't look like he'd just raped anyone."

"Oh really? And how many rapists do you know?" Her eyes were almost black with anger.

"None. But he was happy, and he didn't have a scratch on him. I mean, if she was raped, then why didn't she fight back?"

"He threatened Gideon. He said—"

"Pssh. Whatever. My God, Paige, Gideon is deadly when he needs to be. I mean, that's what he's trained for. And he isn't here—he's on the other side of the world. This guy can't touch him, much less threaten him. I can't believe you're buying Charlie's load of crap. Besides, I saw them together again a few weeks ago."

Paige's eyes opened wide. "When?"

"What?"

"When did you see them together?"

"A few weeks ago at Horton Plaza. They were in the leather store. I saw him behind her, whispering in her ear."

"And then what? What else did you see?"

"Nothing. I left. I couldn't stand the sight of either of them."

"That explains why she's been locked in her house for the past couple of weeks."

"What? She's probably been screwing that guy for the last two weeks." Tyson knew immediately that was totally the wrong thing to say.

Paige stared straight at him like she wanted to slap him. He even saw her hand twitch. She jumped off the chair and started to pace the room.

"God, Tyson. You have such a knack for bad timing." Her teeth were clenched, and the statement came out as a hiss.

Now Tyson started to get angry too. Paige was a smart girl — how could she not see how naïve she was being?

"Do you remember Gabby and Chance's Halloween party? How horrible Charlie looked that night — like the walking dead when she was trying to be an angel?"

Tyson nodded and opened his mouth, but Paige started speaking again before he could get a word out. "I found her upstairs crying. When we went back to my place she told me what happened. She doesn't want anyone to know because she's afraid they'll look at her differently, especially Gideon."

"I still don't believe her. She's covering up!"

"Just shut up for two minutes. God, this is so fucked up!" Paige took a deep breath. "She's not lying. The guy works with Gideon. He came over under the pretext of checking up on her. He told her he knew where Gideon was and that something could happen to him."

Tyson didn't know what to say. Paige seemed so sure. Had he been wrong? Had he just missed catching this guy? No. He was right.

"I convinced her she needed to talk to someone and see a doctor. I took her to L.A. myself for her to see doctors there. She was worried that between Chance and Peter someone would know who she was. She was so broken, Tyson. She didn't sleep for days. That's why I spent those nights with her. Those were the only nights she slept." Paige was on the verge of sobbing.

"What about at the mall? It was the same guy." Tyson wasn't ready to give up.

"Oh my God! Why do you need to be right? Charlie didn't tell me he approached her, but she was doing so much better up until about two weeks ago. Between the therapy, the babies, and the move, she was actually starting to be happy. But now she's sunk back into what she was before. I thought it was the holidays, and Gideon not being here." Paige shook her head. "She was doing so much better."

"Fuck! Are you telling me that not once, but twice I could have stopped this guy from hurting Charlie, and I didn't? Oh, Paige…what have I done?"

Paige laughed — not a cute laugh, a derisive one. "It isn't all about you, Tyson! My God! Are you really so self-centered that Charlie being abused is about you?"

"No! That's not what I meant." Tyson sat on the couch. The weight of everything Paige had told him was just too much. He couldn't deny it any longer. He might be an ass, but he wasn't stupid.

"Then what? Please explain to me how I could actually be in love with someone so shallow! Please, because I'm not feeling all that great about my choice in men right now!"

"I mean…God! Why didn't she tell us? Why didn't she tell me? Why didn't she go to the police?" He fought back tears. Tyson never cried. He wasn't a girl. He was Tyson Fucking Cooper.

No, he was the asshole who may have ruined several lives.

"I told you. She's worried about how Gideon will treat her — how everyone will treat her. Why didn't you tell me what you saw?"

Paige asked the one question Tyson had been dreading. Now he'd have to tell her how truly awful he was.

"Remember that day I went for a drive? You know, when you were at my apartment?" He looked at her, and her head bobbed in affirmation. "Well, that was the day I saw the guy. I was *so* sure Charlie was cheating! I swear! He was smiling and even said hi to me. Oh, God!" Bile rose in Tyson's throat as he remembered the satisfied grin on the guy's face.

"Oh, Tyson. I wish you'd told me." Paige sat next to him, pulling his hand into hers. She was comforting him, and he didn't deserve it. When Tyson finished telling her what he'd done, she was going to leave forever.

"I didn't tell you because I decided this was something for Gideon and Charlie to deal with. I was just going to wait for him to get home, and then tell him what I saw."

His tears began flowing, and Tyson felt like a giant pussy, but he couldn't stop. He'd caused so much pain. Paige had no idea.

"What do you mean you *were* going to wait? Oh, Tyson! No! Please tell me you didn't tell Gideon. Please."

Tyson lowered his eyes. "It was Thanksgiving. When Charlie told us she was pregnant, I heard how excited Gideon was. I couldn't let him think the baby was his. I thought there was a possibility it could be this other guy's." He braved a glance at Paige. "Don't look at me that way. You thought so too. I saw your reaction when I told you she was pregnant and you did the math. I just didn't have the information you had."

"You're right. I was worried it was his. Thank God they aren't."

"I had my mom tell Gideon to call me. I needed to do it in private. And I almost didn't, but in the end I told him Charlie was cheating. Shit!"

"Oh, no, no, no, no. This is bad for him and for her. He could get himself killed over there worrying about this. And she thinks Gideon is upset about the babies."

As much as Tyson didn't want to admit what else he'd done, he knew he had to. She was definitely going to walk out after he told her the next part.

"There's more." Paige looked at him, and he had to take a deep breath. "Tonight when Gideon called, he asked to talk to Charlie."

"What? Then why didn't you let him? What did you do?"

"I love you. I just need you to know that before I tell you." Her expression didn't change, and Tyson swallowed hard before beginning again. "I told him she left."

"You told him what? That's just cruel! Did you see Charlie?"

Paige cried harder, and Tyson didn't know what to do. She was right, it had been cruel. He'd hurt everyone. He had to fix it, but he didn't know how.

CHAPTER 26

When Charlie woke it was still dark outside, and she wondered what time it was. Glancing at the clock, she groaned; it was two in the morning. She rolled back over and caught the shape of someone sitting in the chair in the corner of the room.

Oh my God. It's him. *How did* he *find me? How did* he *get into the house?*

Charlie broke out in a cold sweat and suddenly couldn't breathe. She was frozen, and even if she could have forced herself to move, where would she have gone?

"Lottie?" Chance's voice sliced through the darkness.

Charlie's body instantly reacted, and she began to shake. Her brother got up from the chair, and she watched in the darkness as he moved toward her.

"Lottie, are you okay? What's the matter?"

He was getting closer, and even though Charlie knew it was him, she couldn't speak a single word.

"Talk to me, Charlotte. Please."

"Chance, I—I just…you…" Words tumbled out, but nothing made sense. What could she tell him? That she thought he was the evil who lived in her nightmares?

Then the events of the previous night came crashing back to her—like watching a movie on fast forward, jumping from scene to scene: Evelyn hanging up the phone, Tyson's smirk, Gabby's pity, not being able to get out of the shower. It had been so long since she'd taken a shower that lasted more than the few minutes it took to wash. But last night, she'd never wanted to leave.

The water had run cold, and she was shivering. Her skin had wrinkled from exposure to the water. She slid down the wall and stayed there. Charlie remembered Gabby coming in and pulling her out. Charlie vaguely remembered Chance opening the door, but only because Gabby said his name.

After Gabby found her in the bathroom, there was no way Charlie could keep her secret from her, which meant she wouldn't be keeping it from Chance either. Gabby would tell him. Charlie expected nothing less from her and would never have asked her not to. But she hadn't told Gabby who it was. Otherwise Chance would go after him.

"Shh, Lottie." Chance sat on the bed and wrapped his arms around her. Charlie wished this was something he could help with, that she could cry while Chance promised to beat the guy up like when they were kids. But they weren't kids anymore, and there was nothing her brother could do.

Chance stroked his twin's hair and continued to whisper how sorry he was and how he wished she'd told them sooner. His words were filled with affection, and Charlie took them all in. She took everything he could offer because she needed to know she wasn't totally damaged and she was still loved — if only by her brother.

Eventually, Chance's soothing voice lulled Charlie into sleep, and when she woke again, the light was bright in the room, and Chance was spread out on the bed next to her, snoring. Now that he and Gabby knew, she felt lighter. She made a note to tell her therapist about this. Dr. Lassiter would of course continue to insist that she tell Gideon. And Charlie would once again tell her no. She still couldn't even imagine him knowing.

Rolling out of the bed, Charlie went to the kitchen to make breakfast. Gabby was already there. Of course. The table was set and her sister-in-law motioned for her to sit and start eating. Charlie saw the look in her eyes — the one she didn't want to see. It was pity.

"How are you?" Gabby tentatively touched her shoulder, worried she might jump away from her touch.

"I'm fine. Really. Chance, however, is snoring like a lumberjack in my bed." Charlie smiled, trying to convey that she didn't want or need her sister-in-law to feel sorry for her.

"Yeah, he wouldn't go to sleep last night. He insisted on watching over you."

"I don't need anyone to watch over me. I'm a grownup. I can deal with this on my own." Charlie knew her tone was harsh, but she needed everyone to understand she was still Charlie. The bastard wasn't going to take that away too.

"He's your brother, and he loves you. He feels like he failed you somehow by not being there. And just as a warning, he's extremely angry at Gideon. As much as he blames himself, he blames Gideon more."

"First, why is my life his responsibility? I won't let him blame anyone for this. This is my fault. It's not Gideon's fault. It's mine. I let *him* into the house. I didn't fight *him*. I let *him* do this to me." Charlie was on the verge of yelling and didn't want to have this discussion any longer.

"No. Stop it right now, Lottie." Chance's voice filled the room, and Charlie turned to see him behind her. "None of it was your fault. This was *his* fault. *He* did it to you." The look on his face was hard and serious.

"Chance, please. I don't want to do therapy right now. Just be my brother and not my therapist. I have one of those."

"Fine, then as your brother, I want to kill your husband and his brother, and the guy who did this to you. Hell, I want to kill myself for not being there."

"Okay, how about a combination of the two?" Charlie tried to joke. She wanted her life to be normal, even for an hour. She wanted to eat breakfast with her brother and his wife.

"And as your brother, I really think you need to alert the police," Chance added. "What if he—"

"No," Charlie said, her eyes flaring. She looked slowly from Chance to Gabby. She didn't need to say anything else.

"Fine." Chance tried to smile. "How about this? I'll wait until you need to talk. Until then I'll be your overbearing twin brother who makes sure you know I'm always right here."

The three ate breakfast and pretended things were normal, but at least they all knew they were pretending now. Charlie loved Chance and Gabby for being able to play along with her. Once she was able to live her life normally, she'd talk to them, but it was too much to deal with right now.

After Gabby and Chance left, which took a lot of convincing on Charlie's part, she got dressed. She felt much better once she was wearing yoga pants—the only non-maternity thing that still fit—and one of Gideon's T-shirts.

Just as Charlie sat down on the couch and clicked on the TV, the phone rang. She didn't want to deal with Evelyn today. As much as she loved her and Peter, she just wasn't up to it. She decided to let the answering machine pick up.

Charlie heard her voice tell the caller she couldn't get to the phone and to leave a message. Then the beep rang out. The voice that came next was not Evelyn's, however. It was the operator and Gideon. The operator told him there was no one home, and Gideon was trying to leave a message, but she wouldn't let him.

Without hesitation, although she was still hurting from the previous night, Charlie lunged for the phone.

"Wait! Wait! I'm here! I accept the charges!" she screamed into the phone, hoping she'd picked up in time. "Please!"

"Charlie?" It was the first time she'd heard his voice in over a week, and she wanted to cry.

"Yeah. Sorry. I didn't feel like talking to anyone today."

"Well, you won't have to talk to me very long."

"I want to talk to you. I just don't want to talk to anyone else."

"Oh, well, anyway, I just wanted to call so you wouldn't worry. We're heading in deep today, and there won't be any communications." Gideon's voice was cold and flat.

"Okay. You mean I won't be able to talk to you at all? How long?"

"The rest of my tour. And I'm sure you're relieved not to have to talk to me. Damn it! I can't talk about this now. I just don't want you to worry."

"What the hell are you talking about? I'm sure *you're* relieved not to have to talk to *me.* I mean, yeah, you'll miss talking to your parents and your brother, but your pregnant wife? Screw her!"

"You left, Charlie! You can't tell me you didn't know I was on the phone, and you left. I think it's pretty clear who didn't want to talk to who. So, yeah, screw you."

"I went to the bathroom! I have two little people rolling around inside of me, pushing on everything, so when I have to pee, I have to pee. I was trying to wait, but you kept asking to talk to everyone but me. So I went to pee!"

"Fuck! What's going on? I wanted to talk to you last. I was getting through everyone else, and then I wanted to talk to you last. Tyson said you left." His tone had softened, and Charlie was at a loss.

"Why would he do that? He saw me dancing in my seat. Oh, Gideon. I miss you." She took a huge breath, trying to control herself.

"Charlie, I have to go. I'm sorry. When I can call, I will."

"I love you, Joe."

"Me too." And then he was gone.

Charlie sat for a few minutes holding the phone and crying. Her life was crumbling around her. Four months ago she had a great life, and now she was barely getting through each day. As she got up off the couch, there was a knock on the front door. In a daze after talking to Gideon, she forgot to check who it was before opening the door.

She should have asked.

CHAPTER 27

"Tyson. What are we going to do?" Paige asked as the first traces of light filtered into the apartment.

The couple had been up all night, talking at times and not talking at others. There were long stretches where they just sat and held each other. And in the end, Tyson still didn't know where they were.

"I just don't know right now. Things have gone to shit so fast. And it was all my fault." Tyson was still absorbing what had happened to Charlie, and his guilt over thinking she would cheat on Gideon was eating him from the inside out.

"Tyson, I swore to Charlie that I wouldn't say anything to anyone about this. I had to tell you because you needed to know, but it should have been Charlie telling you. She can't know I broke her confidence."

"Paige, do you think after all the hurt that I've caused I won't go to Charlie and try to fix this?"

"You can't fix this. Charlie's the only one who can. What you *can* do is tell Gideon you were wrong. Tell him Charlie loves him and would never cheat on him. That's what you can do."

At this point, Paige stood on the opposite side of the room, an indication to Tyson of where they were with their own relationship. He realized the situation with Charlie wasn't the only one he needed to fix.

"I have to let Charlie know how sorry I am. There's so much more I can't even tell you right now. There's so much I need to apologize for." His voice trailed off as he grabbed his coat off the back of the couch.

Tyson closed the distance between them and kissed Paige lightly on the lips. He pulled her to him and rested his chin on her head. No matter what had happened in the last twenty-four hours, he loved her, and he wanted her to know that once he'd done his penance, he'd be back. But right then, he couldn't be near her knowing how badly he'd fucked everything up.

"Go away! I don't want to talk to you," Charlie ground out through gritted teeth as she slammed the door.

The door never found its home. Tyson put his foot out to stop it. He pushed the door open again and stepped into the house.

Charlie thought about calling the police but knew she could never hurt Peter and Evelyn that way. "I'm serious, Tyson! Get the hell out of my house!" Three months of anger and hurt bubbled up in her, and Tyson was the perfect target. She'd endured months of sneers and smirks from him, and she was tired. She didn't have any more patience.

"I need to talk to you. I'm not leaving until you hear me out."

Tyson's voice was calm, but full of something else Charlie couldn't place. Sorrow? Regret? No, it couldn't be either of those things. Not Tyson.

"Oh my God! What the hell is wrong with you? Are you trying to drive me crazy? Because honestly, I don't know if there's anything more you could add to this situation to make things worse."

Tyson just stood there, staring at her. Charlie wondered why he wasn't arguing with her. She wanted to fight — fight for her marriage, fight for her sanity, fight for her children…fight for her life.

And yet Tyson was just standing there.

"I'm sorry. I'm so sorry."

"What? Sorry for what? Please, I want to hear you tell me how sorry you are that you told Gideon I left last night — how you made your brother think I didn't want to talk to him. Please, I want to hear this."

She expected him to be surprised at her statement. He didn't know she'd talked to Gideon just minutes ago. But there was no indication of surprise on his face at all. What Charlie did see was what she'd heard in his voice — that tone she couldn't place: pity. Charlie realized instantly that he knew what had happened to her. Paige had told him. She'd trusted her. Her anger grew exponentially.

"I'm so sorry, Charlie."

"Stop it! I don't want your pity. I can't believe Paige betrayed me." Charlie would rather have rather endured more of his smirks. This was the worst form of torture.

"Don't be mad at Paige. She had to tell me."

"Did you force her, Tyson? Did you beat it out of her?" She couldn't take any more. The past two days had been too much. There was nothing left. "Whatever. But don't be sorry for me. Be sorry for trying to drive Gideon away from me. Luckily he called this morning, and despite your efforts to destroy me—or is it him you're trying to bring down? Well, he knows about you, Tyson. He knows."

"Why didn't you tell me?" Tyson's voice quivered like he was on the verge of tears.

Tyson Cooper crying? For me? Charlie thought in complete amazement. "Because I don't want this," she said, waving her arms at him and pointing out his reaction. "I don't want Gideon to know. Do you know what it will do to me to see that look—*that* look—in his eyes every time he sees me? I can't live the rest of my life with that. Please don't tell him."

Charlie watched as Tyson's face crumbled and tears poured from his eyes. She had no idea what to do. Tyson was crying for her. No. Even with Paige around, she knew Tyson hadn't changed *that* much. Tyson was crying for himself.

"I'm so sorry," he choked out again.

"Stop saying that! You didn't rape me! *He* did! Go away, Tyson!"

"Charlie, please come sit down. I want to tell you what happened."

Tyson tried to steer her to the couch, but Charlie didn't want to be anywhere near him. She watched as he sat down and looked up at her. He wasn't going to leave. Of course not. Tyson wanted to hurt her some more. This was his show, and he wasn't going to leave until he was finished.

"I know what happened. I was there! I can't do this again. I'm trying to forget! Don't you get it? Why are you doing this to me?"

"Paige told me because I saw the guy. I'm so sorry." He wouldn't look at her. This was worse than the looks of pity.

"Stop! I don't want to know anything. I'm trying hard to be me again. You've done what you came to do. You apologized. Okay? Now can you please just go?" Charlie felt the familiar sensation of bile working up into her throat.

When Charlie talked with Dr. Lassiter, it was different. She was removed from what happened when she was in therapy. She could talk about it like it was someone else, but now, with Tyson talking this way... No! It was too much. It was too real. Tyson was *not* going to do this to her. She couldn't let him.

Charlie's body betrayed her rationalization. Turning, she ran for the bathroom and made it just in time. When she was done retching, she cupped her hands under the stream of water in the sink and splashed her face, taking a small drink to rinse her mouth. She willed Tyson to be gone when she got back to the living room.

But when she returned, Tyson was exactly where Charlie had left him. His elbows rested on his knees, and his head was lowered as he stared at the floor. Seeing Tyson like this made her nervous. She wasn't ready to feel any of this with him, of all people.

"Charlie, please let me tell you what happened." Tyson stopped for a breath, like he was preparing to tell her something he didn't want to. "I was coming to the apartment that day. I was doing my good brotherly duty and checking on you."

He finally looked up, those oceanic blue eyes full of pain. Sitting in the chair across from him, Charlie gave in. She was too tired to fight any more. Tyson had defeated her, so reluctantly she let him continue.

"He was coming down the stairs from your place. Oh God, I'm so sorry. He was smiling, and I thought…I never would have thought he'd hurt you. I'm sorry." His eyes never left those of his sister-in-law.

"Well, he did. There's nothing you could have done. It was over. So you don't have to feel guilty anymore. You're off the hook. Now can you leave?" Charlie was on the verge of losing it and didn't want Tyson to be there when she did. She wouldn't let him see her fall apart, ever.

"I just keep thinking that if I'd left earlier, or not stopped for gas, or, I don't know. I just didn't know. I was so torn up after I saw that guy. I love Gideon so much. And I thought you did too."

Charlie exploded at his asinine insinuation. "I do! How can you even question that? How?" Where was he was going with this? Why would her being raped make him question her love for Gideon?

"I just left. I wish I'd come upstairs and confronted you then, right at that moment. Then I would have been there for you. I could have been the one you relied on. Instead, I ran. I ran from you and from Paige like a coward. Goddamn it!"

Charlie couldn't speak—she could barely breathe. *Confronted me? He thought I'd done something wrong?* Maybe it was the weight of the past two days, or maybe she was missing something, but Charlie couldn't put the pieces of this puzzle together.

"I just wasn't able to handle it. I mean, the whole thing with Paige was so new, I couldn't talk to her. And the one person I could always talk to was gone—and he was *so* not the person I could talk to about this anyway. So I did nothing."

Then it clicked.

"Wait. You thought what, Tyson? That I invited that animal into my home? That I wanted him to violate me?" Charlie was horrified.

"I didn't know that's what had happened. I only knew what I saw. You didn't tell me. You didn't tell anyone. I thought he was your… Fuck! I'm such an ass! I thought you were cheating on Gideon." Tyson's voice was barely a whisper as he finally got to the point.

Charlie was horrified. He'd thought she was the type of person who'd send her husband off to fight for his country and two weeks later take another man to her bed. She wanted to yell and scream. Yet somehow, at the same time, Charlie felt bad for Tyson. She was torn between hating him for thinking she could hurt Gideon that way and wanting to pull him into a hug and soothe the tremendous guilt he felt. Then Tyson spoke again and what was left of Charlie's life came crumbling down around her.

"I kept it to myself…until…"

Until? What did that mean? He kept it to himself until what? Oh no. What did he do?

Charlie had to force herself to focus on what Tyson was saying. She came in halfway through his explanation.

"…were his. I felt I needed to tell him." He was no longer looking at her.

"Oh my God. What have you done?"

"I told Gideon. I told him you were cheating."

Suddenly Charlie was on her feet and no longer feeling defeated—she was mad. Livid. And hurt. Tyson stood to face her, ready for whatever she was going to throw at him. Charlie had the sense he was trying to take his punishment like a man—like this was some sort of test for him. She hated him in that moment. She wanted him to hurt the way she did.

"What is wrong with you? Are you that little and petty? Are you so jealous of Gideon that you could hurt him like this? Do you think so badly of me that you believe I could be that woman? Do you think I was just waiting for Gideon to leave so I could find a lover? That I'm some kind of whore? God, Tyson!"

Tyson said nothing. Fire burned inside Charlie. This was about more than just the last three months—this was about a lifetime.

"Gideon's a much better man than you! You'll never be like him, and that kills you! So instead of trying to better yourself, you decide to take from him, to tear him down? Why? Oh my God! He could get killed! Your stupidity could kill your brother!" Charlie's hands, resting on the small bump of her belly, balled into fists.

She flung herself at him and began to beat him, pummeling his chest. Tears were hot and wet on her cheeks. And the bastard wasn't even trying to stop her. He let her attack him. He'd given up, just like she'd done, and that made Charlie even angrier.

She knew then that *he* hadn't just raped her, *he* had destroyed her and everyone who cared about her. This was never going to end.

CHAPTER 28

Tyson took every single blow Charlie threw at him. He didn't even attempt to stop her. The entire time she beat on his chest, she cursed him, telling him how much she hated him. She said all the things he wanted her to say.

Finally someone was telling him the truth. Someone was telling him what a jealous, small man he truly was. Everything she said was true. Tyson *was* jealous of Gideon. He *did* want the life his brother had. He wanted people to look at him the way they looked at Gideon—with respect and admiration. But Tyson also loved Gideon more than any other person on the earth and hadn't done any of this to hurt him. He'd thought he was doing it to save his brother from getting hurt. He truly did.

"I hate you, Tyson! I hate you!" Charlie's fists kept beating, and he relished the punishment she doled out. He knew he deserved it.

"I'm sorry. I'm so sorry." Tyson kept repeating those words over and over.

When she began to tire, Tyson wrapped his arms around her, moving her to lie down on the couch. He couldn't protect her all those months ago, but he wanted to right now. He worried about how all this was affecting her and the babies, his nieces or nephews.

It was the first time Tyson had thought of them like that. Up until that moment, he'd refused to think of them much at all, always thinking there was a chance they were the other guy's.

"Charlie?"

She looked at him, all the anger still there. It hurt Tyson that he'd spent the last three months thinking she could have treated Gideon like that. He knew better. He knew she loved his brother.

"What? Is there more you need to tell me that will actually kill me?" Her voice was harsh, and Tyson worried she would never forgive him.

"I'll tell Gideon. I'll tell him I was wrong. I won't tell him about the other stuff."

"Rape, Tyson! I was raped! *He* took so much from me. And now, because of you, *he* will take the very last thing I have. I can't spend the rest of my life with Gideon looking at me like I'm weak and damaged. I won't."

"You have to give Gideon a chance to show you how much he loves you. When I told him what I saw, he wouldn't believe me. He hung up on me. I think even now he has doubts. He loves you. I'll talk to him."

"You can't. When he called this morning, he told me he's going deep. He won't call until they come out — for the rest of his deployment. You can't change this. He, oh God — "

Charlie didn't finish her sentence. It was like watching slow motion as her head swayed for a moment, and then her eyes fluttered closed.

"Charlie? Charlie! Wake up, Charlie!" Tyson didn't want to touch her. He worried he would scare her if she opened her eyes and he was there, touching her. He didn't know anything about the aftermath of rape. He never thought about shit like that. It made him wonder about his career choice. He'd have to comfort people through trauma. He didn't know if he could.

Tyson kept trying to wake her up, but nothing he did helped. He was scared. Over his lifetime, Tyson had felt a lot of emotions, but fear like he was feeling right then had never been one of them. Gideon wouldn't have been scared in this situation — he would have acted. Feeling ashamed, Tyson knew he needed to act. He needed to do this for Charlie, for Gideon, for their family.

While he wanted to take Charlie to the hospital or call his dad, Tyson knew she wouldn't want that. He didn't want to do anything more to hurt her, but he was worried. Her breathing was even. Her pulse was strong and steady, and her color was good. He went into the bathroom and ran cold water over a washcloth. When he returned to Charlie, her eyes were still closed, but she was stirring, which was a relief. He placed the cold cloth on her forehead and sat on the edge of the couch next to her, praying she'd wake up. If she didn't come to soon, he'd have to take her to the hospital.

It seemed like hours since Charlie had closed her eyes, but when Tyson looked at his watch he realized it couldn't have been more than a few minutes.

"Tyson?" His head snapped up at the sound of her voice. "Oh God. We can't get in touch with Gideon." It was as if their conversation hadn't been interrupted by her fainting.

"Charlie, thank God. You fainted. I was so worried."

"What are you talking about? I fainted? You didn't call Peter, did you?"

"No, it's only been a few minutes."

Tyson was taken by surprise when she kicked him and knocked him off the couch. He landed on his ass on the floor. When he looked up at Charlie, her eyes were flaming again.

"Well, thanks for that. But can you now get the hell out of my house? I don't want you around me. You aren't good for me, for us." She brushed her hand over her stomach. "Do you know what you've done? You have Gideon worried about this while people are trying to kill him! He may not come home! He may never see his children! *You* did that!"

Tyson was shocked—not because Charlie wanted him to leave, but because she was angry about Gideon. She hadn't said a word about the rape and how he'd missed the whole thing, how he hadn't been able to save her. All she cared about was Gideon.

"I'll go, but please let me call someone to come and stay with you for a while. I'm worried. I want to make sure you're okay. I'll call Chance."

"No. I don't want Chance."

"Sorry, I thought having someone who doesn't know would be better. Do you want me to call Paige?"

"Chance does know. And if he finds out about this, I won't be able to stand it. He's going to want to kill you, Tyson. Gideon…I don't know what he's going to do."

"You need to calm down. I'll call Paige." This was even worse than Tyson had imagined. He hadn't thought Charlie would forgive him, but he never expected he'd endanger her or the babies.

Tyson called Paige. The phone rang four times before the answering machine picked up. Panic built in his belly. What was he going to do if he couldn't get a hold of her? He couldn't leave Charlie alone, and there was no one else to call. The beep signaled to leave a message.

"Paige? I…yeah…um…"

"Tyson?" Paige picked up.

"Yeah, Charlie needs someone to stay with her for a while. Can you come over?"

"What happened? Is she okay?"

"She seems fine now, but she passed out for a few minutes. I don't want her to be alone, and she doesn't want to go to the hospital. So can you come?" Tyson knew he was begging for more than just having her come to Charlie; he was begging her to remain part of his life.

"Of course I'll come. Give me a half an hour."

"Okay. Paige?"

"Yeah?"

"I love you." Tyson hung up before she had a chance to say anything.

By the time Tyson opened the door for Paige, he was in a panic. One thing he was sure of—the *only* thing he was sure of—was that Charlie would never survive something happening to the babies.

"Where's Charlie? What happened?" Paige immediately tried to calm him, letting her hand drift up to cup his cheek. He wanted nothing more than to absorb her into him, but she hadn't come for him. Quickly pulling away, he turned back into the house with Paige following.

"Thank God you came. She doesn't want me here, and I don't want to upset her any more. I'm so worried."

"Where is she?" Paige asked again.

"In the bedroom. Can you take care of her? Please? I know she trusts you, and God knows I don't have any right to ask you to be part of this." Tyson's eyes never met Paige's as he watched his feet. They still had so much to work through, but right then he had to focus on Charlie and her safety.

"I'm Charlie's friend, Tyson. I want to help her."

"She hates me, Paige. Fuck! I can't really blame her, but I swear I never started out trying to hurt her or Gideon…or you."

Then he looked up at Paige and realized that while he might not be the smartest guy in the world, he was definitely the luckiest. He could read on Paige's face her need to make everything better for him.

"I'm gonna go," he said, hope filling his heart. "I'll call later."

CHAPTER 29

Evelyn looked around the room, finally satisfied with the adjustments she'd made. Everything was perfect, unlike her family.

Sitting in one of the two chairs in the room, she sighed as she tried to figure out when everything had gone so wrong. Gabriella's outburst at Christmas had forced her to look at what was happening around her, and none of it was good.

It wasn't as if she hadn't noticed Tyson acting cool toward Charlie, but she'd thought he was having a hard time with Gideon being gone. After Christmas, Evelyn had to look closer and see what she didn't want to. She was then convinced Tyson was jealous that Gideon and Charlie were going to have a baby. Tyson had finally been coming into his own, trying to be a new man for Paige, and then Charlie announced the news about the baby. That was when Evelyn noticed the change.

It had been almost two months since that awful Christmas dinner, and things had gotten perhaps not better, but more civil. Charlie came by every few days, but she refused to stay more than a few hours.

She'd allowed Evelyn to go to some of her doctor's appointments with her. Each time she heard her grandbabies' heartbeats, her own heart sang with joy. No matter what else was happening, those babies were going to be loved and cared for. Of course, Evelyn kept trying to get the doctor to tell her the sexes of those precious babies, but the doctor wouldn't budge.

Tyson and Paige had also been over a few times during the past weeks. They came for dinner, and everyone would talk and laugh together. But the couple was different now. Before, Tyson was always as close to Paige as he could possibly be, his hand resting somewhere on her body. Now they were comfortable sitting on opposite sides of the table, just talking. And when they left, Tyson's touch was light and tentative as he moved his hand to the small of her back to guide her out the door.

Evelyn hadn't asked him about it. She could tell he wasn't ready to talk…yet. He'd let her know when he wanted to talk about Paige, about his life, or even about his relationship with his brother and Charlie. Evelyn knew better than to press.

"Mom?" Tyson's voice carried up from the entry hall.

"I'm upstairs, dear. Come on up," Evelyn called back to him. A small smile played on her lips. She felt smug in her assessment of her son. She knew him so well. He was ready to talk. Now she just needed to ask the right questions.

"Hey, Mom. Oh, good Lord in Heaven!" Tyson stopped in the open doorway and looked around the room. "Gideon's going to kill you. You know that, right?"

"Your brother will not kill me. He'll see the practicality of having a fully stocked nursery here."

"Yeah, but didn't he say you weren't allowed to buy anything for the babies until he came home? Mom, this is more than the few blankets and outfits you were trying to pass off as gifts for Charlie. This is a whole damn nursery!"

Evelyn was proud of the job she'd done on the room. The identical wooden cribs had matching neutral bedding, with pops of color in muted pastels. The coordinating changing table was fully stocked with diapers, wipes, and anything else the babies might need. In opposite corners of the room were two very different rocking chairs—the rockers Evelyn had used for Gideon and Tyson.

Peter had gotten the chairs out of the attic and had them refinished as a surprise for her. Gideon's was a light oak, strong and sturdy. It fit easily into any room and stood out, even when set into a deep corner. Tyson's chair was a dark cherry, beautiful and polished. This one needed a special spot where it could be noticed. Evelyn loved them both dearly.

"I'm going to be the grandmother, and I can do whatever I want in my own home."

Tyson laughed, and it was the first time in a while that he'd seemed truly happy. "Whatever, Mom." He sat in the empty chair, Gideon's chair.

Silence stretched between mother and son. Then Tyson took a deep breath.

"Mom, I need to talk to you for a minute."

"You know I'm always here for you boys." Evelyn sat back in the chair.

"I know you've seen a difference between Paige and me." He looked at his mother who nodded, encouraging him to go on. "Well, I did something really stupid a while back. That's something for another time. It has to do with Charlie and Gideon, and I'm not comfortable talking about it unless they're here too."

"Tyson, what did you do? Is this why you've been so rude to Charlie?"

When he mentioned Charlie and Gideon, Evelyn saw a flash of Charlie's face on Christmas night — all the pain and hurt as she ran out of the room. Was Tyson responsible for that?

"Mom, when Gideon comes home I'm sure he'll insist on sitting down with the family and pointing out exactly what I did. Right now I don't want to talk about it. No, I *can't* talk about it without them. Just know that I'm trying to fix it. Can we leave it at that for now?"

Evelyn had never heard Tyson so responsible, so grown up, and she felt a lump in her throat. Evelyn's baby was finally a man.

"Okay, I guess I have to accept that and wait for your brother. But you wanted to talk about Paige, didn't you? I like her, Tyson."

"Yeah, me too. The thing is, we've been kind of taking it easy for the past couple of months. Part of it is about what's going on with Gideon and Charlie, but also something happened over Thanksgiving. I want her to be sure she wants to be with me. I mean, I know what kind of guy I've been. You know too. I've seen how you look at me sometimes — like you could see what was waiting for me, and you were disappointed I hadn't found it yet."

Evelyn started to protest, not because Tyson was wrong, but because she needed him to know she was always sure he'd find it one day. She'd always believed in him.

"It's okay. You were right. I've spent so much of my life *not* being Gideon that I never figured out who I *should* be. Does that make sense? So Paige and I have just been dating lately, and it's been great. I mean, I know I love being around her, but I also know I'm not changing *for* her, but more because of her. Here's the thing though, I kind of made her go out with another guy." He lowered his head in embarrassment.

"Tyson Lawrence Cooper! Why would you do something like that?"

"I had to be sure she wasn't missing something by picking me. I know it was stupid, but what was even more stupid was that I showed up on her date."

"Tyson! Good Lord. How can such a smart man act like such a stupid boy?"

"I know, I know. It took everything I had not to throw her over my shoulder and haul her out of the damn café like a caveman. I love her, Mom."

"So what's the problem?"

"I'm scared."

"Oh, Tyson, don't be scared. She loves you. I'm willing to bet she wasn't all that keen on your experiment. She's a smart girl. You can't treat her like she isn't. And that's what you've done. You've questioned her judgment. Fix it, Tyson."

"I want to, but what if it's too late? What if I screwed this whole thing up?"

The twins were kicking again, and Charlie rolled over, hoping they'd settle so she could go back to sleep. The clock read three in the morning. It had become routine for the twins to dance a two-step at this time just about every morning, and Charlie was exhausted. Fortunately, her life pretty much consisted of reading pregnancy books, plus spending a few hours with Evelyn and the rest with Oprah and Judge Judy, so she was able to catch up on her sleep.

As she lay in the dark, waiting for the critters to stop their *Dancing With the Stars* routine, Charlie thought about what they'd be entering into.

So much had changed over these past weeks. Having Gabby and Chance know about *the incident* was a relief *and* another burden for Charlie. It was good not to have to pretend around them, but she could tell they were uncomfortable now. And then there was Tyson's little confession… The thought of Gideon worrying about something so ridiculous sent Charlie into a total tailspin. She still wanted to kill the little prick. He was worried about not helping her at the time of *the incident*, and all she could think was that he may have killed her husband.

Thank God for Paige.

Paige had spent the three days after Tyson's bombshell with Charlie—taking care of her, making sure she actually ate and got out of bed. She'd called Charlie's therapist, trying to get an emergency session, but Dr. Lassiter was out of town for the holidays and could only give Paige another doctor's name. Charlie wouldn't consider going to someone else, so instead

Paige let her cry and express all her fears for Gideon and the babies. Paige smoothed Charlie's hair, rubbed her back, and made tea, but she never told her everything was going to be all right. Charlie knew she wasn't sure it was going to be.

Charlie could tell things were different for Paige and Tyson too. Paige had told her about Tyson's ridiculous idea that she date other people. Charlie tried to be a good friend and listen and give Paige advice, but she couldn't bring herself to worry too much about Tyson. She did feel bad for Paige and wanted to be someone she could talk to, but whenever Tyson came up, Charlie's anger got the best of her, and she had to change the subject.

In those weeks, Charlie tried again to get her life back. She returned to therapy after the holidays, and Dr. Lassiter was pleased she'd been able to confide in more people. The fact that circumstances now dictated that Charlie would have to tell Gideon about everything was something they talked about extensively. Charlie still didn't know if she could stand to see on Gideon's face that look she'd seen from everyone else.

Somewhere during this attempt to get back to normal, it occurred to Charlie that she hadn't seen Zoe since they'd gone to Disneyland. She felt guilty for that, knowing Zoe was missing Jaylon as much as she was missing Gideon. Zoe didn't even know about the babies. But when she tried to call, none of the numbers Charlie had for her friend were in service, and she wondered if she was tired of being alone and had gone home to her parents. All Charlie knew was that Zoe's parents lived somewhere back east.

The thing that helped Charlie the most was the letter she'd received near the end of January. She'd been holed up in the house for a few days, avoiding the "help" of her friends and family. Charlie appreciated their concern, but there were some days she just couldn't be the Charlie they needed her to be. On those days her only option was to lock herself in the house and rest. On one of those days Charlie had gone to the mailbox and nearly keeled over when she saw the letter. It was from Gideon.

She couldn't bring herself to open it for almost a whole day. She just held the sealed envelope in her fist, imagining every possible scenario. Gideon thought she was sleeping with another man, so she didn't see how anything in that letter could be good. She convinced herself he was going to tell her he didn't want her anymore. She decided never to open that damn envelope.

Being a woman, however, Charlie couldn't *not* open the stupid thing, so she did it in baby steps: first opening the envelope, then hours later taking the folded paper out. Another few hours passed before Charlie could bring herself to unfold it, and then right before she went to bed, she read it. The paper shook in her hand as she talked herself into reading the words. Just the sight of Gideon's handwriting made her heart flutter, and the ache of missing him was so strong she actually felt pain.

> Charlie,
>
> I only have a minute. What I said was true. I won't have any comm. or mail for the next few months. I'll be lucky to get this out, but I had to tell you this:
>
> I LOVE YOU.
>
> No matter what happens, know that.
>
> We'll talk when I get home.
>
> Joe

Charlie had cried for hours. It was the only communication she'd had from him, and she couldn't help but think it might be the last.

Now, weeks after first reading those words, Charlie reached over to the nightstand and picked up the letter. The envelope was dirty and wrinkled because she carried it with her everywhere and often fell asleep clutching it. As she held it, the twins calmed and Charlie was able to ease back to sleep. It made her smile to think they were calmed by Gideon's words too.

When Charlie woke again, the room was filled with light. These early-morning wakeup calls from the babies were throwing off her internal clock, and Charlie wasn't all that surprised to see it was almost eleven. She stretched and yawned as she rolled out of bed. Her stomach rumbled, and she decided to skip the shower for now and went to the kitchen for some breakfast.

Charlie stood in front of the open refrigerator trying to decide if chips and dip would be a proper meal when her cell phone buzzed. The vibrating noise as it danced across the counter startled her, and she swore after stubbing her toe as she tried to get to it.

"Nice way to answer the phone."

"Oh my God! Gideon!" Tears pricked Charlie's eyes at the sound of his voice. It had been so long. She glanced at the calendar to gauge just how long it'd been since she'd heard his voice. Well, crap! Wasn't that just perfect—it was Valentine's Day.

"Come open the door, Charlie."

CHAPTER 30

The flight home had been the worst of Gideon's life — and he'd been in a few crashes and had to punch out of a few flights (parachute landings sucked), so that was saying something. Fox had been sitting next to him, and Gideon was glad they were going commercial because the more comfortable flight allowed him to put in his ear buds, crank his iPod, and fake sleep, effectively avoiding Jaylon's questioning glare.

His buddy knew he was torn up. Gideon appreciated that Fox wanted to help, but he didn't want to spend all those hours rehashing what he was going through. He just wanted to get lost in his own thoughts.

As Gideon approached the front door of the little house Charlie had moved into, he realized he didn't have keys, so he hit the speed dial for Charlie's cell.

"Goddamn it!" He heard Charlie's voice, and the thought that she was just on the other side of the door made him nervous. Gideon hadn't decided how this was going to go, and until he saw her…he wouldn't.

When she realized who it was, Charlie's tone immediately changed. All Gideon did was ask her to come open the door, but when he didn't hear any footsteps, he tried again, "Charlie, I don't have a key to this place. Can you please come open the door for me?"

When she opened the door, Gideon's breath caught. She was still the most beautiful woman he'd ever laid eyes on. In that brief second before she launched herself at him, Gideon knew he couldn't ever leave her…them.

Gideon pulled back slightly, and his eyes fell on the small, perfect bump of her belly. He couldn't help but reach out and hold it. *They're mine… they're mine…they're mine…* He kept running those words through his head.

If he didn't believe those words, he wouldn't be able to get through this. *They're mine…they're mine…they're mine…* And then something else a little bigger caught Gideon's eye, and he couldn't help as his smile spread wider. *They're mine…they're mine…they're mine…* His focus was now solely on her breasts, and something changed between them. Charlie pulled away from him—just a fraction, but she pulled away.

"You're beautiful, Charlie." Gideon thought maybe she was worried he didn't find her attractive anymore. That apparently wasn't a problem as he was instantly rock hard, even with the prospect of the brutal conversation looming in front of him.

Suddenly, Gideon felt a wave move under his hands, which still rested on her stomach, and he quickly pulled them back, his eyes wide with worry.

"It's all right, Joe. They're just happy to see you. They must know their daddy."

Gideon moved to lay his hands on his kids again. Never before had he felt something as overpowering as his babies' movements in his wife's womb. Then the reality of what was between them came rushing back.

"Charlie…" He wanted to tell her he loved her and would fight for her and for this family he wanted so badly to be his. The words just weren't there.

"Gideon."

He kept his gaze on his hands as he marveled at the lives growing beneath them, and he tried not to get all nancied out by the whole thing.

"Gideon, look at me, please."

"Damn it, Charlie. I don't know what to do here." The moment of truth was approaching fast, and there was no slowing it down. They had to get some shit sorted out or Gideon was going to explode.

"I know why you're worried, and you don't have to be. I love you."

Gideon's arms wrapped around Charlie as she tried to push her body as close to his as possible. The words she'd spoken had so many meanings, and while his heart was pounding at the surface meaning of the statement, his mind twisted and turned her words until they were a jumbled mess.

The couple stood together for a long time. Charlie never wanted the feeling of him holding her to end. She knew as soon as they let go, they were going to talk.

Charlie cursed *him* for taking yet one more thing away from her. She wasn't going to get to give her husband the happy welcome home other wives were giving their husbands right then. Instead, Charlie was going to have to tell the man she loved more than anything else in the world what had happened to her. While she blamed *him* for the most part, Charlie couldn't help but think this was Tyson's fault too. If Tyson hadn't told Gideon what he thought she was doing, it would have been easy to fake her way through this. She might even have been happy.

Gideon pulled away, his hands slowly sliding off Charlie's belly. Instantly she felt coldness fill the space between them as he began to look around the unfamiliar room.

"So, this is the new place, huh? It's nice," he commented. His voice was so controlled and sounded strange to Charlie. He didn't sound like her Gideon.

"Yeah. I didn't do the nursery though." She wanted him to know his ideas and his participation in their babies' lives were important to her. "I can't say the same for your mom, however. Did you go home first?" The question was loaded with all the things she wanted to know.

"Yeah, I came here." Gideon knew what Charlie was asking, but his reply let her know he still thought of life with her as "home," although his response was without emotion. He was obviously trying to control himself.

"Why are you home, Gideon? I mean, I'm so glad—but it's only February. I thought you'd be gone for two more months?" That wasn't the way she'd wanted the question to come out.

Gideon raised his eyebrows, and Charlie knew he was taking it the wrong way.

"We finished the mission. It was faster than we thought, and there was nothing else for us to do, so they sent us home." All business. That was all Charlie could hear. There was no warmth in his tone.

Charlie stayed glued to her spot near the front door as Gideon explored their new home. A few minutes later, he came back in to the living room and fell onto the couch. He looked so tired. Charlie wanted to crawl into bed with him and lay next to him while he slept. She definitely *didn't* want to have the conversation that was inevitable.

The silence around them was heavy. Neither wanted to acknowledge what they had to talk about.

When Gideon leaned forward, laying his forearms on his thighs and taking a deep breath, Charlie knew it was about to happen. Her stomach started to knot, her hands began to sweat, and the tears that were building made her vision blur. She hoped she wouldn't pass out.

"Charlie," Gideon took another deep breath and Charlie mimicked him, trying to calm herself. She wanted to throw herself at him and beg him to trust her, to tell him she loved him and would never hurt him. But instead, she sat in the chair across from him. They were in the same positions she and Tyson had been in just a few weeks ago.

"I'm not one to put this kind of shit off. I can't pretend that this is all happy-happy, joy-joy," Gideon continued. Normally the use of their word would have brought a smile to her face, but Charlie focused only on the pain floating in Gideon's eyes.

"Gideon, please…" Charlie wasn't sure what she was begging for. She just wanted him to hear her voice, to know she was hurting.

"I think you know about the conversation I had with Tyson a few months ago."

He stopped and looked at Charlie. Charlie simply nodded.

"Yeah, the one where he described in detail how he ran into a very satisfied asshole zipping up as he walked out of our apartment. This is *so* not the kind of shit I need to hear about while I'm getting my ass shot at."

Gideon's tone was cold and detached. He was all SEAL: moving forward on his mission, laying it all out so he could target the enemy. Unfortunately, Charlie was in the bull's-eye.

"Gideon." Charlie tried to hold back the tears, barely able to see him through the haze.

"So I've had a few months to think about this. I need to know. I can't just pretend I don't know. I can't look at you and wonder why you needed someone else, why I wasn't enough for you. I know I left you, but not because I wanted to. It's my job. I do love you, but…"

The "but" scared the hell out of Charlie. The thought that she could keep Gideon without telling him *everything*—it vanished with that one word. She was going to have to tell him about *the incident*…the rape. She would tell him every detail—things she hadn't told anyone, not even Dr. Lassiter. And she was going to have to do it now, before he finished that sentence.

"Gideon, I love you," she began. "I know what Tyson told you. I found out right after you told me you were going deep with no communication. And although I finally understood all those weeks you'd been so distant with me, all the hurt you must have felt, it also scared the hell out of me. To think of you worrying all that time? Oh God! You could have been killed."

The tears finally came, and when Charlie looked at Gideon, she knew he'd offer no comfort for her sorrow. He was so angry that he focused solely on trying to maintain perfect control.

"Yeah, well, I'm home now."

Charlie could actually feel her soul begin to fracture, small fissures threatening to shatter it. She didn't know if even the truth would repair him.

"I didn't cheat on you. I would never cheat on you. It hurts to think you could believe for one minute I would do that to you."

Being defensive probably wasn't going to help the situation, but Charlie couldn't stop. The thought of telling her husband what his fellow sailor did just seemed like too much.

"That's what I thought! I thought you loved me — only me!" His cool demeanor broke and he was up off the couch, his big body hunched in pain. "But what can I think, Charlie? I mean, you were so mad at me for leaving, and then Tyson saw the guy. I know my brother's a dickhead sometimes, but he wouldn't track me down just to lie to me! So did he? Did Tyson lie to me about this?"

"No. He didn't lie about what he saw."

Gideon moved toward the door. Charlie felt like she was watching her life, her future, walk away. She had to stop him. She had to tell him. Nausea washed over her, but she held it off. She prayed for the right words, unsure if there even were right words.

"I was raped."

Charlie's voice was only a whisper, but he heard her. He stopped in his tracks, his hand on the doorknob.

She prayed he wouldn't look at her. She couldn't go on with the story if he were to look at her. "What Tyson saw was after *he* was done. *He* was leaving."

Gideon turned around, his eyes wide. Charlie quickly looked at the floor. She didn't want him to talk, so she continued.

"It was someone from the base. He said you'd asked him to check in on me. God, I never should have let him in. I'm so stupid." She never raised her eyes to his, not wanting to see that look: the one she'd seen in the eyse of Paige, Chance, Gabby, and Tyson. Charlie couldn't stand to have Gideon look at her like that.

Suddenly Gideon was pulling her into his arms, and as much as she wanted to be there, Charlie couldn't tell him her story that way. It was too close, too much to have someone touching her while she explained every-thing that happened that day.

"I love you, Gideon. But I can't do this like this. I can't have you hold-ing me. I'm so sorry. It's just…"

Without a word, he stumbled back and sank into the couch again. Charlie had hurt him by pushing him away, but she had to do it. This was the only way she could tell him.

When Gideon looked up at Charlie again, the anger was gone. When she looked she saw shame and fear — but no pity. He wasn't looking at her like she was damaged.

Sitting in the chair, Charlie lowered her eyes and watched her hands rub over her belly as she told Gideon what *he* had done to her. She heard his gasps and curses, but didn't look up at him. That would have broken her.

"He said he knew where you were, and he could hurt you. He knew more than I did! There was nothing I could do." Charlie sobbed, her whole body convulsing. There was a brush of cloth against cloth, and she knew Gideon had moved off the couch. Then Charlie felt his arms around her as he pulled her into him, rocking her and kissing the top of her head.

"I'm sorry, baby. Fuck! I should've been here. If I'd been here he never could have gotten to you. Who was it, Charlie? What was his name?"

Charlie stiffened. She hadn't said his name since that day. Saying his name would make *him* real.

Gideon tried to soothe her, rubbing his hands over her back. "It's okay, baby. I just need his name."

Charlie didn't want to tell him. Not because she was afraid, but be-cause she didn't want Gideon to hurt *him*. Charlie couldn't lose Gideon now…not ever.

"Charlie, we have to do something about this. I need to know who did this to you."

"C-Cody B-Boyd."

CHAPTER 31

Gideon sat and listened as his wife told him what that animal had done to her. He wanted to kill him. He wanted to be the one who made him breathe his final breath. Dead would never be good enough for the sick fuck who'd hurt Charlie.

Gideon hated himself for what happened to her. And for the first time since he'd joined up, Gideon hated his job for taking him away and leaving her so vulnerable.

Gideon's vision went white hot when Charlie said Boyd's name. The fact that he'd laid his hands on her in any way was enough to earn him a death sentence, and if he'd done what Charlie said, Gideon would have to make it hurt badly when he did it.

For almost three months Gideon had struggled with what Tyson told him. The thought of Charlie with another man drove him nearly crazy. What Tyson had described didn't match what Charlie was telling him, but he saw how hurt and broken she was. How could Boyd do that and then just saunter out? Had Charlie asked him over and things got carried away?

None of it made sense to Gideon's logical, engineering mind. He had to know for sure; he needed to find out from Boyd.

"Charlie, I have to leave. I'm sorry. I know I'm a total shit for leaving, but I, I just have to." Gideon didn't know how much time had passed while the two of them held on to each other. The look on Charlie's face physically hurt him, like someone had punched into his heart and was trying to drag the thing out of his chest. Gideon's heart tried to protest and make him stay to comfort her, but unfortunately, it was already battle weary and couldn't put up much of a fight.

"What are you going to do? Are you coming back? Please, just stay here with me. I need you," Charlie pleaded.

Gideon had to turn away from her or he was going to change his mind. It occurred to him that he didn't have keys to his truck. He was so disoriented. This was not his house, not his Charlie, not his life. Everything was off. Everything was fucked up!

He looked around and found what he was looking for. In the apartment, they'd had a key holder in the kitchen by the phone. Sure enough, it was in the same spot here too. In fact, as Gideon surveyed the house, he noticed it was set up pretty much like the apartment had been. He let out a small, humorless laugh—it reflected how his life was now: It looked the same, but it was completely different. Everything was different.

For the first time since he'd gotten back, Gideon felt at home when he climbed into his truck. It was the one thing in his life that hadn't changed. The drive to the base allowed him time to process some of the information he now had. Gideon wanted to hurt his little brother. The one time he'd asked something from Tyson, and his brother couldn't even man up enough to do that. Gideon wanted to strangle him for not finding out the fucking truth before he decided to be all noble and tell him.

As he walked into the office, Gideon knew no matter the outcome of their "discussion," he couldn't touch Boyd there. It made no difference what the guy said, Gideon already wanted to make him hurt. He wasn't, however, in the mood to be arrested for assaulting a fellow sailor.

Luck was with Gideon as he caught Boyd coming out of the head, zipping up as he stepped into the hall. The scene Tyson had described flashed in Gideon's mind. *This self-satisfied prick walking out of my house after being with my wife…* His hands instinctively balled into fists, and Gideon had to use every ounce of self-control not to lay the fucker out right then and there.

"Hey, Boyd." Gideon tried to hide his building hatred. He was supposed to be able to trust this guy with his life. Cody Boyd was Gideon's teammate, his brother.

"Cooper? I thought you'd be on leave for a few weeks."

Gideon wanted to pound him into the ground. "Yeah, I am. Just had a few things I needed to clear up here."

"Oh?"

Gideon's façade slipped slightly, and Boyd's eyes flashed fear for a split second.

"Charlie and I had a little talk this morning." Gideon stepped closer to the other man, wanting him to know he meant what he was about to say. The look on Boyd's face changed.

Gideon lowered his voice; this conversation didn't need to be public. "She said you paid her a visit. And right now, I need a reason *not* to kill you."

"Look, dude. I didn't want to tell you. I mean, I just went to make sure she was okay." Gideon stood silently, staring at Boyd. His plan was to let him get it all out, see where this went.

"I knew you being gone would be hard on her, and I thought I could help if she needed someone to talk to."

Gideon nodded, indicating for him to continue.

"She came on to me, man." Boyd started to back away.

"That's not what she told me, *man*." Gideon spat out the last word.

"Well, of course she lied to you. She's not going to tell you she slid down my body, grabbed my dick, and told me she wanted to give me a blow job. It's not like she's stupid, dude."

Everything stopped in those few seconds. When the words "blow job" came out of the prick's mouth, Gideon's heart stopped beating. His breathing stopped. His whole world stopped turning.

"Really? What exactly did she say? I mean, word for word."

Cody's face broke into a smirk. He thought Gideon was buying his load of crap.

Gideon wanted to wipe the grin right off his face, but he controlled himself. Later, he'd look back and wonder how he managed not to wrap his hands around Boyd's neck and squeeze the life out of him. His feet stayed glued to their spot and he continually curled and uncurled his fingers into fists as he waited for Boyd to tell him how he'd violated his wife, to tell him how his sick, fucking mind thought raping a woman—Gideon had to swallow back the bile that bubbled up in his throat when he realized the woman was Charlie—was her wanting him.

"She had her hands all over me, and I was, like, 'No. We can't do this.' Then her hand stopped, and she grabbed my package. She looked right at me and said, 'Let me give you the best blow job you've ever had. I promise I can rock your world.' Come on, your wife's smokin' hot. After that, I was rock hard, and since she'd offered…"

Thoroughly pleased with himself, Boyd looked back at Gideon, the fucking grin still in place.

Anger roared through Gideon. *Fucking liar!*

He thought briefly about how Charlie's face would light up when she talked about bringing "joy" to his life, and Gideon's heart broke again. She *never* said blow job; it was always joy. Gideon stood stock still. Every emotion he had flowed over him: relief Charlie hadn't cheated, pain for Charlie's anguish, hatred of the prick in front of him. Gideon suddenly needed to get home and tell his wife he knew the truth.

"Dude, it only happened that one time. I stayed the hell away after that." The monster's voice cracked, offering further proof he was lying.

Gideon stepped in to him and offered his hand, still unsure whether he could control himself—and caring less and less. Boyd took Gideon's hand to shake it. Gideon pulled him into a one-armed hug and whispered in the prick's ear: "I know you're fucking lying. While I can't kill you here and now, don't doubt that I *will* do it." He released Boyd with a small push so he stumbled backward. The look on his face wasn't fear, as Gideon had expected it would be. He looked smug.

"She was the best of all of them. Sweet and tight," he hissed at Gideon. Then, as if he was *trying* to get Gideon to kill him, he added, "I do wish she would've fought more. The orgasm's so much more satisfying for me when I have to work for it."

Gideon's fist immediately went into the wall. He wanted it to be Boyd's face, and he was about to make that fantasy a reality when he heard her voice.

"Gideon, please don't. I need you with me."

Turning around, Gideon found Charlie. Tears streamed down her cheeks, and her hands rested on the bump of her belly. From the look in her eyes he could tell she'd heard every word the scumbag said.

"Cooper, you didn't tell me I might be a daddy!" Boyd's eyes fell on Charlie's pregnant belly.

Gideon snapped. He saw himself breaking the guy's neck, watching the life drain out of him. He wanted to make him hurt. Maybe snapping his neck would be too easy. With all his training Gideon knew just what he could do to kill him slowly. He wanted him to bleed for all the pain he'd caused Charlie, for what he'd taken from all of them.

Fuck it! Gideon thought.

But Charlie threw herself at him, and his body reacted to the feel of her in his arms. He wrapped himself around her, protecting her now, even if he hadn't protected her then.

CHAPTER 32

As he knocked on Paige's door, Tyson worried about the evening ahead. The time he'd spent with his mom had helped him know what he needed to do, and for the first time, Tyson was doing what *he* wanted. His whole life had been spent trying not to be himself because he thought that would never be good enough — he'd never be Gideon.

He'd taken the easier path instead. If no one expected anything of him, he couldn't let them down. Tyson could remember worshiping his brother as a kid. He knew even back then he couldn't compare to Gideon. But he didn't have to. In school, at home, in sports — Tyson never *had* to compete with his brother. He just needed to be Tyson; that would've been enough.

Now he was going to do just that. This time, he was going to do what he thought Tyson should do, not what he thought Gideon *wouldn't* do.

When Paige opened the door, Tyson wasn't sure what to expect. He'd been secretive about what they were going to do, and he knew she was still upset about him showing up on her date. But the thought of another guy near her had scrambled Tyson's mind. When Tyson saw Paige with that guy, he suddenly realized how it must have driven Gideon crazy to know what he'd seen outside their apartment.

Charlie had been right; he was an asshole, and maybe he did want to make Gideon hurt when he told him. He never thought about it that way. Sure, he'd had that twinge of guilt and second thoughts about whether he should tell him, but he'd told him. He didn't have to, but he did. Now Tyson was living with the hurt and pain he'd caused Charlie, and the possibility that Gideon might not come home because of what he'd done.

Tyson immediately noticed Paige was wearing the necklace he'd given her for Christmas. She hadn't worn it since that day, and he took its presence now as a sign he was about to do the right thing.

"Hi," she said shyly. It was strange to be so shy with each other these days. It was as if they were working backward.

"Hi. Paige, before we go, I want to apologize to you."

"Yeah, you're kind of an ass, Tyson. I can't believe you showed up on the date that *you* insisted I go on, but I forgive you. So where're we going? Being told to dress casually for a Valentine's date doesn't exactly instill confidence, I gotta tell ya."

Paige was joking, but Tyson's feeling that he'd screwed things up beyond repair grew slightly stronger. Nevertheless, he smiled wide and grabbed her hand to pull her out of the apartment. "That's still a surprise," he said.

As the couple drove west, their conversation was stilted. Tyson didn't know what to say. He wanted to wait until they got to their destination to bring up the reason for this night. There was a picnic packed in the trunk, and Tyson hoped things would unfold the way he'd planned.

When he pulled into the parking lot at the beach, Tyson watched for Paige's reaction. He was pleased when she recognized where they were.

"You didn't bring me here to make out on Valentine's Day, did you?"

"What? You don't want to spend the night with your feet against the windshield again?" Tyson teased as he got out of the car.

"Why, Mr. Cooper, you thought of everything this time," Paige commented when she saw the basket and blanket in his arms.

Tyson held the door open as she stepped out of the car. "Well, I'd love to take credit for everything, but Evelyn deserves the accolades for the meal. The idea was mine, though."

Tyson took Paige's hand and led her onto the beach. Finding a little alcove, he spread the blanket. As they looked out over the Pacific, blue-green waves crashed against the sand, and the sun started to sink over the horizon. Later, after they'd worked their way through Evelyn's fried chicken and potato salad and were getting ready to dig into the individual tarts she'd packed, Tyson turned to Paige. She froze in place with the plastic fork halfway to her mouth.

"Paige, I need to talk to you."

"No. No, no, no. You're not going to do this on Valentine's Day."

This was not the reaction Tyson had planned. He should've known she'd think he was going to break things off for good.

"Oh, no. That's not it. Shit! I was trying to be all romantic and do this right, but…aww crap!" Tyson took her hand. "Okay. My entire life I've been trying *not* to be Gideon. I don't know if I've ever told you this before, but I always thought Gideon was better than me, that he was more than me."

"Oh, Tyson."

"No, that's not what this is about. I'm only telling you to explain some things. I want you to know that's the reason this whole situation has blown up so much. I don't know if I did what I did to hurt Gideon or to try to destroy something in his life. I just don't know now. But because I've been trying so hard *not* to be Gideon, I've made some big mistakes in my life."

"I don't believe you intentionally hurt Gideon or Charlie. Honestly."

She was going to make him go completely girlie with all this "believing in him" stuff. Tyson never realized anyone believed in him, and now, in just twenty-four hours, he'd found two people who did.

He took a deep breath and continued. "The reason I'm telling you this is because my belief that I could never be Gideon has influenced me so much, in so many decisions I've made, including us."

Paige's eyebrows knit together.

"Let me explain," he said. "I knew from the first time you let me kiss you that I didn't ever want any other woman in my life. I think I even knew then that you were the one I wanted to stand with for the rest of my life."

Although Tyson felt like she could see deep into him, he had to continue. The sun was now moving fast below the line of the sea, and he didn't think his newest mini-flashlight would do the trick for both of them. "Paige, I know I've screwed up so much lately. My past is one I'm not proud of. The reason I wanted to let you go a little was because I didn't want to rush in to this. I didn't want to be Charlie and Gideon. Even though I wanted you from the beginning, even though I probably would've run off to Vegas with you months ago, I didn't. Because that's what Gideon did. But I'm done. I'm done worrying about not being my brother, and I want you. I want you forever."

Paige stared at him, and Tyson was sure he'd screwed up. She was going to go running, screaming into the coming night. In hopes of stopping that from happening, he pulled a small box from his pocket. He opened it and held it out to her.

"Paige Halloran? I can't promise perfection—we all know I'm far from it—but I can promise to love you for the rest of my life and try as hard as I can to be the man you need me to be. Will you marry me?"

Paige sat there, not moving. There was no expression Tyson could discern, and his gut began to broil as he realized he'd fucked up once again.

"Um…uh…" Paige stammered.

"Okay then. I guess I have my answer." Tyson tried to hide his hurt as he closed the small box and slipped it back into his pocket.

"Wait." She reached out and touched his arm.

Tyson looked at her, but the expression on her face didn't make him feel any better. Her forehead was wrinkled, as if trying to find the right words to avoid completely shattering his heart — too late.

"I didn't say no," she whispered.

"But you didn't say yes."

"Tyson…" She seemed to realize there were no words.

"I know. I really do. You're afraid. Given my behavior over the past couple of months, I don't blame you. But everything I said is true. I've wanted you from the beginning. From the first time my lips touched yours and the world stopped spinning for a moment, I knew you were it for me. But if you need more time, that's fine. I'll wait for you."

Tyson had taken out the ring box again and absentmindedly flipped it open while he spoke. He noticed Paige looking down at his hands and couldn't help the small twinge of satisfaction he felt when her breath caught. The ring he'd chosen was perfectly Paige. Instead of a huge block of a diamond, he'd found a ring that was small and delicate with thin, gold prongs that softly cradled a beautiful square-cut stone — big enough to be noticed but not obscenely huge.

"Um…I…"

"See when a guy asks the woman he loves to marry him, this really is *not* the reaction he's looking for." He didn't want to sound like a total pussy, but knew he wasn't succeeding. Paige had broken his heart.

"Tyson," she cupped his face in both hands, forcing him to look at her, "You should know by now, I'm not like most girls. You should've known I wasn't going to jump up and down and squeal like a fangirl when the Beatles landed in America. There's so much running through my head right now."

"You're right. I just thought this'd be all gooey romantic and maybe for once that brain of yours would stop working and you could get caught up in the moment." Tyson looked out at the sun setting. "We better head back to the car. When the sun goes down, we'll be stuck in the pitch black out here."

They packed up the remains of the picnic and folded the blanket before walking to the car as the last rays of sun fell below the horizon. Tyson went to the back to put the picnic paraphernalia in the trunk.

"Tyson?" Paige called from where she waited by the passenger door.

"Yeah?" He'd been taking an unusually long time at the trunk. He didn't want her to see how broken he was.

"How often do you come here? You knew the path by heart."

Tyson slammed the trunk and walked toward her as he answered the question. "I come here to think a lot. There's a big rock over by the cove, and I can just be alone with my thoughts sometimes. In fact, you're the first person who's ever been here with me." As he leaned past her to grab the door handle, Paige threw her arms around his neck and pulled him to her.

"Yes," she whispered as she pressed her lips to his.

The word was swallowed by the kiss, but Tyson heard it. Their kiss took on a whole new meaning, and Tyson could feel Paige's love flow through his entire body. He pulled her body closer to his own, trying to make her part of him. When he finally broke the kiss, they both gasped for air.

"Really?" Tyson couldn't keep the surprise out of his voice.

Paige nodded before attacking him again.

"Let's go home," she said as she turned to get in the car. Tyson let out a low groan when she pulled away from him.

"Oh! Wait!" Tyson kneeled in the open door and pulled the velvet box out of his pocket for the third time. "Paige, will you please marry me and make me happy for the rest of my life?" He slipped the ring on her finger.

"Yes, Tyson. I love you." The ring sparkled in the interior light of the car, and as Tyson looked up at Paige, he saw her tears sparkling the same way. He wiped her cheeks and kissed her softly.

Tyson swore the only tears he'd ever cause her to shed were these diamond ones—tears of happiness.

CHAPTER 33

Gideon was tired, but he couldn't fall asleep. His body ached for rest, but his mind was ready to run a marathon. When he and Charlie had returned home after the confrontation with Boyd, they'd sat and stared at each other for a long time, neither wanting to acknowledge what the guy had said.

Charlie had been the first to speak. "Gideon, there's no way that what he said is true." She reached out and took Gideon's hand. "I was pregnant before you left. I missed my period before *he*…" Charlie paused and Gideon looked at her, waiting. "Raped me."

"I'm not letting him get away with this. We have to do something."

"I don't know. I just want to forget. Can't we just be us for now? Please?"

"Charlie, he told me he's done this to others. We need to stop it."

At those words, Charlie had broken down. Gideon held her until they'd finally crawled into bed, and she'd fallen into a deep sleep.

Now as he looked over at his wife sleeping next to him, Gideon's gaze wandered her still form. He loved every inch of it: her swollen belly, knowing he was responsible for those two small lives; the way her hips had widened just a little; and—good Lord!—her breasts were incredible. Charlie's body was so different from when he left. *She* was different in so many ways. Gideon hated himself for what that prick had done and was plotting his very painful death, but the most important thing was to be there for Charlie. Later. *He* would pay later.

Watching as Charlie's chest moved up and down with the rhythmic breathing of deep sleep, Gideon thought about how horrible the past three months had been. He'd been in total shock after talking to Tyson. Fox had tried to talk to him, but really, there wasn't anything anyone could tell him that would help. He had to process the whole thing on his own.

He'd volunteered for most patrols or scouting missions just to have something else to concentrate on, but he could only work so many hours before he had to take time off. During those hours of downtime Gideon's mind would run wild — playing images over and over like some horrible movie. The images were always the same: Charlie fucking another guy. Gideon knew he wasn't the first to go through this, and he definitely wouldn't be the last. Hell, he saw it happen at least once every tour, but he just couldn't make himself believe it had happened to him.

Those months had been spent in a war. Not a war Gideon could fight with weapons and his team members watching his back, but one that raged inside him. He wanted to believe Charlie loved him — only him. He'd seen it in her eyes, felt it in her touch, heard it in her words. Charlie was his. Her heart would always belong to him and only him. The emotional argument was working hard for the win.

But he kept remembering how mad she'd been when he told her he was leaving. His mind kept running over the way she'd yelled at him for lying to her during their entire marriage. Logically, Gideon could almost understand her doing something to get back at him. Charlie was a woman who fought for the things she believed in, and Gideon had made her believe she couldn't trust him, so she wanted him to feel that same pain.

Christmas pushed him over the line. When Tyson told him Charlie left while he was on the phone, that was the turning point in the war. Logic was the victor in that battle.

No matter how much he loved his wife, Gideon wasn't sure he could spend the rest of his life with her. He'd always wonder when she told him she was going to the store, if she was really going to meet another man. He'd always be suspicious of her motives and her actions. That was no way to live. Gideon knew he wouldn't be going back to a home. He'd return to his life, but not to his love.

And the babies? He'd been so happy about Charlie's pregnancy, but once Tyson shared his little news flash, the doubt crept in, and Gideon didn't let himself even think about them.

It had taken a lot for Gideon to call Charlie that next day. He'd wanted to disappear and say a big "Fuck You!" to the world, but his stupid heart still had a bit of fight in it. If nothing else, Gideon wasn't cruel, and he did love Charlie, so he couldn't stand the idea of her hurting or having her be even a little worried. Thank Christ he'd called.

In that short conversation, Gideon's world flipped once again. If Tyson could pull shit like telling him Charlie had left when she hadn't, why was Gideon so sure he was telling the truth about Charlie cheating? He knew Tyson had had it rough, coming in behind him his whole life, but would he really be so low as to start this shit while Gideon was trying not to get killed at his job? Yeah, he and little brother were going to have a big heart to heart real soon, and Gideon was going to get some shit straightened out.

Unfortunately, he could only talk to Charlie for a few minutes that day, and when he hung up he was more confused than ever. The only thing Gideon knew was he loved Charlie. It was all that mattered, and she needed to know that. He scribbled a note on a piece of scrap paper lying on the table and quickly stuffed it into an envelope. After addressing it, he gave it to one of the guys in camp who wasn't a part of the new mission. Gideon hoped he'd be going home to Charlie when the mission was over, but if he didn't, he wanted her to know he always loved her.

Charlie stirred beside him. Her hands went to her belly, and a grimace crossed her face as her eyes slowly opened.

"What's wrong? Do I need to call the doctor or my dad?" Gideon heard the panic in his voice and felt like a pussy, but these were his kids.

"Calm down, Joe. I'm fine. It's just that your little ones here like to party in the middle of the night," she said, her hands roaming over her stomach. "I was sleeping so good, knowing you were next to me, and to be honest, I'm a little annoyed right now." Charlie's face now presented a huge smile where that frown had been minutes before.

As he pulled her closer, Gideon felt her body tense slightly and a whole new wave of being pissed off washed over him. Gideon rolled her onto her side so he could curl his body around hers. His hands rested on her belly, and she was right, those little critters were moving around like they were trying to break out.

He leaned down to whisper to his kids. "Now you two settle down in there. Your mommy's tired, and she needs to sleep."

Charlie laughed. It was the first time since he'd walked through the door Gideon had heard her laugh, and it was perfect and beautiful.

"Wow, Joe. They know you. They're actually calming down. Usually I'm up for hours when they do this." Charlie yawned, and Gideon was happy when she settled into him. He made her feel safe and comfortable enough to relax, and soon she fell back to sleep.

Some time later, lost in sleep, Charlie rolled toward him, and Gideon was jolted back to reality—his life. Waking up with his wife in his arms was something he'd been dreaming of for months. Even through those horrible months when he thought he'd never hold her this way again, he'd still wanted it.

Gideon's body reacted and he got harder than he'd been in *forever*. The feel of Charlie's body against him and the sight of her breasts moving against his chest were more than he could take. He wanted her, but he worried about so much. Would she let him touch her like that? Would he hurt the babies? Even just wondering this after what she'd been through made him feel like an asshole.

Unable to help himself, Gideon tentatively ran a hand down Charlie's back, continuing to her ass and up over her hip. He felt her stiffen slightly against him. That reaction answered all of Gideon's questions, and he immediately withdrew his hand from her body.

"Joe." Charlie looked up at him.

"It's okay, baby. I understand."

"No, I want to try, but we have to go slow. I can't help the reactions, but I need to be reminded that it's you. If I can't do it, I'll let you know. Is that okay?" Her voice was so small, and her eyes were wide with fear. There was no way Gideon could even try this.

"No, Charlie. We don't have to do anything. It'll be fine. We can work through this in your therapy."

"I've talked about this in therapy. I want this. I want you." Charlie's hand moved down to find his throbbing length, and Gideon couldn't help the hiss that escaped when her warm hand wrapped around him. "I really want to try."

Gideon held her gaze as she continued to stroke him. If they were going to get past this, if Charlie was going to be with him again, she had to be in control, and that was fine. Gideon cursed under his breath at the sensations she was creating in his body. It'd been months since Gideon had felt his wife's hand, and he was worried he was going to lose it before they got any further.

"Charlie?" Gideon breathed out on an exhale. "I want to touch you, baby."

Charlie's eyes held his, and he tried to read them. He wanted to make sure there was no fear in them at all. He'd never forgive himself if he forced something she wasn't ready for. There was nothing in her eyes but love for him and deep want.

Gideon slid his hands up under her tank top to cup her breasts. The feeling of Charlie in his hands again was almost too much.

"God, Charlie. I love you." And…he was done. For the first time since he lost his virginity at fifteen, Gideon came at just the touch of a girl. He felt like such a pussy, but considering it'd been more than four months since Charlie had touched him, he thought he'd get over it. He cursed his poor performance. Here was this beautiful, hurting woman offering herself up to him, and he couldn't get any farther than that.

Charlie's smile was wide. Gideon could tell she liked doing that to him, which eased his guilt and embarrassment slightly.

"See what you do to me, baby?" A giggle filled the air, and Gideon knew it wouldn't take long for him to get back in the game. He was already starting to harden again, just from the feel of her in his hands and the sound of her laughter.

Gideon inched the tank top up Charlie's body and over her head. He smiled when her hands immediately went to her belly, like she was worried he wouldn't want to see her like that.

"Baby. The sight of you carrying my kids is the sexiest fucking thing I've ever seen." Gideon leaned down and placed as many kisses as he could over the swell of her belly as his hands deftly slipped her pajama bottoms down off her hips.

Charlie had tears in her eyes when Gideon looked up at her.

"Oh, I'm sorry. I'm good. We don't have to do anything more. I'm sorry." Gideon immediately chastised himself for being a total degenerate and wanting to have sex with his pregnant wife who just told him…Gideon didn't want to even think about that right now.

"No, Joe. I'm fine. It's just, just…"

"Shh." Gideon moved back up so he could hold her to him. He wanted to make all the hurt to go away. But for the first time in his life, Gideon was helpless.

Charlie looked up into his eyes. Her expression was full of determination as she moved her lips to his. The kiss was soft and perfect, just like Charlie. But soon what had started so carefully turned into something full of need. Gideon felt Charlie's hands move his shorts down his legs, freeing his once again hard-as-a-rock erection. She was in control again, and this time he was just going to go with it. She flung her leg over his hip and pulled herself up to straddle him. He looked up at her, and damn if she wasn't the most gorgeous thing that had ever existed with her pregnant belly and her bigger breasts. Gideon nearly passed out when she lifted up and slid herself down on him, sheathing him in her moist warmth.

Their eyes locked together as Gideon held her hips and helped her move. His hands moved to caress her belly. When he suddenly remembered the babies, Gideon's eyes got wide. Charlie leaned in to whisper, "You can't hurt them. I promise."

"Charlie…oh, God…yesss," he hissed as she moved. Watching her in charge and in control was getting Gideon where he wanted to go fast. He felt the orgasm building, but wanted to make sure Charlie was there too.

"I'm going to touch you, baby. Is that okay?" How he had the cognitive wherewithal to ask the question, Gideon had no idea. But he knew he needed to make sure Charlie was okay.

"Mmm…yeah….Gideon…please…"

Gideon didn't need to be told twice. He moved one hand down over her belly to find the spot he knew was throbbing to be touched. Charlie let out a small gasp as she tightened around him. It only took a few more strokes before Charlie exploded for him. Her eyes closed, breaking their visual connection for the first time. Gideon knew it was because she trusted him and knew it was him loving her.

After he followed her over the edge moments later, Gideon wrapped his wife in his arms and rolled to his side. Charlie's eyes stayed closed, but there was a smile on her face.

In the years he'd fought for his country and all the missions he'd been on, Gideon had never felt a greater sense of pride than he did in that moment. After everything Charlie had been through, she trusted him enough to let him love her this way; that was the most important thing he'd ever accomplished.

Charlie rolled over so her back was to Gideon. Being face to face after such intimacy was too much, and while she didn't want to break the connection, her mind was heading into panic territory. It was too much, too real. While Gideon kept telling her how beautiful and perfect she was, a single tear tracked down her cheek.

"I'm sorry, Charlie. I'm so sorry."

"I'm *not* sorry. I love you, and I love that we can still do that." It was the truth. For months Charlie had been working with Dr. Lassiter to be able to let Gideon touch her in an intimate way again, but until the moment she looked into his eyes and knew it was him, she didn't know if she'd be able to go through with it. But it had been perfect.

"Then why are you crying again? Are you hurt? Did I do something to hurt the babies?"

"No, Joe. I told you—you can't hurt the babies. Do you need an anatomy lesson from your dad?" Charlie teased.

"Can we not talk about my parents while we're naked? It kind of creeps me out." They laughed as Gideon pulled her closer.

Charlie's stomach chose that moment to remind her she hadn't eaten in several hours. Suddenly Gideon was off the bed, and Charlie got a wonderful view of his perfect ass. For the first time in months, she felt the stir of sexual need deep within her. Gideon had initiated their earlier round of lovemaking, and while Charlie hadn't pushed him away, and her body had responded the way it should have, this was something different. This was Charlie wanting her husband. It was just a small twinge deep in her belly, but she was happy to know it was there. Maybe someday she'd be the one initiating their intimate moments.

"Where are you going at four in the morning?" Charlie poked her lip out in a pout.

"I'm going to feed my woman."

"Gideon! You know better than to call me *woman*."

Gideon laughed as he pulled on his boxers and padded out to the kitchen.

Lying in bed in the quiet of the early morning, Charlie sighed. Things had changed so much in such a short time yet again. She was thankful she'd followed Gideon when he left the house the day before. Without a doubt, had Charlie not stopped him, Gideon would've killed her attacker and then gone to jail. Just the idea of losing him nearly caused her to break down. Gideon's booming voice staved off the panic when he came back into the room with a plate full of more food than Charlie had eaten the entire time he was gone.

"What did you make, Joe?"

"Eggs, bacon, waffles."

"You made waffles?" Gideon was not what one would call *proficient* in the kitchen, so the idea that he'd made waffles had Charlie worried about the state of the kitchen.

"Okay, I didn't really make them, but I put them in the toaster."

Charlie laughed. It felt good to laugh. To laugh with Gideon. He set a plate in front of her, but even though she was starving, they needed to talk about some things.

"Joe?"

"Mmm?" he answered, his mouth full of waffle.

"I have a therapy appointment this week, and I think I'd like it if you came with me. Do you think you can?"

"Baby, I'll be anywhere you need me to be. If you want me to come to therapy with you, I will."

"Thank you."

"I also want to go to the next doctor's appointment with you. I'm so ready to find out if we have any stems on the apples in there."

"Yeah, so is your mother. She's been driving the nurses crazy trying to get them to tell her. Oh! Speaking of your mom, does she know you're home?"

"No. I want one more day with you. Just us, locked in this house."

"I like that idea."

"I just have one errand to run today, and then it's all us, baby. No outside world for the rest of the day." His mouth settled into a smirk, but there was something behind his eyes that worried Charlie. She chose to ignore it for the moment and enjoy just being with Gideon. For the next few hours they were simply together. They talked only about the future and made plans for the babies.

"I'm gonna jump in the shower," Gideon finally said, "and then I can run my errand and be back here before you know I'm gone."

When Gideon emerged from the bathroom a short time later, he came to kiss her good-bye, and his hands moved over her belly again. He leaned down to kiss it, whispering, "Daddy'll be back soon. Be nice to your mommy."

Charlie remembered something she'd wanted to ask him. "Hey, Joe?"

Gideon stopped and turned around. "Can we try to get together with Jaylon and Zoe? I kind of lost touch with Zoe after everything happened, and when I tried to call her a few days ago, I couldn't get a hold of her."

"Sounds like a plan. I love you…all."

He headed out the door to do who knows what. Charlie silently prayed he wasn't making good on his promise to take care of Cody Boyd. The door clicked, and like a perfect metaphor, everything clicked for Charlie: *Boyd, Zoe…others.*

CHAPTER 34

Charlie scrambled out of bed. The blood in her veins had gone cold, and she knew she was right. Gideon's words ran through her mind: *Charlie, he told me he's done this to others.*

She grabbed the phone and dialed Zoe's number again and again and again. Each time she got the same message—the number was no longer in service. Charlie was starting to get frantic. She needed Gideon home. His cell number went straight to voicemail, and she realized he must've turned it off. That made Charlie even more nervous, and she wondered again what kind of errand he so desperately needed to do today.

She could do nothing but wait, and she waddled from room to room, constantly stopping at the front window to see if Gideon's truck had magically appeared. When her ankles and calves began to ache too badly, she lowered herself onto the couch. As she curled up to wait for Gideon, she couldn't believe how selfish and stupid she'd been. Of course Cody Boyd had done this before. He'd been perfectly calm through the entire thing. Charlie shuddered and bile rose in her throat as—for the first time in months—she allowed the visual memory of that day to seep back into her mind.

Boyd's demeanor had been polished and practiced. He'd known exactly when to attack and what to say. It hadn't been the first time he'd done it, and it wouldn't be the last. Gideon was right—they had to do something to stop him from hurting anyone else. Because of Charlie's silence, he might have hurt Zoe, and who knows how many others. Charlie's stomach turned, and the waffles that Gideon had so lovingly made for her threatened to make a reappearance.

The phone rang, and Charlie prayed it was Gideon so she could beg him to come home. It wasn't. She swallowed back the fear and anger churning in her stomach as she answered the phone.

"Hi, Evelyn."

Paige was in Tyson's bed again. His future was there with him, and he'd never felt more himself in his life. With Paige, Tyson knew he could be the person, the man, he wanted to be. This time he wasn't doing it for her though, this time he was doing it for himself. Tyson had made decisions, and he was going to talk to Paige about them. She'd now have a say in his future — *their* future.

Tyson's hand drifted over Paige's curves, earning a sigh that sent a flame of desire through his entire body, making him twitch and come to life. When he brushed against her breast she hissed, and Tyson suspected she was feigning sleep, trying to see how far he'd push. His palm moved over to cover her breast, and he rubbed over her perfect pink peak. Another small groan. His hand glided down over her stomach as his lips followed. When his fingers made contact with the sensitive spot between her legs, Paige finally ended her poorly played ruse.

"Damn, Tyson!"

He lifted his head to look at her.

"You are such a faker, my dear. And a bad one at that. At least I know when I make you cum and you're praying my name, it's for real. Because you, Paige, weren't fooling anyone."

She let out a small laugh that quickly turned to a moan as Tyson's fingers moved over the wetness and heat of her core. Her back arched, and he dipped his head to take a pink tip into his mouth, sliding his tongue over it. Paige's hands tangled in his hair, holding him to her, and he loved every damn minute of it.

Tyson began to kiss the soft skin between her breasts, heading down over her stomach. When he stopped to swirl his tongue in the dip of her navel, she giggled. Just as Tyson made it down to the sweet spot at the apex of her gorgeous legs, there was a thunderous pounding on the front door. Paige jumped, her body bowing off the bed under Tyson and slamming her pubic bone against his mouth. Not only did he get a bloody lip, he bit his tongue in the process.

"Oh my God, Tyson! I'm so sorry." Blood dripped from his lip, and his tongue was already starting to swell.

"Thall rwite," he lisped, trying to get off the bed without making things any more awkward. Another pounding on the door startled him, and he fell off the bed, landing on his ass.

He pulled on his shorts before going to see who the fuck was whaling on his door first thing in the morning. He peered through the peephole and almost stumbled back to fall flat on his ass again. He yanked the door wide open, excited at the appearance of the guest.

"Gideon! What—" Tyson never finished the sentence. Before he could get another word out, Gideon's fist came flying at him, landing squarely on his nose. Tyson heard a crunch as his brother's knuckles met the hard bone at the bridge.

Blood ran down the back of Tyson's throat and dripped from his chin onto his bare chest. He saw stars and stumbled back to sit on the coffee table. Gideon stepped into the living room, the look on his face nothing short of murderous.

"We're gonna talk, little brother. Not now. Now I'm going to go back to my house to lock myself in with my wife and love her like I haven't been able to for months."

Tyson stared at him. Even if he could have thought of something to say, the pain that radiated through his entire face wouldn't have allowed it.

"Mom doesn't know I'm home yet. And she better not find out. She also better not find out I was the one who did that to you. If she finds out about *this*, she's gonna find out what you did to Charlie."

Out of Tyson's peripheral vision, he saw Paige come into the room wearing only his shirt and panties. He wanted to cover her up. He didn't want Gideon to look at her. It was an odd fucking thing to be thinking right then. His nose was broken, his lip was split, and he might've bitten his tongue completely in half, but all he cared about was Paige's ass hanging out in front of his brother.

"Hey, Paige." Gideon waved to her.

"Um…hi, Gideon." Paige's voice was barely a whisper.

"You might wanna get some clothes on and take Ty to the emergency room. I think that nose is broken." Gideon was so calm, like he wasn't the one who'd just sucker punched Tyson and broken the damn thing.

"O-O-Okay," Paige replied.

Gideon leaned down to look Tyson in the eye. "You fucking deserved that, and you know it." He turned and walked out the door. Tyson stared at the closed door for a heartbeat and realized Gideon was right. He totally fucking deserved it.

The door eased closed behind him and Gideon leaned against the wall as he felt the satisfaction begin to seep from his body. He'd wanted to hurt someone, and Tyson seemed to be the easiest and most logical target. Now he felt a little guilty, and the throbbing pain in his hand reminded him what a moronic move it had been. The look on Paige's face bothered Gideon the most. She'd looked at him like he was a cruel bully. Gideon hated that look.

A lot of his time as a kid was spent defending Tyson, who had a tendency to piss off the wrong people. Gideon was always bigger than him—hell, he was bigger than most guys he knew—but Tyson's mouth was bigger than anyone's. When Tyson's mouth got him in trouble, Gideon had to come rescue him. Tyson was his little brother after all, and he couldn't let other people beat the crap out of him. That had earned Gideon the title of "bully" at a pretty young age. He'd always hated when kids looked at him with fear in their eyes.

Eventually Gideon tried to get Tyson to realize that if he was going to have a smart-ass mouth, he would have to learn to defend himself. He was tired of being the bully. When Tyson was around ten, Gideon started resolving most of their arguments with a wrestling match on the back lawn. Gideon would more often than not come out with the victory, but there were several times Tyson had gotten the best of him. Tyson became pretty good at defending himself against Gideon and eventually learned that if he shut the hell up, he wouldn't have to fight at all. If nothing else, Tyson was smart. And once he stopped being an asshole, Gideon was able to stop being a bully.

A reel of memories ran through Gideon's head: him and Tyson rolling all over the grass, Mom yelling at them to stop, bloody noses, fat lips, black eyes. He thought back to the last time they'd fought like that—Tyson was just starting high school. The brothers never really hurt each other badly enough to require medical attention, and once they were done, that was the end of it. This time, however, the sucker punch was wrong. And that definitely wasn't going to be the end of it. They were going to have to talk.

A few minutes later, when he'd gathered his thoughts again, Gideon pushed off the wall and shook his hand out, trying to ease the ache of his knuckles as he headed back to his truck. The need to get home to Charlie was pulling him, but he sat in the truck for several minutes before he could get himself together enough to go home. On the way he called his dad to give him a heads up about Tyson. His father's hospital was the closest to Tyson's apartment.

"Hey, Dad."

"Gideon? Where are you, Son?"

"On the Five."

"What? You're home?"

"Yeah, got home yesterday."

"Does your mother know? Wait, I'm going to assume the answer to that question is no, considering I didn't get a frantic phone call from her." His father laughed, and Gideon was glad that he'd called him.

"About that, Dad—could we keep this between us for a day or so? I love Mom, and I've missed both of you, but right now I just want to be with my wife." Gideon could always say anything to his dad and know he'd understand.

"I get it. Don't worry. But you only have twenty-four hours. Your mother misses you terribly, and if she finds out I knew you were home… well, I don't even want to think about the repercussions."

"So, I needed to tell you something."

"Sure, although I was heading down to the ER. Seems your brother and Paige just came in. Rumor is he has a broken nose and a busted-up face. You know anything about that?"

"I might."

"Gideon, what's going on? This family has been slowly tearing apart since you left, and then at Christmas it ripped wide open."

"Tyson was an asshole to Charlie while I was gone, and I paid him back this morning." His dad didn't need all the specifics. It wasn't his place. If Charlie had worked so hard to keep this from them, Gideon couldn't be the one to spill it.

"I'm not going to give you a lecture, Son. But you aren't kids anymore, and you need to talk these things out now. You know better than anyone that violence doesn't change or solve anything."

"I know, Dad. I just…I just…I'll talk to Tyson. I promise." He hated hearing the disappointment in his dad's voice. Peter's respect was something Gideon never wanted to lose.

"I'm going to give your brother some advice now too and check on that broken nose. You better hope your mother doesn't find out you broke his pretty nose, Gideon." Peter laughed, but Gideon knew he was serious.

"Thanks, Dad. Tell Tyson we'll talk tomorrow. Right now I'm going home to my wife."

"Good idea, son. And plan to make an appearance for dinner tomorrow." He hung up.

As the guilt balled in his gut, Gideon knew he didn't want Charlie to know what he'd done to his brother. She'd be upset. While she was still angry with Tyson, Charlie loved him, and for him to be hurt would hurt her. Gideon wasn't a kid anymore, and really, the few seconds of satisfaction from punishing Tyson weren't worth the pain he knew he'd caused his family. It also hadn't resolved their problem.

Gideon walked in, caught up in his own thoughts until he saw the look on Charlie's face. Something was wrong.

"Hey, baby. Are you okay? Why are you out here?"

"I don't plan on spending the next few months in bed, Joe. I've been waiting for you. Why was your phone off? We have to —"

Gideon winced as he ran a hand through his hair and tried to think how to explain where he'd been.

"Oh my God, Gideon! What did you do?" Charlie moved slowly across the living room, her gaze locked on his hand.

"It's nothing. I punched a door." The look Charlie gave him let Gideon know she wasn't buying it, but he wasn't about to tell her the truth. Then he remembered that not being open and honest was what had gotten them in this mess in the first place.

"You didn't go after Boyd, did you? Please tell me you didn't go after him." Charlie's arms wrapped around him, and he felt her body shake as he pulled her closer.

"No, baby. I didn't go after Boyd. Actually —"

"Thank God. Oh, Gideon, we have to get in touch with Jaylon and Zoe."

Charlie headed off on a different tangent before Gideon could tell her the truth. He pushed her back slightly so he could look in her eyes. They were wild with emotion.

"Okay, baby. I'll call Jaylon right now." Gideon pulled his phone out of his pocket.

"No! We have to go there. I need to talk to Zoe. I need her to know she isn't alone."

Gideon shook his head, confused.

"I know in my heart Cody Boyd raped her like he raped me."

CHAPTER 35

By the time Paige came back to the living room, dressed and with Tyson's keys in her hand, Gideon was gone. Tyson could see the fear and worry in her eyes and wanted to wrap her up and cradle her in his arms until that look went away. Unfortunately, the blood drying on his bare chest and the blood-soaked towel pressed to his nose made that impossible.

While Paige had thrown on clothes, Tyson had scrounged for some himself. He was now in an old pair of jeans and flip flops, but still wore no shirt—he'd given up trying to get it over his head. It hurt too much.

"You ready?" Paige asked.

"Ure. Ets o." Between the busted lip from Paige's deadly pelvis, the broken nose, and the towel pressed to his face, his words were jumbled.

The couple headed out of the house, and Paige helped Tyson into the car.

"I ove ooo," Tyson mumbled as they turned onto the street.

"I love you too."

"Air are ee oing?"

"The emergency room—duh. You have blood spurting out of every orifice on your pretty little face. I think medical attention is warranted."

"O! Ot ere."

Paige looked at him like he was speaking gibberish, and he realized he was.

Tyson frantically pointed to the hospital sign as she pulled into the parking lot. "Ot ere! Ad orks ere!"

"Are you kidding me? You're bleeding to death and you're worried your dad's going to find out? Baby, you're a mess. Trust me—he's gonna notice no matter where he sees you."

Tyson was not going to go into that hospital and face his father—wasn't going to happen. He crossed his arms over his chest and silently vowed to stay right where he was until Paige took him to another hospital.

Paige walked around and opened his door. Tyson sat in defiance. Paige sighed. "Tyson Cooper, you get out of that car right now. You're acting like a spoiled child. Be a man."

Tyson looked at her. He attempted to stick his tongue out to complete her description, but pain rippled over his entire face. He let out a loud groan.

"Really. There's no way you'll ever hide this from your parents."

Slowly Tyson unfolded himself from the car and sulked into the emergency room.

Once they were shown to a curtained area, the couple waited in silence for someone to come look at Tyson's nose. He prayed his dad was in surgery. Then they could get in and out before he even knew they'd been there.

"Tyson, I don't—" Paige started just as Peter came around the white curtain.

"I hear someone's in need of a doctor?"

"Dad? You don'th work ER," Tyson said. The swelling in his lip had gone down a little—they'd at least given him an ice pack—but Tyson hated that he was still lisping.

"No, but the Cooper name spreads quickly in this hospital, and when I heard my son was here, I had to come. So you want to tell me what happened, Son?" Peter moved forward and tilted Tyson's head back to get a better look at the damage.

"Walked into a door?" It was a question.

"Yeah, right. Tyson, why don't you try being honest with yourself and those who love you for once?" Tyson never would've expected him to say that. His mom, sure. But Dad? Tyson looked at him, not saying a word. He wouldn't betray Gideon.

"I walked into a door," he repeated.

"That's definitely what you're going to tell your mother, and she'll probably buy it. And while I don't condone Gideon punching you, I'm worried about what you did that made this—" Peter waved a hand over Tyson's face "—a top priority for your brother a day after he came home."

"How did you know?" Tyson and Paige asked at the same time.

"I just got off the phone with Gideon. He wanted to give me a heads up about you and tell me to keep your mom busy so he could have a day with

Charlie. Speaking of which, you both need to be at dinner tomorrow night. I just had to cancel lunch with her to come down here and take care of you, and I'm paying her back with a family dinner and all her kids at the table."

"I don't know if that's going to be thuch a good idea, Dad. I mean, look at my fath. Me and Gid in a room might noth be good."

"Trust me—I let him know how disappointed I am in him. You boys aren't fourteen anymore. You need to find a new way of dealing with your problems. You need to start acting like the men your mother and I raised you to be. I'm pretty sure you both can do that for a few hours." Peter gave a hard stare that made Tyson sit up a little straighter.

"You aren'th going tho thell Mom, are you?"

Paige giggled, and Tyson turned his attention to her. "What are you lauthing at? Until you thee my mom in a full-blown fith of rage, you haven't theen anything."

"No, I'm not going to tell her. I don't like keeping secrets from your mother, but sometimes it's a necessity. I've known the sex of the babies since Charlie's first ultrasound." A sly smile appeared on Peter's lips.

"Theriouthly? Mom's going to kill you if the ever finds out."

"She won't find out." Peter pegged both of them with a stare.

"She won't hear it from us." Paige held her hand over her heart, and Peter laughed. "You're going to tell us though, right?"

"No. Like I said, sometimes secrets are a necessity."

"Damn. I don't think I can wait until…well, shit!" Paige glanced at Peter, her face flushing. "Sorry. I was about to say I couldn't wait for Gideon to come home, but he's home."

Tyson groaned at the reminder that his brother was definitely home. "How could you forgeth?"

"Okay, let's take care of this face," Peter said. He placed his thumbs on either side of Tyson's nose and pushed.

The sound that came out of Tyson's mouth was horrific. He looked over to see Paige weaving back and forth.

CHAPTER 36

"Shit," Gideon hissed between clenched teeth. "I'll call Jaylon and see if Zoe's all right."

"No! We have to go there. I have to see Zoe. Please." Charlie was on the verge of tears, and her heart beat faster than she'd thought possible. Gideon took a few steps forward and pulled her to him, but Charlie didn't want him to comfort her. She wanted to get to Zoe, and if she let her own experience in, she'd never be able to do that. She'd locked that part of her up for the moment.

"Baby?"

It hurt Charlie to pull away from him. She planted her hands against her husband's chest tried to push him out the door.

"Charlotte." He placed both his hands over Charlie's and stopped her from pushing him any further. "We need to think about this. We can't just barge in to Jaylon and Zoe's lives and open up this can of worms. We don't even know for sure that anything's happened to Zoe."

But Charlie knew something was wrong. She just knew it. "This is all my fault. If he hurt Zoe, it'll forever be *my* fault."

"I don't ever want to hear you say that again," Gideon said severely. "None of this was your fault. This is that prick Boyd's fault, and if he did hurt her, it'll just be one more reason for me to break his fucking neck. But we need to know first."

"You don't understand. If I'd done something right after — right after he raped me — then maybe he wouldn't have been able to get to Zoe. If only I'd told someone. If only I'd called the police."

Gideon lunged for her with his arms spread to gather her to him, but Charlie took another step away. If she let him comfort her, she'd lose the fight, and that couldn't happen, not now.

"I'm fine. Really. We have to get to the Foxes'. Let's go. Please."

Gideon opened the door for Charlie.

As they drove to the base, Charlie relived her regrets over everything that had happened. Cody Boyd had taken so much from so many. For the first time in Charlie's life, she wanted to see someone dead, and that was the last thing *he* could've taken from her — her humanity.

Charlie tried to focus on something else, and her eyes made a sweep of the inside of the truck. She caught sight of Gideon's bruised and bloodied knuckles wrapped around the steering wheel and remembered she never did find out what had happened.

"Gideon, what happened to your hand? If you didn't go after Boyd, then who? Or what?"

"I went to see Tyson this morning."

"No. I never wanted this. I don't want what happened to me to tear our family apart. It wasn't Tyson's fault."

"I know that. I just…I just…fuck! I hate this! I hate what that — what he did to you. And I hate that I wasn't here. And I hate that Tyson let me down." His teeth were clenched so tightly that Charlie barely understood him.

"I need you to listen to me. I mean *really* listen to me."

He turned slightly to look at his wife. His brow was furrowed, and his mouth drawn into a tight line.

Charlie took a deep breath. "You're the strongest man I've ever known — not just physically, but on the inside too. And I love you with my whole heart. But I don't want you to protect me."

Gideon looked lost and confused, as if Charlie was speaking a foreign language. In Gideon's mind, protection equaled love. If Charlie didn't want his protection, she didn't want his love.

"Before you left, I loved the life we had. Always knowing you were there to keep me safe made me happy. But then you left — and I know you didn't leave *me*." Charlie addressed that issue before he could open his mouth to argue. "It took two weeks, but I was just starting to realize my own strength."

Gideon's lips twitched. It was obvious he wanted to interrupt, but Charlie couldn't let him.

"All my life the men I love have tried to protect me. Growing up I had Chance, and while I know he thinks I was the bold one, it was him that everyone was afraid of. One time in high school, this guy was spreading nasty rumors about me. Everyone at school was talking. It was bad. Chance had a little 'talk' with the guy one day, and after that, the looks and rumors stopped. He never told me about it, but I heard he went after the guy with no mercy."

She looked over to see Gideon's mouth turned up in a smile. She was sure he was thinking he needed to give Chance a big pat on the back next time he saw him. *Men...*

"The point is, I've always relied on you or Chance to be there for me. Once you were gone, I had to find that in myself—and I was doing it, Gideon. For the first time in a long time, it was me. I had to take care of me. Then...*Boyd*...walked in and took everything. I couldn't stop him."

Charlie shuddered as the memory hit hard. Out of the corner of her eye, she saw Gideon flinch as well.

"So, what? You don't need me anymore?" The hurt in his voice cut straight through her.

"No. That's not what I'm trying to tell you. I love you. You and these two little critters are what matter most to me in this whole world. What I'm saying is I want you to stand *with* me—to support me and be there for me when I break, because what I'm about to do is going to break me. I just want you to be there to love me, to help me. I have to protect *myself* from now on."

Charlie hoped Gideon would understand she still wanted him, but she'd never again let herself be as vulnerable as she'd been that day. Never.

Charlie was the strongest woman Gideon had ever met. And he'd seen female drill instructors that made soldiers pee their pants.

"Okay, I get it. I can't promise I won't still protect you, though. It's what I do."

"I know, Joe, but can you try to let me find my way a little?" Charlie reached over and laid her hand on Gideon's. The warmth of it traveled straight to his heart. He didn't know how he was going to *not* protect her, especially while she was carrying his kids.

"Here's the deal, baby—until those little critters are out in the real world, you're not leaving my sight. After that, I'll make an effort to back off...a little. I love you, and I respect the hell out of the fact that you want to deal with this, but there's no way I'm going to stand by and let something happen to my family again."

"Okay. I guess I can accept that. I know you can't change overnight. I want you to promise me one more thing…" She trailed off, a sure sign she was about to request something he'd object to.

"Anything you want," Gideon forced himself to say.

"Wow, that's kind of open-ended, isn't it? What if I asked you to do something crazy like to quit your job? You just promised me anything I wanted." She was teasing, but Gideon swallowed hard and bit his tongue. That would be the one thing he couldn't do, even for Charlie. He'd thought about it many times since the night he told her he was being deployed, but he couldn't picture himself doing anything else.

"Uh…." Gideon searched for words.

"I'm not asking you to quit your job. I'd never take that from you. What I want is for you to make up with Tyson. You can't blame him. It wasn't his fault I was raped."

Gideon cringed at that word. He hated hearing it.

"It wasn't his fault I didn't tell anyone. Tyson's assumption was just another side effect of me holding everything in — just like the others Boyd may have hurt. The only thing Tyson did wrong was jump to conclusions, and when you step back and look at it, it makes sense. Right now I can't forgive him for what he did to *you*, but you need to forgive him for what you think he did to me."

"Charlie."

"No. You said anything. I want this. Your mom called, and we're going over to your parents' for dinner tomorrow. Tyson and Paige will be there. You can talk then. I figure after today, the whole family's going to have to talk."

"You didn't tell her I was home, did you?" Gideon didn't want to find his mother on the doorstep when they got home.

"I'm not crazy."

"Thank God. My dad knows I'm home though," he confessed, realizing he hadn't exactly told her the whole of what happened that morning.

"What? How?"

"I called him. I had to. I was pretty sure Paige would take Tyson to his hospital, and I thought he needed a heads up."

"You hit Tyson so hard he had to be taken to the hospital? Gideon! Oh my God!"

The guilt he was already feeling amplified a million times at Charlie's words. "I kind of broke his nose." Gideon cringed and leaned away from Charlie.

As they pulled up to the front gates of the base, Charlie stiffened in her seat. Gideon didn't know whether it was because of what they were about to do or because she knew the animal who'd hurt her was probably here somewhere.

Ironically, Gideon had wanted to move on base when a house opened up not long after they were married, but Charlie didn't want to leave their cozy apartment. He'd pushed her a bit because he thought if she were on base, she'd be safe whenever he deployed. But Charlie had been adamant, and eventually he'd given in. Now he realized his rationale was full of holes anyway.

"Baby, we need a game plan," he said as he showed his ID to the guard. "You can't just go busting in there and throwing around that Boyd may have… um…hurt Zoe like he did you," Gideon said as he pulled away from the gate.

"He didn't *hurt* me, Gideon. He *raped* me. I want you to say it. I know it's an ugly word, but it's an ugly thing. I couldn't say it for a long time, and until I did, I was still under his control. You—and the knowledge that what he did wasn't about me, but the power he needed over me—have given me the strength to move on with my life, our life. I have to take that power back, and so do you. So say it."

Gideon looked over at his wife. Her eyes were big and shining with the strength she'd found inside. He'd never seen her like that.

"He raped you. Goddamn it! I want to kill him for raping you." For the first time since Charlie had told him, it hit him full force. Gideon felt like he'd just been kicked in the balls, and all the wind went out of his lungs. He had to pull over for a minute to get control. *Pull your shit together, man.* Even if Charlie didn't need his protection, she definitely needed his strength.

He took a deep breath and looked at her. Then he leaned over and quickly kissed her. What she'd been asking him earlier finally clicked. He couldn't protect her from what was about to happen, but he could be there for her. And she'd be there for him—he knew without a doubt.

"You're my hero, Charlie. I mean that. You're so strong and caring, and I'm going to be here for you when you need me. Thank you for all that you are." Gideon meant every word he spoke.

"Okay," he added, shifting gears. "What are you going to say?" He pulled the truck back onto the road and headed to Jaylon's place.

"I don't know. I want to talk to her alone, so maybe you can take him out for a beer or something."

"Okay. I can do that."

"You can't say anything to him about Boyd or the rape, though," she added.

"Why?" Confused didn't even begin to describe Gideon's reaction.

"Because we don't know if Zoe's told him."

"Baby, we don't know if Zoe was…" He still couldn't bring himself to say the word in conversation. Gideon wanted to be strong for Charlie, but the images that word conjured were too painful.

"Please just trust me on this. I'll know when I see her. Without support from people around her, this will be eating her up."

"You weren't going to tell me, were you?"

"No. If not for Tyson, I don't know if I ever would've told you." Charlie watched as her hands pulled a loose thread on her top.

Gideon couldn't say he wasn't hurt by her answer, but he also couldn't judge her for doing what she thought was right. He'd never fully know or understand the things she went through.

Gideon pulled the car over to the curb in front of Jaylon's house and hopped out. He walked slowly around to open the door for Charlie. There was a lump in his throat. If he started to talk to her, he'd completely lose it. Gideon had a role to play, and he couldn't let Fox see what was going on in his head.

"I'll call you when I want you guys to come back, okay?"

"All right. I love you, baby." *And admire, worship, and adore the hell out of you*, Gideon thought.

"Thanks, Joe. You know I love you too."

Charlie rang the doorbell, and they waited for someone to answer. Gideon had never been so nervous in his entire life—not even when he'd married Charlie. This was going to be a very long and emotional day for everyone involved. Jaylon opened the door after a few seconds and looked surprised to see them standing there.

"Cooper? What the hell are you doing here, man? I mean, hell, we just got home…" His gaze slid to where Gideon's hand was joined with Charlie's and a questioning look crossed his face. Gideon was sure Fox was remembering Gideon's turmoil during the mission. But then he continued.

"Shouldn't you two be locked away somewhere?" His tone was jovial, but there was strain in his voice.

"Well, Charlie was thinking about Zoe and hasn't been able to get a hold of her for a while, so she begged me to bring her over to see you guys." Gideon tried to match Fox's cheery tone. The squint in his friend's eyes meant he knew Gideon was full of shit.

"Zoe isn't feeling very well. I don't think now is a good time." Jaylon's face fell. In that moment Gideon was sure Charlie had been right, and he felt for his buddy.

"I just want to see her for a minute," Charlie said. "I mean, she hasn't even seen how huge I am." Charlie's face was plastered with a smile Gideon knew wasn't genuine.

Jaylon looked confused, and Gideon could tell he was trying to decide what to do. But Charlie wasn't about to give him the chance to keep them out. In an instant, she politely pushed past him into the darkened house. Gideon followed.

All the curtains were drawn, and a stale odor hung in the air. Zoe was on her side on the couch, curled into a small ball. Her eyes were open, but she didn't look like she was seeing anything.

This is bad.

CHAPTER 37

The sight of Zoe on the couch caused Charlie physical pain. When Jaylon didn't want to let them in, she thought she'd been right. Now she was positive.

"Can I get you guys anything?" Jaylon asked after both Gideon and Charlie overcame the shock of seeing Zoe and took a seat on the love seat opposite her. "We're kind of low right now, but a glass of water or a soda?"

"No, thank you." Charlie shot Gideon a look to let him know it was time to get Jaylon out of the house.

"Hey, man, why don't we go over to the club and grab a beer? The girls can catch up. Seriously," he added as Jaylon hesitated, "you don't want to hang around and hear about all the pregnancy stuff. Some of it's pretty gross." Gideon made a face.

Charlie was surprised at how well Gideon was playing his role. He really sounded like nothing was wrong.

Jaylon looked over at Zoe, debating. While he looked like he wanted to go, he was clearly worried about his wife. Charlie had always liked Jaylon, and his concern for Zoe made her like him more. She was certain he could help her through this.

"It's okay. I'll take care of her." Charlie started pushing the guys out of the house.

"Okay. I guess." Jaylon finally gave in. "But only one drink."

He walked over to kiss his wife good-bye, and Charlie's heart broke when Zoe cringed and pulled away. He tried to play it off, but Charlie could see the hurt and fear in Jaylon's eyes as he turned and headed out the door with Gideon. Gideon gave Charlie a weak smile as he pulled the door closed behind him.

Once Charlie heard them pull away, she went to Zoe. She looked so small on the couch. Charlie sat down on the floor next to her friend, setting her hand on the other woman's arm. Zoe flinched under Charlie's touch. Charlie knew it couldn't have been long since Cody Boyd had been there to take from Zoe. *This is my fault,* Charlie thought.

"Zoe, honey?" she whispered.

The broken woman didn't even acknowledge her. Zoe's stare was fixed on some small point in front of her.

"Zoe, I know. I know what he did."

Zoe's eyes got big, but she still didn't say anything. A single tear slid down her cheek.

"You don't have to tell me, but I want you to know what he did to me." Charlie moved a hand down Zoe's arm and took her hand. Zoe squeezed it, and Charlie knew she was doing the right thing.

For the next half an hour, Charlie told Zoe her story. Zoe never said a word, just held Charlie's hand tightly. When she was done, Charlie looked over at her face. It was stained with tears, and her breathing had become ragged.

"He…he…oh, Charlie!" They were the first words Zoe had spoken since Charlie walked in. Charlie wondered if they were the first in days.

"When was he here, Zoe?"

"F-Five days ago."

Charlie felt like the worst person to ever live. If she'd told someone, if she'd gone to the police—even if they didn't believe her, at least Zoe would've known not to open the door five days ago.

"We're going to get you help. I promise. I know someone who'll help you." Charlie's own tears clouded her vision. "I'm sorry. I'm so sorry."

"I c-c-can't tell Jaylon. He'll leave me."

"Oh, Zoe. You need to trust him. I learned the hard way just how tough our men are. I almost lost Gideon because I tried to hide it. Jaylon loves you. I saw his face—he's hurting for you. And when you're ready, we need to talk to others." Charlie had a plan. She wouldn't push Zoe, but she'd need her help.

"No! Even if I tell Jaylon, I can't tell anyone else. What'll they think of me?"

"They'll think you're the bravest person they know. Zoe, I won't push you. I want you to see my therapist, but I'd never make you do anything you don't want to. But, he needs to be stopped. If I'd spoken up all those month ago, he couldn't have done this to you. I'm going to talk to the other wives."

"You don't think…" Zoe's face twisted in horror.

"Yes, I do. Gideon went after him yesterday. He admitted what he did and said there were others."

"Oh, God."

"Can I call the guys and have them come back? I'll stay here with you when you tell Jaylon, if you want me to. If not, we'll leave. Whatever you need, but Jaylon needs to know."

Zoe sat up, and Charlie moved next to her, still holding her hand. Zoe gave a small nod, and Charlie pulled out her phone.

Getting his buddy into the car was like herding cats. When Gideon lost focus for even one minute, he'd had to backtrack and round him up again. Jaylon stopped at least seven times in the middle of the sidewalk, turning around to go back to the house. Each time Gideon physically pushed him forward. Gideon knew his objective, and he wouldn't let Charlie down.

Gideon couldn't blame the guy for being hesitant—Zoe looked really bad. He was pretty sure he wouldn't have wanted to leave his wife's side if she'd looked like that. It occurred to him that Charlie probably had looked *just* like that at one time; he just hadn't been there to see it. A picture of Charlie in the exact same position flashed in Gideon's mind, and his knees nearly buckled with the pain that nailed him square in the chest. It took every ounce of strength he possessed to finish pushing Jaylon to the car. If he'd had to see Charlie like that, Boyd would be dead right now. That was for fucking sure.

Other than the few times Gideon had to redirect his friend away from the house, neither man had spoken a word since leaving. Gideon didn't know what to say. He'd promised not to tell him what had happened. Not that he didn't want to. He hoped eventually, when Zoe did tell her husband, he could be there to keep his friend from going after Boyd. As much as he wanted the prick gone from this earth, Gideon couldn't let one of his buddies fall with him.

The club was pretty deserted in the middle of the day, and the two men took seats at the bar. The bartender looked up from the beer he was pulling to flash them a smile. "Hey, Lieutenant. Long time no see. I'll be with you in a minute." In Gideon's single days he'd been a regular, and the whole staff knew him.

"No problem. We're in no hurry." Gideon glanced over and saw Jaylon's lip curl at his comment. He was already itching to get back to Zoe.

"What can I get you two?" the bartender asked moments later as he made his way over, wiping his hands on the towel tucked into his waistband.

"Couple of Buds. Thanks," Gideon answered, not even asking Jaylon what he wanted.

A few minutes later, they each nursed a beer in silence. Finally Gideon couldn't take it anymore. "So, can you believe the Chargers tanked it again this year? And to lose to the Raiders? Dude, I'm almost embarrassed to be a fan." He hoped the inane sports babble would at least break the ice.

"Um…"

"Oh, that's right. You're a Raider fan. I think I can accept that as long as you don't claim to be part of the 'Raider Nation.' Because then I'd have to seriously rethink our friendship." He tried to get a rise — get Jaylon to show any emotion other than the worry currently on display.

"What the fuck are you talking about, Cooper? You show up out of nowhere with the wife you were sure had cheated on you last I knew. And did you not see *my* wife? You're rambling on about football? Seriously?"

"I know. I'm sorry. I just didn't know what to say. Do you know why she's like that?"

"No. I came home, and that's exactly how she was. I can't even touch her. If I go near her she flinches and starts crying."

A flash of anger sparked in Gideon's eyes. He knew what was wrong and wanted the bastard who did it to hurt. He tried to drive the thought from his mind before Fox noticed. He was a second too late.

"What? Why did you look like that? Do you know something, Cooper?"

Gideon took a long pull from his beer and tried not to look at his friend. Charlie had trusted Gideon to keep his buddy calm, and he was failing miserably. He couldn't hide his feelings any longer. Gideon was raw and angry and guilty — and all those things were painted on his face.

Faster than Gideon thought possible, Jaylon had him pinned against the bar with a hand on his throat. He squeezed tight enough that Gideon had a hard time drawing in air.

"What the hell do you know about Zoe? I saw it in your face. What did Charlie do to her?" Jaylon clenched his teeth as his eyes focused only on Gideon.

Out of the corner of his eye, Gideon spotted two huge military police-men coming toward them. He lifted his hand to wave them off. He didn't want his buddy to get jacked up over this. It wasn't Fox's fault. It wasn't even Gideon's fault. It was that fuckhead Boyd's fault.

"Fox, you gotta let me go man. See those MPs? They want to peel you off me and haul your ass to the brig. You can't let that happen." Gideon watched as Jaylon's expression changed instantly. His hand dropped, releasing Gideon.

Gideon took a deep breath and looked at his friend. He couldn't blame him for his reaction. If he thought someone he knew had hurt Charlie, Gideon would've done the same thing. In fact, he'd done just that to Boyd and Tyson.

Jaylon stepped away, his eyes lowered to the floor. Gideon wanted to tell him everything was okay and he shouldn't worry about Zoe, but he couldn't. There were too many facts he didn't know. Clapping a hand to his shoulder, Gideon tried to convey to Jaylon that he wasn't pissed off about being choked. He was about to try to calm the situation further when his phone vibrated in his pocket. He prayed it was Charlie.

"Hey, baby. You okay?" He wanted to hear Charlie's voice—to know she was still holding it together. Gideon silently vowed again to be her support.

"Yeah, I am. Can you and Jaylon come back?"

Gideon hoped he could find a way to prepare his buddy without coming right out and telling him. "Sure. We'll be there in a few." He threw a twenty on the bar and turned to Jaylon, who hadn't looked up since letting him go. "Come on, man. Zoe needs you right now."

Fox's head snapped to attention, and he looked Gideon in the eye. "This is going to be bad, isn't it?"

"Yeah. I'm not going to lie, and I can't be the one to talk to you about it, but yeah, it's going to test all your commitment. The commitment you have to your job, your country, yourself—and to the life you've built and want to have with Zoe. I know it did for me."

The two men walked out in total silence after that. There was nothing more to say.

Charlie held Zoe as she trembled. She worried Zoe wasn't going to get through this, and as selfish as it was, Charlie needed her to tell Jaylon.

If Zoe could tell him, they could move on and talk to others. She had to know how many more there were.

Zoe's body stiffened when they heard the car doors slam a few minutes later.

"I-I can't do this, Charlie. I…I just can't." Zoe began to panic.

"I'm right here. I can't guarantee how Jaylon will react, but he's a good man. He loves you, and I know he won't hurt you. You have to trust him."

Charlie tried to be encouraging, but she knew was what a hypocrite she was. Here she sat trying to convince her friend to trust her husband, when for months Charlie hid her own rape from everyone who loved her.

The sound of the key in the door seemed to echo in the house. Zoe took a deep breath, and Charlie did the same. When the door inched open, Charlie could see Gideon looming behind Jaylon in the doorframe. The angry red marks on his neck captured her attention. She caught Gideon's eye, and he gave an almost imperceptible shake of his head to let her know now wasn't the time.

Zoe had dropped her head to stare at the floor. Charlie knew exactly what she was thinking—she'd done something to deserve having her world collapse around her. Again Charlie's guilt consumed her. She'd been weak and selfish. How many other lives had *he* destroyed because of her?

Charlie watched as Jaylon hesitantly approached. Even Gideon, who'd moved only slightly into the house, looked worried about how this was going to play out.

"Zoe? Baby? Please tell me what's wrong. I love you. Nothing you tell me could change that."

Zoe shook her head.

"Boo, I'm so scared here. I don't know how to help you." Jaylon tentatively slipped a finger under her chin to lift her head so she'd look at him. Tears streamed down her face. Zoe's entire body shook as Jaylon brushed his thumb over her cheek to clear away the tears. Charlie wrapped an arm around her to calm her tremors.

"Zoe, I'm here. You're safe. Jaylon can help. Go ahead and tell him," she encouraged.

"Oh my God! I can't…I can't," Zoe wailed.

"Yes, baby, you can. I won't let anything hurt you. I promise." Jaylon was in tears, and Charlie wanted to leave her friends to their grief, but Zoe needed her to stay.

"He…he…I thought…he said he knew you…and you asked him to come…"

Charlie took a deep breath as Zoe started her story. She prayed Jaylon wouldn't try to speak. If he interrupted, Zoe would never be able to get it out.

"Oh, Jaylon. He said you told him to come, and then he…why? Why did he do this to me?" Zoe's voice held so much pain Charlie could feel it radiating through her own body.

It took a few more tries, but eventually Zoe got her story out. The details were similar to Charlie's, and she had to hold her breath and force herself to keep her eyes open for fear she'd relive it too.

"You keep saying he said he knew me. Who did this to you, Zoe?"

"He said his name was Cody." As soon as the name was out of her mouth, Jaylon was up and heading for the door. He didn't get far. Gideon caught him by the back of the neck and pinned him to the wall. Jaylon struggled against Gideon's hold, but even though they were both trained Navy SEALs, Gideon had a considerable height and weight advantage and was able to keep the other man where he was.

"I can't let you do it, man. I won't watch you throw your life away on that piece of shit. Trust me, I know what you're feeling," Gideon said calmly.

Charlie was surprised by how in control he was. While Zoe told her story, she'd been watching him and knew he was seeing it happen to her.

"What the hell do you know about how I feel? You don't know shit! Now let me go, or so help me I'll kill you after I take out that prick!"

Jaylon worked hard against Gideon's grip, but Gideon was just stronger. For the first time since Charlie had known Gideon, she realized he really was deadly. She'd never been able to comprehend that he could actually kill people until now.

"I know because I almost killed him myself yesterday. I know because what my brother saw and decided was Charlie cheating on me so many months ago was Boyd leaving our apartment after he'd raped my wife. I know because I was where you are right now not twenty-four hours ago. So you need to calm the hell down."

Jaylon looked over at Charlie. She nodded.

"Now you need to be here for your wife. You need to get her some help. You can't do that if you're locked up for going after Boyd. This isn't over. He's going to pay."

Charlie shivered at the malice in every word Gideon spoke. He was deadly, and he wanted to protect not only Charlie, but his friends as well. She couldn't have loved him more.

"Zoe? I've been talking to someone for a few months now," Charlie explained. "Would you like to talk to her? She's helped me a lot. I know I'll never get over this. It's a part of who I am now, but I'm dealing with it every day. And every day brings something new for me to overcome. But I'm still here…"

"Wait—what do you mean months?" Jaylon asked. Gideon released him and he came back toward the couch where Zoe and Charlie still sat.

"Cody Boyd raped me two weeks after you left." Charlie saw the moment Jaylon realized what she'd said.

"What do you mean? Why is he still out and able to do this to other women?"

"Jay, please, don't," Zoe begged in a whisper.

"I never told anyone," Charlie confessed. "I was too ashamed. I was scared I'd done something to cause it to happen, and if Gideon found out he wouldn't want me anymore." Charlie saw Jaylon's face, and for a split second she wanted Gideon's protection again.

"So it's your fault this happened to Zoe? This is all your fault!"

Gideon was suddenly at his wife's side. She didn't even remember him moving. "Okay, that's enough. I know this is a lot to handle—believe me I do—but the only person to blame for this is Boyd."

Charlie felt a pain in her stomach. Not even thinking, she placed a hand over her belly. Gideon noticed, and Charlie saw panic in his eyes.

"What's wrong, Charlie?"

"Nothing. One of the babies just must've kicked too hard. That's all." She tried to reassure him. "Zoe, I'm going to call my therapist right now and see if she can meet you and Jaylon today, if you want. And I think seeing your doctor would also be a good idea."

Zoe nodded, and even though she flinched slightly, she did relax a little when her husband stepped over to take her hand.

Charlie knew what Jaylon said was true. She'd always be partially to blame for Zoe being hurt, but she was going to do everything she could to help her. She was going to do everything she could to help all the women Cody Boyd raped because she didn't tell.

Charlie called Dr. Lassiter and explained the situation. The therapist agreed to see the Foxes and said she'd wait in her office for them to arrive.

As Charlie leaned over to the coffee table to write down directions to Dr. Lassiter's office, she felt another sharp pain rip through her belly. Once again, her hand automatically went to her stomach, and she gasped. When she finally calmed herself and the pain subsided, Charlie noticed everyone focused on her.

"Okay, I'm done, Charlie. What the hell was that? And if you say nothing, I'll throw you over my shoulder and take you to the base hospital right now."

"I just had a little pain. That's all. I swear, it's gone already." She handed the directions to Jaylon and stood to leave. Charlie wanted them to get on the road immediately, before they changed their minds about talking to someone.

As they left their friends, Charlie leaned against Gideon a little more than she normally would. She was exhausted, and the last twinge of pain had scared her. "I think maybe we should go to the hospital," Charlie whispered.

"What's wrong, baby?" Gideon's voice had lost all the calm he'd worked for earlier when trying to reason with his friend. Now he was panicked. She needed him calm.

"I don't know, but I want to see my doctor. It's probably nothing. You know there are so many new things every single day with these two."

Charlie tried to be casual, worried that Gideon would make good on his threat to take her to the base hospital. That idea was not appealing. She'd much rather see her own doctor than a stranger. Having an unknown man touch her would do more harm than good.

After helping Charlie into the cab of the truck, Gideon ran around and jumped in the driver's side. His phone was already to his ear as he headed to the front gate and off base.

"Come on, come on. I know you're still there," he mumbled as he listened to the ringing on the other end. Charlie smiled at how perfect he was and how much she loved him. The smile quickly faded as another wave of pain rolled through her.

"Damn it!" Gideon hung up and dialed another number. "I need you to page Dr. Cooper. This is his son. Page him. Now!"

"Gideon, calm down. Please." She reached out and touched his arm. The worry in his eyes as he looked over at her was almost as painful as the... contractions?

No, no, no. It's too early. They aren't supposed to come for four more months.

CHAPTER 38

There was no way on this earth Gideon was going to be calm. Charlie was in pain, and no matter what she'd said earlier, he had to protect her and the babies. He sat with the phone to his ear listening to the horrible Muzak crap. "Like a Virgin" was never meant to be instrumental. Despite his annoyance, Gideon found himself tapping his fingers to the song, which irritated him even more. Then he started singing along, trying to calm himself.

"Are you singing 'Like a Virgin'?" Charlie asked. Gideon couldn't tell whether she was in pain or angry. Fortunately, the music ended as someone answered on the other end.

"This is Dr. Cooper."

Relief washed through Gideon at the sound of his dad's voice. "Dad, something's wrong with Charlie."

"What do you mean, Gideon? What's wrong?"

"She's having pains. It's the babies."

"Okay, don't panic. It could be a million different things."

Gideon looked over at Charlie and watched as she tried to hide another pain. "Bring her in, and I'll call her doctor."

Gideon turned to Charlie. "Dad's going to call your doctor. Who is it?"

"Gideon, I know who Charlie's doctor is. Don't worry. I'll get her here no matter what."

"We're on our way right now." Gideon flipped the phone closed and tried to concentrate on getting Charlie to the hospital.

"What did he say?" Gideon noticed Charlie's voice was a little weaker than it had been a few minutes ago when she'd scolded him.

"That it could be one of a million things and not to worry. I fucking hate when doctors tell you that."

As he drove, Gideon went through all the things he'd done wrong in the forty-eight hours he'd been home. He was sure he was the reason something was wrong with Charlie and the babies. Not only had Gideon accused her of cheating on him and forced her to relive what that prick had done—he couldn't breathe for a minute while those images flashed through his mind—but then Charlie had to pull him off Boyd. And then they'd had sex. What if that's what had caused all of this? What if he was the one to force yet another horrific torture on Charlie?

The cherry on the top had to be Charlie taking on Zoe's pain. Her guilt was so overwhelming, Gideon could almost feel it himself. He vowed he'd never let her be alone again. He didn't care what that meant. He only knew he could never leave her again.

Gideon suddenly realized he had not only Charlie to worry about, but also those two little critters. He was going to be totally screwed for the rest of his life—but in the best way possible. And God help him if they were girls. He'd never sleep again.

Please, God. Don't let anything happen to them. Please, God. Don't let anything happen to them… He repeated the mantra over and over as he sped along the freeway, glancing sideways at Charlie from time to time. She seemed to have calmed some, and Gideon felt a little better.

He pulled up to the emergency room doors, stopped the truck, and jumped out to run around and get Charlie. She was already opening her door. She really should've known better than to think he was going to let her walk. Gideon scooped his wife up and headed through the sliding doors.

"Gideon! I can walk!" Charlie protested.

"I know you don't want me to protect you, but like I told you—until these two are out, you're just going to have to—" Gideon couldn't finish his sentence. He looked up to find the last person he ever expected to see.

Tyson and Paige waited in the small, curtained room after Peter was called away. Tyson's face felt better and the swelling in his lip was waning—not that he thought he could return to any rigorous activity any time soon.

"Oh, God," Paige sighed as she pushed her head into Tyson's chest.

He wrapped his arms around her. "Paige, please. I know this seems bad, but it's not really. Trust me, Gideon did far worse when we were kids."

"I'm not talking about the broken nose. Although I think he was wrong, I knew you wouldn't be able to avoid Gideon's wrath for long. I knew eventually he'd take his anger out on you."

"Then why are you still so upset? Dad knows the best plastic surgeons in the state. The nose will be fine for the wedding," Tyson teased.

"Yeah, because that was my main concern."

"Then what's up?"

"I'm just a little overwhelmed," Paige said. Then she took a deep breath and smiled. "After this morning's encounter with my pelvis of death, you aren't going to stop…you know…are you?" She looked up at him and batted her lashes.

"Paige, you're ridiculous." Tyson's voice lowered an octave before he spoke again. "I love you. There's nothing that would make me not want you. I love to taste you. I'll—"

At that moment Peter pulled back the curtain to make his entrance as he returned to the room. Tyson sat on the cot with Paige standing between his legs. She jumped back when Peter came in, her face bright with a blush. Peter chuckled at the two of them—like teenagers who'd been caught on their parents' couch without all their hands visible.

Tyson wondered how much of that conversation his dad had overheard. After thinking about it, he decided he didn't want to know.

"I was going to offer to take the two of you to lunch for a little celebration, but that page was your brother," Peter said. "He and Charlie are on their way in."

"Why? Why are they coming here?" Tyson got up off the cot, instantly worried.

"Charlie's having some pain. That's all I know."

"Oh no," Paige choked out. "How can things get any worse?"

"Don't panic. Like I told Gideon, there are a million things that could be going on."

"Well, we have to stay and make sure she's okay." Paige's voice was small and broken, her worry obvious.

"I don't think that would be a good idea," Peter said. "Gideon usually takes a while to cool down, and I don't think Charlie seeing Tyson in the shape he's in would be all that great either."

"Good point, Dad." Tyson took Paige's hand and pulled her to him. Peter opened the curtain, and the three headed to the exit. They rounded the corner into the main foyer of the emergency room and pulled up short at the sight of them.

"Shit!"

"Uh-oh!"

"Damn!"

After hanging up with Peter, Evelyn sat feeling sorry for herself for all of about two seconds. Her husband had stood her up, her sons had lives she wasn't part of anymore, and her daughters-in-law were either too busy or tired of her. Eventually she decided if her family wouldn't come to her, she'd go to them. She grabbed her purse and left to have lunch with her husband.

When she arrived at the hospital, Evelyn went to the doctors' parking area to make sure Peter's car was there. She held her breath as she searched. Evelyn trusted Peter and knew in her heart he'd never do something behind her back, but when her husband started acting different — like he was hiding something — she started to worry.

Peter's excuse for canceling lunch had been some sort of emergency, but Evelyn hadn't heard of her husband taking an emergency case in years. Usually when an emergency surgery came in, one of the younger surgeons took it. Peter generally did scheduled procedures. After thirty years, he had some seniority.

Evelyn sighed with relief when she saw his car parked in his usual spot. She suddenly felt guilty for not trusting him. After finding a parking space, Evelyn went in to the ER. The doors opened, and she stepped into the main hallway. Sitting at the nurse's desk was a young, cute little brunette. Evelyn instantly didn't like her. She felt bad about that. The poor girl hadn't done anything wrong…yet.

"May I help you?" she asked, her tone clipped.

"Yes, I'm looking for Dr. Cooper." Evelyn smiled at her, ignoring the way the woman was obviously sizing her up.

"Dr. Cooper is with a patient right now. I'm sure he'll be wrapping up any minute if you want to wait."

Evelyn smiled and turned to the waiting room. She froze. Walking through the door was Gideon — carrying Charlie. A million things went through her head: Why was Gideon here? Why was he carrying Charlie? Why were they at the hospital?

Before Evelyn could say anything, they saw her, and Gideon stopped dead in his tracks. She was hurt by the expression on her son's face. He looked like seeing his mother was the worst thing that could've happened to him. She wanted to ask what was going on but wasn't able to get a single word out before she heard three different voices to her right.

Turning, she saw not only her husband, but Paige and Tyson.

Evelyn's vision began to swirl, and she could hear the clock ticking away the seconds. Then she felt herself slip away. She'd never fainted before, but somehow she knew that's what was happening.

CHAPTER 39

One minute Evelyn had been standing, and the next she'd crumpled to the floor. Peter ran over and scooped his wife up to take her to a room. Gideon, still carrying Charlie in his arms, followed his father back to the exam area.

Charlie caught sight of Paige and realized the man next to her with a bruised and swollen face was Tyson. His lip was split open, and Charlie would not have even recognized him. She was horrified Gideon had done that to his brother. Tyson was an ass, and while *she* would have loved to beat the crap out of him, and had actually tried, she never wanted Gideon to hurt him. They were brothers; it wasn't right. She made the decision that for the family she needed to make amends with Tyson. Gideon needed it to happen. At that moment, however, there were more pressing issues to deal with.

"Gideon, put Charlie down on that bed, please," Peter instructed. Charlie was in awe of Peter's calm when there was about to be a huge scene right in the middle of his hospital. She glanced at her husband and understood for the first time where he got his strength. A small smile crept onto her lips.

"What are you smiling about?" Gideon asked, his brows pulled together.

"Nothing." Charlie kissed his wrinkled forehead as he laid her down on the bed across from Evelyn's. Gideon shook his head as he turned back to his mother, but he never let go of Charlie's hand. Evelyn had started to stir and her eyes fluttered open.

"Oh my God. I'm dreaming," she said as she looked at Gideon. "Or is it a nightmare?" She looked around at the rest of her broken family. Evelyn's gaze finally settled on Peter. "Peter Aloysius Cooper. What the hell is going on here?"

The tiny space was silent. Charlie had never heard Evelyn swear, and while "hell" wasn't a big swear word, she was still stunned. Tyson and Gideon looked at each other with amusement. Tyson's smile looked a little painful, but still he seemed to think the whole thing was funny.

"Oh, the full name? You are in so much trouble, Dad," Gideon said.

"Yeah, you might get grounded." Tyson tried to laugh, but he looked like it hurt.

"Dr. Cooper, you have a call on line five. Dr. Cooper, you have a call on line five," a disembodied voice announced over the intercom.

Evelyn glared at her husband. Tyson and Gideon tried to stifle their laughter as their father shot them a warning look. Paige and Charlie looked on, not knowing what to think.

"Evelyn, dear, I have to take this. It should be Charlie's doctor, and she really needs to see her. I love you, darling."

Charlie's mouth dropped open. Her father-in-law had just thrown her under the bus to save himself. Peter stepped out to get the phone, and Evelyn's eyes immediately fell on Charlie. *Yep. That's exactly what he did. Coward!*

"Charlie, what's the matter?"

"Um…" Charlie knew better than to answer that question.

"She's having pains," Gideon answered for her. That was a mistake. Evelyn's head moved ever so slightly to look at Gideon. Charlie had never seen her mother-in-law look like that. She was a little scared.

"You. Why are you here? I mean home. Why are you home and I don't know about it? How long have you been home?" Evelyn's tone conveyed how deeply hurt she was.

"Mom, calm down. You just fainted—we don't want you to go out again." He was scared of his mom too.

"Gideon, I'll deal with you later." She looked over at Paige and Tyson, who'd tried to push themselves against the farthest wall. "And what happened to you, Tyson?"

"Um…" Like Charlie, Tyson didn't want to answer the question. His attempt to protect Gideon made Charlie soften toward him—a fraction. He then made the mistake of shooting a quick glance over at his brother. It didn't get past Evelyn.

"Your brother did that?"

No one knew what to say. Charlie tightened her grip on Gideon's hand. She wanted him to know she was there for him. It was Charlie's turn to be strong.

"Mom, there are a lot of things—" Gideon was cut off by the reappearance of Peter. Right behind him was Dr. Miles, Charlie's doctor. Charlie exhaled in relief. Finally she was going to get some answers.

"So, Charlie, I hear you're having a little pain," Dr. Miles said.

"I wouldn't say 'little,' but yeah."

Dr. Miles and Peter laughed, but Gideon seemed to be working up to a good tirade. Charlie gave his hand a squeeze to ease him.

"Well, let's take a look and see what's going on. Other than the pain, are there any other problems? Bleeding? Pain anywhere else?" Dr. Miles asked as she pulled the curtain around Charlie's bed to give at least the appearance of privacy.

"Don't think I'm done with any of you," Evelyn warned. "But right now, my grandbabies are the most important thing. Just be prepared. When we go home tonight…" She didn't have to finish that sentence.

"So tell me what's going on, Charlie."

"I keep getting these pains in my stomach. And then they kind of go away and about fifteen minutes later I get another one. Please tell me I'm not having these babies right now."

A tear escaped as she spoke, and Gideon squeezed her hand tightly. It was too early. She'd read all the books. With medical intervention, the babies might survive. She'd seen stories about babies born even earlier making it, but Charlie didn't want that. She wanted perfect, healthy babies.

After checking Charlie over—heartbeat, temperature, pulse—Dr. Miles stepped back and grabbed the curtain. "Okay, let's get you undressed, and I'm going to get an ultrasound machine in here. We'll have a look and see what those little buggers are doing." She turned and left. Charlie quickly undressed and put the gown on. She was nervous.

On the other side of the curtain, Charlie heard Evelyn scolding Peter for not calling her the instant Tyson came in to the ER. Listening to them calmed Charlie. Life was going on.

After a few minutes, the curtains opened again and a nurse came in pushing the portable ultrasound machine. Just behind her, Charlie saw everyone's eyes as they looked in. They all had the same look of fear, and in that instant, her good feeling disappeared.

The doctor pulled the curtains around them to do an exam before the ultrasound. Poor Gideon, Charlie thought he might pass out when he saw what the doctor was doing. His grip on her hand increased, and his eyes grew wide.

"You aren't dilated at all. Also no effacing, so as I suspected, you're having Braxton Hicks contractions. They're common around this time, and you might have them again before you actually go into labor. It's just your body practicing."

Charlie was embarrassed. After reading all those books, how could she not have known they were Braxton Hicks?

"So how are we going to know when they're real ones?" Gideon asked.

"Trust me. When they're true labor contractions, Charlie will know. They'll be much stronger and will probably last longer."

Charlie gave Gideon a terrified look. Screw all that big, brave crap she'd spewed in the car earlier, she wanted him to take care of her.

Gideon's thumb moved over the back of her hand. "It'll be okay, babe. I'm here."

"Can you have these babies for me, Gideon?" Charlie's voice was a harsh, but she was scared.

The other side of the curtain erupted in laughter.

"Now there's something I want to see—big, bad, Navy SEAL Gideon pregnant and doing that breathing crap!" Tyson barked.

"Tyson, stop," Evelyn scolded, but not soon enough.

"Shut it, Tyson. Or I'll shut it for you," Gideon growled.

"Boys," Peter broke in.

"Okay. Not to interrupt this family love fest or anything, but how about we have a little look-see at those babies. I'm assuming now that Gideon's home we want to know the sexes?" Dr. Miles asked.

"Yes!" everyone shouted at the same time.

Once the doctor began running the ultrasound wand over Charlie's belly, Gideon's eyes became glued to the monitor. The smile on his face sent a tingle through Charlie's body. He was obviously trying to hold back tears. Charlie loved her husband more than she thought possible.

"Well, here's a foot, and one, two, three more." Dr. Miles pointed at the tiny screen. "And looks like they have all their toes. Strong heartbeats. I see twenty total fingers, so we're good there. And if you look right here, you'll see we have two little boys."

"Ah, more boys," Evelyn said from the other side of the curtain.

"Sorry, Mom!" Gideon called.

"No, Gideon, don't be sorry. I'm so happy. As long as those babies are healthy, I'm fine. Besides, there's always next time."

Gideon leaned down and kissed Charlie softly on the forehead. "I love you, Charlie Cooper. You amaze me. Thank you." His voice was heavy with emotion, and tears began to stream down Charlie's cheeks. After everything that had happened, she never thought she'd be this happy again. The two little boys on the screen had changed everything.

"I'll print these for you two. Go ahead and get dressed, Charlie. I want you to rest today, but other than that, everything looks fine." She shook Gideon's hand and patted Charlie's bulging belly before she left the room.

Charlie dressed quickly and gave Gideon the signal to open the curtain. Now that they knew everything was okay with the babies, they'd have to face the rest of the family, and now was as good of a time as any.

As Gideon pulled the curtain back, Charlie heard a demanding voice from the lobby.

"I don't care. Tell me where Charlie Cooper is. That's Cooper as in *Dr. Peter Cooper.*"

Charlie recognized her sister-in-law's voice. The nurse pointed, and Gabby's head swiveled to where the group was gathered. In an instant she was striding toward them, Chance following behind.

"Who?" Charlie demanded, looking at her family. This was not a situation she wanted Gabriella to be part of.

"Sorry," Paige squeaked from the corner. "I thought if you were going to have the babies you'd want her here."

"Oh my God, Charlie. Why aren't you lying down? She should be lying down, right?" Gabby looked at Peter for confirmation.

"Gabriella," Peter said, "Charlie's fine. The babies are fine."

"Thank God. I was so worried when Paige called." Gabby sighed.

"I'm ready to get out of here. I think our little party is starting to draw attention." Charlie gestured to the other patients now staring in their direction.

"What happened to you?" Gabby asked Tyson, the venom in her voice not hidden in the slightest.

"Long story," Gideon answered for him. Both Chance and Gabby looked over at Gideon and from the smiles that broke across their faces, Charlie was sure they knew he'd gone after Tyson.

"Welcome home, Gideon." Chance shook Gideon's hand and clapped him on the back.

"All right, I think it's time we go," Peter suggested.

"Good idea, Dad. I'm going to take Charlie home to rest. She's really going to need it to handle me and the boys." Gideon's booming laughter filled the entire emergency room.

"Boys? We're having boys?" Gabby asked. Everyone nodded. "Damn! I wanted a couple of nieces. Oh well, I guess boys will like all the good rides at Disneyland instead of that princess crap." Everyone, other than Evelyn, laughed as they headed to the exit.

"Okay, Paige and I are going to head out too. Those pain killers should kick in soon," Tyson interjected.

Evelyn gave Gideon a look, and they all knew if he'd still been a child, she would've punished him severely for what he'd done to his brother. But Charlie had to hand it to Gideon—he had the good sense to look ashamed.

"How about I take my beautiful wife to a late lunch?" Peter asked.

"That would be wonderful." Evelyn smiled, but quickly continued. "I expect everyone at the house *tonight*. We're going to sit down as a family and fix all of this. I will not have those boys come into a world of violence and anger." Evelyn caught each one of her children with a meaningful glare. "You and Chance too, Gabriella. You're both part of this family."

Chance cursed under his breath, and Charlie stifled a laugh.

Peter followed Evelyn from the hospital to her favorite restaurant, The Shore. The view of the Pacific from the patio was amazing, and Evelyn was sure it would take her mind off of all that was happening with her family. It didn't.

While Peter tried to be charming, and even a little frisky, she couldn't help but wonder how much he'd known that he hadn't told her. Had he known the emergency patient he was going to treat was their son? Had he known Gideon was home? And if he was keeping all of that from her, what else was there?

The cute, young nurse at the ER popped into Evelyn's mind. Was Peter keeping more secrets? She knew that would never be true—she'd always trusted Peter completely—but knowing he'd been keeping things from her caused something deep down to rear its ugly head.

"Evelyn, darling," he said, holding her hands in his across the table. "I love you. I'd never keep anything from you I wasn't ethically and legally bound to."

"So you admit you knew…what? What did you know, Peter?" Evelyn tried to pull her hands away from his grip, but he held them more tightly.

"I knew Gideon was home. He called me this morning, so I've only known for a matter of hours. They were coming for dinner tomorrow night. He wanted some time to spend with his wife, Evelyn. How could I deny him that?"

"I'm his mother, Peter," Evelyn stated, and even she could hear the shrill tone in her voice. She'd been betrayed by both her husband and her son.

"Yes, and he's a grown man with a wife and a soon-to-be family of his own. He loves you, darling. I know he'd never purposely hurt you, but he needed time with Charlie."

Peter looked his wife right in the eye. Evelyn knew what he was saying was right, but she wasn't happy about any of it. When had her son — the one she'd carried for nine months, the one she'd rocked to sleep, the one who's knees she'd bandaged — become a man? Evelyn hadn't been told about this. No one asked her if she was ready to give up being the most important woman in his life.

"No matter how old he gets, I'll always be his mother, and I should've been told he was home." It was childish, but Evelyn wasn't going to give up that easily.

People at the restaurant started to notice Peter and Evelyn as their conversation became more and more heated. Between Peter's work in the medical community and Evelyn's in the general community, both were well known around town, and the last thing Evelyn wanted was to be gossip for the church social club.

"Peter, I don't want to talk about this any more right now," she said in a low whisper, trying to make sure no one was still staring. Evelyn had worked too hard over the past twenty-five years — or more — to establish her family in the social hierarchy of La Jolla to be brought down by an airing of her family's dirty laundry in public.

"Whatever you want, darling, but I want you to understand that your sons love you. And I promise you, whatever happens tonight that will never change. Know this, Evelyn Cooper, our boys are men now — strong, smart men who've found wonderful, loving women to share their lives with. They'll always be part of us, but in the end it's you and me, babe." He placed a light kiss on Evelyn's knuckles before releasing her hands.

She narrowed her gaze at him. Evelyn was proud of her boys. She wanted nothing more than for them to be happy. That they'd found the other pieces of themselves to spend their lives with should've made her happy—it was everything she'd ever wanted for them. But she didn't know how to let go.

CHAPTER 40

Charlie gazed at Gideon as he held her hand and backed the truck out of its spot in the hospital parking lot. For the first time in several hours she looked content — tired, but content. Knowing the babies were okay had taken a big load off both of them. Now Gideon was going to go home to take care of his wife.

Just as Charlie's eyes closed, her phone began to chime. Gideon immediately braced himself for more drama, because damn, but when it rained on him it poured. He couldn't help but think somehow all this had been waiting for him. Up until now, everything in his life had gone almost perfectly. So this was just the price to pay.

Gideon's eyebrows went up when his wife said "Paige?" He turned his attention back to the road and tried to ignore the conversation. Charlie's voice was light, and she had a smile on her face — that was all he needed to know. Gideon let out a breath. It wasn't another tragedy they needed to tend to. When she laughed out loud, Gideon turned back to her.

"Gideon, we need to turn around," Charlie said, causing panic to spark in his veins.

That's what he got for thinking everything was finally good.

"Why? What's wrong? Do we need to go back to the hospital?"

"No, baby. I'm fine. I promise. Your brother, however, is passed out in his car, and Paige needs help getting him up to his apartment."

Gideon's heart rate dropped back to normal. "Tell her to leave him there!"

"Gideon Isaac Cooper."

He knew then he'd be dragging his dead-to-the-world brother up to his apartment.

"You turn this car around right now, or I'll name these babies after your father and my brother — their middle names," Charlie threatened.

"Aw, shit. Fine." Gideon gave in.

"We'll be there in a few, Paige," Charlie said into the phone.

"I can't believe I have to go carry my brother up to his apartment," Gideon grumbled as he turned the truck around.

"Stop being such a baby." Charlie's hand rubbed along his arm.

The truth was, Gideon wasn't angry about helping Tyson. No matter what he'd done, Tyson was his brother. He glanced over at Charlie, amazed. After everything his brother had put her through, she wanted nothing more than for Gideon to forgive him and have everyone be a big, happy family again. Gideon just wasn't so sure that was an ending he could give her. They were all changed because of what Boyd had done, and that change was permanent.

As they pulled into Tyson's apartment complex, Charlie pointed out a truly frustrated, totally disheveled Paige sitting on the curb. Gideon laughed at the sight. He parked next to Paige's car and got out to look at his brother. Tyson was out cold.

"You sure you didn't knock him out, Paige? I mean, I know that mouth of his can get him in trouble."

"Wow. I've never seen anyone so out of it," Charlie said as she came to stand next to Gideon.

"Well, he took three painkillers at the hospital, so I'm guessing he's going to be out of it for a while. I've tried everything to wake him up. I swear. Even the Prince Charming kiss thing."

"Don't worry. I'll throw him over my shoulder and haul his ass upstairs. It's like carrying a body out of a hot zone."

"Gideon!" Charlie scolded.

"What? I didn't say a *dead* body."

He received two glaring looks from the women in front of him.

"Just pick him up and take him upstairs," Charlie huffed, her hands on her hips.

"Thanks, Gideon," Paige offered as he leaned into the car and easily lifted Tyson out before slinging him over his shoulder. Tyson barely stirred as Gideon kicked the door closed and turned around.

"Gideon! That looks uncomfortable. Do you have to carry him that way?" Paige asked as she trailed behind him.

"You wanted me to help. I'm helping. You don't like the way that I'm doing it—" he stopped at the bottom of the stairs and made a motion to set Tyson down "—then you can carry him yourself."

"No. I'm sorry. Please just get him upstairs."

At the top of the stairs, Gideon had to wait for Paige and Charlie to catch up. Paige was helping Charlie climb the stairs, and Gideon had to hide the smile that quickly spread across his lips. She was just so damn cute with her swollen belly and the flush of her cheeks from climbing the stairs. She actually waddled. Of course he'd *never* tell her that, but he loved it.

Paige slipped past Gideon to unlock the door, and he took the opportunity to lean in and kiss his wife. Charlie flashed a gorgeous smile that didn't quite make it to her eyes. Actually, she looked like she was ready to follow Tyson into dreamland.

Paige unlocked and opened the door, holding it as Gideon hauled Tyson in. He pointed to the couch and told Charlie, "Sit. I want you to relax for a few minutes while I take Sleeping Beauty to his bed." He was surprised when she listened and plopped herself down.

As Gideon turned to follow Paige to Tyson's bedroom, he saw Charlie stifle a yawn. In Tyson's room, he dropped his brother on the bed, where he bounced a few times before finally settling on the mattress. Even with all that jostling, Tyson was still completely asleep.

"Gideon! Could you at least pretend to be a little concerned about your brother?"

"That wasn't part of the bargain. I agreed to carry his stupid ass up here. Never was I going to be nursemaid for him." Gideon got that Paige loved Tyson and was concerned for him, but he was still pissed about what Tyson had done to Charlie.

"Well, if you haven't figured it out, he wouldn't be where he is if you hadn't broken his nose."

"Good point. And now that I've redeemed myself by tucking him in, I'll take my wife and go home," Gideon replied.

"Thank you, Gideon. I really do appreciate your help," Paige offered as they headed back to the living room. Gideon stopped short, causing her to run into the back of him. "What the hell?"

"Shh…" Gideon held a finger to his lips and gestured to Charlie on the couch. In the short time he and Paige had been in the other room, Charlie had succumbed to the exhaustion that had hovered over her for the past couple of hours. Lying on her side, she had her knees curled up under her belly and her hands folded under her head. Gideon went to the couch and was about to pick her up when a small hand on his arm stopped him. He raised an eyebrow in question.

"Let her sleep," Paige whispered. "She needs to rest, and you'll only be waking her up to go right back to sleep." As much as Gideon didn't want to admit it, Paige was right. Charlie falling asleep so quickly proved it.

"Come on." Paige tugged his arm, pulling him toward the kitchen. "I'll get you a beer."

"Thanks, but do you have a Coke or something?" He'd had the beer with Jaylon earlier, and with the evening in store for them all, he didn't want to get started drinking again now. He might not be able to stop.

"Sure, come on."

Gideon followed Paige into the kitchen where she pulled a Coke out of the fridge and poured it into a glass for him. After setting it on the table, she reached in and got a beer for herself. Gideon sat down, and Paige sat across for him. As Gideon took a sip of soda, he wondered what the hell he and Paige were going to do for the next couple of hours.

"So here we are," Paige said before tipping her beer back to take a healthy swig.

"Yep."

"You know that was a total sucker punch, right?"

"Yeah, it was," he agreed.

"Just as long as you know."

There was a lengthy silence, but strangely it wasn't uncomfortable. Usually Tyson's girls felt the need to prattle on, but Paige really was different.

"So, I didn't get to talk to you very much before I left. Tell me a little bit about yourself. I mean, judging from that diamond you're sporting, you're going to be my new sister soon?"

"Yeah." She looked back up at Gideon. "What do you want to know? I'm pretty simple. Come from a small town in Minnesota, only child."

"How did you end up with my dickhead brother?"

"Gideon. Don't talk about Tyson like that, please."

"I'm sorry. He only almost ruined my life and my family. I might be a little bitter," Gideon countered, not willing to give up his anger just yet.

"Tyson was just trying to protect you. He isn't the only one at fault, you know," Paige argued.

"Don't even try to blame Charlie. I'm not ready to dislike you simply for your choice of fiancé, but you start blaming Charlie and we might have a problem."

"Can you stop being so angry for just a minute? I know that sounds impossible, but please try."

Gideon nodded slightly, not sure if he could actually do it.

"I'm not blaming Charlie completely. I was the one she told, and she swore me to secrecy, so I had a hand in everything getting all tangled and out of control too. I get it. We all have secrets, and had both of them not been keeping secrets, things might have happened differently." She stopped and took a breath. "Tyson really was trying to protect you. Put yourself in his place. If you'd seen what he saw, what would you have thought?"

That point hit home. After hearing Tyson describe what he saw, Gideon had believed him, and that was secondhand. If he'd *seen* Boyd that day, he would've thought the same thing.

"Okay, I'll admit what he saw looked bad, but why didn't he tell you? Why didn't he talk to Charlie? Instead he chose to treat her like shit for months and then spill it to me without all the facts."

"I can't answer those questions, Gideon. And believe me, I felt the same way. When Tyson told me what he saw that day, and I realized what he'd done in telling you, I was angry. It made me question how I could be with a man like that. I wondered if I was being shallow and just wanted to be with Tyson for his looks."

Tears started to gather in the corners of Paige's eyes. She'd been through a lot in all this mess too. Gideon finally realized someone outside the three of them had also been affected by what happened. The violence Boyd inflicted on Charlie had a ripple effect, and it reached so far out they might never know the full extent of what he'd done.

"Tyson loves you. Once he found out what really happened he was horrified. *That's* why I love him. Because no matter what, he was trying to be a better man—he was trying to be you. There are a lot of 'ifs' in this whole thing, and none of us can go back and change any of it. All we can do is heal."

"Damn, you really make it hard for me to stay pissed at Tyson," Gideon said. He paused to listen as Charlie stirred for a moment in the other room, moaning in her sleep. "Charlie doesn't blame him for anything other than telling me what he thought happened. She wants me to forgive him. The only thing I can do is say I'll try." Gideon gave Paige a small smile, which she returned.

"That's all I can ask of you. I really do understand hurt and betrayal."

I open my eyes to the bright overhead lights. Where am I? My hands and feet are strapped to a bed with bars on either side. I'm in a hospital room. I can hear the beeping of machines and notice wires that lead from the machines to my stomach.

I can see the huge swell of my belly and let out a sigh of relief that my babies are okay.

The door opens and a man with a surgical mask and gown comes into the room. I can tell the babies are almost ready to come, and I'm happy the doctor's here. As he approaches my bed, there's something in his eyes that isn't quite right, but I can't place it.

"Where's Gideon?" I ask.

The doctor just looks at me, not saying anything.

"Please, can you find my husband? I need him here with me," I beg.

Still the doctor just looks at me. There's something so familiar about his eyes, but as much as I struggle I can't place it.

Tears start to well at the thought of going through this without Gideon. I need him with me. As tears slide down my cheeks, the doctor finally speaks.

"Oh, don't cry. And if I was you, I wouldn't scream either. I don't want to hurt you. I just want to take care of your needs."

The door opens again and another masked man and two women enter.

"Well, let's have us some babies!" the new man says, and I realize the man in front of me isn't the doctor, it's Cody Boyd. His words echo in my head, taking me back to that night. I try to get out of bed, but the restraints hold me in place.

"Naughty, naughty, Charlie. I thought you were smarter than that," he whispers in my ear, sending a chill down my spine.

Things are hazy, and suddenly there's one cry and then another filling the room.

"Look at my boys!" I hear Boyd say. That's more than I can take. These aren't his babies, these are Gideon's boys.

"NO!"

CHAPTER 41

"No!"

Tyson was jolted awake by the sound of screaming. Disoriented, it took him a few seconds to figure out where he was. The last thing he remembered was leaving the hospital with Paige.

The scream Tyson heard was a woman's. Thoughts of Charlie's story flitted through his head, and he launched himself off the bed. His legs, however, hadn't gotten the memo and almost gave out on him as his feet hit the floor. He caught himself before he landed on the ground and continued moving forward. If Paige was in trouble, that's where he needed to be.

Tyson's mind was still foggy from the medication as he looked out the bedroom door into the living room. The sight in front of him was not anything he'd expected to see. There on the couch was Gideon with Charlie wrapped in his arms. He stroked her back and whispered into her hair. Charlie's body heaved with sobs that were muffled in Gideon's chest.

"What happened?" Tyson finally oriented himself enough to ask. All eyes landed on him, and he suddenly felt uncomfortable in his own home.

"Bad dream," Gideon muttered, not relinquishing his hold on Charlie.

"Are you okay, Charlie?" Tyson asked, earning a death glare from his brother.

"What the fuck do you think?" Gideon snapped.

"Gideon, please," Charlie begged. "Thank you, Tyson. I'll be fine. Just need a minute. It's been a few weeks since I've had one that vivid," she quietly explained.

Suddenly the pain and hurt she'd been through over the past months slammed into Tyson all over again. "I'm sorry," he said, meaning it for more than just her haunting dream.

Tyson didn't notice that Gideon had exploded off the couch until he was pinned against the wall. Gideon's entire body weight pushed against him.

"Gideon!" Paige and Charlie shouted at the same time.

"Don't," was all Gideon said through clenched teeth. "You don't talk to her about that."

"Or what? Are you going to break my nose again? Go ahead, Gideon." Tyson pushed his brother back, surprised when he moved.

Charlie and Paige rushed over and pulled Gideon farther away from Tyson.

"I'm sick of this macho shit, Gideon. Tyson is your brother!" Paige was in Gideon's face. Tyson wasn't sure if he was more impressed or more scared that she was standing up to a trained killer. Either way, he felt his nuts shrink up into his body as he realized his girlfriend felt the need to protect him.

"Yeah, my brother who let me down on so many levels in such a short time," Gideon spat back.

"Enough!" Charlie's voice echoed through the apartment, and everyone instantly stopped. "Gideon, I want this fixed now. We're going to your parents' in two hours, and I'll not have the two of you fighting when we face your mother. You get it?"

Gideon sheepishly nodded.

"Tyson, you and Gideon need to sort out whatever it is you've got happening. And I mean everything."

Silently Tyson nodded too.

"Okay, here's what's going to happen," Paige started as Charlie came to her side, hands on hips. They were an intimidating pair. "We have dinner at your parents' in two hours. I'm going to take Charlie home to get cleaned up. Don't worry, Gideon, I'll stay with her while she gets changed and then we'll stop at my place before heading to your parents'."

"I'll not have this hanging over us tonight," Charlie added. "There's too much other crap that's going to come out as it is. And, Gideon, you touch Tyson again, and you don't even want to know what the punishment will be like," she finished.

After a few "yes dears," the men walked the women out to Paige's car.

"I'll see you at your parents'. I love you." Paige gave Tyson a small peck on his sore lips, and he had to try not to wince at the pain.

"Please don't leave me here with him—"

Paige's mocking smile stopped Tyson right in the middle of his sentence.

"Tyson, you need to grow up. He's not going to hurt you. You heard Charlie—he touches you and Lord only knows what she's going to do to him."

"Fine. Leave me." Tyson smiled so she'd know he was kidding, but realized that wasn't the best idea when pain lit up his entire face. Paige laughed and got in the car.

Gideon was trying to get out of the whole thing too. His attempt was going about as well as Tyson's had.

"Suck it up and make up with your brother. I love you," Charlie said to Gideon, who'd pulled out the big guns and was pouting, lip poking out and all.

"Come on, baby."

"Say good-bye to Daddy, boys." Charlie laughed as she got into Paige's car.

Gideon and Tyson stood there like idiots as their women drove away.

"What now?" Tyson asked.

"I guess we have some things to straighten out. I mean, I'm all kinds of pissed off at you, but I'm more afraid of Charlie and Mom than I am of you, so let's do this."

Tyson knew his brother was right. Gideon may have broken his nose, and no doubt could break almost every other bone in his body, but Paige could break his heart, and that was way worse. So the two headed back to the apartment.

"Hey, what the hell were you and Charlie doing here anyway?" Tyson asked.

"Paige needed help getting your passed-out ass upstairs. And Charlie threatened to name my sons Aloysius and Mortimer if I didn't."

"Oh man. Where did Mortimer come from?"

"It's Chance's middle name."

"Oh shit! I can't wait to see Chance again." Tyson laughed.

"I wouldn't go there, Tyson. He may seem quiet and easygoing, but I have a feeling he's almost as pissed off at you as I am and would be more than happy to re-break that pretty nose of yours. I wouldn't push my luck."

Once back inside, the brothers stood around just sort of looking at one another for a long while. Neither knew where to start or what to say. Gideon finally sat at the kitchen table.

"You want a beer?" Tyson offered, following him into the kitchen.

"No. I think sober is the best way to go at this. Plus, with what's on tap for tonight at Mom and Dad's, I might need to save the drinking for then."

"Good point." Tyson pulled out the chair across from his brother and sat down, forgoing the beer.

"Okay, go ahead." Gideon looked Tyson right in the eye and waited.

"What?"

"Apologize…I'm waiting." He leaned back and folded his arms over his chest.

"Apologize to you? What the fuck for? I'm the one with the broken nose, dickhead! You need to apologize to me." Tyson's voice got louder as Gideon's eyes got wider.

"And you treated my wife like a whore! You let her get raped, Tyson!"

"Bullshit! This isn't my fault, and you know it."

"What the hell was so important that you one, couldn't get to the apartment a few minutes earlier, or two, go up and talk to Charlie? Huh, Ty?" The vein in Gideon's neck was popping out, and Tyson knew he was restraining himself. Charlie's threat still hung in the air.

"Well, as long as we're going to point fingers, Gid—where the fuck were you? Why is *your* wife suddenly my responsibility? What, off playing war with your buddies? One of which, I might remind you, is the guy who hurt Charlie," Tyson shot back.

"It's my job. I was off serving my country. You were here. You could've protected her. No, you *should've* protected her." Gideon's face fell slightly as his anger began to fade.

"Gideon, if I'd been there earlier, nothing would've changed. The guy would've come back another time. There's no way I could've protected her every minute."

"I want to kill the fucker. It's taking every ounce of strength I have not to take him out."

Tyson looked up at his big brother and for the first time in his entire life saw him crying. Tyson had seen him with a bone sticking out of his arm during a football game in high school. He'd seen him get dumped by more than one girl. But he'd never seen Gideon shed a single tear.

"I'm sorry. I do feel guilty for not protecting her. I feel like a shit for not talking to her and for jumping to conclusions. And most of all, I hate that I hurt you." Tyson felt like a total sissy, but deep down he knew this had to be done before they could even try to get back what they'd had.

"That's what I don't understand. Why? Why didn't you talk to her?" The hurt and fear in Gideon's stare almost took Tyson's breath away.

"I just didn't know how," Tyson told him truthfully. "I mean, what am I going to say? 'So Charlie, I saw the guy you're screwing while Gideon's gone. What's up with that?' I just didn't know how."

Gideon nodded, tears spilling down his cheeks. "I went to find the prick. I was going to kill him." His voice was barely above a whisper. "He described what he did to her, Tyson. He told me…fuck…he told me how good it was. That she didn't fight him the way he'd hoped…the way the others had."

Tyson's expression clearly reflected his shock. The fact that Gideon had had his hands on this dickhead when he'd said that and the guy was still breathing was astonishing.

"And you didn't hurt him?" Tyson finally asked.

"No, I was about to. I was about to kill him when Charlie showed up. She looked so hurt and sad, and she begged me not to. She said she needed me."

Actual sobs broke from Gideon's chest, and Tyson felt his own eyes begin to well up. He realized his earlier comments had been right on—Gideon had been so defensive because he blamed himself.

"You know Charlie doesn't blame you," Tyson said. "Hell, she doesn't even blame me."

"Doesn't matter. I should've been there. I should've protected her from that piece of filth." Gideon looked up at Tyson and seemed to realize for the first time how beat to hell his brother's face was. "Shit! Did I do all that? I'm sorry, Tyson."

"Um…"

"I just…I couldn't do anything to Boyd, so I took it out on you. Don't get me wrong. I wanted to hit you, badly, but I sucker-punched you and for that I'm sorry."

"So let me get this straight. You aren't sorry for hitting me, only that I didn't get a chance to fight back?" Tyson laughed.

"Well, I was still pissed at how you treated Charlie, and I probably would've got you out in the back yard at Mom and Dad's eventually. I just don't know why you told me. I tortured myself for months." The teasing was over for the moment.

"I swear I wasn't going to tell you. I was going to wait, but when Charlie announced she was pregnant, I just…I wanted to protect you," he admitted.

Gideon's head snapped up and his gaze fell on his younger brother, hard and questioning. "What? Why would I need you to protect me?"

His tone was indignant, like he'd been insulted—like the idea that Tyson could ever be strong enough to protect him was out of the realm of possibility. That familiar feeling Tyson thought he'd buried deep inside started to surface.

No, I'm not going to let that happen. I don't have to be Gideon—or anti-Gideon. I just have to be Tyson. "I didn't want you to come home and be blindsided when she told you or when the babies were born and they weren't yours. You know, all my life I wanted to be like you. Fuck that! I didn't want to be *like* you—I wanted to be you. I thought you were the greatest guy who ever lived. I knew I could never live up to you though, so I became the womanizing asshole, Tyson Cooper. Just this once, I wanted to do what was right, and I fucked that up too." Admitting that to his brother was one of the hardest things Tyson had ever done.

Gideon was speechless. He sat and stared at Tyson for a long minute before getting up out of his chair. As his brother approached, Tyson's entire body tensed. He thought he must've pissed Gideon off so badly that he was willing to face Charlie's wrath.

When Gideon thrust his hand out Tyson flinched, then noticed it wasn't balled into a fist but was extended in an offer of peace. Tyson stood up and took his brother's hand—and he pulled him in for a hug…a man hug.

When Gideon stepped back, he was frowning. "I'm still not ready to totally forgive you, little brother. But I get it better now. I'm not perfect, and neither are you. You need to find your own way. I've done what was right for me in my life; you need to do the same."

"I know. I really am sorry about everything, Gid. I promise you, now that I have Paige in my life, I see things so differently. I see what you have with Charlie, and I can't tell you how pissed I'd be if you did something to fuck that up."

"Good to know. Now let's figure out what we're going to tell Mom tonight so she doesn't kill both of us and leave Charlie and Paige widows at such young ages." Gideon laughed, and Tyson knew even if it didn't happen right then, one day things would be okay between them again.

Almost two hours later, after a quick stop at Gideon's so he could get cleaned up, Gideon and Tyson pulled up just behind Paige's car in the driveway of the Cooper house. Jumping out of the truck, Gideon practically ran to help Charlie out.

"Baby, are you okay?"

Tyson watched his brother's hands sweep over her belly. Gideon's eyes were big with worry. Charlie laughed before letting him know that they were all perfectly fine.

"So, you two figure out what you're going to tell your mom?" she asked as they headed to the front door.

"Sure," Gideon said with a smile on his face. "I'm just going to direct attention to you and your baby-oven there and then point out that I'm the father of her grandsons. She won't be able to be mad at me then."

"Don't be so sure about that, Gideon." The voice that spoke was full of love, but with enough authority to make them shake in their shoes just a bit.

"Mom! I didn't know you'd be waiting at the door for us. Are we late?" Gideon gave Evelyn a kiss on the cheek as he slipped past her, acting like he hadn't just been caught plotting.

"No, but Gabriella and Chance are already here. I want everyone in the living room right this minute. We're going to fix this family here and now. No one leaves this house until things are right."

CHAPTER 42

Evelyn followed her four children into the living room. Gabriella and Chance stood up to greet the rest of the family, and then they all took seats on the two couches. Peter sat in one of the wingback chairs. Only Evelyn stood. She wanted there to be no mistake about who was running the meeting. Glancing around at the family, Evelyn was trying to decide where to start when Gabriella raised her hand.

"Gabriella, dear, you don't have to raise your hand if you want to speak," she told her.

"Well, I just didn't want to do anything that might get me in as much trouble as all of them are." Gabriella swept her hand around the room to indicate the rest of the family.

Evelyn smiled—but only a little.

"Okay, so I realize this motley bunch has totally screwed things up, but why exactly are Chance and I required to be here?"

"You and Chance are part of our family. Chance is Charlie's brother; you'll be the aunt and uncle to my grandbabies, and I have a sneaking suspicion both of you know what has happened in the short time Gideon was gone—why this family is suddenly so broken." Out of the corner of her eye she saw Gideon grab Charlie's hand and pull it to his lips. Then she knew just where to start.

"Evelyn, maybe we should have dinner first. Let the kids relax a little bit," Peter suggested.

"No. Until I get every last story, no one eats. I'm sorry, but for the past few months I've watched Charlie with dark circles under her eyes, barely eating, and that beautiful smile from the first day I met her all but gone. At the same time, Tyson has been nasty and cruel, Paige felt the need to leave him, and I've barely heard from Gideon. Something is wrong, and I want to know what it is. I want it fixed."

"It's not that easy, Mom." Tyson spoke from his seat next to Paige.

"I'm sure it's not, Tyson. But until we all sit down and talk about it, it will never be right. I have a feeling that each of you has talked separately, but not as a group to get it all out on the table."

"Evelyn is right. As much as I want to settle a few things the way that Gideon did—" Chance glanced over at Tyson, smiling slightly "—the fact is, this whole thing affects all of us in some way, and it needs to be out."

"Easy for you to say, Chance. It isn't your issue. It didn't happen to you," Gideon all but growled at his brother-in-law.

"No, Gideon. It happened to my sister—while you were gone." The venom in Chance's voice was surprising. He'd started to rise off the couch before Gabriella grabbed his arm to keep him in place. The accusation of his words hung heavy in the air.

"Boys," Gabriella said. "I think we need to stop playing the blame game and let Charlie decide what happens next."

Evelyn immediately looked at her daughter-in-law, and the expression on her face broke Evelyn's heart. Charlie was torn between her brother and her husband. But then her expression changed from fear and embarrassment to hard determination.

"Chance is right. This whole thing just kept getting bigger and bigger because no one was talking. And I think now is the time to get everything out there," Charlie said. She reached over and patted Gideon's cheek, her love for him painted on her face.

"If you're sure, baby. You don't have to say anything you don't want to," Gideon told her. She nodded slightly as she acknowledged his concern, but then turned back to the rest of the family and took a deep breath.

"Evelyn, Peter, I think you're the only ones who don't know what happened." Charlie stopped, her eyes closing for a moment as she took a deep breath. "I was raped. Two weeks after Gideon left, a man who works with him knocked on my door. I was stupid enough to let him in the house, and he raped me."

"Baby, please stop blaming yourself." Gideon tried to pull her closer, but she refused. She needed to do this on her own.

"Not your fault, Lottie," Chance commented as his glare slid to Gideon.

Evelyn couldn't help her reaction. She let out a huge gasp, and tears welled in her eyes as they landed on Charlie's distended belly.

"No, Evelyn. The babies are Gideon's. I was pregnant when he left, but I didn't know until I had the exam after the rape." Charlie's voice was so calm and even; she could've been talking about a day at the beach.

"Are you sure?" Evelyn's hand flew to her mouth when she realized what she'd just said.

"Mom! What the hell is that? Charlie was…raped, and your biggest concern is whether or not the babies are mine? What if they weren't? Would you want them any less?" Gideon had risen to his feet.

"Gideon! I don't care that you're a grown man. You will not speak to your mother like that." Peter was on his feet too.

Charlie laid a delicate hand on Gideon's arm, encouraging him to sit back down. He complied easily, and it was then that Evelyn realized Peter's observations at lunch had been right—in the end, she had to let him go. He was a man, a husband, and about to be a father. He belonged to Charlie now.

"It's all right, Gideon." Charlie looked over at her mother-in-law before continuing, "Actually, Evelyn, I'm positive, but I plan to have DNA testing done as soon as they're born."

"What?" a chorus of voices rang out around the room.

"I have to do it. Yesterday when the man who attacked me saw I was pregnant, he insinuated that they might be his. I can't take the chance that he'd come after my sons. I won't let that happen. The sooner we prove what I already know, the safer the babies will be."

"I'll kill him first," Gideon whispered.

Charlie turned to him and gently took his face in her hands. "No, you won't. We had this discussion already, and I need you. I can't do this by myself. I need you to stand with me and face this. It's going to get worse before it gets better."

The strength of the woman Gideon had chosen to share his life with knocked Evelyn Cooper over. She had to sit as her knees went weak and everything started to sink in.

"Charlie, I'm so sorry. I wish you'd told us. I wish I could've done something to help you all those months ago," Evelyn said as tears slid down her face. "You're so strong. I know why Gideon loves you so much, and I couldn't have picked a better wife for him." She truly meant every word.

"Thank you, Evelyn. That means a lot to me. But I need to warn all of you, I'm going to the Judge Advocate General with this. He has attacked more than just me, and I suspect once we start looking we aren't going to like what we find. One of my friends was raped by him just days ago, and I can't let this go any longer." Tears fell in great drops from Charlie's eyes. Gideon pulled her into his side and held her there.

"You know we'll support you whatever way we can," Gabriella offered.

"I have to stop him. I can't raise my children to stand up for themselves and others if I never do. The thing is, when this all starts coming out, I can't imagine Boyd taking things easily," Charlie added.

Evelyn walked over to Charlie and Gideon, pulling them into a hug.

"We're your family, Charlie, and we'll be right here for you no matter what. We love you, dear."

Evelyn went to the other wingback chair, sat down, and looked around. Her gaze settled on Tyson, who'd been uncharacteristically quiet through this whole thing. His bandaged nose and two black eyes made it clear there was more to this story.

"So, can we eat now?" Tyson asked when he caught his mom looking at him. "I'm starved. How about you, Paige?" He made a move to get up off the couch.

"Don't even think about it, Tyson," Evelyn warned.

A charming smile tried to make its way onto his face.

"I'm your mother. That little smirk doesn't work on me. You should know that by now."

"Yeah, Tyson, why don't you tell Mom about your role in this whole mess?" Gideon taunted.

"Does this have anything to do with Tyson's broken nose, Gideon?" Evelyn asked.

"Um, yeah, you could say that."

"Then, Tyson, I believe it's your turn to add to the revelation of why my family has been slowly falling to ruins." Evelyn turned back to her youngest son and waited for him to begin.

Tyson took a deep breath. "I saw the guy after he'd…hurt Charlie."

"What? How?"

"I'd gone over to check on Charlie, and I saw the guy come down the stairs. He was doing his pants up." The last part was barely a whisper. "I thought Charlie was cheating on Gideon."

"Tyson! How could you think such a thing?" Evelyn was appalled. How could anyone look at the two of them together and think for one minute she'd betray him like that?

"I saw what I saw, Mom. The guy was happy. He didn't have a mark on him. Charlie never said anything about it. What else could I think? What would you have thought?" Tyson leveled his mother with a stare.

"Okay, I can see that. Miscommunication on both of your parts; it makes sense. Still doesn't explain why your brother felt the need to physically attack you."

"For a while after, I kept my thoughts to myself. I didn't know what else to do. But then Charlie announced she was pregnant, and I couldn't let Gideon think the baby was his. So I told him."

"Oh, Tyson. That's why you wanted Gideon to call you?" She'd thought he wanted advice about Paige.

Tyson simply nodded before beginning again. "I didn't know what had happened, and I never talked to Paige about it. I wish to God I had. Charlie had confided in her, and if I'd only talked to her that first day, none of this would've happened."

Evelyn wanted to take him in her arms, but knew, as with Gideon, it wasn't her place anymore. Instead she watched as Paige took his hand and held it close to her heart, whispering words only Tyson could hear.

"Why did Gideon attack you?" Evelyn asked after a few minutes.

"That you have to ask him about," Tyson replied. The room was quiet as attention shifted to Gideon.

"I went after Boyd, but Charlie wouldn't let me touch him. I was pissed off, I was feeling guilty for leaving Charlie vulnerable to this, and I needed to blame someone. Tyson had treated my wife like a piece of trash for months, and by telling me his theory he put my life in jeopardy. I wanted someone to hurt." The honesty of Gideon's words was hard to take in.

"Gideon! I can't believe you took all that out on Tyson! He's your brother."

"You're right. He's my brother, and he hurt me more than anyone else ever could," Gideon shot back. "But I've apologized. I just didn't know what else to do."

"You two are grownups now. You can't take care of things by rolling around on the back lawn," their father weighed in.

Evelyn looked over at Peter, who'd said so little throughout all of this. She blamed him in part for Gideon going after Tyson. All those years of him telling her, *Boys will be boys, darling. Just let them fight it out.* "I swear on everything I hold near and dear in this world, if I *ever* hear of the two of you fighting again, I'll take you both over my knee," Evelyn said severely.

"Grow up. Both of you. Tyson, you need to take some responsibility for the months of being nasty to Charlie. You should've talked to her. And Gideon, just because you need an outlet for your anger doesn't mean you can attack your brother. Be the men I raised you to be."

"Yes, Mom," the two replied in unison.

"Now, I want to know what we need to do. Charlie, what can I do to help you?"

"Nothing, Evelyn. I have to do this on my own. I just want all of you to be prepared when you hear things about me that you know aren't true. They may say them in your church group, Evelyn. Or at the hospital, Peter. Just know that I love Gideon, and nothing you hear is going to be true."

"We know, dear. You don't worry about us. I'm more embarrassed about my sons' behavior than anything coming down the road. Are you going to be okay?"

"Eventually. I'm better than I was yesterday, and tomorrow I'll be a little better, but this is part of who I am now." Charlie's voice was strong.

For several moments, everyone sat and stared at one another. Then, in the quiet of the large room, Evelyn heard Charlie's stomach growl. The group erupted into uneasy laughter.

"Sorry. The boys are hungry." Charlie blushed.

"Man, I wish I could use that as an excuse," Gideon boomed.

"Seriously, can we get something to eat?" Tyson piped up.

"Fine! But if I discover there's more you all aren't telling me, what you saw of me tonight will be nothing compared to how I am then," Evelyn warned. She stood and headed for the kitchen to find some menus. "I'm ordering pizza. What does everyone want?"

The rest of the evening was quiet as the family sat comfortably in the Coopers' living room. Gideon joked a little as his hands moved over Charlie's rounded belly, a smile on his face. Tyson and Paige sat together, his arm around her protectively. It was relaxed and easy. It was family, and as Evelyn watched them all, she was thankful Gideon was home and her family was being repaired.

At eleven o'clock Chance stood, pulling Gabriella up with him, and announced, "So, we're going to head out."

Suddenly everyone seemed to realize how late it was, and there was mumbling about going or getting to bed.

"Before we all scatter to the four corners," Chance added, "I just want to make sure I have all of this straight. Today we found out that Gideon is home early, Gideon put the smack down on Tyson…" He stopped for a moment and shot Gideon a look of respect that Evelyn didn't appreciate. "Gideon and Charlie are having twin boys, and Charlie was hurt in a way so unimaginable that I want the guy who did it to suffer like never before. Did I get it all? Anyone got anything else they want to confess? 'Cause I don't think I can survive another day like this."

The family broke into genuine laughter, which was a perfect way to end the long and draining day.

As all the kids were walking out the door, Peter announced, "In light of today's events, you all are off the hook for dinner tomorrow."

"What? Peter, you can't just do that," Evelyn protested.

"Darling, look at our family. They're exhausted. Let them have a day off." He turned back to the group gathered in the doorway. "Now go before you all have to watch me convince your mother that I'm right," Peter threatened.

"Ew!" Everyone groaned and headed for their cars.

CHAPTER 43

Gideon looked at his watch for, like, the hundredth time in the past five minutes and wondered again where the hell Chance was. His other hand was being crushed by Charlie's grasp. Gideon knew he had to pull his shit together because there was no way in hell he was going to admit his wife was hurting him.

"I can't do this, Gideon. I want to go home." Charlie looked up at her husband, fear etched across her face. It had been three months since Gideon came home and learned what had happened to his wife, but suddenly he felt helpless again.

"Too late, baby. I'll be here for you, though." He tried to smile, hoping to help her out a little bit.

"Yeah, but you're not the one who has to do it," she shot back.

"Where the hell is that brother of yours? He needs to be here." Gideon tried to change the subject. There was no use talking about backing out. It wasn't a possibility at this point. Charlie let out a long sigh. "I wish I knew what kind of freaky connection you and Chance have," Gideon said.

"It's a twin thing," she replied, tapping her finger against her temple before letting her hands fall to rest over her huge belly. "You know these two will have a strong connection too. I don't want you to freak out when F —"

"Ahh!" Gideon looked to make sure no one else was around. "We said we weren't going to call them by their names until they're born. I don't want to hear shit from anyone about what names we picked. I mean, it's bad enough that every time we see my mom she tries to convince us what a great name Aloysius is."

Charlie laughed and Gideon felt relieved that if nothing else, he was distracting her from what was happening.

"I think we should just go with my original idea of Gideon Jr. and Gideon the Third," he offered, hoping to keep her laughing.

"Not going to happen. We have the boys named, and that is that." She crossed her arms over her chest, but she was smiling. Gideon leaned in and brushed his lips over hers. He felt her relax into him. That was his job—making her feel loved and protected. And he was damned good at it.

"Come on—we could call them Junior and Trey!"

Charlie's laughter floated in the air around them, and he was thankful to hear it again. For a time after that infamous "family meeting," he wasn't sure Charlie would laugh again…

…The days that followed Cooper Family Share Night were extremely difficult for Charlie. Watching her during that time nearly broke Gideon. Again he wondered what would've happened if he'd had to witness the days, weeks, months following the rape. He didn't know how Charlie was still functioning. He was damn proud of her.

The team was on a month's leave after spending almost four months on assignment, and for that Gideon was eternally grateful. He was able to spend time with Charlie and help her get through the hard tasks she felt she needed to do. The added bonus of not having to look at the smug grin on that prick's face didn't hurt either.

Over the next few weeks, Charlie talked to Zoe daily, making sure she was getting the help she needed, including medical attention, which like Charlie she'd been reluctant to seek. Charlie's guilt ate at her, and if she could've taken all the pain from Zoe, she would've in a heartbeat. But the best she could do was be there for her friend.

Charlie was also trying to convince Zoe that she needed to go to the JAG with her. Since Charlie's attack didn't occur on base, she was worried the military authorities wouldn't be able to do anything with just her. And at this point, she didn't want to tip Boyd off by going to the police.

Over the next two weeks, Gideon and Charlie also met with the other two married members of the team. Lieutenant Walker was especially hard for Gideon. Walker had planned on getting out when they returned home because he didn't want to leave his family anymore, and this could send his guilt into overdrive. As soon as he opened the door and Gideon saw that dead look in his eyes, he knew Charlie had been right. Boyd had been seeking out the wives of his own deployed team members, and he'd found Lieutenant Walker's wife.

Just like with Zoe, Charlie insisted that Gideon take Walker out so she could be alone with his wife. The two men had never been close outside the job, but that was about to change—quickly.

"What the fuck happened while we were gone, Cooper?" Walker was never one for beating around the bush. Gideon just couldn't answer him. "I mean, I came home and Ginger was catatonic. The baby was the only thing that looked like it had been taken care of in weeks. In fact, the only thing that gets her up is to take care of the baby."

"This is something she's going to have to explain to you, Lieutenant. I'm sorry." Gideon stood back to wait for the inevitable outburst.

"I just want to know what's wrong with my wife." Instead of attacking as Jaylon had done, Dallas slumped in his seat in a posture of total defeat. All Gideon could do was set a hand on his shoulder and let him know he wasn't alone. "Some days I hate this fucking job, Cooper. You know that?"

"Yes, sir. I definitely know what you mean."

Once back at the house, it was like déjà vu. Gideon had to hold his team leader back so he wouldn't go out and kill Boyd. Charlie offered her therapist's name and number as she'd done for Zoe, along with encouragement to see a doctor, but the guilt was again overwhelming for her.

Charlie later told Gideon that Ginger had opened up once she'd described what Boyd did to her. The attack on Ginger had occurred just after the new year. She and the baby had gone to visit her family in Georgia for the holidays. They'd been gone almost three months. But only a week after they'd returned Boyd had shown up at her door. That made Gideon wonder what Boyd had been doing between the beginning of October, when he'd attacked Charlie, and January, when he got to Ginger Walker.

All the stress was quickly revealed not to be good for Charlie, and Gideon constantly worried that contractions would start for real. He tried to talk her out of pursuing the case against Boyd until after the babies were born, but she wouldn't hear of it.

"I've already waited too long. He's ruined more lives because of that. I couldn't stand it if he was still preying on women," she explained. Gideon couldn't persuade her to let it go for a few months, so he had to support her as best he could.

It took a few more weeks—and a lot of talking and convincing—to get all the women together. But Charlie felt they needed to talk as a group before they could go to the JAG and tell them what had happened. The road to getting their justice was going to be long and brutal, and they needed to know they had someone standing with them. Charlie knew supporting one another was the only way they'd make it.

The day finally came when Charlie felt all of them were strong enough, together, that they could go talk to the people who could help them. That was the worst day for Gideon in the whole thing. None of the women wanted their husbands with them when they talked to the guy at the JAG office. Instead, the men were delegated to sitting in the lobby.

They sat in silence for hours, watching people go in and out of the office. Gideon recognized a few people from the Office of Special Investigations and a few from Naval Criminal Investigative Service as they passed the lobby on the way to the conference room where the women were explaining to total strangers how Boyd had violated each of them.

Three days of meetings and questions passed before anything was decided. The only reason the JAG finally decided to do something was that leave for the four affected SEALs was about to run out, and they had to go back to work. The fear that one—or several—of them would kill Boyd when they saw him again was, most likely, the final factor in the decision to move forward. Given who the men were, it was surprising Cody Boyd's body hadn't turned up on a beach somewhere already.

Boyd was moved to a different unit and put on base restriction to allow for a thorough investigation. The military process moved more quickly than a civilian one would have, but there was no way the Navy was going to rush something this big. They wouldn't want to look bad if things fell apart. Very few people went to a court-martial who didn't see the inside of the brig in the end. The JAG made sure they had their *i*s dotted and *t*s crossed before they ever went to trial…

"Chance." Charlie's whispered words pulled Gideon back to the present.

"It's about time. Your sister needed you, man. Where the hell have you been?" Gideon knew Chance hadn't intentionally come late, but he was nervous and needed someone to yell at—that someone definitely wasn't going to be Charlie.

"Gideon," Charlie scolded as she slapped at her husband's shoulder to move him out of the way. "Don't mind him, Chance. Thank you so much for coming."

"You know I wouldn't leave you today." Chance was trying to look brave, but Gideon could see the worry and fear on his face. He wasn't ready for what was about to happen any more than Charlie was…or Gideon, for that matter.

"Work that twin thing on her, Chance. We don't have a lot of time." Gideon slipped an arm around Charlie's waist.

Just then, the door opened and a uniformed man stepped into the hallway. "Charlotte Cooper?" he called in a professional voice that sent chills up Gideon's spine.

Charlie looked up at the man. There was fear in her eyes.

"You've been called to the witness stand." He stepped back, indicating that Charlie needed to enter the room.

Charlie made an effort to pull herself together. Gideon wanted to take her and run in the other direction.

"It'll be okay, Lottie." Chance leaned in and hugged his sister before she could slip through the door. Charlie took a deep breath, attempting to absorb whatever good thoughts Chance was trying to convey to her.

"Baby? I want to be in there with you," Gideon whispered.

"I know." Her eyes met Gideon's; he saw how much she loved him and how determined she was to do this.

"Ms. Cooper? They're waiting for you," the court representative said, breaking the connection between the couple.

Gideon had to let her go in there and face *him* alone, and it hurt all the way to his soul. Once that door closed, he couldn't protect her.

Charlie watched Gideon and Chance as the door slowly slid closed and finally clicked into place.

Get it together, Charlie. You have to do this. You have to stop him. Her stomach tightened. She only hoped she wouldn't be sick. That she hadn't been able to eat anything that morning was a point in her favor. But the twins were restless, and their constant movement only served to magnify the nervous flips of her stomach.

Turning around slowly, Charlie took in the room. It was terrifying. Her knees shook as she tried to wrap her mind around what she was doing. This wasn't even the actual court-martial. That thought caused Charlie's ears to ring and sweat to bead on her upper lip — she was going to have to do this again.

In the military world, something similar to a grand jury hearing, called an Article 32 hearing, was required before proceeding with a court-martial for something as serious as rape and battery. The difference — and the thing that made Charlie so nervous — was that Cody Boyd was allowed to be there with a lawyer. His lawyer was allowed to question Charlie too. She honestly wasn't sure if she could talk about the things *he* had done to her while *he* stared right at her.

The room was only slightly larger than the conference room in the JAG office where Charlie, Zoe, Ginger, and Kelly Klausen, the young wife of another of Gideon's teammates, had spent three days going over and over every detail with different types of investigating officers. The women told their stories a dozen times to at least sixty different people in those days, but sitting alone in front of Boyd was a completely different situation.

At the front of the room was a small table with a man Charlie recognized as one of the JAG investigators. He wasn't working on their case, and she wondered what he was doing there. The only other people in the room were Cody Boyd — Charlie's heart raced in her chest — his lawyer, the JAG attorney prosecuting the case, and the young officer who'd called Charlie into the room.

"Ms. Cooper, please come sit down." The man at the front table motioned to an empty seat near him. His deep voice rang out authoritatively, and Charlie guessed he was going to be in charge of the proceedings.

"Mrs.," Charlie corrected as she slowly made her way to the front of the room.

"I'm sorry?"

"Mrs. Cooper. My husband is Lieutenant Gideon Cooper." Charlie let the pride in her husband show in her voice. Cody Boyd may have taken a lot from her, but *he* couldn't take her husband or her babies or how much all of them meant to her.

Charlie dared a quick glance at Boyd. *He* smirked as his eyes roamed over her belly. She crossed her arms protectively over her boys. They'd never even know of this man, and *he* would never lay his eyes on them. Charlie had promised herself.

"Right. I'm sorry. Mrs. Cooper, please sit. Make yourself comfortable."

Charlie rolled her eyes slightly, not meaning to offend him, but really—could he have been more insensitive? How could she ever be comfortable in the same room as the monster who'd raped her?

"I mean, well, please sit," he corrected, pausing to take a deep breath. "Now, Mrs. Cooper, do you understand why you're here? What this proceeding is about?" the officer asked.

"Yes, I do," she replied.

"Okay then, let's go ahead and get started."

Charlie was sworn in, and then the JAG attorney asked her to tell her story. The lump in her throat was so huge she was sure one of the babies had crawled up there. Her stomach heaved, and she thought she was going to be sick. *No, you're not, Charlie. Don't let* him *do this to you. You're stronger than* he *is.*

Boyd sat with that self-satisfied smile plastered on his face, and Charlie wished she'd let Gideon hurt *him* that day. She wished she'd been able to hurt *him*. Never in her life had Charlie wanted someone to be hurt—killed even—but she really did wish for that as she sat in the room with men staring at her, waiting to hear all the tiny details of her rape.

Taking a deep breath and without looking at *him,* Charlie focused on the back wall and told her story. The tears began sometime after she started; she wasn't sure when. She didn't bother to wipe them away.

Charlie was acutely aware, however, of the exact moment the first real contraction hit. The clock on the wall read 11:13. She'd just explained how Boyd had pushed her to the floor when the pain of the contraction caused her to suck in a huge breath. Nobody even noticed. They probably assumed it was because of the emotions she was reliving.

Charlie finally got to the end of her experience and told how Boyd had warned her not tell anyone before leaving. That's when the second contraction rolled through her body—11:20. She was breathing heavy, her hand resting over her belly, when it occurred to Charlie that she really was in labor.

"Mrs. Cooper, what did you do after the alleged attack?" Boyd's attorney stood right in front of Charlie, and she couldn't remember when he'd gotten up from the table.

"I'm sorry? Could you repeat the question?" Her voice was quiet, and she did the math to see how long it had been since the last contraction. Seven minutes.

"What did you do after the alleged attack? Did you go to the police? To a doctor?" There was an ugly tone in the man's voice, and Charlie decided this was one of those times she wanted Gideon to protect her.

"No. I didn't tell anyone."

"Why is that? Because you didn't want anyone to know that while your husband was serving his country you were sleeping with a fellow sailor?"

Another wave of pain shot through her belly.

"Uh…I have to go," she whispered, too low for anyone to hear.

"What? I'm sorry, I didn't hear that," the snide asshole practically yelled at her.

"I said, 'I have to go,'" Charlie repeated, louder.

"So now, after accusing my client of this awful crime to cover up your infidelity and allowing it to get this far, you've decided you don't want to keep the charade going? Is that what you're trying to tell us, Mrs. Cooper?"

Charlie glanced at the clock again. It was 11:25, and she was having yet another contraction. They were getting closer. These were different from the smaller tremors that had been pulsing through her body over the past three months. These were the real thing—she just knew it.

"No, you ass! I'm about to have two babies, and I'd prefer to be in a hospital rather than in this room with the man who raped me!" Apparently her answer was loud enough to be heard in the hall because the doors burst open and both Gideon and Chance came flying into the room.

The officer in charge seemed to be at a loss. Charlie was pretty sure he'd never had a woman go into labor with twins during one of his proceedings. Gideon finally reached her and his arm slid around her to help her out of the room.

"Hot damn! I didn't know we were having twins, darling. Name one after me." Boyd laughed.

Anger flashed in Gideon's eyes, and Charlie was thankful he was more worried about the babies and her than getting to Boyd. Gideon's arm tightened at her waist, and Charlie allowed herself to lean into him a little.

"Don't worry, baby. I gotcha," Gideon whispered lovingly in his wife's ear. All fear seemed to wash away with just those words. Gideon was there with her, and he'd take care of his family.

Charlie had completely forgotten Chance was in the room until she heard the sound of chairs toppling over and a table sliding. Looking over, she saw Boyd on the floor and Chance standing over him, shaking his hand out. The other men in the room had rushed to pull Chance back.

"You even look at my sister again, and I'll kill you," Chance hissed.

"Nice…threatening me in front of a room full of military officials? You must be as dumb as she is," Boyd said as he turned and spit blood out of his mouth.

"Fuck you. Gideon may not be able to touch you, but I'm a civilian. Oh, they can throw me off base, and you can go to the police, but really, do any of you want *that* kind of publicity about what's going on? I mean, if I got arrested it might get out how your man here—a man *you* trained to hurt and kill people—has been terrorizing the women left behind when you send their husbands on top secret missions." Chance shrugged out of the light hold the clerk had on him.

Charlie's water chose that moment to break, and the sound of the fluid hitting the tile floor caused everyone to turn in her direction. Every man in that room, including her husband, gagged before turning away.

"Gideon, I think we need to get to the hospital. Now."

Gideon's eyes were double their normal size. He was frozen as he watched the room erupt in chaos. Charlie could tell he was torn between jumping Boyd himself and getting her the heck out of Dodge. Fortunately, he picked getting to the hospital, and he carefully maneuvered her around the puddle in the middle of the floor. Charlie saw him fight another gag, and even as another contraction rocked her body, she had to smile. It looked more like a grimace, and suddenly Chance was back at her side. The two men guided her to the door.

Just as they reached the entrance, Boyd spoke again. "Don't worry, darling. I'll be up to see my babies once this is all cleared up."

Charlie pulled against the tugging of her husband and brother to look back at the animal who'd taken so much from her. *He* now thought *he* could take her sons? *Not in my lifetime*. All eyes in the room were on Boyd. Even his attorney had a look of disgust on his face.

Seeing Charlie's stare, Boyd couldn't help himself. "Hope we have a pretty little girl," he sneered.

Gideon nearly jumped over the tables trying to get to him, letting a string of obscenities fly as he went. It took Chance and three other men, including Boyd's lawyer, to hold him back. Unlike when Chance went after him, they were ready this time. While this scene played out, Boyd's evil smirk never wavered.

He thought *he* was going to get away with all of this. Charlie couldn't believe *he* thought *he* was smart enough. She looked at *him* again, and his gaze sent a shiver up her spine. She suddenly realized it wasn't that *he* thought *he* was smart enough — *he* thought people would believe all these women had wanted *him*. Charlie's stomach clenched. She couldn't believe the arrogance. She had to get out of that room.

Finally pulling Gideon and Chance out — Charlie was a little pissed off that the woman in labor had to be the sane and rational one in the situation — they all headed toward the parking lot.

"By the way, Chance," Gideon said, "that was outstanding." He held his fist out for Chance to bump it.

"Thanks, man. It felt good, but I think I may have broken something," Chance said, shaking out his hand, which was already starting to swell and turn purple.

"Very nice, Chance," Charlie said. "Gabby is going to be pissed." Charlie watched her brother's face blanch slightly.

"Shit. But...but...I was defending you. That makes it okay, right?" Gabby really was going to be angry, but knowing the reason behind what happened, combined with Charlie giving birth, might distract her.

"So, are you two Neanderthals done with all the chest thumping? I mean, I'm about to have two babies pop out of me here." Charlie gestured to her swollen belly. It was like they'd completely forgotten she was in labor.

"Who's going to drive? I don't think I can," Chance said, holding up his hand again. Charlie was glad they were going to a hospital where he could get that looked at — and that he didn't have any future plans to be a surgeon or concert pianist.

"Charlie?" Gideon turned to his wife and laughed.

He thought he was so funny. Charlie was definitely not in the mood for funny and made sure the look she threw him indicated it.

"O-O-Okay, I'm driving." He opened the passenger door for Charlie to climb in — not an easy feat since she looked like she was smuggling a beach ball under her shirt. The situation was made even more awkward by the fact that Charlie had dressed up for the hearing and was wearing a skirt.

"What about my car?" Chance asked after they were all squished into Gideon's truck and heading to the hospital.

"For crying out loud, Chance! You have a broken hand, and I'm giving birth. I think we have a few things that are more—" She didn't finish the sentence because an extremely painful contraction hit, causing her back to spasm and her body to bow off the seat.

"Do the breathing, Charlie," Gideon offered. "Hee hee haw, hee hee haw," he demonstrated. Charlie rolled her eyes.

"Yeah, Gideon, how about I grab your balls and squeeze and you try that lame-ass breathing to relieve the pain. Tell me how well that works."

Chance chuckled, and Gideon turned slightly to glare at him.

"Shit! Baby, I don't know what to do for you. Christ, I don't know if I can do this." Gideon's face was contorted with pain and worry.

"*You're* not sure *you* can do this?" Charlie's voice was getting louder the longer they were in the car. "I'm sorry, are you the one who has to push two—*two*—heads out of your vagina? Huh, Gideon? And judging by the size of that melon that you have, I can only imagine what that's going to be like!"

"Uh, Lottie, could you not talk about your vagina? It kind of grosses me out," Chance squeaked.

Lucky for Chance, Gideon pulled up at the hospital right then and Charlie didn't get a chance to tell him to go fuck himself before Gideon lifted her out of the truck and carried her through the sliding doors.

"Yo! We're having a couple of babies here!"

CHAPTER 44

"Maternity is on the third floor," the nurse informed Gideon and directed him to the elevator.

"Call up there and tell them Charlotte *Cooper* is on her way up, and they better be ready for us," Gideon fired back.

Normally Charlie was uncomfortable with him throwing his father's name around, but at a time like this, she wasn't about to argue. And if it got them what they needed faster, then what the hell? *Throw that Cooper name around all you want, baby!*

Looking over Gideon's shoulder Charlie saw Chance just staring at them.

"Chance! Will you get your hand checked out and then call Gabby?" she asked, trying not to sound like a shrill witch as pain shot through her abdomen.

"Don't worry, Lottie." Chance smiled, then the elevator doors closed and blocked Charlie's view of him.

Another contraction rippled through Charlie, the worst one so far. Gideon still had her cradled in his arms, and she curled her fingers around his bicep and dug her nails into his flesh.

"Damn, Charlie. That hurts."

"Really? Well, the incredible case of blue balls you'll have for the rest of our marriage is going to hurt even more. Because if you think that you're getting anywhere near me again—" Just then the elevator doors slid open and what seemed like the entire staff stood staring.

"In labor, are we?" one sweet, older-looking nurse asked. She reminded Charlie of a nice grandmother and instantly made her feel a little better. "Shoo," she said to those who'd stopped to watch Charlie's breakdown. "You all can go back to your jobs now. I've got this."

"Trust me, honey." The nurse patted Gideon on the shoulder as she motioned for him to follow her. "They all threaten the same thing when that first really bad contraction hits. And it's only going to get worse. But eventually most of them end up right back here again in a few years."

"I sure hope so," Gideon mumbled under his breath.

"Epidural," Charlie breathed out. "Now!"

"Sure, dear," the nurse offered in a sweet, motherly voice. "Let me call down to anesthesiology and get someone up here while we get you settled in your room." After she hung up the phone, she indicated for Gideon to follow her again.

Gideon still hadn't put Charlie down, and she was beginning to feel ridiculous. When they got to the room, the nurse turned back to the couple. "I'm Maeve. I'll be your nurse for the delivery. I've already called your doctor and your father." She looked at Gideon. "They're both on their way. Dr. Cooper was finishing up in surgery, but I left a message with his secretary."

"Thank you, Maeve," Charlie replied. "Gideon, I think you can put me down." She patted his arm and kissed him softly on the cheek.

"You sure, baby? I mean, I'll do whatever I have to so I don't end up with a giant case of blue balls for the rest of my life." His eyebrow shot up in question.

"Shut up and put me down." Charlie laughed. Gideon knew she'd never be able to spend the rest of her life without loving him again.

"Go ahead and put this gown on, dear, and climb up in the bed. Dr. Carson will be here in a few minutes for your epidural." Maeve left, closing the door behind her.

Charlie quickly undressed and put on the hospital gown before getting into the bed. Her eyes traveled over all the equipment pushed against the walls, and a shudder traveled up her spine as she thought of something happening to the boys.

The door opened after a quick knock, and Maeve reappeared. Her grandmotherly appearance was deceiving. Charlie soon realized she knew exactly what she was doing. Charlie quickly found herself hooked up to a monitor and her enormous belly wrapped with another strap to monitor the babies' heartbeats.

"Ohh, those are some healthy babies you have there, sweetheart. The heartbeats are strong," Maeve commented as she looked over the data already pouring from the machines.

Much to Charlie's relief, her doctor came in next. "You're doing well, Charlie," she said. "Only two centimeters dilated, but the babies are still high." She looked at the information spitting out of the collection of machines and quickly hid a small frown, but Charlie saw it.

"What's the matter?" When Charlie spoke Gideon's head snapped up to stare at the doctor.

"Nothing's wrong. Like I said, I'm just surprised the babies are still high, but you're definitely contracting. Don't worry, we'll keep an eye on it."

As she finished speaking, Charlie sucked in another deep breath as a contraction rolled through her. All medical eyes turned to the machines. Charlie's went to Gideon who was staring at Dr. Miles and Maeve.

"Someone better start telling us something," Gideon barked.

"Just a dip in the heart rates. It's the first one. Nothing to panic over. Labor is as stressful for them as it is for the two of you. Just relax and the anesthesiologist will be in any minute now. I'll be back to check on you when he's done. Don't worry." She laid a hand on Charlie's shoulder and gave a little squeeze before leaving the room.

Charlie looked over to see Gideon pacing. She'd never seen him so nervous. This was a man who went on missions that could get him killed and was responsible for the lives of the men he worked with. Gideon didn't get nervous.

After a few minutes there was a quick knock on the door, and a doctor peeked in. "Mrs. Cooper?"

"Yes?" Charlie had never seen this doctor before, but as another contraction washed over her, she hoped to God he was the man who was going to take away the pain.

"I'm Dr. Carson. Someone said you might want an epidural, but—" he glanced at Gideon, who was now looming over him threateningly "—if you no longer need me…"

"No! Gideon, move away from the man with the good drugs," Charlie instructed. "Don't mind my husband, doctor. He's not nearly as scary as he looks. He's really a pushover."

"Not really, I could kill you with one finger, but if you can make her feel better, then do it." Gideon took a few steps back, but kept his gaze locked on the anesthesiologist. Charlie wondered if she'd have to send Gideon out of the room when the doctor gave her the epidural. He might take the poor man out if she even flinched.

"Gideon, you don't actually have a weapon—do you?" Charlie tried to make her voice light.

"Now, baby, you know I always have a weapon on me." Gideon's face lit up with a huge grin. Charlie wasn't sure if he was joking. From the look on his face, the doctor wasn't either.

"Don't worry. He's kidding." *I think,* she silently added.

Dr. Carson worked quickly and efficiently to get the drugs into Charlie's system. Soon they flowed through her body, easing the intensity of the next contraction. Charlie breathed a sigh of relief.

"Babe, why don't you go get something to drink and start calling the family? I feel really good right now," Charlie told her husband, waving him out the door.

"Are you sure, baby? I don't want to leave you."

"This is going to be a long night. Go get a breath of air. Hey, check on Chance for me."

Gideon leaned down to brush a soft, sweet kiss across Charlie's lips. "I love you, baby. Don't start without me," he whispered before heading out the door.

Finding the remote control, Charlie flipped through channels for something to do. She was floating with the relief the epidural had provided and barely noticed the next contraction—until the doctor, Maeve, and two other nurses burst through the door.

"Charlie, did you just have another contraction?" Dr. Miles asked.

"Um…yeah?" She wasn't sure what was happening, but wished she hadn't sent Gideon out.

"Okay, the babies' heart rates dropped again. I don't like this at all. I think we need to go in and get them." The doctor's voice was calm, but Charlie was beginning to panic. She wanted Gideon. She needed him there with her.

Suddenly, Charlie was unhooked and the bed tilted back. The nurses pulled down the IV bags that were giving her fluids and the much-needed anesthesia. Everyone seemed calm, but that didn't help Charlie at all.

"Yes, Mom. Charlie's really in labor. I'm not playing a joke on you." Gideon couldn't believe his own mother would think he'd joke about something like this.

"Oh, Gideon. I'm so excited. Where's your father?" she asked.

"They said he was in surgery. The nurse left a message with his secretary." He scanned the vending machine for something to take the edge off. Better to tear into a bag of Doritos than the doctors in the room.

"Okay, well, I'm on my way, darling. Tell Charlie not to have those babies until I get there."

"Yeah, I'll do that, Mom. I'm sure if she just crosses her legs that'll do the trick."

"Gideon!" she scolded. "I'll call Tyson and Paige too. I love you, Gideon. I'll be there in a little while." Evelyn hung up.

Gideon settled on cheese crackers with peanut butter and a Diet Coke before heading back to Charlie's room.

As he entered the room, Gideon froze. The whole place seemed overrun with medical personnel, and he couldn't even see Charlie anymore. It took all his strength not to start knocking people out of the way to get to his wife.

"What the hell is going on?" He was trying to stay calm — really — but seeing what seemed like chaos breaking out around his pregnant wife made it hard to find that quiet place inside himself.

"Here, you need to change into these." A nurse pushed a set of blue surgery scrubs into Gideon's hands.

"I'll ask again — what the hell is going on?" Gideon almost yelled this time.

When the nurses moved the bed, it turned so he could see Charlie. The fear in her eyes sent a chill through him. He knew he had to be the strong one in this situation. Charlie, as brave as she'd been over the past months, looked like she was going to lose it any minute.

"The heartbeats dropped again during a contraction, and I'm concerned the cord may be wrapped around one of the babies' necks. I want to do an emergency C-section," Dr. Miles finally explained to Gideon.

His heart nearly stopped. These babies were the only thing that had kept Charlie going all this time, and if anything happened to them…

"Okay." There was nothing else to say.

"Gideon?" Charlie's voice was so small and scared. He was afraid to look at her. His heart couldn't handle seeing her like that. Charlie helpless and scared was the one thing that could break him.

"Don't panic on me, baby. I need you to stay calm so I don't do anything stupid like threaten to kill the doctor," he whispered, placing a light kiss on her forehead. She must've thought he was kidding because she smiled up at him. Gideon was not joking in the least.

They started to roll her out the door, and Gideon saw her turn her head as a tear ran down her cheek. He needed to get in that room with her.

Quickly changing into the scrubs, Gideon practically ran down the hall to the operating room. He nearly knocked over his dad as he rounded a corner too fast.

"Whoa! What's going on, Son?" Peter reached out to steady him. Gideon could hear his breath coming fast and worried he was starting to hyperventilate. He knew his body well after so much training and realized if he didn't stop and get a hold of himself, he was definitely going to pass out.

"They…they took Charlie…cord…operate…" he panted, hoping his dad would get the gist of what was happening.

"Okay, Son. You need to stop. Charlie needs you on your feet." Gideon could see his dad, but his voice sounded like it was in a tunnel. The walls in the hall started to sway.

The sun filtered through Tyson's closed eyelids. The only good thing about waking up was feeling Paige in his arms. It was the only way he wanted to wake up for the rest of his life—with Paige's warm body pulled close to him.

Paige stirred, inadvertently brushing her perfectly rounded ass against Tyson's rock-hard morning erection. Well, it was noon, but his body didn't know that. He was so hard that the sensation caused his body to tighten. Just from that small contact, he almost came.

Leaning over, Tyson buried his face in her waves of luscious hair, just inhaling Paige.

"Mmm, Tyson, stop poking me with that thing." Paige's voice was deep and groggy from sleep—and sexy as hell.

"Marry me, Paige," Tyson whispered as he pulled her even closer, allowing his hardness to graze her lace-covered bottom again. She let out a low laugh that blanketed Tyson's skin in goose bumps.

"Did all the blood in your head go to your groin? I've already said I'd marry you. In fact, it's been more than three months now that I've been sporting this rock on my finger." She lifted her hand, wagging the ring in front of his face.

"I know that. I meant I don't want to wait," he said. "I'm going to graduate tomorrow, and I want the new chapter in my life to begin with us. I want you to marry me this summer before I start med school."

"Stop talking crazy, Tyson," Paige said, her tone full of laughter.

Tyson sat up. "I'm not. Listen."

Paige rolled over and looked up at him.

"My parents have a huge Fourth of July party every year. We could do it then. I want to know you're going to be with me forever."

"I am *so* not sharing my wedding anniversary with a national holiday," she laughed. "No. Let's stick to the plan."

"Well, since I haven't been briefed on said plan, I don't know if I can stick to it."

"I want to wait until after I graduate. You know that. Getting my degree is important to me."

"You can still finish school, Paige. It's not like I'm going to chain you to the stove and get you pregnant on our honeymoon." Tyson let out an exasperated breath. He'd never tell her he'd thought a lot about her pregnant with his child lately, especially since they'd been spending more time with Gideon and Charlie.

"I don't want to end up like Charlie," Paige said quietly. Paige and Charlie were the best of friends. That was the last thing Tyson had expected her to say. The look of shock on Tyson's face spurred Paige on. "I mean… shit, I don't want this to sound bad, but Charlie only had a semester left and now…"

"She's going to go back to finish her degree, Paige. I mean, she didn't stop just because of the pregnancy." He hated thinking of the other reason that Charlie had missed her last semester. "She totally could've finished this semester and graduated this year too."

"Could have, but she didn't. Do you think having two babies to take care of is going to make it any easier to go back and finish? Do you really think she'll finish?"

"She doesn't really have to. Gideon can support them, and Charlie can take care of the kids. Christ, I'll be able to support our family too. I'm going to be a doctor. You don't even have to finish school."

As soon as they were out of his mouth, Tyson knew those were the wrong words. Paige was out of the bed in an instant.

She turned on Tyson. Even with fire in her eyes and her hands on her hips she was the sexiest woman ever. Ways to remedy this situation began to run through Tyson's head, but seeing Paige standing there, all he wanted to do was pull her back into bed and take her over and over.

"I know you'll be able to support our family. This isn't about me doubting your manhood. This is about me doing something for me. I don't want to be reliant on you for my entire life. What if something happens with us? What if you start screwing your young, cute nurse?"

"That's not going to happen. I don't even see other women," Tyson argued.

"Not now, but what about in ten years? Things happen, and if they do, I want to be able to make my own way. I'd think with everything we've all been through lately you could understand that." She looked angry and lost at the same time.

Tyson needed a way to bring her back.

"Come back to bed." He pulled the sheet back, hoping to entice her and end the argument. "Honestly, I just wanted to make sure you didn't change your mind about marrying me. I know I'm an ass sometimes—"

"You think?" A smirk slid across her perfect lips. Tyson longed to get those lips working—on him.

"Okay, I deserved that. But see, that's my point. The longer we aren't married, the more time you have to realize how much better you are than me and walk away. If we're married, I think it would be harder for you to leave me." Tyson smiled at her, embarrassed that as stupid as it sounded, he'd spoken the truth.

"You're an idiot, Tyson Cooper. I'm going to marry you. I love you. But I'll have my degree first. It's a promise I made to myself a long time ago—nothing will stop me from graduating from college. If you want to get married the day after I graduate..."

She was moving back toward the bed. Tyson would respect her decisions and wait until she graduated. "Fine," he said. "But do you think you could finish in the winter semester?" he asked with a sly grin.

"No. We'll get married next June. There, that's settled. Your mom will be happy. Besides..." She stopped at the edge of the bed and slowly lifted her T-shirt over her head. "You may find some pretty doctor wannabe who tickles your fancy in med school next year. I wouldn't want you to be stuck with me."

"Fuck that! There's no other woman I want, Paige. Just you. Now get your ass back in this bed."

Paige's eyes glazed over, and her thumbs hooked into the sides of that white lace she claimed was panties, but really only served to frustrate Tyson. At the precise moment when Paige pushed her panties past her hips and Tyson got a glimpse of the Promised Land, his phone began to ring. Paige stopped. Tyson groaned.

"I'm not answering that. There's absolutely no reason to answer it. Continue, please."

Of course the answering machine kicked in, and then the whole morning went to hell.

"Tyson? Tyson? Oh, gosh. Well, I just got off the phone with your brother, and Charlie's having the babies!" Evelyn's voice was higher than Tyson had ever heard it. "Okay, so I'm on my way to the hospital. Get there when you can. Love you, and Paige too."

The sound of his mom's voice echoing in his head, again, when he was trying to get laid was never a good thing. Tyson's erection instantly deflated, and Paige's panties switched direction. Tyson let out another groan. There'd be no lovin' to start the day.

CHAPTER 45

*W*here's *Gideon? He should be here.* Charlie couldn't see him among all the people in green with masks over their faces. They calmly wandered around the room while she lay helpless on the bed. She tried to remind herself this wasn't the dream she'd been having. Gideon was here… somewhere. And Boyd was not.

Charlie recognized Maeve's kind eyes as she put another warmed blanket on top of her. She patted her shoulder and whispered, "It's all right, dear. Your husband had a little accident. He's coming right now though."

"Wh-What happened." Charlie's teeth chattered in the cold of the room.

"Um, he fainted." Charlie couldn't see Maeve's mouth, but the sparkle in her eyes told Charlie she was smiling under that mask. "The bigger they are, the harder they fall."

Charlie almost laughed. She tried to imagine her big Navy SEAL of a husband, a man who bragged he knew eighty-two different ways to kill someone, passing out because he was about to be a father. She was *so* not ever going to let him live that down.

The doors swung open and Charlie saw Gideon holding an ice pack to his head as he strode into the room. She couldn't wait to tell his brother, or hers for that matter. They'd torture him until the twins went off to college.

"I'm so sorry, baby. I kinda had an accident." He blushed.

Charlie didn't have the heart to make fun of him. "Are you okay, Joe?"

"I'm fine. I almost ran over my dad, though. Then, like a big pussy, I hit the tile—hard." He winced as he ran his fingers over his scalp. "I'm here for you now. Are you okay?"

"Actually, I think I am. Knowing you're as scared as I am has made this a little bit easier, I think. I trust my doctor." Charlie believed about half of what she was saying, but knew Gideon needed to hear she was okay.

Less than five minutes later, while Charlie held Gideon's hand, she heard the first cry fill the room, followed shortly by a second. Gideon peeked over the sheet they'd put up to block her lower half from view.

"Good Lord, baby. They're perfect. I swear. I've never seen anything so wonderful in my entire life." Gideon leaned down to brush a kiss across Charlie's forehead.

"Where are they, Joe? I want to see them." Just watching Gideon brought tears to her eyes, and she didn't think she could stand another minute of not seeing her sons.

"They're getting cleaned up, dear," Maeve told her. "They're gorgeous—and healthy it would seem."

"Yeah," Dr. Carson said as she came to pat Charlie's arm. "I'm glad we went to get them though. The cord wasn't wrapped around anyone's neck, but it was blocking the birth canal, and they'd have been in real distress soon enough. This way we got them before there was too much stress or trauma." Although Charlie thought there'd been an awful lot of stress and trauma, she was thankful her boys were safe.

Moments later, a nurse appeared around the barrier with two bundles in her arms. "You can have them for a minute, then we have to take them to the nursery for a checkup and a few tests." She handed the babies to Gideon. Charlie was worried he wouldn't know how to hold them, but he cradled them in his arms perfectly, tilting them up slightly so she could see.

They took Charlie's breath away. With little pink faces and tufts of blond curls—they were perfect.

"Okay, Mommy, why don't you let me take them to get all their testing done. They look very healthy, and I don't anticipate them having to go to the NICU, even though they're a few weeks early."

"Don't let him name them," Charlie yelled after the nurse. Gideon laughed. "Make sure they do the DNA testing, Gideon. I don't want *him* to get near them. Ever," she whispered.

"I know. I've already had them do my swab, and they have instructions to do the boys. There's no way he'll get to them. In fact, I found out just before they brought you in here that despite what happened during your questioning today, they're going to formally charge Boyd, and he'll be locked up until the actual court-martial. Apparently there are women coming out of the woodwork from every base he's been stationed at. The JAG guy said they have three more women so far and interviews set up with two more."

"Good. Now go see if any of our family's out there. Tell them we're all fine." Charlie let go of his hand. "I love you, Gideon Cooper."

"Goddamn, I love you, Charlie Cooper."

Charlie nodded, suddenly so tired and emotionally drained she only wanted to sleep. Charlie felt Gideon kiss the top of her head just as she let her eyes close.

One last thought flitted through Charlie's mind before she drifted off: *I'm a mother now.*

There was nothing for Charlie to worry about. Just as Gideon told her, the nurses had the instructions and knew to swab the boys and run the test. There were some sideways looks when he told them what he needed, but Gideon didn't care. It was none of their business—let them think whatever they wanted.

Before calling his mom, Gideon had called the JAG office to make sure Boyd was still restricted to the base. He didn't want to worry about him coming to the hospital and upsetting Charlie. Gideon had breathed a sigh of relief when he was given the even-better news of Boyd's arrest.

Every member of the family was standing in the hallway when Gideon came through the doors. As he looked around at them, he thought about how lucky his sons were to have all these people to love them. They all started talking at once, and Gideon had to hold a hand up to stop them from shouting over each other.

"Everyone's fine," he started. "There was a small problem with one of the cords blocking…um…the exit."

"But they're all healthy?" Evelyn asked. Gideon looked over at his parents and could tell it had taken everything his dad had to keep his mom in place all this time—Peter's hair was even disheveled. Gideon laughed as he pictured him holding his mom back.

"Yeah, Charlie's sleeping right now, but she's fine. And I think we may be able to see the boys any time now." Gideon started heading down the hall toward the nursery, knowing the whole group would follow.

Feeling a hand on his shoulder, Gideon glanced over at Tyson. It had been hard over the past three months, but things were better, and he was glad his brother was there. They reached the big glass window and spread out across the front of it. A nurse looked up and, recognizing Peter, instantly went to the beds marked *Cooper*. She wheeled them over closer to the window so everyone could see them.

"Okay, everyone, I want to introduce you to my sons: Finley Connor and Rory Gideon Cooper."

CHAPTER 46

"Come on, guys. Help the old man out here." Gideon had resorted to begging his six-week-old sons. "I need you to work with me. Mommy will be home any minute with the 'go ahead' from the doctor, and it's been a long time, guys. Really, is it too much to ask that you both sleep for a few hours?"

Rory's response was to spit up what looked like the entire bottle he'd swallowed not fifteen minutes earlier. It was like *The Exorcist* or something. Finn, on the other hand, took on a look of extreme concentration. Gideon knew that look. *Crap!* And he meant that both figuratively and literally.

"Aw, come on boys. What are you trying to do to me?"

The twins stared at Gideon—one covered in spit up, the other starting to smell like the diaper pail threw up on him—and he knew he had to take care of both situations quickly. There was nothing romantic about coming home to stinky, dirty babies.

It had been way too long since Gideon had his hands on Charlie's body. He knew she thought she was still out of shape from having the boys. But no matter what, she'd always be the most beautiful and perfect woman Gideon had ever seen. And he wanted to touch her again.

Up until about two weeks before the babies were born, things had been progressing nicely. Gideon had started to notice that when he touched Charlie intimately, it took less time for her to relax and allow him to love her. But the stiffness was still there, and it hurt. He couldn't say it didn't. And now Gideon was afraid the six-week break had set her back so far she'd pull away all over again.

Gideon missed the Charlie he'd had before he left. He missed the Charlie he'd caught pleasuring herself in the bathtub, the Charlie who sent him naughty pictures of herself in lingerie, the Charlie who seduced him while wearing his uniform.

That bastard had stolen all of that from him.

The Charlie Gideon had now was tentative and quiet when they made love. She always had to hold eye contact with him, never allowing herself to fall into it and just enjoy. Gideon didn't know if she'd ever initiate sex again.

Gideon had just finished changing Finn and was putting him back in his bouncy seat when the baby let out a squeak as if to say he was getting with the program. And Rory was a total team player with his little thumb securely tucked in his mouth and his eyes closed in sleep.

"That's my boys. You know what Daddy's trying to get done here. You want to help Daddy get some today, right?"

"Gideon Isaac Cooper! What are you saying to my sons?" Charlie asked from the doorway.

Gideon knew he was in trouble. "Um…well…uh…" Finn was more with the program than Gideon had realized. He must've known his mom had come in, and that little squeak was a warning, not support. Gideon couldn't wait for the boys to talk. He'd get away with so much more when they could actually tell him Charlie was standing behind him.

"That's what I thought. Step away from my sons." Charlie's voice was stern, but Gideon could hear the laughter she was holding back. "Gideon? Why does Rory have spit up all over him? Why didn't you change him?" Charlie looked at her boys, and Gideon knew she was counting fingers and toes.

"I was about to," Gideon defended. "Look, I even have this." He waved a handful of clothes at her. "But when I came back from changing Finn, Rory was asleep." Gideon moved to stand closer to Charlie, wrapping his arms around her waist. "I was trying to get the boys to work with me and sleep so that if the doc gave us the okay, we could…you know."

"No. What, Gideon?" Her voice was lower than normal, with a hint of lust.

Gideon leaned in close to whisper in her ear. "I need to be with you, baby. I'm so hard I could cut diamonds over here just thinking about having you naked in bed."

Charlie inhaled quickly as her husband's hands slid from her waist over her hips and pulled her in closer to him. Evidence that he'd been telling the truth a moment ago pressed against her abdomen.

"So do we have a green light, Charlie?"

"I'm not telling you." She smiled up at Gideon, toying with him.

This was one of those times that put Gideon in a quandary. He didn't know whether she was playing because she was worried about being with him or because she was trying to be coy and alluring. He didn't want to push her if fear was the issue.

To make things worse, Charlie had been dealing with Boyd's hearing the past three days. They'd decided not to have her testify after finding the women from the other bases where he'd been stationed. According to the lead prosecutor from the JAG office, it was better not to include her rape in the charges against him for the court-martial. Because Charlie's assault occurred off base, if for some reason Boyd was not convicted in the court-martial, they'd still have her case the civilian authorities could prosecute.

Charlie had been dropping the boys off with Evelyn and spending the days at the base with Zoe and the other women. She said she wanted to be there to support them. Gideon admired the hell out of her for putting herself through all of it just to help the others. But it also meant she'd been thinking more about the rape recently, and he knew that made it harder for her to be close to him. He felt like a bastard for even wanting it.

Glancing at the boys, Gideon smiled to see that Finn had closed his eyes like his brother. His boys were working with him. Now he just needed to work out how much he should push.

His mind was made up. He had to have Charlie. He couldn't let this opportunity slip away. The boys usually slept for about two hours, and that was plenty of time to ease Charlie back into being naked and sweaty with him.

"Come on, baby," Gideon whispered. "Let me show you how much I love you. Let me show you how beautiful you are."

"I don't know, Joe. I should put the boys in their cribs."

"They're fine. If you try to move them, they'll wake up."

"Gideon…" Charlie let out a big breath as Gideon slid his hands up and cupped her breasts, gently moving his thumbs over her nipples, surprised when they instantly hardened.

"Baby, you're so beautiful. Just let me love you. Slow and perfect. I promise." Gideon was practically begging and didn't even care. He loved Charlie with everything he had, and he wanted her to know exactly how much.

Gideon felt the precise moment when Charlie gave herself over. Her body relaxed against him. Not wanting to lose the momentum he had going, Gideon quickly picked her up to carry her to bed.

"Gideon!" she squealed.

"Shh," he warned. "Please don't wake the boys."

"We have to go slow, Joe." She lowered her eyes. It broke his heart.

"Baby." He dipped his head to look Charlie in the eye. "I just want to be with you. You don't have to worry about a thing." Kissing her gently on the mouth, Gideon headed toward the bedroom. The clock was ticking, and he didn't want to waste any more time. He knew as soon as he got Charlie in the bedroom, she'd relax and allow him to show her how much she meant to him.

Gideon set Charlie on the bed and moved away from her. As much as he wanted to undress her, that was one of the triggers. He had to allow her to find the place she needed to be and do it herself. Instead of taking her clothes off, Gideon pulled his own T-shirt over his head and tossed it on the floor. His eyes focused on his beautiful wife, watching as her gaze slipped over his bare chest, her eyes darkening slightly.

And there it was. She wanted him. It was the look Gideon waited for every time they'd been intimate since he'd gotten home; the look that let him know she was there with him, not back in time with *him*. Then Gideon knew he could touch her without feeling her flinch away. There were guidelines to go by, but this was the first step toward having Charlie the way he needed her.

Charlie's eyes followed as Gideon undid his pants and moved them down over his hips. Moments later, he stood next to the bed in only boxer briefs. Charlie was still fully dressed. She was killing him.

"Baby, I'm gonna need you to catch up with me here," Gideon begged.

Slowly, tortuously slowly, Charlie began to lift her shirt up over her head. The sight of her breasts under the lace of her bra nearly made Gideon explode. It had been so long. Although he'd seen his wife naked hundreds of times, ever since the babies came, she'd been hiding herself from him. He knew she was worried her body had changed. Like he could give a flying fuck about that—her body was perfect. She'd given birth to his sons and that had only served to make her more beautiful.

"You're the most beautiful woman I've ever laid eyes on, baby." Gideon wanted to touch her. He wanted to run his tongue over every inch of her body, but knew he couldn't just jump on her. He had to go slow. Even if she'd been flirting earlier, he had to respect her and love her the right way.

"Stop it, Gideon. You don't have to lie to me. I'm half naked, the doctor gave us the okay, and the boys are asleep—pretty much a sure thing here." There was a blush on her cheeks and tears in her eyes.

Gideon moved to the bed, never letting his gaze fall from hers. Lying down next to her, he pulled her close, burying his face in her hair. He wanted her so badly, but not this way, not with her thinking he was being dishonest simply to get in her pants. Not that he hadn't done that in the past—but never, ever with Charlie. Charlie always got the truth.

"I'm not lying to you," he finally said. "No matter what, you'll always be the most beautiful woman ever to me. You've given me so much over this last year and a half. Every day I look at you and our sons and thank God for all He's given me."

Charlie's body moved against Gideon's, and he really was trying to be good. He wouldn't hurt her for anything in the world. Charlie's hands entwined in Gideon's, and she pulled them to her waistband.

"I want you to make love to me. I want you to show me how beautiful you think I am, please," she whispered, barely loud enough for Gideon to hear.

"Are you sure about this, baby?" He was hesitant.

"I am. I need this. I don't know if I can completely give up control, but I want this…now." Her eyes were bright, and Gideon knew she meant it. He couldn't sense any fear, only want—for him.

Carefully, Gideon maneuvered her pants down over her body, revealing lacy underwear that matched her bra. She looked like perfection there on their bed, waiting for him.

After loving each other for as long as they could before the real world came crashing back, Gideon allowed Charlie to relax and take a shower while he dealt with the boys a while longer. She was glad he'd given her the time he knew she needed after they'd made love. It still wasn't easy and natural, but having Gideon be so understanding helped.

Once the boys were settled, Gideon fell into bed, exhausted from the emotional and physical toll of the day. He'd never taken care of the boys for a whole day before, and the house looked like a football team had run through it. But Charlie decided to let that go and crawl into bed beside her husband. The house could wait. She wanted to feel the security of Gideon holding her as she slept. Only that would make things right.

Later, Charlie rolled over to watch her husband sleep. He was the most perfect man she'd ever known. She was pretty sure God had put him on this earth just for her. Then, glancing over his shoulder at the clock, she groaned and rolled out of bed.

The twins were getting better, but they still weren't sleeping through the night. The four a.m. feeding was the hardest for Charlie. She didn't know how Gideon slept through their crying, and she honestly wasn't sure he was sleeping—not faking it so he didn't have to get up. She couldn't blame him too much though. He did have to go to work every day. Charlie, on the other hand, had the luxury of catching a quick nap when the boys did. Of course, first she had to make sure the house was picked up, the Diaper Genie emptied, the next bottles ready and in the fridge, and a load of laundry started. So she got maybe fifteen minutes to close her eyes. And she wouldn't change a thing.

As Charlie sat alone, feeding Finn while Rory sat in the swing watching the mobile go around, her mind focused on the past days and Cody Boyd's court-martial. She ached for the women who had to testify.

Gideon understood she needed to be there, as did the rest of the family. Charlie was lucky to have Evelyn to watch the boys. She'd promised to not let what Cody Boyd had done to her affect the lives of her sons, but she had to do this. And Evelyn seemed to love having them with her for a few hours each day. In fact, it was almost impossible to get them back.

Today's session would be different, though. The panel's decision was expected, and all the women were being allowed into the room. She was going to be there too. *He* may not have been on trial for what *he* did to her, but she was as much a part of this as any of the others.

Charlie hadn't seen Cody Boyd since the day she'd gone into labor and *he* had said all those ugly things. Fear that the monster would try to claim her sons had been at the forefront of her mind that day. The way *he* had leered at Charlie and his unwavering belief that she'd *wanted him* to do those things worried her. Charlie hated to admit it, because she'd never want *him* to use it as a defense, but she truly thought *he* was insane.

The family didn't understand why they'd had the DNA test done when the twins were born. Evelyn kept saying all anyone had to do was look at the two of them and they'd know they were Gideon's. It was true. They were like minis of their father with their blond curls and steel gray eyes. But the DNA tests were the only pieces of empirical evidence Charlie had to fight against Boyd. There would never be any doubt in the eyes of the law that *he* had no claim on her sons. Ever.

Now, sitting in the dark with her babies, Charlie had time to think about seeing *him* once again. Her stomach turned and tears began to pool behind her eyes. She hated that just the thought of seeing *him* could do this to her. She hated *him*.

Once both of the boys were fed, changed, and back to sleep, Charlie debated getting back in bed with Gideon and letting him chase away her fears. It would be so easy to revert back to the old Charlie, the Charlie who hid behind her husband. She decided, however, that she couldn't do that — not this time. Today Charlie wouldn't hide. She might not be testifying, but she needed to stand up and be heard by all the others, by Cody Boyd, and, most importantly, by the panel of men who'd decide his fate. Charlie didn't see how they could do anything but find him guilty. The only question would be what kind of punishment he'd get.

Charlie watched out the big picture window as the sky lightened. When she heard the alarm go off, she got up and made coffee for Gideon. As she sat and listened to the normal morning sounds of her home, Charlie took comfort in the decisions she'd made. By the time Gideon came out of the bedroom, looking incredibly sexy in his "uniform" of a black T-shirt and camos, she was perfectly at peace with her life.

While she'd still need therapy for a long time and certain smells or images could still send her off into that dark place for a bit, Charlie knew she'd get through. She was going to let herself be happy, let herself be loved.

CHAPTER 47

Gideon knew Charlie would never miss the proceedings today, so instead of trying to talk her out of it, he was supportive.

"So," he started, and then didn't seem to know what to say.

"Yeah," Charlie offered. Not much help in moving the conversation along. Charlie knew he wanted to say something awe inspiring and *uber*-supportive, but he sometimes couldn't find the right way to express his feelings.

"Are you taking the boys to my mom's?" He grabbed a cup and poured himself some coffee.

"Yeah, in fact I probably should jump in the shower. Can you get the boys if they wake up?" Charlie asked. She kept her responses short and focused. All her attention went toward facing the day, and the conversation seemed off after the previous day's total abandoning of all barriers.

By the time Charlie got out of the shower, Gideon had the boys fed, dressed, and their diaper bag ready to go — not that they needed to bring a single thing to his parents' house with the fully stocked nursery Evelyn had there.

Gideon helped get the babies in the car and kissed Charlie good-bye before he left for the base. She wouldn't be far behind. The court-martial was set to start at nine, and Charlie wanted to be there early enough that she could talk to the JAG officer about what she wanted to do.

As usual, Evelyn was excited to see her grandsons and eagerly took both carriers from Charlie — then practically pushed her back out the door.

Charlie arrived at the Headquarters Building on base, where the court-martial was being held, early enough to catch the JAG prosecutor in the hallway. She asked him if she'd be allowed to speak if Boyd was found guilty.

"Mrs. Cooper, that's a very unusual request. We kept your case out of this for a reason, and I'm afraid if we were to allow that—"

Suddenly, the entire building erupted in total chaos. Several men rushed past Charlie and the JAG prosecutor, weapons drawn, shouting, "Get out of the halls, people. We have a situation outside. We need everyone out of this hallway!"

The officer ushered Charlie into a small conference room off the main hallway and closed the door. She could hear men running through the building and shouting. Charlie waited there by herself for several minutes. Being alone in a room with a door that could be locked while Cody Boyd was in the same building caused her heart to beat double time. The thought that *he* could waltz in and hurt her again never left her mind.

When the door finally opened again, Charlie's heart felt like it had stopped for a split second before she saw Zoe walk in.

"Oh, thank God," Charlie breathed. "What's going on? Why are we in here?"

"I don't know," Zoe said as she entered the room, followed by the other women who'd been raped by Boyd. Charlie was relieved to see all of them. At least now if Cody Boyd were to walk into the room, *he* wouldn't get out with his manhood intact.

"I need all you ladies to stay here. We have a situation outside that we need to get under control, and we can't have any civilians hurt," a uniformed marine with a very big gun told the women before closing the door again.

Small, tentative conversations started up around the table. Everyone glanced at the door whenever the sound of heavy boots running past echoed from the hallway. The voices outside the door were muffled, and there were so many of them that none of the women could figure out what was happening.

Twenty minutes had passed and no one had been in to check on the group of women. Then the door opened, and Gideon stepped in. He completely ignored every other person in the room as he made his way to Charlie, scooping her up out of the chair and burying his face in her hair.

"What the hell is going on, Gideon?" Charlie asked through her shock.

"Oh God, Charlie. I was so worried. We got the word, and Jaylon and I ran out of the office immediately. No one would tell us anything. We just didn't know…" There were tears in his eyes, and the look on his face was one Charlie hadn't seen since the day he came home and thought he'd lost her.

When she finally glanced around the room, Charlie found Jaylon holding Zoe in much the same way Gideon held her.

"Gideon? What happened? Are we being attacked?" Every face was turned to Gideon and Jaylon.

"We got a call about twenty-five minutes ago that there'd been gunfire at the Headquarters Building. We were put on alert in case of a hostage situation." Gideon paused, swallowing hard before pulling Charlie in closer to him. "They didn't give us any details. Fox and I couldn't wait for the rest of the team. We hauled ass over here."

"Gunshots? Hostages? Oh my God. We've been locked in this room. No one's told us anything."

"I know, baby. They couldn't. They did the right thing here. As much as you hate being kept in the dark and locked up, it was protocol. Protect the civilians." His grip on her tightened, and Charlie almost couldn't breathe.

The room was silent except for the sound of footsteps from the hall. All the yelling and running had stopped. Whatever had been going on seemed over now. Charlie looked up at Gideon. His face was grim: his lips drawn in a tight line, his brow wrinkled with worry.

"For the love of all things holy, tell us what the hell happened," one of the women said from between clenched teeth. Charlie knew she'd been raped by Cody Boyd three years ago at another base.

"It was all but over when we got here," Gideon said.

"Just spit it out," another woman hissed.

"I can tell you what I know. They don't want to tell you all, but fuck that. I think you have every right to know." Gideon stopped to take a deep breath. "They were bringing Boyd into the building this morning. He was being escorted by MPs when he was shot on the stairs outside."

"And?" Charlie prompted. *He* was shot? What did that mean? Was *he* dead, wounded, suffering? She had to admit, none of those things would bother her that much. Then she felt horrible—*he* was a human being.

"He's dead." Gideon voice was emotionless. Charlie had the feeling he was on autopilot, waiting to react to her reactions. She was numb.

The room was silent for a long minute. No one had been ready for what Gideon told them.

"I don't believe you," Ginger said.

"It's the truth." Jaylon spoke for the first time. "I swear to you, we saw his body. There were two nice holes in his head." His voice held a hint of disdain.

Kelly sat at the table with tears streaming down her cheeks. Charlie knew hers was probably the appropriate response—a human life had been taken. Although maybe Kelly's were just tears of relief. Charlie knew she couldn't bring herself to grieve for *him*. Through the stunned silence, a collective feeling of freedom washed over the room.

Charlie was still held tightly in Gideon's arms when she realized she was crying. *No!* She wouldn't cry for *him!* She wouldn't cry that *he* was gone! Her whole body began to tremble. If Gideon hadn't been holding her, Charlie would've been on the floor.

"Come on, baby. I'm taking you home. We don't need to be here," Gideon whispered as he led her out of the room.

"Wait! Who? I mean who k-k-killed him?" a voice Charlie didn't recognize asked.

"Honestly, I don't know. And I don't care. I, for one, am not going to question how karma works." With that, Gideon turned and walked Charlie down the hall away from the front of the building to the parking lot in the back. Once they made it to her car, he leaned back against the door and held her, letting Charlie sob against him.

Charlie now realized she wasn't crying for *him*, she was crying simply to allow her body to rid itself everything that had been bottled up all these months. She was free — no more worrying every time there was a knock on the door, no more nightmares that *he* was going to come back. No more. None of the women *he* hurt were crying *for him*. They'd all mourn everything *he* had taken from them, but not one of them was sorry *he* was dead.

Gideon held her, whispering that it was okay, everything was over. This was one of those times she allowed him to protect her. Everything was too new, too out of control. Charlie needed Gideon to hold her up. She was strong, but this was too much.

Charlie didn't remember a lot about the drive home. There were people, cars, and news cameras everywhere on the base. The one thing she did remember was Gideon's string of obscenities as he tried to maneuver past them all to get off base. The next thing she knew she was on the couch and her husband was on the phone with his mom, trying to calm her and explain what had happened. Apparently the media were covering the shooting, and Evelyn had been trying to call to make sure they were okay.

The couch dipped as Gideon sat down next to Charlie and pulled her to him once again.

"My mom's going to keep the boys a while longer. She and my dad will bring them home later. We have all day. Just let me help you." His warm breath brushed over her neck as he spoke. Charlie took comfort in his familiar touch and the sound of his voice. She sank into Gideon's embrace, losing herself in just being held.

The sun was beginning to lower into the ocean when Charlie finally roused herself enough to look out the front window. She hadn't even noticed the passing time as she sat with Gideon's safe embrace protecting her from the world.

"Thank you, Gideon," she said, snuggling into him. *Thank you for not making me talk about what happened,* she silently added. *Thank you for allowing me to just take comfort in you. Thank you for being here.*

"I want to know more," Charlie said after another moment.

"What do you mean? He's gone, Charlie. He can't hurt us any more. What more could you need to know?" Gideon tried to maintain the control in his voice.

Charlie didn't want to hurt him, but it wouldn't be real to her until she knew what had happened. "I just need to know. I can't explain it."

There was a knock on the door, and Charlie jumped. Even though Gideon had told her Boyd was dead, she couldn't stop the thought that it was *him.* That's why she needed to know. Gideon had felt her reaction too, and she heard him sigh as the understanding hit him. He wanted to protect her, but the only way to do that was to let her know the truth.

Gideon opened the door to find his parents, each with a baby in their arms. The boys were wide awake and cooing happily. For the first time in hours, Charlie smiled. Nothing in the world could make her happier than to have her boys and Gideon with her.

"Oh, Charlie," Evelyn said as she reached and pulled her into a one-armed hug.

"I'm okay, Evelyn. It all happened outside the building. I was inside." Charlie tried to comfort her mother-in-law as she took Finn from her.

"Come in. We were just about to turn on the news," Gideon offered. "Charlie needs to know all of it. Hell, I guess I want to know who did it too," he admitted.

Closing the door, Charlie directed everyone into the living room. But before they made it three steps into the other room, there was another knock at the door. Charlie opened it to find Chance and Gabby. Her sister-in-law rushed in and pulled Charlie into her arms, placing a small kiss on Finn's head as she did.

Chance waited patiently for Gabby to release his sister. After several long seconds, she finally stepped back, wiping tears from under her eyes before a smile appeared on her face.

"Now where is my other beautiful nephew?" Gabby called as she headed into the room with the rest of the family.

"How are you, Lottie?" Chance asked as he pulled Charlie into a hug. "And don't lie to me, 'cause you know I can tell."

"It's getting better. I'm glad you're here, though. We were just about to see what the news people are saying about it, and I could use some extra support," she admitted.

"That's what I'm for. Let us be here for you, Lottie. We want to help. You don't have to handle this alone."

"Thanks, Chance. That's a lesson I've learned the hard way." Charlie held on to him a little longer than she probably should have, but he was comforting. Finn's squirming was the only thing that made her let go.

"Ah…what's wrong….um…" Chance stammered, looking at the baby.

"Finn, Chance. This is Finn. Jeesh! You'd think you could learn to tell your nephews apart," Charlie joked. Everyone, Evelyn included, still had a hard time telling them apart sometimes.

"I know—I suck," Chance shot back with a big smile.

Before Charlie and Chance could turn to join the rest of the family, there was yet another knock on the door.

"Come in, Tyson," Charlie called.

Sure enough, the door opened to Tyson and Paige looking nervously at her.

"I guess we're the last ones?" Paige asked.

Charlie simply stepped forward and pulled her into a hug. The two didn't say anything. Paige had become Charlie's best friend over the past year, and she had to know the conflicting emotions Charlie was fighting.

When they finally let go, Tyson tentatively stepped up to Charlie. They hadn't had much actual contact recently. Even though progress had been made in their broken relationship, they remained distant.

Charlie met Tyson halfway, and to his credit, he made the first move, pulling her to him in a light hug.

"Charlie, I know this is hard for you. I want you to know we're always here for you. Don't let the past keep us apart. You need all of us."

He was right. Charlie needed her whole family. Tyson's words touched her more than any of the others. Once again the tears started.

"Tyson! Damn it! What did you say to her?" Gideon came storming into the foyer, ready to save the woman he loved from his brother.

"Nothing…aw Christ! I swear I just told her we were here for her."

"Tyson didn't do anything." Charlie sniffled, trying to stop the tears. "Everything's fine." She grabbed Gideon's arm to pull him back into the living room and smiled up at Tyson to let him know she was trying. He shook his head as he put his arm around Paige, a smile playing on his lips.

The TV was already on and turned to the local news. The family was mesmerized by what they saw on the screen. The news anchor spoke over footage from earlier in the day. Uniformed men scrambled around as a stretcher covered with a white sheet was loaded into an ambulance. Then the scene changed to a newscaster in a blue suit. The now-quiet Headquarters Building filled the background.

"We're working to get more details, but it appears Ensign Cody Boyd was shot on his way to court-martial proceedings this morning. He was set to receive the results of a full court-martial in which he was accused of raping several fellow military members' wives."

"Yeah, we know that much," Gideon barked at the TV. Charlie put a calming hand against his arm. He took a deep breath and looked down at Rory, who'd fallen asleep cradled against his chest.

"A spokesman for the base is now confirming that the shooter turned the gun on himself immediately after killing the victim and is also dead. Our sources say the shooter was a former Naval officer whose wife claimed Boyd attacked her five years ago in Virginia Beach."

The group was silent. Charlie ran through the other women who'd testified about what Boyd had done. The oldest incident was the woman from three years ago.

"Gideon, there was no one who said anything about five years ago."

"Apparently when she reported the incident, she was told nothing could be done because Boyd said it was a consensual relationship. According to our sources, the woman committed suicide shortly after that," the reporter added.

He had gotten away with it all those years ago and knew *he* could do it again. All *he* had to do was lie, and no one would believe the woman — or so *he* thought.

"The shooter used a high-power rifle and delivered two precise shots to the victim's head. It's being reported that he was dead almost instantly," the reporter continued.

As Charlie looked around at her family—the husband she was over-the-moon in love with, her sleeping son in his arms, his twin cooing in her own arms, and the rest of the people who loved them—and thought about the other women Cody Boyd had taken so much from, one phrase ran through her mind…

And justice for all.

EPILOGUE

Four Years Later...

Charlie looked up from her seat in the hospital room to see her family once again gathered. She thought back to that day almost four years ago and remembered how certain she'd been that she'd never be back in the maternity ward — ever.

Her attention was drawn to the open door of the small room everyone had crammed into and the figure of Maeve, Charlie's favorite nurse, standing there holding her sons' hands. Charlie rolled her eyes. Gideon was supposed to be watching those two, not the nurse.

Charlie could only imagine what they'd gotten into. At almost four years old, they had a curiosity typical of small boys. That, combined with their ability to work together, could be catastrophic in a hospital. Two days ago she'd forgotten to lock the pantry and they'd managed to dump out all of the flour and sugar...then topped it off with an entire bottle of maple syrup. She sighed thinking of how much she was going to make Gideon pay for not watching them.

Looking over at her husband talking to his father, Charlie had to giggle at how much trouble she was about to get him in. Calling him out in front of his mother was probably the worst thing she could do.

Gideon waved his hands in the air as he relayed a story — one she'd heard several times over the past three days — to Peter, who laughed right along with him. Charlie knew every inflection in his voice, every gesture. She was still amazed by the happiness that radiated from him these days. It had taken some time to get there...

…After Boyd's death, Gideon's entire team had been torn apart and in turmoil. Each of the affected men had to find a way to deal with the aftermath of both the shooting and what Cody Boyd had done to their families. And the damage went beyond Gideon's team. Several of the men from other bases decided to leave the service, blaming their absence for what happened to their wives. Some of them publicly praised the shooter.

Lieutenant Walker left the SEALS and the Navy, as he'd already planned, and he and Ginger relocated their family a few hours north to L.A. Walker was hired as a military consultant for a movie studio. Gideon still talked to him from time to time and reported to Charlie that Walker seemed to enjoy still feeling connected to the military without having to leave his family. Walker wasn't comfortable talking much about his wife, though, and Gideon could only ask so many times. But at least Charlie knew Ginger was surviving.

Jaylon, who couldn't bear to leave the military, was able to transfer to a desk job out in Miramar. Zoe never went back to school, and Charlie hated that it was one more thing *he* had taken from her. They had a new baby girl now, and Zoe was still going through therapy. When they spoke these days, Charlie could tell how much the combination of talking to someone and becoming a mother had helped Zoe. And their friendship had helped both of them. Most people couldn't understand everything they'd been through, but having each other helped so much.

Gideon, unlike Jaylon, had had a hard time figuring out what to do. Charlie watched him for months after the shooting as he fought with himself over his future. He loved serving his country. And he loved his family. The guilt he felt over what had happened was eating him up.

The only thing that had saved Gideon during those weeks after the shooting was that with the decimation of his team and the publicity generated over the whole incident, he hadn't been sent out on any missions. Charlie couldn't deny she was relieved — she wasn't sure either of them would've survived that.

Though it pained Charlie to watch the man she loved struggle, she knew she couldn't help him make the decision. She wouldn't tell him what to do. This was something only Gideon could decide.

He finally accepted a job in the civilian world at an architectural firm. His background as an engineer was highly sought after, and he had several offers that would allow him to more than support his family. In fact, with the salary he was slated to earn, they could've bought a nice house in La Jolla near Peter and Evelyn. But Gideon was miserable.

For weeks, as his separation date approached, he'd come home from the base and not even want to play with the boys. Charlie could tell he wasn't going to be happy leaving the Navy. Gideon was a SEAL. It was more than his job—it was a part of who he was. But this was his decision, she told herself, and she was selfish. She liked the idea of him being home for more than a few months at a time. She liked the idea of him not being shot at. She liked the idea that he'd picked his family over the SEALs. She just didn't like what it was doing to him. Charlie feared they couldn't survive either choice.

Then one day about a week before he was set to process out and start his new job, Gideon came bounding in the door, a huge smile on his face. Charlie hadn't seen him this happy since the day the boys were born.

"Charlie, baby, I need to talk to you." His voice was cautious and Charlie watched the light in his eyes dim just a bit when he looked at her holding a sleeping Rory. Charlie was afraid to know what had made him so happy.

"What is it, Joe?" There was a hitch in her voice.

"I got an interesting phone call today." He paused. He was trying to be dramatic, but Charlie had had all the drama she could handle for a lifetime.

"Just tell me what happened." Charlie looked up into his eyes. They were dancing with excitement. "Please?"

"I haven't had you begging in a long time, baby." Gideon grinned and those dimples made Charlie's knees weak. "Okay, so I got a phone call at work today. Apparently someone had been under a rock for the past few months, and the Commander over in BUDS training just heard I was getting out. He said he thought it would be a criminal offense to let a SEAL like me leave the Navy, and with the world the way it is today, they needed every good man they could get."

Charlie's stomach started to flip flop. She didn't like the way this was going. She knew the man Gideon was, and that the military would be better with him than without him, but she couldn't bring herself to be okay with him staying in. She couldn't think of one circumstance that would make her change her mind.

"They want me to stay in and be an instructor at the SEAL training school. Do you know what that means, baby? It means I get to be a SEAL, and I get to stay with you and the boys."

That would be the one circumstance Charlie could live with. Gideon could do what he loved and be with who he loved.

Gideon leaned down and brushed his lips over Charlie's. "Now let's go celebrate while the boys are still sleeping."

As if on cue, Rory opened his eyes and looked right at Gideon. Instead of crying like he'd normally do, he laughed—a big belly laugh that woke his brother. Finn joined in, and soon the whole family was laughing.

The celebrating may have been postponed, but Charlie would always remember that as the moment she knew they were going to survive—Cody Boyd didn't win…

"…and then the kid has the nerve to say he went to Annapolis, and he's well versed in how to break down and service his weapon. So I told him, 'Son, you may be able to do this blindfolded, but if your ass is sitting in the jungle with the enemy firing on you, there ain't no amount of crap you learned at Annapolis that's going to help you. Now pick up your fu—"

"Gideon Cooper!" Evelyn warned. "Do *not* finish that sentence, young man." Evelyn might have given up some of the control over her sons' lives over the past few years, but she was still their mother.

"Sorry, Mom." Gideon gave his mother a peck on the cheek. "Sometimes I forget I'm not trying to weed out the ass…um…less-qualified men, and I get carried away. You know the only thing those kids listen to is lots of yelling—some very colorful yelling." His face lit up with the true joy he'd found in his new career, and he launched into yet another story Charlie had already heard. Charlie smiled too in response to his happiness, but her mind went elsewhere…

…The women Boyd had hurt so badly, both physically and mentally, suffered the aftereffects of everything in a different way than the men. This was the reason behind the support group and Charlie's change in careers. While she loved working with kids, *the incident* had truly shaped her life's path.

Charlie finally finished college, cramming in classes to get her degree in social work. She'd taken a lot of social science classes already because of her years spent studying to be a special education teacher, but she'd had to do another full year of classes to complete her new major.

With her diploma in hand, Charlie started a small clinic that provided military wives with assistance they might need while their husbands were gone. She helped them find childcare and jobs and organized support groups for them. The best thing was that while the clinic specialized in working with military wives, word quickly spread, and eventually Charlie's clinic helped the spouses of many of the men and women who served their communities. The wives, and even a few husbands, of police and firefighters would come just to talk to others like them — people who lived every day worrying about the ones they loved.

Once Chance got his degree and finished his post-grad work, he came to the clinic once a week to hold counseling sessions. What had happened to Charlie not only affected her and Gideon's careers, but Chance's too. He decided to focus on treating people who've been through trauma, and he was wonderful. He treated every one of the women at the clinic with total respect…

Charlie stroked the bump of her belly as she tried to devise the perfect way to get Gideon in the trouble he deserved for slacking in his duties as daddy — although he was usually a great dad to the boys. He'd play ball with them, and she constantly caught the three of them huddled together, plotting and planning some sort of adventure that didn't involve her or her mothering ways.

The best thing about Gideon as a father, however, was the respect he was teaching the boys for women and girls. Never did Charlie hear him use a degrading term. He always treated the women in his life with complete love and admiration. A few weeks previous, when the twins came home from the clinic — which included a small daycare center to give women whose husbands were gone an occasional hour or two to themselves — they told Gideon a story about another little boy who was mean to a little girl. They said he was hitting her and calling her names. Gideon told them it's never okay to hit, and most especially not a girl, and the only names they should call a girl were "honey" and "sweetie." The next day, the teacher in the daycare was laughing because Rory and Finn were walking around calling all the girls "honey" and "sweetie"—even her.

"Hey, Joe?" Charlie called across the room to get his attention. She wasn't about to get up to waddle over there.

"What's up, baby? You need something?" He looked at his wife with all the love in the world, and she almost felt guilty that she was about to bring down the wrath of Evelyn—Nana Possessed.

"Well, it's getting kind of late. Maybe we should call Gabby and Chance to come and get the boys." As soon as Charlie said the word "boys" Gideon realized he'd let them get away from him.

"Shit!" He spun in a circle, quickly scanning the room. Charlie tried not to laugh, knowing they were right outside the door. He needed to be taught a lesson, though. He couldn't let down his guard for even a second or they'd be gone. He was lucky it had happened in a pretty safe environment. The whole staff knew the miniature Gideons were Dr. Cooper's grandsons, so they kept an extra-close eye on them.

"Gideon! What on earth has gotten into you? Your language—I might need to wash your mouth with soap, young man." It took just a heartbeat for Evelyn to realize Gideon was frantically searching for her grandsons. "Where are my babies?" she asked, quickly joining his search. "Oh no. Where are those boys?"

Charlie saw Maeve peek her head around the corner of the door. Only because Charlie was worried about Evelyn actually losing her mind, or hurting Gideon, did she nod to let her know it was okay to send them in.

"Momma, Momma!" Rory, the crazy little man, came running, trying to climb in Charlie's lap. Unfortunately, Charlie's lap had disappeared about four months ago. "Lookie what the nice lady over there gave us." He held out his loot.

In his tiny hand was a new bedpan filled with tongue depressors, Band-Aids, and a load of other things Charlie was sure had been scattered around the two when Maeve found them.

Peter smiled as he leaned down to scoop up Finn, who was much quieter and more reserved than his brother. Charlie was pretty sure he was the brains behind most of their adventures—even the ones involving their father.

"Well, wasn't that nice of Nurse Maeve?" Peter asked. Finn nodded furiously before whispering "Thanks."

"Oh, they're just so adorable, Dr. Cooper. I found them in the supply cabinet checking things out." Her smile was warm and comforting.

"Hey! Who started this party without us?" Gabby asked as she came through the door. The room kept getting smaller and smaller.

"Auntie!" Rory ran across the room to jump into her arms.

"Dude, what about me?" Chance came in behind Gabby with his arms open and ready for his nephew. Rory, of course, took that opportunity to jump into his arms as well.

Finn tugged on his grandfather's ear to get him to bend his head to him. Charlie couldn't hear what he said, but assumed it was something to do with wanting to go see his Uncle Chance. The bond between the two of them surprised her every time she saw them together.

Although the twins looked like miniatures of their father, Finn definitely had Chance's personality. He would fight to the end for any of his family—something he ended up doing more often than Charlie would like because his brother had more of his other uncle in him than she was happy with.

The only ones missing were Tyson and Paige, but their absence was completely understandable. They'd been married for just over two years now, and Tyson was about to move on to his residency in pediatrics. He'd decided to specialize in pediatric cardiology, against Peter's warnings. And while he was working his ass off, he loved every minute of it. The focus he had was something no one ever thought they'd see from Tyson.

Tyson and Charlie's relationship was still a work in progress. Charlie had forgiven him, but every time she saw him, all the memories of those horrible months would flood her, and she had to work to move past them. She didn't blame him for anything—they'd both made mistakes—but dealing with the memories was always harder around Tyson.

After graduation, Paige decided to stay at the university and work toward her master's degree and eventually her doctorate in economics. While doing that, she'd been working in the registrar's office, dealing with "comeback students." Paige came to the clinic twice a week to work with some of the women and help them put together resumes. She also used her expertise to run seminars about going back into school after an extended absence.

Tyson suddenly filled the doorway, a smile on his face and green scrubs hanging loosely on his tired body.

"I'm a dad!" he announced. "Paige and the baby are both doing great."

"Congratulations, Ty." Gideon wrapped his arm around Tyson's shoulder. "If you need any advice, you know you can come to your big brother."

"What, on how to lose your kid?" Charlie asked, earning a laugh from most of those in the room. Evelyn didn't find humor in the situation, however, and Charlie saw her glare at Gideon.

Tyson looked dazed, and he was definitely confused about the joke. He was tired and elated and couldn't think straight if his life depended on it.

Before Tyson could get his bearings, a nurse pushed into the room behind him with a rolling crib.

"Maeve asked me to make a quick pit stop on the way to the nursery," she said as she was practically shoved out of the way so the crazy Cooper family could get a good look at its newest member.

"He's beautiful, Tyson," Charlie commented as she came to stand next to him.

Uncharacteristically, he reached over and grabbed her hand, giving it a tight squeeze. When Charlie looked up at him, there were tears in his eyes. She squeezed Tyson's hand back, and his smile widened.

"This is Isaac Thomas Cooper," he said, introducing his son. Even at just minutes old, they could tell he was a Cooper boy through and through. All three boys were going to be the cause of much heartache in the greater San Diego area—that Charlie could absolutely guarantee.

After a few minutes, the nurse took the baby down to the nursery with Tyson following behind, the smile never leaving his face.

Another Cooper was now in the world, and he was lucky enough to be born into a family that would love and support him through anything. Charlie looked over at Evelyn and caught the slightest hint of a frown on her face before she realized Charlie was looking and pulled it into a smile.

"What's wrong, Evelyn?" Charlie asked quietly.

"Oh, nothing. It's silly." She waved her daughter-in-law off.

"No, tell me," Charlie insisted.

"Don't get me wrong, I love all my boys." She paused and looked lovingly at Finn and Rory who were giggling as Chance made faces. "But when do I get to have a girl?"

The whole room erupted in laughter. Only Evelyn would be mourning the lack of girls when she was surrounded by such handsome, strong, smart, funny men.

"Well, Momma and Daddy said we were gonna have a sister," Finn announced with all the authority in the world.

"That means a girl, right?" Rory looked around at all the grownups in the room as they stared at Gideon and Charlie.

Charlie nodded, smiling at Evelyn. She never should've trusted the boys with that secret. Gideon and Charlie had known for a few months, but since Paige and Tyson had decided not to find out the sex of their baby, they didn't want to steal their thunder. The only reason Rory and Finn knew they were getting a sister was that they'd caught their parents talking about names and were worried their little brother was going to be called Jenna or Abby.

Evelyn squeaked as she pulled Charlie into a tight hug and whispered in her ear. "I thank God every day that Gideon found you. You're my daughter. You were meant to be my daughter. I love you."

A tear slowly slid down Charlie's cheek as Evelyn released her. Gideon pulled her into the comfort of his body and lightly kissed the tear away. There was nowhere else in the world she felt more comfortable than in his arms.

This was their future, their family. While the past and everything that happened all those years ago had shaped who they were now, they would never let it define what they would become.

ACKNOWLEDGMENTS

Thanks to my family, who inspire me and make me laugh on a daily basis. They deserve an award for putting up with me while I write and edit.

Big thanks to those who support me with all their love and encouragement. E, without you I wouldn't be doing what I love. To Kim and Kindra, who were there in the beginning and helped me work through some of the tougher scenes. And Ebony, who was always there to keep me going by telling me how much she loved this story.

Finally, thank you to my Omnific family—and I call them family because they had to put up with me. Bev and Jess, you helped make this story what it is, and I love it! Coreen, you worked your magic again.

ABOUT THE AUTHOR

Jessica McQuinn, co-author of *Passion Fish*, is a mom of two very active kids. They keep her busy running from activity to activity, but it is in those moments that she finds inspiration and has no problem pulling out a notebook to write down a few lines for her next book.

Married for twenty years to her high school crush, Jessica lives in Utah with her family. As a family they enjoy taking advantage of the extremes that can be found there. From skiing in the winter to hiking the mountain trails in the spring and summer, the whole family loves to be together.

Jessica has been writing all her life, but it wasn't until her kids started school that she decided to think that she could do it and actually share it with others. Now she hopes that you will enjoy the result of the process that has helped her find herself again.